The Dac

Book six of the Vete

CW00417612

By: Willi

Visit the author's website ht

William Kelso is also the author of:
The Shield of Rome
The Fortune of Carthage
Devotio: The House of Mus
Caledonia - Book One of the Veteran of Rome series
Hibernia - Book Two of the Veteran of Rome series
Britannia – Book Three of the Veteran of Rome series
Hyperborea – Book Four of the Veteran of Rome series
Germania – Book Five of the Veteran of Rome series

Published in 2017 by FeedARead.com Publishing – Arts Council funded
Copyright © William Kelso. Second Edition
The author has asserted their moral right under the Copyright, Designs and Patents Act, 1988, to be identified as the author of this work.

A CIP catalogue record for this title is available from the British Library.

To: Annetta and Simon, Generation X

1

ABOUT ME

Hello, my name is William Kelso. I was born in the Netherlands to British parents. My interest in history and in particular military history started at a very young age when I was lucky enough to hear my grandfather describing his experiences of serving in the RAF in North Africa and Italy during World War 2. Recently my family has discovered that one of my Scottish and Northern Irish ancestors fought under Wellington at the Battle of Waterloo in 1815.

I love writing and bringing to life the ancient world of Rome, Carthage and the Germanic and Celtic tribes. It's my thing. After graduation, I worked for 22 years in financial publishing and event management in the city of London as a salesman for some big conference organizers, trying to weave my stories in the evenings after dinner and in weekends. Working in the heart of the original Roman city of Londinium I spent many years walking its streets and visiting the places, whose names still commemorate the 2,000-year-old ancient Roman capital of Britannia, London Wall, Watling Street, London Bridge and Walbrook. The city of London if you know where to look has many fascinating historical corners. So, since the 2nd March 2017 I have taken the plunge and become a full-time writer. Stories as a form of entertainment are as old as cave man and telling them is what I want to do.

My books are all about ancient Rome, especially the early to mid-republic as this was the age of true Roman greatness. My other books include, The Shield of Rome, The Fortune of Carthage, Caledonia (1), Hibernia (2), Britannia (3), Hyperborea (4), Germania (5) and Devotio: The House of Mus. Go on, give them a go.

In my spare time, I help my brother run his battlefield tours company which takes people around the battlefields of Arnhem, Dunkirk, Agincourt, Normandy, the Rhine crossing and Monte Cassino. I live in London with my wife and support the "Help for

The Dacian War – Veteran of Rome Series

Heroes" charity and a tiger in India.

Please visit my website http://www.williamkelso.co.uk/ and have a look at my historical video blog!

Feel free to write to me with any feedback on my books. Email: william@kelsoevents.co.uk

If you expect Trajans war in Dacia you like me will be dissaponted This is a fictitious navel.

The Dacian War
Book six of the Veteran of Rome series

Chapter One – The Contract with the Immortals

The Island of Vectis. Early autumn 105 AD

The wide sandy beach was deserted apart from a single solitary figure. It was morning and a strong fresh salty breeze was blowing in from the west. Silently Marcus stood gazing out at the grey sea, his stern face, tough, old and weather beaten. He looked worried. The white tipped waves came crashing, hissing and surging up the beach towards him, encircling him as if he was a rock and threatening to swamp his old army boots in icy cold water. The wind tugged at his grey beard and his long black cloak, roaring in his ears and whipping grains of sand into his body. His two hunting dogs were splashing and chasing each other through the surf, barking excitedly. Ignoring the dogs and the elements he absentmindedly reached down to his belt, fumbling for the pouch in which he'd kept his Hyperborean smoking herbs. But the pouch was no longer there. His craving for the herbs had made him forget again. His supply of smoking herbs, which he'd brought back from Hyperborea, had run out weeks ago, and there was no chance of getting anymore. Instead with an annoyed, irritable gesture he pulled his cloak tighter around his shoulders.

There was no point in denying it, he thought. He worried about Fergus, his son. He missed Fergus. It had been too long since he had seen him. The boy had marched off to war in faraway Dacia with a vexillation of the Twentieth Legion and he hadn't been there to say goodbye to him. Grimly Marcus turned to look up the beach. He had not been there to say his farewell, to give the boy some final last minute advice and to wish him well. Marcus's face darkened. He knew what Fergus was marching towards. For fourteen year's he had served on the Danube frontier with the 2nd Batavian Auxiliary Cohort and the thought

4

that Fergus was going to participate in a new Dacian war made his stomach turn over. But the worst was that he was completely helpless. There was nothing he could do to help his son, nothing he could do to protect him. All he could do was sit and wait for news and trust that all would be well. It was intolerable.

Slowly Marcus raised his head and looked up at the sky, his rugged face, defiant, cold and hard like granite.

"Hear me immortal gods," Marcus said silently as he gazed up at the sky, "Hear me for I have something important to say. I shall make an agreement with you on these terms. I ask you to keep watch over my son. His name is Fergus and he has red hair just like mine. I ask you, immortal ones, to keep him alive and safe. I ask that one day he shall come home to us alive and well." Marcus paused and took a deep breath. "And in return, when you deem the time and place is right, I shall repay you in the manner of my father, Corbulo. I shall willingly give you my life, to do with, as you see fit. This I swear."

For a moment, Marcus stared up at the sky. Then a defiant gleam appeared in his eyes.

"But if you accept my offer and fuck me over and allow my son to die," Marcus hissed, "then to hell with the lot of you and I will curse you all, useless immortal pricks. Do not think that I fear you or the furies. No man who respects himself does."

As he fell silent Marcus turned his eyes back towards the sea. If the gods had accepted his offer they would send him a sign. He would have to keep his eyes open.

A month had passed since Priscinus had dared attack the farm on Vectis and now Priscinus was dead, poisoned in his own home, a murder that had been arranged by Dylis. Staring out to sea Marcus slowly shook his head in bewilderment. He had not believed his sister capable of such ruthlessness. Dylis, his sister, thought she had done the right thing by arranging the murder. It had solved the immediate threat but it had not settled the legal dispute over the ownership of his farm and land on Vectis. It had made the dispute worse. She hadn't known how well connected Priscinus was. She didn't understand that the Governor of Britannia would not tolerate the murder of a close friend. There would be consequences, consequences that were beyond the capability of a troop of retired Batavian soldiers to handle. Dylis however had not understood. He had tried to explain it to her but she had refused to listen. She had called him a coward, a man who lacked the balls to do what was necessary to defend his farm and land from a hostile takeover. The argument had descended into a bitter quarrel and for the past three weeks Dylis had refused to speak to him or even remain in the same room as him.

Across the wind-swept beach a figure was slowly coming towards him. It was Kyna, his wife. Marcus turned back to stare out across the grey sea as Kyna came up to him, her long white stola cloak flapping in the breeze. Her head was covered by a shawl which hid her silver-grey hair that was tied back and fixed with a bone fibula. For a moment, the two of them said nothing as Kyna paused at his side and turned to gaze out across the sea. In the surf the two hunting dogs suddenly came bounding towards her and excitedly bustled around her legs, shaking the water droplets from their coats. Affectionally she reached down to give the dogs a pat on their heads.

"Are you worried about Fergus?" Kyna asked as she straightened up. "Is that why you have started coming out here on your own?"

"What else is there for me to do?" Marcus growled irritably as he stared out to sea. "Jowan, Dylis and Cunomoltus are more than capable of managing the farm on their own. They do not need my help and besides I am no farmer. The slaves are content, the children have good teachers. What is there to do for me around here? So yes, I have time to worry about our boy. I have time to worry about everything and nothing."

"You are the head of this family. A family needs a leader and you are that man, you will always be that man," Kyna replied with a little resigned shrug.

Marcus remained silent as he stared out to sea.

"I worry about our son too," Kyna said at last, her voice calm and strong, "When you were away all those years with your Batavians, I worried about you too. I know what it feels like to wait for news, to fear the worst and to be unable to do anything about it. You have no idea how many sleepless nights I had when you were away. But all you can do is endure it. There is no other way."

At her side, Marcus remained silent. Then at last he stirred, glanced at Kyna and gave his wife a little agreeing nod.

"I shall write Fergus a letter," Kyna said as she slipped her fingers into Marcus's right hand, "and maybe in a few months or so we should get a reply. The boy has a sensible head. He will be all right and there is a girl waiting for him back at Deva. When he was here just before you returned from Hyperborea, he told me her name was Galena and that she is expecting his child."

"I bet he has a girl waiting for him in every army camp he's been in along the frontier," Marcus growled. Then he turned to Kyna and a faint smile appeared on his rugged face. "The letter is a good idea. I will get the Batavians to deliver it to Fergus. Some of the cohorts are taking part in the Dacian war."

Kyna gave her husband a little answering smile.

"You need to speak to Dylis," Kyna said lightly, "this quarrel between you two is not good for anyone."

The smile abruptly vanished from Marcus's face.

"What do you propose I do?" he snapped. "That woman does not want to see sense. She doesn't even want to be in the same room as me."

"I don't know," Kyna said with a weary sigh as she looked away, "she refuses to speak to me too. But this situation cannot continue. You must do something, Marcus."

Marcus muttered something under his breath and turned to stare at the waves surging up the beach.

"She didn't realise who Priscinus was," he growled at last. "The man was a close friend of the Governor of this Province. The Governor will not let his friend's murder pass by without an investigation." Marcus's face darkened. "We have a prosperous farm, Kyna, which means that our home and business are coveted by others. Priscinus will not be the only man who will have his eye on our farm. We cannot afford to make an enemy of the Governor. What happens if the Governor decides he likes our place so much, he wants to take it for himself. What then can we do to stop him? We will be homeless and destitute."

"I understand," Kyna nodded, lowering her head, "I understand." Marcus sighed and tightened his grip on his wife's hand.

"I told you before," he said in a quieter voice, "I have ambitions for us. I want to raise this family, us, up in the world. I want to become a member of the Equestrian Order, a knight. It is the knights who effectively run the Empire. They get awarded all the premier military and commercial positions in government. They are men of respect, men who have made something of themselves through guts and hard work. That's who I want us to be. We built this farm into what it is today. We made it prosper. No one else did that. And now our farm and land are such, that we qualify for membership of the order but admittance still needs the Governor's and the Emperor's approval. And how are we ever going to get that approval if the Governor of Britannia is our enemy?"

"Governor's come and go, don't they?" Kyna shrugged.

"They do," Marcus growled, "but if there is a cloud of suspicion hanging over us that we were involved in the murder of an important citizen, then no one will want to touch us. In these matters, reputation is all important and ours hangs on a slender thread."

"I don't know about reputation," Kyna said, "all I know is that Dylis and you must make peace with each other. It is driving us all insane."

Marcus grunted and the two of them fell silent. At their feet, the two hunting dogs went racing off, splashing through the incoming waves in a mad dash for a piece of flotsam.

Gripping Kyna's hand, Marcus turned to study his wife.

"Did you really come all the way out here just to tell me this?" Marcus asked.

Slowly Kyna shook her head, her thoughts seemingly faraway.

"Ninian has come," she replied, "he is waiting for you at the farm. He says that he has important news and wishes to speak with you."

"Ninian?" Marcus muttered with a sudden frown, "now what does he want?"

Chapter Two – The Murderess

Beyond the stepping stones that bridged the gurgling river, the earth rose steeply to form a natural embankment and through the trees beyond, Marcus caught a glimpse of the neat red roof tiles of his farm. A whisper of smoke was curling up into the sky from the kitchens. Limping slightly from the wound he'd received in the fight with Priscinus a month ago, Marcus helped Kyna across the stepping stones and the two of them silently climbed up the embankment and headed towards the main house, accompanied by the hunting dogs. As they entered the small wood, Marcus paused to stare at the forest floor which was covered in a beautiful carpet of yellow flowers. Then abruptly he stooped and with the two remaining fingers on his left hand he picked a few of the flowers from the earth and held them up for inspection.

"For Dylis's twins, girls like flower's, don't they?" he said, glancing at Kyna.

Kyna gave him a wry smile. "So, do I," she replied.

"You have to earn them," Marcus said with a twinkle in his eye, "You asked me to solve matters with Dylis and that is what I am trying to do."

Suddenly Marcus froze and the colour in his face drained away. Sitting watching them high up on the branch of a tree was a golden eagle, it's talons grasping the branch. The animal's sharp, fearless eyes were staring straight at him.

At his side Kyna gasped in surprise and delight as she too caught sight of the bird.

"The ruler of the skies," Marcus muttered as he respectfully gazed up at the eagle. Then abruptly he looked away as he realised what this meant. The eagle was the sign he had been waiting for. The Gods had accepted his offer.

"Let's go," Marcus said quietly as he reached out and took his wife's hand. Kyna shook her head with a good-natured smile as Marcus started walking again. Through the trees the farm suddenly hove into view. The fine stone Roman villa, barns and out buildings enclosed a courtyard on three sides and next to the house a herd of cattle stood idly munching grass in an enclosed field. From somewhere out of view he could hear a party of slaves singing to themselves as they worked. Excitedly the dogs scrambled away through the trees towards the farm and, a moment later Marcus heard the barking of another dog. He paused as he suddenly caught sight of the crude wooden palisade that Jowan and the slaves had built to protect the farm from Priscinus and his men. He had considered pulling it down now that Priscinus was dead but somehow hadn't managed to convince himself that that would be wise. Studiously avoiding looking at the burnt and ruined wheat fields beyond the farm, he strode around the low palisade and V shaped ditch towards the main gate. Those same wheat fields had once been a glorious golden colour and had promised a fine harvest only a month or more ago, before Priscinus had set them on fire and ruined that year's entire harvest. The destruction had been terrible and it still depressed Marcus when he turned to look at his wasted and blackened fields. At the front gate to his property, standing on top of a small wooden watchtower, the slave on lookout, dipped his head respectfully as he caught sight of his master and mistress. In the courtyard one of the slave girls was tending to a stranger's horse.

"Tell the twins that I picked these flowers for them," Marcus said, handing Kyna the fine yellow flowers he'd picked up in the wood. "And this one is for you," he muttered in a quieter voice as he handed his wife one of the flowers, "after all these years, still the prettiest girl of them all."

Ninian was standing beside the window looking out over the blackened and ruined wheat fields, when Marcus accompanied by Cunomoltus, his brother and Jowan, Dylis's husband entered the long rectangular dining room of the villa. The agent hastily stepped forwards and greeted Marcus with a respectful nod before stretching out his hand, which Marcus clasped in the legionary fashion. Ninian, their broker, agent and go-between with the merchants of Noviomagus Reginorum, Chichester was a fat, fleshy man with a quick friendly smile.

Marcus was just about to speak when there was a sudden commotion behind him and Dylis forced her way into the room and defiantly folded her arms across her chest as she caught sight of Ninian.

"My lady," Ninian exclaimed with a wide friendly grin as he stepped towards her and quickly planted two kisses on Dylis's cheeks. "I have served you and your family for a long time and as always, I am honoured by your presence."

"Thank you, Ninian, for coming all this way from Reginorum," Marcus said clearing his throat and ignoring his sister, "it's a long journey, I know. You are welcome to stay and dine with us tonight."

"That is kind of you Sir," Ninian replied with a respectful nod. "But I must return at once after I have spoken with you. Business presses I'm afraid."

"What news do you have for us," Dylis asked quietly fixing her steely eyes on Ninian and at the same time giving him a small encouraging smile.

"Well," Ninian said carefully glancing from Marcus to Dylis, "I have good news and some not so good news." Ninian coughed. "The good news is that the merchants and priests in Reginorum are willing to do business with you again if you were to pay a thousand Denarii donative to the Temple of Neptune and Minerva. The priests also wish that you Marcus come to the Temple and pay your respects to the gods. If you do this, they have promised to forget what happened with Priscinus and the priest who was killed."

"So, they no longer want us to hand over Petrus for defiling the Temple and for insulting the priests," Cunomoltus said hastily.

"It seems that way," Ninian replied nodding.

"A thousand denarii, they don't seem to value the lives of their priests very highly," Dylis scoffed in an angry, contemptuous voice. "But what about our burned and ruined fields? Who is going to compensate us for that?"

"And the not so good news," Marcus snapped ignoring his sister.

Ninian forced a nervous smile onto his face as he glanced from Dylis to Marcus.

"The not so good news," Ninian sighed and raised his eyebrows. "Priscinus's family are in mourning. Priscinus was most likely murdered by one of his own slaves. That is what his family believe. One of their female slaves vanished straight after his death. She ran away and they suspect that it was this slave who poisoned Priscinus. She had easy access to her master. The family have put out a sizeable reward for the woman's capture. Notices are going up all over the Province. The family say that the woman has identifying marks, marks that cannot be hidden or destroyed. And there is more," Ninian held up his hand as Cunomoltus was about to interrupt. "Priscinus was a close friend and ally of the Governor of Britannia. The Governor is said to be deeply troubled by the murder of his friend and has ordered an investigation. I have heard that he is sparing no expense to find the murderer." Ninian sighed again. "The Governor has appointed an investigator to look into the case, a man called Cunitius. Cunitius is a former tax collector and is said to be an expert at tracking down runaway slaves and fugitives. He and his staff are already at Priscinus's house gathering evidence." Ninian paused and then slowly turned to look at Marcus. "Yesterday I heard that Cunitius is planning to speak to you about the murder. He will be here within days. He has questions for you. I thought I should warn you before he arrives."

The room fell silent as Ninian took a deep breath.

"Thank you Ninian," Marcus said at last in a sombre voice, "You have proved yourself once more a good friend. We are grateful for the warning."

Ninian raised his hand to scratch his cheek. "This man, this Cunitius," he said fixing his eyes on Marcus, "this man is the Governor's personal representative. Cunitius is not conducting this investigation because he is interested in justice or upholding the law. He is working for the Governor and Priscinus's family. He will only be interested in furthering their interests. This is not the sort of man who you can meet with a sword in your hand or behind a closed, barricaded wooden wall. You don't mess with this man, Marcus, he is not in that league. He has the authority of the State behind him. Do you understand what I am saying?"

"I know what you are saying," Marcus growled, "and don't worry when he comes here with his questions, we shall give him the reception he deserves."

Ninian nodded, giving Marcus a wary look before turning to give Dylis an affectionate smile.

"This woman, the slave who is suspected of murdering Priscinus," Marcus asked, "does anyone know where she is? Have there been any sightings?"

Ninian shook his head.

"None that I know about," he replied. "She has vanished but she will be found. How long can a runaway survive without food, money or shelter? The Governor is throwing all the resources of the State behind her capture. As I said, he is sparing no expense. The reward for her capture is significant."

"Then maybe it would be best if we found her first," Marcus replied giving Cunomoltus a quick glance. "If as you say, Cunitius is indeed only interested in furthering the interests of his employers, then if he finds her before we do, he will torture her and force her to implicate us in Priscinus's murder. The Governor of Britannia is not our friend. I am sure that he would gladly take away our farm and land and give it to one of his allies and friends. We must not provide him with an excuse." Marcus paused and then slowly turned to look at Dylis. "We can't allow that to happen. I won't allow that to happen. We need to find this slave. Would you not agree sister?"

In the doorway Dylis remained silent as she stonily refused to look at her brother.

"But how will you find her," Ninian shrugged glancing at Marcus. "Where do you start looking? You don't even know what the slave woman looks like."

"Please keep your eyes and ears open for us Ninian," Marcus said with a grateful look as he stepped forwards and placed his hand on the fat broker's shoulder. "Our family is lucky to count you as a friend."

When Ninian had gone, Marcus turned to look at Dylis. His sister was picking at her finger nails in a tense and nervous fashion as she stared out of the window. In the doorway to the dining room Cunomoltus and Jowan, both looking glum, were leaning against the wall waiting for Marcus to speak.

"If Cunitius finds the slave woman and forces her to talk," Marcus said in a quiet sombre voice as he addressed Dylis, "the woman will reveal the role that you played in Priscinus's murder. She will tell him that it was your idea. That it was you who provided the poison and that it was you who paid her to do it. When that truth is revealed, we, all of us here, will be doomed."

"So why don't you just hand me over to Cunitius and say I acted alone," Dylis hissed, turning to stare at Marcus with a cold, bitter looking face. "Surely you have the balls to sacrifice your own sister for the greater good. And there was no need to lie to Ninian. He has always had our interests at heart."

"Dylis," Jowan interrupted in protest but Dylis rounded on her husband and silenced him with a single furious look.

"No, we will not be handing you over," Marcus growled, sizing up his sister. "We are family. We do not give up on each other. That is what Corbulo wanted for us and that is what I want too. We will find another way. We will overcome this. No one is going to take away our farm and land. This is our home and we are going to fight for it like we have done many times in the past. Now come with me, all of you."

Silently Marcus led the way out of the dining room, through the hallway with its fine mosaic floor before turning down a narrow corridor that led to the villa's sleeping quarters. A series of small rectangular bedrooms, their doorways covered by curtains, lined the corridor. Inside the rooms stone beds were built into the walls, upon which lay straw mattresses and scattered personal belongings. At the end of the corridor was another room, this one fitted with a proper wooden door. From his pocket, Marcus produced a key and inserted it into the lock. He turned to glance at Dylis, Jowan and Cunomoltus as he unlocked the door.

Inside the small rectangular, windowless room a woman was kneeling on the cold stone floor. She looked like she was praying for her eyes were closed and her hands were clasped together whilst a small wooden cross on a chain was wrapped around her fingers. Two torches, fixed to the walls, bathed the room in a reddish flickering light and a plate with some discarded food stood beside the door. Hastily the woman rose to her feet as she caught sight of Marcus.

"I am sorry that we must keep you like this," Marcus muttered as he gave the woman an apologetic nod, "But it is for your own safety, and ours, you understand. Priscinus's family are searching for you everywhere. They have hired a man to track you down, an expert so they say, but we won't allow him to find you."

"I know why I am here, Sir," the slave woman replied lowering her eyes. "God has sent you to protect me."

Chapter Three – We are all agreed

"So, what are we going to do, Marcus?" Kyna asked looking up at her husband. It was late in the evening and the whole family except for Efa and the four children had gathered at one end of the long dining room and were sitting around the open hearth. Marcus raised his cup of wine to his lips and drank. Then he turned to look at the anxious, tense faces watching him.

"The woman cannot stay here," he said, fixing his eyes on Dylis, "She can't spend the rest of her days hidden in that room and if we allow her to remain and work on the farm it is only a matter of time before someone notices her and goes to collect the reward that is on her head. It has been three weeks since you brought her here, sister. She must go. She must disappear."

"Her name is Esther," Dylis snapped, her eyes blazing. "And if you kick her out you will have to get rid of me as well. I gave Esther my word that I would look after her. That was our deal. That is why she agreed to help me. She has put herself in mortal danger for us."

"Why don't we just kill her and dump her body in the marshes," Cunomoltus exclaimed with a shrug, "If she is dead she won't be able to reveal the role that Dylis played in Priscinus's murder. No one will ever know."

"You are an animal," Dylis hissed.

"No one is going to kill her," Marcus said in a tired voice.

"All right," Cunomoltus replied ignoring Dylis as his fingers played with the bronze phallic amulet that hung around his neck.

"How about we cut out her tongue then? That way she won't be able to speak if she is ever caught."

"No," Jowan interrupted with a shake of his head. "She will still be able to point at people and write down names, if she knows how to write. Cutting out her tongue won't silence her."

"Then we cut off her hands as well as her tongue," Cunomoltus retorted.

Beside the crackling fire a strangled animalistic noise erupted from deep within Dylis's throat, but before she could turn the noise into words Marcus banged his fist down hard on the table making Kyna jump in fright.

"Enough brother," Marcus cried out in an angry voice, rounding on Cunomoltus. "No harm is going to befall Esther. No one is going to touch her. I don't agree with what Dylis did but now that it has happened we must honour the promise that Dylis made. We have no choice. We cannot go back on that promise, however much I would like to, for that would be dishonourable. Dylis gave that woman her word that she would look after her and because of that Esther has put herself in mortal danger for us. We owe her and we are going to keep our promise. All of us here owe Esther for what she did, misguided as her actions may have been. And we are all honourable people. So, the least we can do is get Esther to somewhere safe where she can start a new life. Where she can start again and be free from the fear of being caught. That is in our interests as well. No one must know about the role that Dylis played in Priscinus's murder. That is what I mean when I say that she must disappear. We are here to discuss where she should go. Now I want to hear ideas, everyone, come on."

"Send her to the marshes," Cunomoltus grunted in disgust as he reached out for his cup of wine and drained it in one go.

Marcus ignored his brother and turned to look at the faces around him. For a long moment, the only sound in the room was the crackle and hiss of the flames in the hearth as they feasted on the wooden logs.

"We could send her to Londinium, Marcus," Jowan said at last in a careful voice. "You have many friends in the city. They could help us."

But Marcus shook his head. "No, not Londinium," he muttered, "that would be right under the Governor's nose. It's too close, too dangerous. Too many ambitious people willing to have a go at getting that reward. No, I am thinking that she must leave Britannia all together."

Once again, the room fell silent except for the roar of the flames. Then suddenly Marcus felt a hand touch his own. It was Kyna.

"Why don't we ask Esther where she wants to go?" Kyna said quietly. "She should, after all, have a say in what happens to her. It would be our payment for the debt that we owe her."

Marcus grunted in surprise. He hadn't thought about that. Quickly he turned to look at Dylis, Cunomoltus, Petrus and Jowan but the others seemed to have no visible objections.

"Petrus, go and fetch Esher and bring her here," Marcus growled tossing the key towards the young man.

A little later Petrus returned leading the slave woman gently into the dining room and as he did, Marcus rose to his feet and politely gestured for the woman to sit down beside the hearth. Esther was clad in one of Kyna's dresses and her black hair hung loosely around her shoulders. In her hand, she was tightly clutching her small P shaped wooden cross. Her face still showed the outlines of the bruises that Marcus had first noticed on her when he and Dylis had visited Priscinus's villa. Nervously and silently Esther shuffled over to the fire and sat down on one of the wooden stools. She looked around forty years old.

"I see your bruises are still not fully healed," Marcus said in a gentle voice, "Your master was a cruel man and it is a good thing that he is dead."

"If it is God's will that I remain ugly, then it is God's will," Esther muttered, lowering her eyes to the floor.

Marcus nodded and for a moment he was silent.

"You and I and this family," Marcus said at last with a sigh as he looked at Esther, "like it or not, our fate is bound together now. We are good people Esther. We are going to look after you, we owe you that much for what you have done. But you cannot stay here on this farm. Priscinus's family and the Governor of Britannia have employed a man to find you. They have issued a big reward for your capture. So, you are going to have to disappear. You are not going to be able to stay in Britannia. We have gathered here to discuss where you should go. So," Marcus sighed, "it is only proper that we ask you first where you would like to go? Maybe you have family in other provinces? Maybe you have relatives who can help us?"

The room fell silent as all eyes turned to stare at the slave woman sitting on her stool beside the crackling fire. Esther was staring at the floor, her fingers fidgeting tensely with her little wooden cross. Then abruptly she looked up at Marcus and there was a sudden defiance and a surprising strength in her eyes.

"I was born in Rome," Esther said slowly, "and I have always dreamed of going back to the city. I suppose it is my home. So, I want to go to Rome."

"Rome," Marcus raised his eyebrows as he stared at the slave woman. "Rome," he repeated. "Do you still have family in the city?"

Esther shrugged. "I have always been a slave. I was only a child when I was sold to a man who took me to Britannia. I have never been back. If I have family in Rome, I do not know who they are. My mother died giving birth to me. She was a slave herself. My father," Esther took a deep breath and looked away,

"I never knew my father either. My mistress in Rome, of the family who owned my mother and who raised me in their home, I remember her being kind to me. She told me one thing - that my father was a Christian priest; a trouble maker and that he was crucified in the arena for his heresy. That was just before I was born, during the reign of the Emperor Nero."

"So, you are a follower of the Christian God?" Marcus muttered glancing quickly at Petrus.

"I am," Esther replied lifting her head. "I believe what my father believed. Priscinus forbade it of course but I practised in secret, for no one shall stop me from believing in the word of God. It is all that I have in this world."

"In this house, you are free to believe in what you like," Marcus growled, "as long as you do not cause trouble or deny others their beliefs. Did you know that our Petrus here is a Christian like you?"

"I have spoken with him, master," Esther replied giving Petrus a quick, grateful look. Then Esther turned to look at Dylis and for the first time a warm affectionate smile appeared on her face. "And I am grateful to you too Dylis, for you have kept your word. May God watch over you."

"All right," Marcus growled irritably raising his hand in the air, "I am not your master, Esther. From now on you should consider yourself a free woman. But we still need to decide on where you should go. Rome may be a good choice. It is the largest city in the world. They say it has over a million inhabitants; that's nearly thirty times the size of Londinium. It should be easy to disappear in such a vast place and it is far away from your former master's family, but we do not know anyone who lives in Rome and if you have no family there, then where do we start?"

"That's not entirely true," Petrus suddenly exclaimed raising his finger in the air, "I know someone who lives in Rome. Well, when I say I know him, I have never actually met him but I have a contact. A man, I am reliably informed, who may be able to help us. His name is Abraham. He is a Christian priest and he is reliable, a good man. That's what my Christian brothers tell me. They have regular contact with our brothers and sisters in Rome."

"Can we for fucks sake please stop talking about bloody Christians," Cunomoltus interrupted, shaking his head in disgust. "Christians are nothing but trouble and if their numbers keep on increasing they are going to cause all sorts of problems. You cannot have one set of people who deny the existence of all the gods and expect the rest of us to be happy with that. At some point, there are going to be riots, civil war."

"Shut up," Dylis hissed, glaring at Cunomoltus.

Marcus, ignoring his brother and sister, was thoughtfully stroking his chin as he studied Petrus from across the room.

"How large is the Christian community in Rome?" Marcus asked.

Petrus grinned as he gazed back at Marcus. "Well, well, for the first time you have shown some interest in what I have to say, Marcus," Petrus remarked. "I must be going up in the world."

"Just answer the question before I change my mind about you," Marcus replied, his face darkening. "You are not too old for me to still beat the shit out of you, boy."

"My brothers in Londinium say there are around five thousand of us living in Rome," Petrus sighed avoiding Marcus's annoyed gaze. "The Emperor Trajan seems to sort of tolerate us for now but who knows when the next State sanctioned persecution will come." Petrus turned to look at Esther and gave her an encouraging smile. "But you should know that Nero failed in his attempt to eradicate us."

"Five thousand Christians in a city of a million," Marcus muttered turning his eyes towards the floor. For a moment, he was silent as he seemed to be considering something. Then he looked up at Esther.

"All right," Marcus nodded as he seemed to make up his mind. "All right, we shall go to Rome and we will use Petrus's contact, this man Abraham, to help you vanish into the city's Christian community. Once settled in the city you should be safe and able to start a new life. No one will know who you are. That is all that we can do for you."

On her stool, Esther was staring at Marcus in silence. Then slowly and with infinite dignity she rose to her feet and came towards Marcus before reaching out for his hand and kissing it.

"I am grateful Sir," Esther said quietly. "I am grateful for what you are willing to do for me. I shall not forget this."

Marcus nodded and looked away.

"Then we are all agreed," he said. "All then that remains is to decide who will go with Esther. I think it should be myself and Petrus."

"I too wish to come to see Rome," Dylis interrupted.

"No," Marcus said sharply shaking his head. "You will stay here to protect the farm and look after Efa. There is no one better qualified than you to do this. That is the job I need you to do."

Marcus took a deep breath as he squared up to his sister's hostile, defiant face.

"I am tired of quarrelling with you, sister," Marcus said in a sudden, changed voice. "The business with Priscinus is in the past. We must now look to the future. So, we will handle the challenges that the gods send to test us and we shall prevail.

And when I return from Rome I shall instruct the lawyers at the bank to draw up official documents that give you half ownership of this farm and land. We shall own this farm jointly, together, on the one condition that Fergus, my son shall be sole owner of this place after we both die. Our father, Corbulo would approve. He would not want us to fight amongst ourselves. He would want us to be united. He would want us to be friends. We are his people after all and we should listen to him."

"Don't worry about us Marcus," Jowan said hastily. "We shall look after the farm and Efa. We can handle it."

Ignoring his brother in law, Marcus's eyes remained fixed on Dylis. His sister however refused to meet his gaze. For a moment, she sat fidgeting with her finger nails. Then abruptly and without saying a word she rose and left the room. A few moments later she was followed by the others until only Marcus and Kyna remained sitting beside the crackling fire.

"Well that went well," Marcus sighed as he took a sip of wine from his cup.

At his side Kyna laid her hand on his, running her fingers over her husband's mutilated left hand.

"That was well done," Kyna said quietly. "She will come around, Marcus. I know she will. But you must give her some time. You said exactly the right things."

"Women," Marcus said shaking his head as he took another sip of wine. "Gods, they are complicated. They exhaust me."

Kyna chuckled as she affectionately laid her head against Marcus's shoulder. "I could say the same about men," she muttered. "I still remember the time when I and Fergus were held as hostages by Agricola and you went off to Hibernia with your father leaving us behind. And another thing," she said in a resigned voice. "When you returned from Hyperborea you promised me that you would not be going away again. And yet here you are, just having promised to escort another woman, a stranger, to Rome. I should really be jealous but I just don't have the energy anymore, husband."

Slowly Marcus turned to look at his wife and sighed.

"You are right," he muttered in a weary voice, "But I must go. What choice do I have? This matter must be settled. Our family's fortunes depend on it."

"Efa is fragile, Marcus," Kyna said quietly as she rested her head against his shoulder. "She is not going to get any better. I fear that her days in this world are drawing to an end."

"I know, I know," Marcus replied as he reached out and wrapped his arm around his wife. "But Efa is a tough old lady. Don't underestimate her. I shall try and return before Saturnalia."

For a moment Kyna lowered her eyes and looked away. Then she reached up to kiss him.

"I know you will," she whispered, "for you always come back to me," she purred kissing him again, "and you must go. I understand, but sometimes I wonder when I shall really have you all to myself. When that day truly comes, I shall go to bed without a care in the world."

Chapter Four – The Boy who was abandoned

Inside the barn, Marcus crouched on the straw covered floor as he concentrated on fitting the hippo sandal to one of his horse's hooves. The beast snorted nervously and tried to back away but Marcus soothing voice seemed to calm her down. Beside him, little Armin and Dylis's three children, the twin girls with yellow flowers in their hair, were watching him as he worked. It was around noon and two days had passed since Ninian's visit. Marcus sighed as he raised his hand to wipe the sweat from his forehead.

"Mother says that you are going to Rome," one of the girls said suddenly. "She says that you are going to be gone for a long time."

"She says that Rome is the largest city in the world," Armin chipped in. "She says that it will take you a whole day just to walk from one end to the other. She says that she is happy that you are going."

"She says that, does she," Marcus said, turning to look at the children and raising an eyebrow. "Well I wouldn't know about Rome because I have never been to Rome. But I am sure it will be big. They do not call it the capital of the world for nothing."

"Will you see the Emperor?" one of the girls asked quickly.

"I doubt it," Marcus replied, "Trajan will be on the Danube with the army. He is a busy man, the Emperor. He has a war to fight against the Dacians."

"When will you come back uncle?" little Armin asked.

"It's hard to say but I shall try and return for Saturnalia," Marcus said giving Armin a little wink. "And I promise that I shall bring each of you something back from Rome; a present. But you must pretend that it is a surprise, all of you."

The children turned to look at each other as excited smiles appeared on their faces.

Marcus was about to turn his attention back to the hippo sandal and the horse's hoof when suddenly from outside the barn the warning bell rang out. Smoothly Marcus rose to his feet and reached out for his belt, from which hung his gladius short sword and pugio army knife.

"Go back into the house children, go," Marcus said hastily, his face darkening, as he strapped his belt around his waist.

Outside in the courtyard Marcus turned to stare in the direction of the front gate. The slave on guard duty up on top of the wooden watch tower was still ringing the bell, but from where he stood Marcus could see nothing. With a slight limp, he started towards the front gate and as he did he saw Cunomoltus and Petrus hastening towards him clutching a spear and a hunting bow.

"Riders approaching master," the slave called out in an excited voice as he caught sight of Marcus. "They are carrying some kind of banner."

At the front gate, Marcus squinted, staring down the track that led away from his farm. A party of six riders on horseback were slowly walking their horses towards him. They did not seem to be in a hurry. The men were clad in long brown travelling cloaks, their heads covered by hoods and they were armed. They were led by a big, broad shouldered man holding up a simple wooden staff at the top of which was fixed a bronze image of a face that glinted in the sunlight. And as the riders came towards the gate Marcus grunted irritably as he recognised the banner.

"What is it?" Cunomoltus muttered, tightening his grip on his spear.

"That's an imperial banner," Marcus growled, his face darkening. "There are only three in the whole province. It is the image of the Emperor. To show contempt for that banner is to show contempt for the Emperor himself."

"Trajan is an arsehole," Petrus hissed as he stared at the approaching riders. "He deserves a bit of contempt."

"I shall do the talking," Marcus snapped turning to shoot Petrus a warning look. "I don't want to hear a word from you boy."

Petrus looked away without replying but the contempt on his face was clear.

When the riders were a few yards from the front gate they reined in their horses and the big, broad shouldered man clutching the imago banner lowered his hood. He was a hard-looking man of around forty. His nose was broken and his head was closely shaven. He said nothing as he turned to gaze at Marcus, Petrus and Cunomoltus, sizing them up with calm, intelligent eyes. And as he stared back at the man Marcus suddenly felt the uneasy yet familiar sense of approaching danger.

"I have come to speak to Marcus," the man said in accented Latin.

"I am Marcus and this is my farm. Who are you?" Marcus growled in reply.

On his horse the big man with the broken nose fixed his eyes on Marcus. His face betrayed no emotion whatsoever.

"My name is Cunitius," the man replied quietly. "I am here to investigate the murder of a Roman citizen by the name of Priscinus. I have a few questions for you."

Marcus nodded. Then he turned to gaze at his blackened and ruined fields that stretched away to the edge of the forest.

"On whose authority, do you claim to do this?" Marcus snapped.

"You already know that," Cunitius replied swiftly and calmly. "My authority to investigate this case comes directly from the Governor of Britannia himself. So, stop wasting time and start cooperating. It is my understanding that you and Priscinus were recently involved in a land dispute and that blood was shed. So, are you going to invite us into your house? I have to ask you a few questions."

"You may ask your questions," Marcus replied sharply. "But you shall do so from on top of your horse. We do not permit friends of Priscinus to come onto our land."

"Ah," Cunitius said slowly tilting his head back and turning to look at the ruined fields on either side of the dusty track. "So, it is true. They warned me that hospitality was in short supply in these parts. But you are wrong Marcus. I am no friend of Priscinus. I never even met the man and if you are worried that I shall be biased in my investigation, then I assure you that I will not be. I just want to see justice done."

"Justice," Marcus sneered angrily flinging up his arm and pointing at his ruined fields, "There is your justice. That is all that is left of my fields and crops after Priscinus burned them. It is he who started this dispute, it is he who came with an armed force of men to drive me and my family from our land. But we showed him what is what. That prick was still alive when he ran away from here. That's all I know. I did not kill him but if I had the chance again I would."

On his horse Cunitius was studying Marcus carefully.

"So, you deny having anything to do with his murder?" Cunitius asked.

"I think that is what I just said," Marcus growled.

Cunitius nodded and turned to look down at the ground. Then he sighed. "I think you still have the wrong impression of me, Marcus," he said in a quiet voice. "I am no friend of Priscinus. I am just doing my job as instructed by the Governor." Cunitius looked up and his eyes found Marcus's. "And I am good at my job. I am the best in fact. It may take me a while but I always uncover the truth and before this is over, I will get to the bottom of this case. That's what I do and I never fail."

"Good," Marcus replied, "and like I said, Priscinus was alive when I last saw him. He and his men were running away in that direction," Marcus snapped pointing away down the track.

As he gazed at Marcus a little smile appeared on Cunitius's lips. "I think I am going to like you, Marcus," Cunitius said at last in his quiet voice, "They said that you would be a difficult man to deal with but I think you are all right. You don't trust me, I understand. You think that I am just some mercenary or messenger sent here by your enemies. But you are wrong, my friend. I am my own man. I am no one's fool. I am just doing a job for which I was hired."

Cunitius paused and as he stared at Marcus the smile on his lips grew. "You should really know something about me before you judge me. Maybe then we shall get on better. I was not born into a wealthy or powerful family," Cunitius exclaimed. "No, I worked my way up just like you. I never knew my father and when I was twelve my mother abandoned me. She left me to fend for myself."

In his saddle Cunitius leaned forwards, his hard face with its broken nose staring straight at Marcus.

"I was homeless and I was starving and I had nowhere to go. I was twelve. But I wanted to live so I joined a street gang. We stole food from the merchants, we lived on the street, we fought other gangs. It was a brutal existence, but I survived."

On his horse Cunitius face had darkened and abruptly the smile vanished.

"And do you know what I learned during those years," Cunitius snapped, "I learned to tell when people are lying to me. I became so good at this, that eventually through good fortune, I was employed as an informant for the Imperial Tax Collector's Office and then as a tax collector. And now I am employed by the wealthy and the powerful to track down people, runaway slaves and investigate murders. So just like you Marcus, I am good at what I do. I have come from the bottom and I have made something of myself. And now I am sitting here looking at you and I am thinking, why is this man lying to me?"

Behind the closed gate, Marcus remained silent as he held Cunitius's gaze. Then he stirred and glanced at his ruined fields. "You and I have nothing in common," he replied with a little shake of his head, "And I am not lying to you. I did not kill Priscinus."

"But someone did," Cunitius snapped quickly, "And I think that you know who did it. I am particularly interested in finding a woman, a slave by the name of Esther. She is around forty years old, a follower of the Christian faith, so I discovered. She belonged to Priscinus's household, she was his property but she ran away immediately after the murder. The woman has conspicuous identifying features, according to Priscinus's family, and it is she who most likely poisoned Priscinus. She was the last person to see Priscinus alive. There is a reward out for her capture with a description of what she looks like. It will be all over the Province by now. But she is just a slave. The real question that interests me is, did she, Esther, act alone or was she used by someone else to get to Priscinus? You can see why I am here, you have a motive, Marcus."

On his horse Cunitius sighed and looked away. "This is a serious case. A prominent Roman citizen has been murdered and I am authorised to tell you that any obstructions to my investigation will be reported to the Governor of Britannia with all the consequences that will cause. Do I make myself clear?"

Marcus turned to gaze at Cunitius and for a long moment he was silent as he studied the investigator.

"As we seem to be getting to know each other," Marcus said at last, "do you have a family? Is there a wife and children waiting for you back in the place you call home? Are you a family man, Cunitius? Do you like to read your children stories before they go to sleep?"

Cunitius frowned as the question seemed to catch him off guard.

"I never had the time for a family," he snapped.

"I thought so," Marcus replied. Then he sighed. "I shall let you know if I hear anything about this slave woman who you are looking for. You shall have my full co-operation. Was there anything else that you wished to ask me?"

Cunitius turned to look away as a glimpse of disappointment flashed across his face.

"Very well," he snapped in an annoyed voice, "Yes there was just more thing. Have you any plans to go away, Marcus? It may be necessary for me to return if I have more questions and it would be helpful if you remained here."

"If I do have to go somewhere," Marcus said swiftly, "I shall send you a message to let you know where I am going."

On his horse Cunitius did not reply as he stared at Marcus. Then with a final little contemptuous smile he gestured to his companions, turned his horse around and started to ride away down the track, kicking up a small cloud of dust as he went. And as Cunitius rode away Petrus farted.

"What a cock," Cunomoltus said taking a deep relieved breath as he stared at the retreating riders.

"We should have left for Rome yesterday, Marcus," Petrus said, "Why wait until that prick showed up? Now he has had a good look at us."

"And I have had a good look at him," Marcus growled. "It is always good to see what your enemy looks like and now we know what we are up against." Marcus took a deep breath and sighed. "He suspects us of involvement in Priscinus's death but he has no proof. For that he needs to find Esther which we must prevent at all costs."

"But why ask him about his family?" Cunomoltus said with a frown as he turned to glance at Marcus. "That was a bit odd."

"A man like that, with no family, no one to care for and look after," Marcus snapped turning to glare at his brother, "has nothing to lose. That makes him a most dangerous man."

At his side both Petrus and Cunomoltus did not reply. Then as the riders vanished from sight Petrus turned to Marcus.

"So now what?" he muttered.

"We leave for Rome tonight under the cover of darkness," Marcus said lowering his voice, "but before we go there is something that I need to know."

Chapter Five – The Black Cross

Marcus, Cunomoltus, Petrus, Kyna and Dylis stood gathered in the corridor of the villa and were gazing down at Esther who was sitting on her bed in her room. Esther, her head downcast, looked pale and nervous as her fingers played with her small wooden cross.

"We shall be leaving tonight on horseback," Marcus said in a grave voice turning to glance at Dylis. "I want to get away under the cover of darkness. Cunomoltus, brother, I want you to wait for a week after we have gone and then send a message to Cunitius at Priscinus's farm, telling him that I have unexpectedly been called away to Deva Victrix. Tell him that there is urgent news from Fergus and that I will be gone for a while."

"And what is the real plan?" Dylis muttered, folding her arms across her chest.

"It is possible that Cunitius or the Governor will have sent men to watch all the major ports, Rutipiae, Reginorum, Londinium," Marcus said carefully. "So, we shall be avoiding those places and harbours. Instead Cunomoltus will accompany us tonight and return to the farm with our horses in the morning. We will make our way to Plautius's farm on the north-west coast. From there I have arranged for a small boat to ferry the three of us across to the mainland. Once on the mainland we shall turn west and head for the old trading post and port at Hengistbury Head. The place is small and isolated enough and it's not too far away. At the old trading post, I know a man who will be able to help us. He's a retired Batavian soldier from the Ninth Cohort. He's a merchant now. We shall stay with him tomorrow night and on the following day, with a little luck we will find a ship in the port that is willing to take us across to Gaul. From there we will obtain horses and make our way overland to Rome. Then once we are in the capital we will meet with Abraham, Petrus's contact and arrange for Esther to disappear into the city's Christian community."

The others glanced at each other but no one said a word.

"Thank you, Marcus, you are a righteous man," Esther replied suddenly from her room. She had risen to her feet and was looking straight at Marcus, her face resolute. "I am ready to go. I have prayed to God. He will be with us on this journey."

"Yes well," Marcus grunted, sizing her up, "I don't know about that, but there is one more thing. I have heard a lot of talk about you having some clearly visible identifying features on your body, but when I look at you I can't see anything. What are these people talking about? I need to know."

Esther did not reply as she gave Dylis a quick alarmed look. At Marcus's side Dylis hissed in annoyance and then moved towards Esther. Without saying a word, she turned Esther around so that her back was facing the onlookers. Then gently and carefully she undid Esther's dress, peeling away her clothes, so that her naked back was exposed and as she did so, Marcus groaned. Covering nearly the entirety of Esther's back was a fantastic tattoo of a large, P shaped black cross. The four ends of the cross were immaculately decorated with strange symbols, a dove, a fish and an anchor.

"Fucking hell," Cunomoltus exclaimed as he stared at the tattoo. "If we could remove it," Dylis snapped, standing to one side, "we would but this is a tattoo, it won't just wash out. It is something that cannot be got rid of. So, Esther must keep herself covered, do you understand?"

"What the hell were you thinking woman? Did it really have to be so large?" Cunomoltus blurted out, but his words were interrupted by Petrus who gave him a shove.

"Shut up," Petrus hissed, "This is faith."

"This kind of faith that will get you killed," Cunomoltus retorted.

Marcus suddenly felt someone tug at his arm. Looking round he saw that it was Kyna. There was a resigned and sad expression on her face.

"You need to speak to Efa before you go," Kyna said in a hoarse voice. "If for whatever reason you are delayed on your return journey, this may be the last time that you will see her. She is weakening Marcus. She is growing fragile. She doesn't have much time left."

Marcus looked down at Kyna's hand and then nodded.

"I will speak with her," he murmured.

***

Efa sat in her comfortable chair on the porch overlooking the vegetable garden, watching the slave girl's at work. Her white hair was neatly bound back and fixed with a fibula and a fine silver necklace decorated her neck. She looked frail. It was late in the afternoon and the sun was a golden ball in the blue sky. In the garden the slaves were singing to themselves as they worked. Despite the heat of the day, a blanket was draped across Efa's legs and waist. Beside her on a small wooden table stood a jug of water and wine. She glanced up at Marcus as he came and sat down on the porch beside her, and for a long moment the two of them were silent.

"They have beautiful voices," Efa said at last, as she gazed at the slaves. "I like sitting here listening to them sing. It reminds me of when I was young."

Marcus nodded but did not say anything.

"So, when are you leaving?" Efa asked turning to look at him.

"Tonight," Marcus murmured, "We must leave under the cover of darkness. I have told Kyna that I shall try and be back for Saturnalia."

"So, this is goodbye then," Efa sighed, "and you are worried that when you return I shall not be here. Well that is just stupid," the old lady said in a sarcastic voice. "You should know me better than that."

"You are ill, Efa," Marcus muttered, "Remember what the doctor in Londinium said."

"I don't give a damn about any doctors," Efa retorted. "They pretend to know everything and yet they know nothing. I don't believe a word of what they say. So, stop worrying about me and focus on what you must do Marcus. I shall be here when you return. I am the least of your worries."

A little smile appeared on Marcus's lips as he looked away.

"If you say so, Efa," he replied. "This man," Marcus sighed, "this Cunitius who is searching for Esther. He is a dangerous man. He is going to be trouble."

"He won't beat you," Efa said in a sharp, derisive voice. "You are Corbulo's son. Nothing will stop you Marcus. I know it in my bones."

Marcus nodded and then reached out to lay his hand on top of Efa's hand and for a moment the two of them were silent.

"I just wish," Efa said at last in a changed voice, "that I am still here to see the whole family together again one final time. That would be truly something. To see you and Fergus and all of us here together, eating, talking and laughing under the same roof. That would make me very happy. It has been too long since we were all together."

Efa sighed and turned to give Marcus a sad little glance. "That was Corbulo's wish you know," she said. "He wanted us all here, reunited and together like a family should be. I hope it will happen one day. So, don't worry about me, Marcus. I shall make an offering to the gods for your safe passage and return."

***

It was dark when the four horses and their riders quietly slipped out through the front gate of the farm and went trotting away westwards. In the night sky the half-moon cast its pale light across the deserted fields and woods and from somewhere in the forest an owl was hooting. A few hundred yards from the entrance to the farm, beside the track and hidden amongst the trees of the forest, the watcher stirred with sudden excitement as he caught sight of the four horses coming towards him. In the darkness, they would never see him, he knew, but nevertheless he moved behind a tree as the four riders came past his position before disappearing into the gloom. As they swept past the watcher tried to pick out faces but it was too dark to be sure yet one of the riders appeared to be a woman. His employer had been right to place a watch on the farm. Silently the watcher turned to gaze in the direction in which the riders had vanished. Then quickly he stooped to awaken a second man who was asleep, his back leaning against a tree.

"Hurry," the watcher growled, "Ride to Cunitius and tell him that Marcus is on the move with three companions. They just rode out into the night. He may have the woman with him."

The second man hastily struggled to his feet and turned to peer up the dark track.

"Are you sure it was him?" the second man blurted out.

"Who else would be leaving the farm at this hour?" the watcher snapped. "Now hurry, get moving. Cunitius will want to know about this."

"And what are you going to do?" the second man hissed.

"I am going to follow them and see where they are heading," the watcher replied, "and try and confirm whether he has the woman with him. That reward is going to ours, brother."

Chapter Six – The Hunted

The salt marshes stretched away along the sea coast, a desolate scene of musty smelling water pools, muddy sand banks and a vast tangle of tall reeds that swayed gently in the cool morning breeze. It was dawn and to the east the sun was rising into a fine, cloudless blue sky. Marcus sat crouching in the prow of the little boat as it slowly nosed its way deeper into the myriad of narrow, hidden waterways and channels. As they pushed on into the swamp a couple of geese, disturbed by their approach, flew up into the air with outraged honks.

At the back of the little boat that had ferried them across the straights from Vectis to the mainland, the boatman was standing up and using a long wooden pole to propel them up the channel. Marcus turned to glance at Petrus and Esther who were sitting behind him. Esther, her body wrapped in a dark cloak with a hood covering her head seemed to be asleep, her head resting against Petrus's shoulder. As Marcus gazed at her, Petrus gave him a confident wink. Ignoring Petrus, Marcus turned to stare at the towering white cliffs of distant Vectis, which rose from the sea like the prow of a gigantic ship and as he did he suddenly felt a sharp pang of sadness. Slowly he shook his head and squinted at the distant cliffs. He had lost count of the times he'd made the journey from his island home to the mainland and never had he experienced such sadness, but today he did. Today, he felt it more than ever. Was he never going to be able to settle down and grow old in peace? Marcus sighed and forced himself to look away. Cunomoltus should be nearly back at the farm by now with the horses and if his plan worked it would be days before Cunitius realised what had happened by which time it would be too late.

"This is as far as I go, the beach is over in that direction," the boatman growled as the boat glided gently onto a sand bank.

Marcus swung his legs over the side of the boat and his feet sank into mud flat. Steadying himself he reaching out to help

Esther out of the boat. She was quickly followed by Petrus who was carrying a large pack on his back.

"We're heading for Deva Victrix," Marcus growled as he tossed the man a single bronze coin. "In case anyone asks."

The boatman caught the coin and raised it in the air to give it a careful inspection. Then without replying, he cast off using his long wooden pole.

"Come on, let's go," Marcus said quietly turning to his companions. Then briskly he started out across the mud towards the gravelly beach.

"Do you think he will give us away?" Esther asked in an anxious voice.

"I don't know but it's a possibility," Marcus snapped as he waded through the water, "If he knows about the reward for your capture he may be tempted and I am sure he got a good look at your face. We must be careful."

"So, what's the plan from here?" Petrus said in a cheerful voice as they reached the firmer ground.

Standing on the beach Marcus paused and turned to gaze westwards. There was no one about. They were alone.

"I told you before," Marcus snapped irritably, "We have a ten mile walk to the port. We will follow the beach and coast and stay away from any villages. The fewer people who see us the better. At Hengistbury Head I know a man who will be able to help us. We will stay with him tonight. Tomorrow we will find a ship that will take us across to Gaul."

"These Batavian's of yours are everywhere," Petrus replied sourly. "But how do we know if we can trust him, Marcus? If this reward for Esther's capture is widely known, maybe he will be tempted to turn us in. You are taking a big risk in trusting this man, this Batavian friend of yours."

Slowly Marcus turned to glare at Petrus.

"We have a long journey ahead of us," Marcus growled, "So don't make me regret taking you with me, boy. Now start walking."

"Don't call me boy," Petrus replied sulkily, as he adjusted the heavy pack on his back and started to follow Marcus and Esther along the stony beach.

***

It was approaching noon when Marcus called a halt and the weary travellers left the path and gratefully sank down onto the forest floor. Lowering his pack to the ground from his sweat soaked back, Petrus rummaged inside and produced a loaf of hard black bread and a lump of cheese. Marcus however did not seem interested in the food or in resting his feet. He looked concerned as he leaned against a tree and gazed back down the path along which they had just come. Soon after they had set out from the beach he had heard a horn ringing out in the distance. It was just a feeling, some animalistic sense of danger but he couldn't shake it. The feeling that they were being followed had started to grow on him.

"What's the matter?" Petrus asked seeing the troubled look on Marcus's face.

But Marcus shook his head.

"Nothing, boy," he growled, his eyes fixed on the path that disappeared away into the trees.

Sitting on the ground, Petrus took a deep frustrated breath. "I told you before," he snapped, "don't call me a boy. I am twenty-eight years old, for fuck's sake. Did you know that I once saved Corbulo's life in Viriconium and that I helped him find his way, navigating by the stars when we were lost in the woods? I know how to handle myself, so for the final time, stop calling me boy."

Slowly Marcus wrenched his eyes away from the path and turned to glare at Petrus.

"You get us into trouble, that's what you do," Marcus hissed irritably. "Your stupidity managed to make enemies of the priests in Reginorum and that nearly cost us our farm and home. Don't think I have forgotten. And your insolence is most annoying. You have no respect for anything. That's why you are a boy."

"I respect Christus," Petrus retorted with a hurt look. "And for what it is worth I grew to respect Corbulo. He wasn't that bad in the end."

"I do not care for your God," Marcus growled glancing at Esther.

"As far as I am concerned, Cunomoltus is right, you Christians are trouble makers. One day your God is going to cause endless struggle and loss of life."

"So why are you taking Esther to Rome? Why are you even here?" Petrus said angrily. "If you don't like us then why don't you go back home and I will take Esther to Rome by myself."

Marcus looked away.

"You would never make it," Marcus replied sharply. Then he sighed and slowly shook his head. "Esther did a great service to our family at considerable personal risk, misguided though I believe it was, and it is only right and honourable that we now do the same for her. That is what honour means, boy. Without honour and self-respect, a man is nothing."

"Marcus, the philosopher," Petrus said in a bitter, mocking voice.

"Marcus is a good man, Petrus, even though he does not believe in God," Esther said suddenly in a quiet voice, "God has sent him to keep us safe. That is why he is with us. Do not mock him for you are mocking the will of God."

Petrus muttered something under his breath as he gave Esther a quick furtive glance.

"And you," Marcus said, turning to look at Esther, "Enough of this talk about God. As far as I am concerned you are no longer a slave. When we reach Rome, you are going to be a free woman, so start acting like one or else people may become suspicious."

Esther lowered her eyes to the ground and for a long moment she was silent. Then gathering her cloak around her, she got up to her feet.

"I don't know what it means to be free," she replied, "I have been a slave all my life, I don't know anything else but servitude."

"Don't worry Esther," Petrus said in a calm voice, "I shall teach you what it means to be free. There are no slaves amongst the followers of Christus."

***

It was an hour later, whilst the three of them were walking across a clearing, that Marcus suddenly halted and turned sharply to stare back in the direction from which they had just come. Had that been the blare of another horn in the distance? Amongst the trees of the forest nothing moved and all was silent. To the south, the sea was just visible, the waves glinting in the fierce sunlight.

"What is it Marcus?" Esther asked seeing his troubled face.

"Something doesn't feel right," Marcus replied grimly. "I think we are being followed."

Then before the others could reply he gestured for them to leave the path. Hastily the three of them took shelter in a hollow in the open rolling ground. Lying on his stomach Marcus quickly turned to Petrus.

"Get your sling out and load it," he growled.

Hastily Petrus did as Marcus had asked and Marcus turned his attention back to the edge of the forest, which they had just left behind. For a long time, the three of them were silent as they lay stretched out on their stomachs on the ground, hidden by the terrain. At the edge of the clearing nothing moved and Marcus was about to give up and rise to his feet when suddenly a figure, clad in a long brown travelling cloak appeared on horseback amongst the trees. Marcus tensed. The man had a curved horn made of bone hanging from around his neck. The rider paused and carefully gazed out across the clearing. He didn't seem to be in any hurry and he was armed with a sword and a small round shield was slung over his back.

"You were right," Petrus whispered, giving Marcus a quick alarmed glance.

"When he starts out into the clearing, I want you to bring him down with your sling," Marcus murmured without taking his eyes off the rider. "Do you think that you can do that?"

Petrus was silent as he seems to be sizing up the distance. Then he nodded.

"Who is he?" Esther whispered.

Marcus did not reply as he stared at the figure. Then, with a little gentle nudge the horseman urged his horse out into the clearing and began to come towards them. As he drew closer to the spot where the three of them were hiding, Marcus's right hand came to rest on the pommel of his sword.

"Now Petrus, take him!" Marcus hissed.

Without hesitating Petrus rose to his feet, his sling already whirling above his head. The rider just had enough time to emit a startled cry, when with a fast twist of his wrist Petrus released the small stone. The projectile went hurtling towards the stranger and with deadly precision smacked into the rider's head. The force of the blow knocked the man clean off his horse and he hit the ground with a loud thump. Even before the man struck the ground Marcus was up and charging towards him. As he reached the fallen rider Marcus could see the blood streaming from the man's head where the stone had hit him. The rider was groaning as Marcus yanked his army pugio, knife from his belt and knelt beside the fallen horseman.

"Time to start talking arsehole. Why are you following us?" Marcus snapped as he pressed the cold steel blade up against the man's throat. A moment later he was joined by an anxious and worried looking Petrus and Esther, who crouched in the grass beside him.

In reply the rider just groaned and his eyes remained closed, as the blood from his head wound covered half his face.

"I could have killed you if I'd wanted to," Petrus hissed, boastfully bringing his face close to that of the horseman, "Another inch to the right and my stone would have killed you outright. Yes, I am that good. So, start talking, if you still want to live."

"Who sent you to follow us? How did you know where we were," Marcus cried.

On the ground the rider groaned and then slowly his eyes flickered open.

"Cunitius is going to catch you," the man whispered weakly. "He is going to toast your balls over an open fire. He is only a few hours behind me. He will be here soon. You are not going to outrun him or outwit him. Your pathetic escape plan has failed."

Abruptly Marcus swayed backwards as if something had hit him. Then surprise turned into alarm.

"How does Cunitius know where we are? How did he find us so quickly?"

In the grass the horseman stirred and weakly tried to wipe the blood from his face but Marcus pressed his hand back down onto the ground.

"Tell me," Marcus said with sudden patience. "Tell me and we shall let you live."

The man gurgled up some blood from his mouth and then slowly and painfully he turned his head and looked up at Marcus with a contemptuous expression.

"You have no idea," the rider whispered, "You have no idea of how much shit you are in. Cunitius has dozens of men watching every port, every town. He had men watching your farm last night. He knows everything and he loves a man hunt. You are never going to get away."

"Does he have men watching the port at Hengistbury Head?" Petrus snapped.

On the ground the wounded rider said nothing as he slowly turned to stare at Petrus and at Petrus's side, Marcus lowered his eyes.

"We are watching every port, even Hengistbury Head," the man whispered, staring up at Petrus with a mixture of resignation and defiance.

Crouching on the ground Marcus suddenly leaned forwards, grabbed hold of the man's hair, yanked his head backwards and with a swift smooth movement, cut the man's exposed throat, silencing him forever.

As the blood came gushing out Petrus recoiled and turned to stare at Marcus in horror.

"You are an idiot," Marcus hissed turning to Petrus with a cold, hard look, "Why did you have to mention Hengistbury Head? Why did you have to give away where we were going? This man's dead because of what you just said. If we had left him here alive he would have told Cunitius where we were heading. And you still question me why I call you a boy."

Angrily Marcus rose to his feet, silently cursing Cunitius as he turned to stare at the forest and the rider less horse that was grazing in the grass some distance away. His anger however was fast becoming overwhelmed by a rising sense of alarm that bordered on panic. If the scout had spoken the truth it meant that he had underestimated Cunitius. He had underestimated the resources the man commanded, the speed with which Cunitius had reacted and he had underestimated his skill and resolve at tracking him down. Abruptly he turned away so that Esther and Petrus could not see his face and as he did so Marcus bit his lip in frustration. Then his cheeks blushed with sudden embarrassment as a new realisation dawned on him. Cunitius had played him for a fool. The visit to the farm the other day had been meant to flush Esther out from her hiding place. Cunitius must have suspected that he was harbouring Esther all along and the visit had been meant to encourage him to make a break for it. And now the hunter had him exactly where he wanted him, alone and out in the open. The scout had been right. They were in deep shit and he Marcus, had allowed it to happen. He'd been played for a fool.

Behind Marcus and still crouching on the ground, Petrus was staring in stunned, embarrassed, silence at the bloody corpse lying in the grass.

Sharply Marcus turned around to gaze at Esther, his face hard and cold, and as he did, she seemed to sense his purpose and rose to her feet, meeting Marcus's gaze with a strange, quiet strength.

"I understand why you would wish to kill me," Esther said in a quiet, strong voice, as she gazed at Marcus, "And I shall not stand in your way if we are in danger of being caught. But you should know that this is not the will of God. He has sent you to me to protect me. That is why you are here. You are a good man, Marcus. I knew it from the first day that I met you, but I also know that you will kill me without hesitation if it means that you will protect your family."

On the ground, Petrus rose swiftly to his feet, looking startled as he turned to look at Esther and then at Marcus.

"What are you talking about?" Petrus blurted out. "No one is going to kill you Esther. I won't allow it."

"But it makes sense," Esther said in a resigned voice, "If I am dead then there will be no one to reveal the role played by your family in Priscinus's murder. With my death, all the evidence disappears. Marcus is right to consider the option and if it's likely that we will be captured, then he must do it. He knows that is right and I know it too. More people will die if I am taken alive."

But Petrus shook his head as he protectively stepped out in front of Esther and his hand came to rest on his knife that hung from his belt.

"I won't allow you to do it, Marcus," he hissed, his face set into a determined expression.

Marcus was still staring at Esther and for a long moment he said nothing. Then with a little annoyed grunt he replaced his army knife in his belt.

"No one is going to catch us," Marcus snapped, "Do you think that I am going to let a prick like Cunitius beat us?"

Chapter Seven – The Frisian Run

It was late in the afternoon when Marcus, who was in the lead, suddenly raised his fist in warning and crouched down behind a large moss covered boulder. Behind him Esther and Petrus hastily did the same. Ahead of him through the scattering of trees and reeds the flat, marshy expanse of a large inland harbour had become visible. The water channels were interspersed with wetlands, mud flats and sand banks and in one of the deeper navigable channels a flat-bottomed ship, with a square leather sail was slowly making its way out of the harbour and towards the sea beyond. Its bank of oars gracefully and silently propelled the vessel towards a narrow winding channel, some fifty paces wide, that formed a gap in the coast line. Carefully Marcus surveyed the scene with an experienced eye. He had never been to Hengistbury Head but he knew enough to know what he was looking for. On the higher ground to the south of the inland harbour, a cluster of thatched round houses stood perched on the top of a ridge protected by a wooden palisade. Smoke was rising from the iron blast furnaces that were operating on the promontory and down in the harbour several shallow draft sea-going vessels lay drawn up on the gravel beach. The smell of burning charcoal hung in the air and in the distance a dog was barking. From the village he could hear the dull metallic pounding of a blacksmith at work.

Hengistbury Head was an old port, so old that no one could remember when it had first come into existence, but it didn't compare to the new docks and harbour facilities at Londinium or Rutupiae. But as he carefully studied the terrain, Marcus could see why the ancients had chosen this place. The sheltered harbour provided an excellent anchorage for ships to wait out storms and to the north, feeding into the harbour, were two rivers which would give access to the fertile farming land to the north. The plentiful supply of iron ore and salt, he'd been told, had once made this a good, strategically placed trading post. But now the place was in decline, overtaken by the development of Londinium as the province's principal Roman port. Marcus grunted as he turned to study the headland itself. On its western, landward side, access to the settlement was sealed off and protected by a double earthen embankment. They would not be getting into the village that way which left him with only one option. He sighed wearily. He would have to brave the waters and swim across the narrow channel that separated the sea from the inland harbour.

Behind him Petrus and Esther crawled up to his position beside the rock and turned to gaze at the small settlement across the wetlands.

"All right," Marcus muttered turning to them, "it's too dangerous for the three us to try and enter the village. So, you two are going to stay here and hide whilst I go into the port and contact my friend and find out what is going on. You are to stay here until I return, even if it grows dark. No fires, no noise, you don't move until I return, got that?"

Esther and Petrus nodded obediently.

Satisfied that they had understood, Marcus turned to stare at the ship that had entered the narrow seaward channel.

"What happens if you don't return?" Petrus said quietly.

"Shut up, boy," Marcus hissed.

***

It was an hour later when soaked to the bone and shivering from the cold sea water, Marcus paused to study the fortified settlement of thatched round houses, barns and workshops. A few people were going about their business but he could see no one who looked like he was one of Cunitius's henchmen. Yet they had to be here. The scout had said they were watching every port. Slowly Marcus ran his hand across his face and beard. Then with a weary, resigned sigh he forced himself out into the open and began to stride purposefully towards the village. He had only met the retired Batavian soldier from the Ninth Cohort once, when the man had come to Reginorum on business. He should have planned this better he thought as he passed on through a gap in the stockade and entered the settlement. Petrus was right, he was placing an awful lot of trust in a man he'd didn't know very well. Grimly Marcus pressed on ignoring the people around him. But if he had learned anything from his army career with the Batavian Cohorts, it was that the Batavians were incredibly loyal to each other. Surely the veteran would help him and of course he would pay the man.

No one however seemed to pay him any attention, despite his soaking wet clothing. And as he strode through the jumble of smelly, crude, wicker-walled buildings with their conical thatched roofs Marcus kept his eyes open. Then at last he saw what he was looking for. One of the Briton round houses had a sign above its entrance door that read

Clodovicus, iron tools and weapons merchant, buy the best in Britannia

Marcus paused at the entrance to the hut and glanced around but he could see nothing suspicious. Quickly he pushed aside the leather apron that covered the doorway and entered the building. Inside the place stank heavily of charcoal smoke. At the very centre of the round house, beside the central pole that held up the roof, a fire was crackling within a protective ring of stones. A man of around fifty and a young girl with long flowing blond hair were crouching around the fire tending to their evening meal. They rose hastily to their feet as Marcus entered.

With relief Marcus recognised the retired veteran he'd first met in Reginorum. The Batavian was a big powerfully built man with long black hair which he'd tied back into a ponytail. A tattoo of a galloping horse disappeared up his arm. Seeing Marcus, the man's eyes narrowed suspiciously. Then he relaxed as he seemed to recognise Marcus.

"You?" Clodovicus exclaimed speaking in the Batavian language, "Well this is a surprise. What are you doing here Marcus? You are a long way from home. Come to buy some of my stuff?"

"Not exactly," Marcus replied in the Germanic language of the Batavians, "I need your help Clodovicus. It's important and I need you to be discreet."

For a moment Clodovicus said nothing as he studied Marcus with growing interest.

"Well, well, Marcus, hero of the 2nd Cohort, has come to me for help. This is an honour," Clodovicus said slowly. Then a broad smile appeared on the big man's lips and he laughed and grasped hold of Marcus in a big, friendly bear hug. "Don't look so worried, man. There is not a Batavian veteran who wouldn't help you. Thunder and lashing rain, so Wodan cometh," the Batavian exclaimed as he let go of Marcus, "Isn't that what you boys in the 2nd used to shout? Of course, I will help you Marcus. Are you in trouble? Why are you soaking wet?"

In response Marcus glanced at the girl with the blond hair who was staring at him. The girl looked no older than sixteen or seventeen. Seeing Marcus's gaze, Clodovicus raised his hand in a dismissive gesture.

"Don't worry about her," Clodovicus said in his guttural Germanic language, "She doesn't understand a word of what we are talking about. She doesn't speak the language of my homeland. You can speak freely."

"Your daughter?" Marcus ventured hesitantly, as he stared at the girl who was gazing back at him.

Clodovicus laughed again and slapped Marcus on his back.

"My wife," the big Batavian veteran exclaimed with a little twinkle in his eye, "Well legally she is my slave but I treat her like a wife. Spent most of my retirement money on buying her and my ship down in the harbour. But now we fuck, nag and fight like any other married couple. She threatens to leave me now and then, but she never will because she knows that I am not a bad man." Marcus turned to look at Clodovicus. "I had to swim to get here," he said as he moved towards the fire and started to warm his hands. "I need to find a ship that will take me across to Gaul and I need to go as soon as possible."

"Sounds like you are in trouble," Clodovicus replied, as the smile on his lips slowly drained away.

"I have heard that the harbours across the whole south coast are being watched," Marcus muttered as he stared into the flames.

Behind him Clodovicus glanced at the doorway. Then he turned and crouched beside the fire and calmly began to finish his meal.

"You are right," the veteran muttered at last, "Strangers arrived a few days ago, there are at least eight of them. They are working together with the customs officials down in the harbour. They are searching every ship that leaves the port. Nothing can leave until it has been approved by them. I have heard that they are looking for a woman, a runaway slave who goes by the name of Esther. Even the customs men are said to scared of them. They told me that it is the same across every port in the province. Whoever is looking for this slave woman must have employed hundreds of men. I have not seen anything like it since I came here. It is a right pain in the arse to have those arseholes rummaging through my boat."

Marcus knelt beside the fire, still staring into the flames, as he warmed his hands.

"They are looking for me," he murmured, "The slave woman is with me and I need to find a ship that will take us across to Gaul. I need to go as soon as possible. The men searching your boat and watching the harbour all work for a man called Cunitius. He in turn is employed by the Governor of Britannia. They are powerful, dangerous men and I have the misfortune of having them as enemies."

At his side Clodovicus paused whilst spooning food into his mouth and turned to stare at Marcus.

"Shit," he muttered, "That's bad my friend. So, the runaway slave with the reward on her head is with you. Why not collect the reward yourself?"

"Can you help me or not?" Marcus growled impatiently.

Clodovicus sighed and wiped his chin with his hand. "It's difficult Marcus," he said in an even voice, "Even if I managed to get you and your slave onto my ship, my boat would be searched and you would be discovered. These men are being very thorough. Two of them accompany every boat that leaves the harbour. They stay on board all the way until the ship has cleared the harbour and is out to sea. It is impossible to slip past them. It cannot be done."

Looking disappointed, Marcus nodded as he continued to stare into the flames and for a few long moments the hut was silent.

"It is none of my business why these men and the customs officials are looking for your slave woman," Clodovicus said at last as he finished his meal and pushed the dirty bowls across the straw covered floor towards the slave girl. "And I am not going to ask you why. Frankly if you have the Governor on your back then I do not want to know about your troubles."

Then the big man turned to study Marcus and there was a sudden hardness and seriousness in his eyes.

"There may be a way in which I can help you," he said quietly, "but if I do help you, I need to know that you will keep your mouth shut about what you will witness. It's not entirely legal and if this gets out, then I am the one who will be in trouble. Do you understand? So, can I rely on you Marcus?"

"Ofcourse you can rely on me," Marcus said looking up at Clodovicus.

For a moment, the big Batavian veteran was silent as he glanced at the blond slave girl. Then carefully he raised his fingers and stroked his chin.

"Hengistbury Head used to be a great port, a big important trading centre," Clodovicus said in a quiet, dignified voice. "Before my time, the merchants based here used to have an extensive network of trading partners across the sea in Gaul, in Armorica. They say that the trade routes across the sea have been used for hundreds of years. People grew rich and family fortunes were made on either side of the channel and with this trade came a powerful common interest, an alliance between the Briton tribes and their maritime counterparts in Gaul. So, when many years ago, Rome invaded Gaul, the Briton tribes were amongst the first to lend their support to their trading partners." Clodovicus sighed as he studied Marcus carefully. "Now I am no historian but I have heard it said that the trading and cultural contacts were so important that this was the reason why Julius Caesar himself came across to Britannia to teach the Britons a lesson. Caesar wanted the Britons to stop helping their Gallic trading partners."

"What has this got to do with me getting across to Gaul?" Marcus asked sharply.

Clodovicus held up his hand in a patient gesture.

"But since the Roman conquest of Britannia and the founding of the ports at Rutupiae and Londinium," Clodovicus said, "this place has gone downhill. The trade with Gaul has been diverted to the new Roman ports. Hengistbury Head is in decline. The young are leaving. There are no jobs, no work. There is no future for this place. Things are looking bleak."

Clodovicus was staring at Marcus now, a hint of defiance in his eyes. Then conspiratorially he leaned towards him.

"But we, the remaining inhabitants here, are not just going to take that lying down," the big Batavian veteran hissed, "Fuck that. People must survive. We must make a living and we have not forgotten who our true allies are. So, we have founded a new industry that has taken over from the old one."

Carefully Clodovicus wiped his chin with his hand.

"Tomorrow night during the darkest hour of the night," Clodovicus said quietly, "if all has gone as planned, a Roman ship will be anchored out to sea, a mile from here, just off the coast. She will spend some time unloading cargo onto the beach. Then she will sail for her home port at Gades in southern Hispania, via the Gallic port at Burdigala. Now I have friends here whom can arrange for you and your slave to go aboard this ship during the night, no questions asked, but it will cost you a considerable amount of money. I cannot say how much, for it will need to be negotiated with my friends and the ship's captain."

Marcus was silent as he stared at Clodovicus. Then abruptly he looked away.

"Smugglers," he muttered. "So, this is the new industry that you and your friends have founded. You have become smugglers."

"Brilliant isn't it," Clodovicus grinned. "The Roman ship that should be off our coast tomorrow night operates on the Frisian run," Clodovicus murmured, "She transports wine and olive oil from Gades to trading partners amongst the Frisii and returns with salt, slaves and amber gem stones. The Frisii are the northern neighbours of the Batavians. They live around the sea marshes and on many small islands to the north along the German coast. The Frisii are a free tribe beyond the borders of the Empire. The Romans consider them allies though and they like to trade. Now if the Frisii merchants had to sell their stuff through the normal regulated Roman trading posts along the Rhine frontier, they would have to pay one quarter tax on their goods. One fucking quarter, that is how much the Roman customs officials demand in tax from any barbarian who wishes to sell their goods in the Empire. And only hard, cold cash is accepted."

A sly little smile had appeared on Clodovicus's lips. "So, we have an arrangement," he hissed. "The captain of the Roman ship trades with the Frisii, charging them only one tenth in tax. The Frisii are happy to sell to him at that rate and the Roman captain pockets the tax that would have otherwise gone to the state. The captain then sails across the sea to Hengistbury Head, where we help unload some of his Frisian cargo, without the knowledge of the port customs officials. Once the goods are inland no one will know or care where they came from. The captain of the Roman ship then lands the rest of the cargo at Burdigala in Gaul where he has a similar arrangement with some of their locals. The Roman customs officials have no idea what is going on and they never will. Fuck them."

"I can see why the Frisii are happy with this scheme and why the captain of the Roman ship does well," Marcus said with a frown, "But how do you profit from this venture?"

"You are clearly not a merchant" Clodovicus snorted with a hint of contempt in his voice, "The Roman state needs money, loads of it so that it can continue to pay its soldiers and maintain the roads amongst other things. So even within the Empire a merchant must pay a tax when bringing his goods across provincial borders. The tax varies between one fortieth and one twentieth of the value of the goods and on top of that there is a harbour charge. So, that my friend is our bonus profit margin when we sell the goods that we shall be picking up from the beach tomorrow night."

Marcus was silent as he stared at Clodovicus. Then he turned to gaze into the flames.

"All right, arrange it," he murmured at last, "And I shall pay passage for three people."

"So where are you going, Marcus?" Clodovicus asked, studying him. "Where are you and this runaway slave woman heading?

"It is best that you do not know," Marcus growled, "For your own security. We are being hunted by a very clever and bad man."

Chapter Eight – The Stupid Boy

Marcus crouched in the soggy mud and stared out to sea. In the darkness, he could see nothing and the only sound was that of his own breathing, the soft whispered nattering of his companions and the gentle lap of the waves as they came ashore on the stony beach. The sea marshes stank of rotting plants and now and then an animal or a fish moved amongst the tall reeds and narrow waterways. Stoically Marcus batted away a mosquito and turned to glance at his companions who were crouching behind him. They had been here all day, hiding in the marshes since before dawn and the enforced stay was beginning to grow wearisome. In the gloom, he could just about make out Petrus, Esther and Clodovicus's friends whom had joined them around noon. Clodovicus himself however had remained in the village and Marcus had been surprised to see his slave girl, with the long blond hair, join the smugglers as they waited for the Roman ship to appear. She and Petrus had quickly struck up a friendship and in the darkness Marcus could hear the two of them whispering. The noise they were making was beginning to get on his nerves.

Suddenly from out of the night Marcus heard a bird call. For a moment, it died away and then it came again. Behind Marcus one of the smugglers quietly rose to his feet and made the same sound. For a while nothing happened. Then close by the reeds began to move apart and a moment later the figure of a man appeared.

"Marcus," a voice whispered from out of the darkness, "where is Marcus?"

"I am here," Marcus growled as he recognised Clodovicus's voice.

In the gloom the figure moved towards him, cursing softly and squelching through the mud. Then Clodovicus was crouching beside him, his breathing laboured.

"If the Roman ship has not been delayed they should be here soon," Clodovicus muttered, steadying himself on Marcus's shoulder. "But there is no way of knowing for sure whether they will come tonight. Any one of a hundred things could have held them up. We just have to wait."

For a moment, he paused to catch his breath. "But there is a problem," Clodovicus whispered at last. "I saw him. Cunitius, the man whom is searching for you. He is here in Hengistbury Head. He and his men are waiting for a pack of hunting dogs to arrive. They believe you are around here somewhere. Don't ask me how they know. The dogs should be here by tomorrow. And if those dogs have Esther's scent then they will find her. Nothing can escape a trained hunting dog when he has your scent. So, if our Roman ship does not arrive tonight, then you should think of another plan and you must do so quickly, Marcus."

At Clodovicus' side, Marcus turned to stare in the direction of the sea.

"My father," Marcus murmured, "Corbulo, once outwitted a pack of trained hunting dogs that were on his trail. The Roman ship will come. We will wait."

"If there is no sighting by dawn, you must run, Marcus," Clodovicus replied as he anxiously patted Marcus on the shoulder and then started wading back towards the smugglers.

Marcus did not look round as Clodovicus moved away. Instead idly, his right hand came to rest on the pommel of his Roman army short sword. Esther had been right. If they were about to be caught he would have to kill her. Grimly he lowered his eyes as he felt the cold, hard steel of the sword. There would be no honour in killing a defenceless, pious woman who had done nothing wrong. There would only be shame and the shame would bite deep and long. It would poison him. Carefully he raised his head and gazed up at the night sky, but the moon and the stars remained hidden from view. Were the Gods testing him? Was this all part of the price that he had to pay for the bargain he'd struck with the Gods? Grunting with sudden contempt Marcus abruptly looked away. Well if this was part of the price he had to pay to keep Fergus alive then he would endure it. He would rise above it all, for his son's survival was vastly more important than his own.

Suddenly from out to sea a light appeared and as it did an excited whisper rose in the marshes. Marcus tensed as he stared at the pin prick of light. Quickly the light was joined by a second light and a moment later the two lights began to move up and down.

"That's the signal," one of the smugglers called out softly, "They are here. Raise the answering torch."

From the marshes one of the smugglers hastily raised a wooden pole on which hung a solitary oil lamp and swiftly waved it around.

"Let's go," Clodovicus called out in a quiet, excited voice. A moment later the band of smugglers rose from their hiding places amongst the reeds and began racing towards the stony beach. Marcus, Esther and Petrus joined them and as they made it up onto the beach, Marcus could see that Clodovicus and his smugglers were already at the water's edge, wading into the gentle surf.

"Look Esther, we're going to make it," Petrus whispered in an excited voice, as he adjusted the heavy pack he was carrying.

Marcus was silent as he paused and crouched on the stony beach and stared into the darkness. A few moments later one of the smugglers gave a quiet warning cry and from the gloom a rowing boat suddenly appeared. Four men were handling the oars and packed in between them were a large pile of sacks and tall ceramic amphorae. With a smooth grinding noise the rowing boat glided up onto the beach and as it did the smugglers swarmed over her.

Petrus rose to his feet as he was about to join them, but a sharp command from Marcus made him sit back down again. In the surf the Roman ship's crew and the smugglers were talking in hushed, urgent voices as a multitude of hands swiftly helped to unload the boat's cargo and bring it up onto the beach.

It was only when the cargo had finally been unloaded that Clodovicus detached himself from the men working in the surf and came towards Marcus accompanied by his blond slave girl.

"The captain has agreed to take you to Gaul," Clodovicus said in a hushed voice as Marcus rose to his feet. "You pay him half now and half on arrival in Armorica or Burdigala whichever you prefer. No questions asked. Have you ever been to sea before Marcus?"

"I have," Marcus muttered as a tight grin appeared on his lips, "I have sailed further than you could ever imagine."

Clodovicus shook his head, his happy face beaming.

"I am sure you have. Now go my friend and safe travels to wherever you are heading. I shall not ask you where you are going."

"Thank you Clodovicus, I shall remember this favour," Marcus said in a relieved voice, as he stepped forwards and hastily embraced the retired Batavian veteran.

"They are going to Rome," the blond slave girl exclaimed innocently as she turned to look at her master. "Petrus told me whilst we were hiding in the marshes. He told me that Rome is the capital of the world and that it is the largest city ever built. They are going to Rome, Clodovicus."

65

Chapter Nine – Portus Augusti

Twenty-four days later…

Marcus stood on the main deck of the merchant ship and gazed in fascination at the harbour that was now less than a mile away. Across the calm azure sea, the fierce Mediterranean sunlight glinted and reflected from the water trying to dazzle him, and there was barely a breath of wind in the air. The square sail hung listlessly from the mast and the gentle slap of the waves against the ship's hull and the creaking of the ship's timbers was the only noise. At Marcus's side, Esther and Petrus, Petrus sporting a black and bruised eye that had nearly fully healed, stood steadying themselves with one hand against the main mast, as they too stared at the magnificent harbour with silent respect.

"Portus," one of the merchant sailors said as he noticed them staring at the artificial harbour.

Marcus and the others did not reply.

Jutting boldly out into the sea were two elegantly curving moles that enclosed the new and magnificent harbour of Rome, called Portus. They seemed to be reaching out to the small cargo ship as if wishing to pull them into a protective embrace. In the middle of the harbour entrance, set exactly in between the two curving stone moles, a small artificial island had been created on which stood a fine-looking lighthouse. Beyond the moles and inside the harbour of Portus, Marcus could make out dozens of ships of all shapes and sizes. A near constant stream of vessels was entering to the right of the lighthouse whilst other ships were leaving through the gap to the left.

"Impressive isn't it," the sailor chuckled as he caught the look on the faces of the three passengers. "It took them twenty years to construct those moles and the light house. Trust me, this harbour will still be here in a thousand years. But wait until you see the inner hexagonal harbour and the canals that connect Portus to the Tiber. That's the true genius of this place. Trajan employed ten thousand labourers to build them and it was only completed a couple of years ago. Without Portus, Rome, could never have grown to be the capital of the world. You will find nothing like it in the whole Middle Sea and I have been everywhere."

Marcus acknowledged the sailor with a little silent nod but his eyes remained firmly fixed on the harbour. Twenty-four days had passed since he, Petrus and Esther had boarded the smuggler's ship. Their journey had been uneventful and had gone as planned, a quick night time dash across the sea to the coast of Gaul and Armorica, that had reminded Marcus of the great crossing to Hyperborea, and then onwards along the shore to the Atlantic port of Burdigala. Once on land in Gaul they had ridden on horseback over the excellent roads until they had reached the ancient Greek port of Massalia. From there they had found a cargo ship that was heading to Rome and had boarded it as fee paying passengers. And now they had finally arrived at Portus, less than a day's walk from the walls of the city of Rome.

"When we reach the city, I shall find us some accommodation," Marcus said quietly turning to glare at Petrus. "All I need you to do is to arrange for us to meet your contact, Abraham, the Christian priest. That's why you are here. Can I trust you to do that?"

In response Petrus sighed and reached up to lightly touch his bruised eye. "I told you that I will arrange it," Petrus replied in an irritated voice, "but I will need a few days. Rome is a big place."

"And don't fuck it up this time," Marcus growled as he turned back to gaze at the port. "I told you, one more time..."

"Yes, yes," Petrus interrupted with a weary shake of his head, "one more fuck up and you will carve a bloody Christian cross in my forehead. Do you have to repeat yourself all the time? I get it. I am not stupid. I will arrange the meeting with Abraham. It will be fine. Everything is going to be all right. There is no need for more violence. Now can we please talk about something else. You are driving me insane."

Annoyed, Marcus sucked in his breath but he remained silent as he stared at the stone lighthouse that loomed over the harbour entrance. He had still not been able to fully forgive Petrus for the appalling breaches of security that the boy was prone to. Petrus had been boasting when he'd told the slave girl where they were going. An innocent gesture perhaps but it had infuriated Marcus. Petrus's tendency to boast was becoming a serious problem. So, once they had gotten settled on the smuggler's ship the first thing Marcus had done was to give Petrus a black eye for revealing their destination to Clodovicus and his girl. There was only a small chance that Cunitius would ever find out, but it was still a chance, and it had been completely avoidable.

Suddenly Marcus became aware that there were tears in Esther's eyes. Quickly she raised her hand to her face to wipe them away and as she did she glanced hastily and apologetically at Marcus.

"Rome," she gasped in a quiet, emotional voice, "I always dreamed of returning to the city where my family once lived and died. I am close to them now. I can feel their spirits. They are here."

***

With a loud splash the merchant ship's anchor crashed into the water and swiftly vanished from view. Marcus rubbed his right hand across his bearded face and sighed as he turned to gaze at the packed, noisy and busy harbour. Huge grain carriers of over a thousand tons, belonging to the Alexandrian grain fleet, rode at anchor inside the protective embrace of the moles. Further away, close to the entrance to the brand new, inner, hexagonal shaped harbour were the smaller merchantmen of less than two hundred tons; oar-powered galleys; small and fast

Liburna, fishing vessels and the odd naval warship. On land the huge stone merchant warehouses lined the waterfront and along the quayside a long line of cranes were unloading the precious cargoes, which were being whisked into the storage houses or onto flat bottomed river barges for transport up the Tiber to Rome. A column of charcoal smoke was rising into the blue sky from a furnace out of sight and the smell of garum, fermented fish sauce, polluted the fresh salty sea air. Out on the water, numerous smaller craft bobbed up down as they moved in between the larger ships and the waterfront. Marcus slowly shook his head in awe. He had never seen anything like Portus before. The harbour was vast, dwarfing the simple port in Londinium and as he gazed at the names of the vessels and studied their pennants flying from the tops of their masts, he had the impression that the whole world had come to sell their goods in the city of Rome.

Suddenly he gasped loudly in surprise and took an involuntary step forwards across the deck. Alarmed, Petrus and Esther turned in his direction but Marcus ignored them. His eyes were fixed on a vessel at anchor beside the quayside of the inner harbour and as he stared at the ship, the frown on his face was slowly replaced by a delighted grin.

"What is it?" Petrus called out.

"That ship over there," Marcus said with a strange growing excitement in his voice as he pointed at a small battered looking merchant vessel, "that's the Hermes. It's the fucking Hermes! That's the ship that took me across the ocean to Hyperborea. Of course, I should have known that Alexandros, would be here. He told me he was going to Rome. How could I have forgotten that."

For a long moment, Marcus gazed at the Hermes with a fond expression, lost in a hundred memories. Then sharply he turned towards his two companions.

"Before we head into Rome I must say hello to an old friend."

***

The Hermes looked in a bad state of disrepair as the little lighter carrying Marcus, Petrus and Esther approached. Marcus sat at the front of the tender and fondly gazed up at the Hermes's battered hull, worn timbers and improvised mast. The ship's red sail had been furled and the eye painted onto her hull was barely visible. He could see no one up on deck and the door to the deck-house at the stern of the ship was shut. The ship looked deserted. Had something happened to Alexandros and his family? Had they sold the Hermes? Shifting his gaze to the roof of the deckhouse, Marcus's gaze lingered on the helm and the two massive steering oars. How many freezing cold and drenched nights and days had he spent up there guiding the Hermes across the vast, endless expanse of ocean without a single sighting of land? With a sigh, he turned to look up at the proud pennant flying from the top of the mast and depicting the face of Hermes, the messenger of the Gods.

"Alexandros, Alexandros, are you there?" Marcus cried out in a loud voice, as unsteadily he rose to his feet and reached out to grasp hold of the wooden hull of the Hermes.

On board the Hermes there was no reply. Marcus called out again but once more his cry was met by silence from aboard the small merchant vessel.

"Doesn't look like your friend is home," Petrus said, sitting behind Marcus in the small lighter. "Come on, we should head into Rome before it grows dark."

"Shut up," Marcus snapped with sudden emotion in his voice, "I said that I would say hello to an old friend and that is what we are going to do."

"But if they are not here…," Petrus exclaimed, hunching his shoulders and raising his exasperated hands in the air.

"Marcus, is that you," a young man's voice said suddenly from close by. Startled, Marcus turned and looked up straight into Jodoc's face. The young man was standing on the deck looking down at him with a calm but perplexed expression.

"Jodoc," Marcus said, his voice tightening in surprise, "yes it's me. Can we come aboard?"

On board the Hermes Jodoc remained silent as he gazed at Marcus and as the awkward silence lengthened, Marcus felt a sudden unease. In his excitement at looking forward to seeing Alexandros again he had forgotten about Jodoc. He had forgotten about the bitterness and conflict that had once existed between him and the son of the druid Caradoc. Jodoc had blamed him for his father's death and although they had been somewhat reconciled since, Marcus was not entirely sure whether Jodoc had truly moved on.

"Well this is a surprise," Jodoc said as a weary, unhappy and resigned look appeared on his face and he folded his arms across his chest. "I hadn't expected to see you again. But life is shit so I suppose letting you come aboard can't make things any worse. If you want to know where Alexandros is, he is inside the cabin sleeping off his hangover. The old man does nothing but drink himself silly these days and the women are ashore, thank the Gods. My wife and I quarrel all the time and her mother always takes her side. My child screams all night and prevents us from getting any sleep. So, like I said, life is shit. Welcome on board. What are you doing here anyway?"

The question seemed to catch Marcus off guard and for a moment he hesitated.

"We are here on business," Marcus replied evasively as he looked away. "I recognised the Hermes's pennant in the harbour. Thought it would be good to come by and say hello."

"Really," Jodoc said with an unconvinced voice as he turned to glance curiously at Petrus and Esther sitting in the small tender. "Business, right."

***

"Juno's arse, Marcus," Alexandros bellowed in a loud disbelieving voice as he staggered blearily to his feet and raised a hand to his head. With a broad grin, Marcus stepped forwards and embraced the big Greek captain. Alexandros stank heavily of stale wine and sweat and he seemed to have put on some weight.

"Good to see you again old friend," Marcus said as he released the big man and stepped back to examine Alexandros.

In response Alexandros groaned, blinked and adjusted the black eye patch over one of his eyes. Then he peered at Marcus and slowly a wide smile spread across his lips.

"Shit, it really is you," the Greek captain exclaimed. "For a moment, I thought that I was dreaming. Ah, my head hurts."

"You look like shit and I see you have started drinking again," Marcus said with a gentle disapproving shake of his head.

"Yes well," Alexandros sighed and cast a quick glance at Jodoc who was leaning against the doorway into the small deck house. "What else is there to do? No one wants to hire the Hermes for any cargo runs. They don't trust the old girl to make it to the next port. We have been stuck here in Portus for months now. Nothing to do but drink and listen to that young whelp over there argue with my daughter."

"Calista is just as stubborn as her father," Jodoc retorted sourly before abruptly turning on his heels and vanishing out onto the deck.

Marcus watched the young man go. Then slowly he turned back to Alexandros.

"What about the meeting with the Empress, Pompeia Plotina, Trajan's wife," Marcus said quietly, "Did you ever manage to get an audience and tell her about our journey across the ocean to Hyperborea?"

"The Augusta," Alexandros replied wearily closing his good eye and groping for a jug of water on the deck, "Trajan has given her a new title. She is the Augusta now. But did I get an audience? Fat chance. I tried Marcus, I tried very hard but I never even got within a half a mile of her. Her officials refused all requests for an audience. And now they have forbidden me from asking again. They threatened to have me thrown to the dogs if I showed my face again at the Imperial Palace."

Alexandros paused to pour the entire contents of the jug over his head. And as he stood forlornly in the middle of the small deck house with the water dripping from his beard, black eye patch and clothes, he shook his head in a depressed gesture.

"No one believes me, Marcus," he sighed, "No one believes me when I tell them about the crossing of the ocean and what we saw and witnessed. They all think that I am mad. They don't take me seriously. In the taverns, they have started to make fun of me."

Annoyed, Alexandros clenched his hand into a fist as he turned to stare at Marcus, passion suddenly blazing from his one good eye.

"But fuck them, fuck the Augusta too. They were not there with us. Remember that storm Marcus, the one that split the mast and sent poor Caradoc overboard. Remember those icebergs; remember those great white bears and the natives with their bone weapons. I think about Hyperborea all the time. But a fat lot of good it does me."

Marcus nodded as he lowered his eyes to the ground. "So, what will you do now?" he muttered.

"Ah, I don't know," Alexandros replied with a depressed groan. "If the Augusta will not listen to what I have to say, then I shall have to find another important person who will. But who is prepared to listen to me and more importantly believe me? I don't know any important people in Rome."

"You and your family are welcome to come and live on my farm on Vectis," Marcus said. "We have a good life there."

But Alexandros quickly raised his hand in the air as a little grateful smile appeared on his lips.

"Thank you," Alexandros replied hastily. "That is a kind offer but I belong at sea. Farming would be no life for me or my family. We are sailors. It's in our blood and like fish we need the water. I shall die at sea and be buried at sea and I will be happy with such an end."

Alexandros sighed. "Don't worry about me Marcus, my luck will change eventually, it always does, like the wind and the seasons. I just need to be patient."

Marcus grunted and turned to look around the deck cabin. "You are right, your luck will change if you help it to change," he muttered. "Nothing is given for free in this life and you must earn your good fortune. I have kept the agreement we made, not to mention a word of our journey to Hyperborea until you have managed to get an audience with someone who matters. You just need to up your game, my friend. Stop drinking, smarten yourself up and befriend the right connections."

Marcus turned to face Alexandros. "I am going to be in Rome for a few days on business. We will be taking lodgings in the city but I will make sure that I come to say goodbye before we return home to Vectis. And if I get the chance I shall try and arrange for an audience with the Augusta. Rome deserves to know about our journey across the ocean."

Alexandros nodded and stepped towards Marcus and grasped him affectionately by the shoulder.

"It is good to see you again Marcus," the Greek captain exclaimed warmly. "I would like that. Just a word of warning if you are travelling into Rome. There have been riots in the city in the past few days caused by disruption to the Egyptian grain supply. Several people were killed in the last riot. Emperor Trajan has left Rome for his Dacian war and the Prefect in charge of the city's grain supply has made a mess of things. The populace doesn't like it when they are denied their free bread handouts. So be careful Marcus. The mob doesn't care who you are when they are out to vent their frustration."

Marcus stepped out of the cabin and into the bright daylight and as he did, his face darkened as he caught sight of Jodoc talking with Petrus and Esther.

"We are leaving," Marcus called out in a loud voice. "Let's go."

As he clambered over the side of the Hermes and into the small transport Marcus caught Jodoc watching him with a sly, thoughtful expression.

"I hope you kept your mouth shut about the real reason why we are here in Rome," Marcus hissed turning to Petrus as the tender started to pull away from the Hermes.

***

Trajan's brand new inner harbour was a triumph of engineering. As Marcus led his two companions along the crowded and noisy quays towards the canal that connected Portus to the Tiber, he kept glancing at the hexagonal shape of the basin and the row upon row or river barges and ships that lined the quaysides. Some of the barges were heavily laden with timber, others with rocks, amphorae, gravel, marble and one was carrying several gigantic stone-carved columns. Marcus raised his eyebrows as his eyes feasted on the activity around him. It was clear that Portus had become far more important than Rome's other and original harbour, Ostia, but at what cost? The new harbour and connecting canals must have cost a fortune to construct. As he looked around him, Marcus suddenly became aware of angry shouts coming from down an alley. Abruptly he paused in the street. A group of children no older than twelve were taunting and abusing a cripple with no legs. The man was angrily trying to defend himself but the children were fearless and were taking it in turns to hit the man with wooden sticks, laughing as they did.

"Have some respect, I served in the legions," the old cripple screamed at the children but they took no notice.

Marcus's eyes narrowed angrily and with a few strides he crossed the street, roughly grabbed two of the kids by their necks and sent them tumbling into the dust.

"Get out of here," Marcus roared, his face contorted with rage as he rounded on the remaining members of the gang. "Have you no shame, you cowards!"

Startled, the children fled away down the alley and on the ground the cripple groaned as he watched them go.

"Thank you, Sir," the old man, who looked around fifty, murmured squinting up into the sunlight as he looked up at Marcus. "That wretched gang do this every day."

"You are a veteran?" Marcus replied gesturing at the stumps of the man's legs.

"I am," the man replied with a hint of pride. "First Italica Legion, Sir, until some fucking Roxolani raiders cut my legs off. I have been begging ever since my discharge Sir. But those children think I am some kind of animal that they can play with."

Marcus turned to stare down the alley along which the gang had fled. Then he fished for something in his pocket and produced a silver coin. Crouching down he placed the coin in the cripple's hand.

"For your misfortune," Marcus muttered, "I have never been to Rome before but tell me how come the Emperor Trajan allows his veterans to be treated in such a fashion? It's a disgrace that men who have served their country should end up begging on the streets."

On the ground the beggar was staring at the silver coin. Then hastily he slipped it into his pocket and glanced around to see if anyone had noticed the exchange.

"Bless you Sir," the man murmured, "It is just the way things are. There are hundreds of us veterans begging in the streets of the city. Fortune looks the other way. Most of the men I know have mental problems. They are not right in the head if you know what I mean Sir."

Marcus sighed and looked away. Then he rose to his feet.

"Did you serve Sir?" the veteran called out, squinting as he looked up at Marcus.

"I did," Marcus replied. "Twenty-three years in the 2nd Batavian Cohort. I fought at the battle of Mons Graupius in Caledonia with Governor Agricola."

"Ah," the cripple nodded, "Mons Graupius, Caledonia. You have come from the north then. Good man. I have heard about the

Batavian Cohorts. They have a worthy reputation as did General Agricola."

Marcus acknowledged the veteran with a little silent hand gesture and was about to walk away but the cripple hastily caught him by his leg.

"A good deed deserves a good deed in return," the veteran exclaimed quickly. "I may have no legs but I have not lost my honour, Sir. If you are new to Rome, you should know that some of your boys have set up home in the Subura. It's a poor shit hole of a district within the city walls, nothing but whores, cheap wine shops and badly constructed insulae, apartment buildings, but if you ever need any help go to the tavern called the Last Truffle and ask for Valentian. Tell him that Honorius sends him a generous customer."

Chapter Ten – The Capital of the World

The walls of the city of Rome were like nothing Marcus had ever seen before. Stunned into silence he, Petrus and Esther came to a halt at the side of the road and gazed across the river at the huge and mighty fortifications, thirty feet high, that ran along the top of the Aventine hill. It was growing dark, but despite the fading light the city was clearly visible and it was enormous. Truly gigantic; like a fat man's belly. Rome seemed to have long ago spilt over its ancient boundaries and expanded beyond the city walls, for the suburbs, endless rows of buildings, streets, multi-storeyed insulae, apartment blocks and industrial buildings stretched away in every direction, covering the ground in brick, mortar, stone and concrete. And over it all hung the faint whiff of a pungent, unpleasant smell. On the tow-path beside the green, placid waters of the Tiber, a team of oxen plodded dutifully along, dragging a heavily laden river barge upstream towards Portus Tiberinus, Rome's river port. Slowly Marcus turned to study the quays and waterfront up ahead. The river harbour, hemmed in to the west by the ridge of the Janiculum and to the east by the vast urban sprawl of Rome, had been squashed into a small, flattish, congested and low lying area that seemed prone to flooding. He could see that efforts had been made to raise the embankments. Dozens of barges and small ships lay moored up against the embankments on either side of the Tiber and even now the place was a noisy hive of activity. Labourers, horses, mules and cranes were all working feverishly to help unload cargoes and transport them into the rows of huge, vaulted concrete storerooms that were packed tightly into the flat, low lying land on the eastern bank. The Portus Tiberinus and the Emporium to the south of it looked congested and Marcus could see why. There simply wasn't any more space left for the river port to expand. All the available space had already been taken. Beyond the quays, his eyes came to rest on a stone bridge that spanned the river, it's elegant stone arches boldly planted into the middle of the current; the fine Roman stone work proudly diverting the river around them.

"It's big," Petrus muttered as he stared across the river at the city.

"I think that must be the Aemilian bridge over there," Marcus replied gesturing at the stone bridge in the distance. "We will cross the river and enter Rome there. Once in the city stay close to me and watch your belongings. This place reeks of money and where there is money there will be crime."

"Where are we going to stay tonight, Marcus, it's getting late?" Esther asked, as she raised the hood of her dusty cloak over her head.

Marcus sighed and wearily turned to look back down the Via Portuensis, the brand-new road that connected Portus directly with the city of Rome. It had taken them four long hours to walk all the way to Rome and now he was tired, sweaty and hungry. But Esther's question had been much on his mind for he didn't know anything about the city of Rome and entering this vast, unknown metropolis without knowing what to expect, made him uneasy. As he silently contemplated the decision he had to make, a column of empty, horse drawn wagons came rolling past heading in the direction of the harbour some fifteen miles away. The wagon driver's eyes were fixed on the road and no one paid them the slightest bit of attention.

"The river captain in Portus," Marcus said, carefully clearing his throat as he watched the wagons trundle away down the road, "he told me that if a man wished to disappear in Rome and not attract any attention to himself, then he should head for the Subura district. So, that is where we will go. We will find a room to rent and in the morning Petrus will go out to make contact with Abraham, the Christian priest. The Subura is in the heart of the city. The captain said it was a rough, lower class district but he also said that it was where all the migrants go when they first arrive in Rome." Marcus paused and then turned to Petrus and Esther. "So, if anyone asks, that's who you are, just another immigrant flocking to Rome in search of work. Got it?" Marcus turned to look at Esther and as he did his tough, hard face softened a fraction. "If all goes as planned," he muttered, "we will find you a place within the Christian community of Rome and we will be saying goodbye within a few days."

Esther's face was unreadable as she turned to gaze at the walls running along the top of the Aventine hill.

"Thank you, Marcus," she said at last in a quiet, subdued voice. "God was truly wise when he sent you to protect me. And you have my solemn promise; what happened in Britannia shall remain solely between you and me. You have nothing to fear from me. I will be true to my word as God is my witness and I shall include you in my prayers."

Marcus nodded, looked away but said nothing.

***

The Aemilian bridge was broader and longer than Marcus had expected it to be and a little way upstream, in the gathering gloom, he was just about able to make out Tiber island and the Temple of Aesculapius, the god of healing. Tiber island split the river into two streams and the Temple itself, he'd been told, was said to be one of the oldest buildings in all of Rome. As he peered at the Temple, Marcus suddenly blushed as he realised that this must be the place where so many years ago, Corbulo, his father had come to ask the Gods, who ruled the destinies of men, for forgiveness for the way he had treated his family. His father had told him the story many years later of how, before he had left Rome for Caledonia in search of Marcus, he had waded out into the river and had allowed the soothing waters of the Tiber to cleanse him of his shame and guilt. And as Marcus now stared at the island in the middle of the Tiber he felt his cheeks burn. He had forgotten. Rome was not just the capital of the world or some vast indifferent metropolis. It had once been Corbulo's city, his father's home.

It was nearly dark when the three of them joined the crowd of pedestrians and labourers who were returning home. As they crossed the Tiber and approached the eastern bank, Marcus suddenly caught sight of a squad of soldiers from one of the urban cohorts. The men, clad in legionary armour and armed with spears and shields were keeping a careful watchful eye on the crowd as they streamed across the bridge and as Marcus stared at the policemen, he saw them pick out a man from the crowd and take him aside. Quickly Marcus glanced at Petrus. He too had noticed the incident and was fidgeting nervously with his fingers. But as they drew level with the city guards nothing happened and within a few swift moments they were back on firm ground and lost amongst the swelling, bustling crowd of commuters.

As they left the crowded river harbour behind and entered the Forum Boarium, the ancient cattle market of Rome, the stench of the city hit them full on and involuntarily all three of them raised their hands to their noses. The pungent smell was eye wateringly strong and rancid.

"Fuck me, this place stinks," Petrus hissed in outraged disgust as he glanced around at the people going about their business. "This is incredible. How can they stand it?"

Marcus ignored Petrus as he led the way across the crowded market and deeper into the city and as they headed in the direction of the Forum he noticed the shabby beggars sitting crouched along a wall, holding out their grimy and pleading hands to the passers-by and the bawdy puppet show that had attracted a small crowd of laughing and amused onlookers. No one seemed concerned by the smell. The inhabitants of Rome must have got used to it.

As they entered the Forum, Marcus paused to gaze about in quiet contemplation. The Forum Romanum was the political centre of Rome, the very beating heart of the Empire and the place from where Rome ruled the world. It was here that the

Senate met and on its western side, perched grandly on top of the Palatine hill was the vast, forbidding complex of the imperial palace. As Marcus looked around he could see that there were surprisingly few people about and the spaces, where the city's merchants, lawyers and bankers set up their stalls during the day, were empty and deserted. It was getting late. Burning torches had been placed along the steps leading up to the huge Temple of Jupiter Optimus Maximus that stood proudly on the top of the Capitoline hill. And as he stared up at the Temple, home to the patron god of Rome, in the flickering firelight, Marcus noticed the magnificent four horse chariot on top of the roof.

A patrol from the urban cohorts came marching past in a single file, the policemen's heavy hobnailed boots clattering across the paving stones and their spears pointing up at the dark, star covered heavens. They paid him no attention.

"Friend," Marcus called out as a man appeared in the gloom hurrying past them. "Friend, which way to the Subura? We do not know the way. We are new to the city."

In the darkness, the pedestrian hesitated but he seemed to relax as he caught sight of Esther.

"The Subura," the man frowned. "Just go straight ahead and when you come across the Temple of Janus take the Argiletum, the street of the book sellers. That will take you right into the centre of the Subura." The man hesitated again. "But are you sure you want to go there? No one goes to that district at night unless you have a death wish. The Subura is a dangerous place. It's rough."

"Thank you," Marcus replied, "We will be fine."

"It's your life," the pedestrian said with a weary shake of his head as he hurried away.

Crossing the Sacred Way, Marcus led them across the Forum until in the darkness he suddenly caught sight of an imposing building. The Temple of Janus, the God of boundaries was smaller than the grand Temple of Jupiter up on the Capitoline hill and surprisingly its doors were open.

"The Temple doors are only closed when Rome is at peace," Petrus muttered as the three of them came to a halt in the darkness. "I heard about this. They are opened and left open during times of war."

"Trajan's Dacian war," Marcus murmured as he stared at the building. "They are open because Rome is at war with Dacia. That must be why."

As the three turned into the Argiletum, the street narrowed dramatically until it was only a few paces wide. The brick terraced buildings on either side of the street were several storeys high and packed into every available piece of space. All the shops were locked up and barred and in the darkness not a single flicker of light showed from within the merchant's homes. There was no one about. At the end of the street however Marcus could hear singing. Marcus raised his hand to his nose as the three of them advanced down the deserted street towards the noise. The stench was growing worse and as they approached the end of the Argiletum, the noise of singing, laughter, screams, yells and music grew louder. Idly Marcus drew back his long travelling tunic so that his sword and army knife were on clear display.

The Subura seemed to live up to its seedy reputation. Along the narrow street, people spilled out onto the pavement from the multitude of taverns, whorehouses and tall tenement buildings, some five or six storeys high. The darkness was lit up by the flickering torch light from within the buildings and the street was noisy and chaotic. Drunks staggered about urinating carelessly against the walls of buildings and as Marcus carefully led his two companions through the rowdy crowds of revellers, he noticed a couple having sex down an alley, uncaring about who could see them. In another alley, a man lay face down on the ground without moving. As they passed a tavern someone emptied a bucket of shit and urine onto the street from a third-floor window and Marcus had to jump aside to avoid being splattered. A moment later a brawl erupted a few paces away, spilling out into the street and from somewhere close by Marcus heard the noise of glass smashing to pieces. Silently he pushed on down the street, ignoring the silent seductive glances of the female and male prostitutes who lounged about in doorways and alleys and who tried to catch his eye. The Subura however was not only filled with taverns and whorehouses though. Here and there Marcus saw the advertising signs of cobblers, wool merchants, barber shops and iron mongers but all the merchants' premises were shut and locked up for the night and there was no sign of any police from the urban cohorts.

Nearly all the revellers appeared to be men. The only women about seemed to be either prostitutes or slaves. Catching sight of a well-dressed man staggering along the street with his arms around a female and male prostitute, Marcus hailed him, stepping out to block the man's path.

"We're looking for a room to rent," Marcus said. "Do you know anywhere around here where we can go?"

The man was clearly drunk and swayed lightly on his feet supporting himself against the two prostitutes. Then he burped and gave Marcus a crazy, happy grin.

"Sure, Janus runs a decent hostel," the man said slurring his words. "He's just down there on the left. He may have some rooms free."

Marcus acknowledged the man with a little silent nod but as he was about to push on down the street, the well-dressed man lurched forwards and pointed a finger at him.

"Say, you are not Jews, are you?" the man hissed crunching up his face before bursting out into laughter and swaying off down the street supported by his two whores.

At Marcus's side Petrus slowly shook his head in disbelief.

"And I thought the taverns in Reginorum were bad," Petrus whispered. "This place is nothing but a heap of filth, heaped on filth."

Marcus however was not listening. Purposefully he started out down the narrow, congested street, his eyes searching the signs that hung above the doorways of the tall, rundown looking apartment buildings. Then at last he spotted what he was looking for. A sign above a door read.

"Janus's Hostel, rooms for rent, decent prices and good food. Foreigners welcome."

Beside the five storey insulae building and down an alley, a feral looking dog was hungrily gnawing on something whilst at the same time trying to keep another dog from stealing his prize.

Without hesitating Marcus barged through the doorway into a small dimly lit hallway. A stairway led upwards into the building and a couple of oil lamps were hanging from the walls and behind a wooden counter a fat man of around forty, with grey thinning hair, seemed to be asleep with his head leaning against the wall. He was snoring. Startled, he woke up as Marcus banged his hand on the wooden desk.

"I was told that you may have a room to rent," Marcus snapped, carefully letting the man get a glimpse of a couple of coins in his hand.

For a moment, the innkeeper's eyes stared at the coins. Then sharply he looked up at Marcus and studied him for a moment as if sizing him up. Then the man's shifty eyes glanced at Petrus and finally came to rest on Esther.

"Would that be for an hour or longer?" the man said with dirty smile, revealing a mouth filled with a row of hideously rotting teeth.

"We will need the room for a few days," Marcus growled. "That's all. I will pay you half now and half when we leave."

"Not from around here are you," the innkeeper said as he turned to look at Marcus. "Let me have a guess. Retired veteran come to Rome seeking a good time. I only say that because you don't look like a poor man and no one with any money or sense comes to this part of Rome if they aren't looking for a good time. So, what is it?"

"We will get on much better if you mind your own fucking business," Marcus snapped. "So, do you have a room we can rent or not?"

The fat innkeeper leaned back in his chair and sighed. Then he gestured towards the stone stairs leading up into the building.

"Top floor, room number one is free. The rent will include food. We serve the best in the whole street. The cook finishes at nightfall. And you will need this, its dark up there," the innkeeper said, handing Marcus a small oil lamp.

The top floor of the crumbling apartment block was lit by a solitary oil lamp fixed to the wall and in its dim light Marcus could see a small landing with two doors. From behind one of the doors the noise of wild party was bellowing out onto the landing. Silently he strode across the landing, unlocked the other door and stepped into the room beyond. In the pitch darkness, he could see little. Behind him Esther suddenly screamed and turning around he saw a rat shooting across the floor and vanishing off down the stairs.

With a weary sigh, Marcus stepped into the room and held up the small oil lamp that the innkeeper had given him. In its faint light, he could see that the room was completely bare apart from a single dirty looking mattress that lay in the corner. One of the sides of the room opened out into an open window and through it he caught sight of the moon and stars in the night sky.

"I think I will pass on the food," Petrus muttered as the three of them entered the room and Marcus closed the door behind them. "I have a feeling that being the best in the street is not going to add up too much."

"Esther will take the mattress," Marcus snapped. "Petrus and I will sleep on the floor. And remember," he said, turning to face his two companions. "There is a reason why we came here. In this place, no one cares who you are or where you are from. It is ideal cover."

"Do you really believe that Cunitius will follow us here to Rome," Petrus exclaimed turning to give Marcus an incredulous look. "You are paranoid, old man. That arsehole lost us when we got away from Britannia."

"Nevertheless," Marcus growled, "I don't like taking unnecessary risks. We must be prepared. Who knows what that man is capable of."

"He got under your skin, didn't he," Petrus said taking a step towards Marcus. "Cunitius actually managed to scare you when we were in Hengistbury Head. Well, well, I didn't think I would see the day when I would see the great Marcus running scared of anything."

"Shut up," Marcus hissed in an annoyed voice, "Of course I get frightened, I am just a man like you but the difference between you and me is that I don't dwell on it. Now both of you get some rest, we have a busy day tomorrow."

"I think I will pass on the mattress," Esther said quietly as she gingerly prodded the mattress with her shoe. "The thing looks like it is invested with lice."

***

As the others sat down wearily on the bare floor and Petrus unpacked the supplies they had purchased in Portus, Marcus strode across to the open window and gazed out into the cool night. In the moon and starlight, he was surprised to see that he had a fantastic night time view of the city of Rome as it stretched and rolled away over the dark hills. In the gloom his eyes picked out the massive oval shape of the Colosseum that seemed to dominate the city around it. Turning to look left and right he saw that the slight, sloping tiled roofs of the tall insulae buildings vanished off into the darkness. In the neighbouring room the loud grunting sounds and cries of multiple people fucking was clearly audible through the thin walls. Marcus sighed and closed his eyes. He already knew that he didn't like Rome. The city was too crowded, congested, smelly and dirty but he would have to endure it. Tomorrow Petrus would find Abraham, the Christian priest and if all went well, they would leave Esther in his care and then set out for home, mission accomplished. And as he thought of the pristine meadows and forests of Vectis and his peaceful and well-ordered farm a stab of homesickness grew inside him. What would he not give to run his fingers through Kyna's hair and feel her warm body beside him? What kind of man left all that behind to come here to this shithole.

The sound of their neighbours fucking had finally subsided when some instinct made Marcus open his eyes and rise to his feet and turn to look at the door. The hour had to be deep into the night. On the floor beside him both Esther and Petrus seemed to be asleep, curled up and covered by nothing more than their travelling cloaks. Warily and silently Marcus rose to his feet and crept towards the door. Had that been a noise outside? Carefully he placed his ear against the door and as he did he heard it again, a little sound that had no right to be there. Someone was standing outside the door. Taking a deep, silent breath Marcus pulled his army pugio knife from his belt and then with a quick movement, he flung open the door. Two men were standing on the landing right outside the door. They seemed to have been listening and both were armed with knives and they looked like they were sober. A startled cry erupted from one of them as Marcus caught the man by his neck and with a violent shove sent him staggering backwards and then crashing over the side of the balustrade and down the stairwell. The second man cried out and came at Marcus, his knife slashing through the air and aimed at his chest. Dodging the blow, Marcus caught hold of the man's knife arm and lashed out with his heavy army boot, catching the man square in his balls which sent him sinking to the ground with a deep painful moan. Then before he could recover Marcus's boot caught him hard and square on the jaw sending him tumbling back down the stairs where he collapsed into an unconscious heap. Hissing in rage Marcus, replaced his knife in his belt, strode across the landing and descended the stairs. And as he did the neighbouring door opened a crack and an anxious face peered out.

"Stay inside," Marcus roared and abruptly the door closed.

Grasping hold of the unconscious man's leg he started to drag the man down the flight of stone stairs, the man's head hitting the steps with a rhythmic and bloody thud as they descended to the ground. There was no sign of the other man. The second mugger must have already fled. As Marcus dragged the unconscious man down the stairs more doors in the apartment block opened, but as the inhabitants caught sight of Marcus dragging his assailant down the stairs they hastily shut their doors again. The fat innkeeper was on his feet and staring at Marcus in disbelief as he came down the stairs dragging the criminal behind him. Calmly Marcus let go of the man's leg, stepped around the wooden desk and before the innkeeper could react he grasped hold of the man's head and slammed his face painfully down on the counter.

"The next time you send a couple of cut-throats to my room," Marcus bellowed, his face contorted in rage, "I will slice open your throat and throw your body to the dogs outside. So, do we understand each other?"

The innkeeper, his face pressed against the desk squealed in terror as Marcus pressed his face hard into the wood.

"All right, all right," the innkeeper yelped in a terrified voice. "I get it. I get it."

"Hell Marcus," Petrus exclaimed clutching his knife and looking alarmed from where he was standing on the bottom of the stairs, "To what kind of shit hole have you brought us?"

Chapter Eleven – Bad Boys

Marcus sat slumped on the floor of the bare apartment room, his back leaning against the wall, and stared at the door with a bored expression. Petrus had already been gone for hours and outside the noon sun had dipped and had begun its long journey towards the western horizon. The room was hot and in vain Marcus slapped at a fly that was buzzing annoyingly around his face. All morning he had been cooped up in this room with nothing to do but watch the door. The thugs had however not returned and all had been quiet. Beside the open window, Esther was gazing out across the city of Rome and, from far below down in the street, he could hear the advertising cries of the merchants and shopkeepers. On the opposite wall, some previous tenant of the room had covered it in crude and rude graffiti.

Suddenly he heard movement outside on the landing and a moment later a little knock on the door. Raising himself Marcus gestured for Esther to step away from the window and get behind him.

"It's me, Petrus," a muffled voice muttered from behind the door. A moment later Petrus quickly entered and closed the door behind him. He turned to Marcus with a relieved, hopeful look, nodding as he did.

"Well?" Marcus growled as he studied him.

"I found them, my Christian brothers," Petrus said with a little triumphant note in his voice, "it wasn't easy but I did it. They are quite secretive. Bit suspicious of outsiders but I think they trust me now. You can't blame them though. Rome is a hostile city to Christians and Jews. They are still burning Christians in the Colosseum, those who refuse to revert to paganism."

"Did you speak to the priest? Did you speak to Abraham?" Marcus interrupted.

Petrus sighed and shook his head. "No, they wouldn't let me see or speak with Abraham. Like I said they are very protective of their priests. But I did leave a message for him and if he wants to meet us he will let us know in due course."

"In due course," Marcus said his face darkening, "how long will that take?"

"Maybe a few days," Petrus replied evasively, "I was told to come back on the Sabbath. They said they would have an answer for me then."

"Great," Marcus replied turning to glance at the open window. "And when you met these brothers of yours, did they ask you why you wanted to meet Abraham? Were they not curious about who you were?"

Beside the door, Petrus hesitated. Then he nodded. "Yes, they wanted to know why I wanted to meet him. I told them what you suggested I tell them, that I needed some advice, advice that only Abraham could give me."

"Good man," Marcus grunted in satisfaction. "Then all we can do is wait until we have the Christian priest's reply."

Turning to Esther, Marcus gave her a reassuring look. "You and Petrus will stay here. Don't leave this room and don't let anyone in whilst I am away. You have plenty of food and drink and if trouble comes up those stairs, you get out through the window. I have already had a look. It is possible to escape across the roofs of the buildings if you must. I won't be long."

"Where you going, Marcus?" Petrus frowned.

"I am going to pay a visit to the Last Truffle," Marcus replied from the doorway, "the tavern suggested by that veteran in Portus. If there are Batavian's staying there then they may have some advice for me on the lay of the land." Marcus paused and then turned towards Petrus. "I don't know this city and I don't like not knowing what we are up against. Maybe the Batavians will be able to fill me in."

"Still worried about Cunitius," Petrus asked raising his eyebrows.

Marcus did not reply as he closed the door behind him and started down the stairs. As he emerged into the ground floor hallway he saw that the innkeeper was not at his post and that another man had taken his place.

"Good day to you Sir," the man said, glancing up at Marcus.

"Fuck off," Marcus replied as he went out through the doorway and into the narrow street.

***

The Last Truffle was a small discreet-looking tavern on the ground floor of a tall apartment block, which opened onto an alley just off the main street of the Subura. Marcus paused as he caught sight of the wooden sign above the door. Further down the alley a pile of stinking, decomposing rubbish was partially blocking the way. The alley itself stank of stale urine and vomit and a pair of rats were busy inspecting the rubbish. In the narrow, crowded and congested main street, people were pushing past each other as they went about their business. On the ground floor of the tall tenement buildings the numerous small workshops, food markets, barber shops and manufacturing outlets were open and doing a brisk trade with customers and slaves looking for bargains for their masters. The noise of the crowd and a dozen different professions filled the street. And over it all hung an ever-present putrid stench. Casting a final glance around him, Marcus entered the alley and approached the entrance to the tavern. Pushing through the doorway he emerged into a large and gloomily lit room. Against the far wall a man was standing behind the bar. He was dipping a cup through a hole in the bar and reaching down into the barrels and amphorae that were stashed underneath the wooden bar. Incense filled the room relieving the smell from the streets and in the far corner, a staircase led up to the floors above. Beside the stairs, a closed door seemed to lead onto a back room. A few customers were hunched over drinks, sitting around a wonky-looking table in the corner. They briefly looked up as Marcus entered before returning to their conversation.

"I am looking for Valentian," Marcus said as he approached the bartender. "I was told that I could find him here."

"Is that so," the bar tender replied, calmly placing his cup on the bar and folding his arms across his chest. The man was clean shaven, with a tough square jaw and he was wearing a short-sleeved tunic. His arm muscles bulged out of his tunic and he had the broken nose of a boxer. He looked around forty. For a moment, he carefully studied Marcus.

"I am Valentian," the man replied. "Who told you to come here?"

Marcus dipped his head and muttered a quick, polite greeting. "Honorius told me about you," he said. "He says that he sends you a generous customer."

Behind the bar Valentian's eyes narrowed suspiciously.

"Honorius said that, did he. A generous customer," he repeated.

"Well, what can I do for you? Some wine perhaps?"

Marcus shook his head.

"My name is Marcus," he said. "Honorius told me that some Batavian veterans like to hang out around here. I was hoping to have a word with them. Do you know where I can find them?"

"No Batavians around here I'm afraid," Valentian said swiftly, as he turned away and started to clean one of the cups on the bar.

"Are you sure," Marcus asked. "Honorius seemed pretty certain that they were here. I served twenty-three years with the 2nd Batavian Cohort and I am new to Rome, so I was hoping to meet some old comrades."

Behind the bar Valentian did not reply as he continued to clean his mugs with a piece of cloth. Then he frowned and turned to peer at Marcus with a pained expression.

"If you are lying to me Marcus," he replied, "I won't take it kindly. No one gives a shit about you and I will not be responsible for what happens. You should know that life is cheap around here. The Batavian's don't like people disturbing their privacy. You have been warned."

Then before Marcus could say anything, Valentian gestured with his head at the door that led to the back room.

"They are in there," he said curtly. "But you leave your sword and knife here. Those are the house rules."

"What?" Marcus snapped.

"Trust goes both ways," Valentian said with a smirk, as he held out his hand. "You will get them back when you leave."

Reluctantly Marcus undid his sword and pugio from around his belt and handed them over to Valentian. Then without another glance at the barman he strode towards the door, opened it and stepped into the back room. A blast of incense wafted into his face nearly making him choke. The backroom was smaller than the bar and completely windowless. Several flickering oil lamps along the walls provided the light and in the middle of the room several men were sitting around a circular table. A pile of gleaming coins was piled up in the middle of the table beside several jugs and cups of wine and one of the men was holding up and shaking a cup that seemed to contain dice. Two stark naked women were sitting in a corner picking at their nails in boredom. As Marcus stepped into the room everyone turned to stare at him in surprise.

Calmly Marcus closed the door behind him as the men, annoyed at the intrusion, loudly pushed back their chairs and rose to their feet.

"Forgive for me disturbing your gambling, boys," Marcus growled turning to face the men around the table. "But I hear that you once belonged to the Batavian Cohorts. Is that so?"

"Who the fuck are you?" one of the men with a hideous scar across his face snapped, taking a step towards Marcus. "Who invited you? This is a private gathering."

"Valentian told me where to find you," Marcus replied raising the palms of his hands to show that he meant no harm. Then he paused and switching to the language of the Batavian's.

"My name is Marcus. For a short while I was acting commander of the 2nd Batavian Cohort when we were camped at Luguvalium in Britannia. I served and fought with Agricola at Mons Graupius. I spent fourteen years on the Danube frontier."

With a grim smile, Marcus held up his mutilated left hand where only two of his fingers remained. "I received this in a skirmish with Dacian raiders. It could have been worse though, it could have been my right hand."

Around the table the men hesitated and glanced at each other. Then the man with the scar raised his hand and rubbed his chin. "2nd Cohort," he snapped replying in the Batavian language, "We are from the 1st but strangely I have never heard of you."

"Maybe you were too young," Marcus replied as a little smile appeared on the corner of his lips. "Anyway, it doesn't matter I can see that you are busy so I will make this short. I am new to Rome and I need some advice. What do you boys know about the Christian community here in Rome? I am seeking to contact these Christians but no one seems to know them."

"Christians," the man with the scar exclaimed, "We don't know any Christians apart from the ones we see being executed in the Colosseum. Why would you want to meet them? They deny the existence of our Gods."

"I remember your name now," one of the Batavians with a dark beard and a shrunken face suddenly exclaimed in his native language as he pointed a finger at Marcus. "You are the officer who gave that speech. What was it? Something like shit here come those damned Batavians again."

"That's right," Marcus replied with a little nod. "Thunder and lashing rain, so Wodan commeth. Maybe you knew some of the officers of the 2nd; Adalberht, Lucius, Hedwig? Adalberht and Lucius are dead now but Hedwig still lives near Aquae Sulis in Britannia."

For a moment, the room fell silent as the men around the table stared at Marcus. Then the man with the shrunken face grunted. "I know this man," he said sharply and confidently in the Batavian language as he turned to his comrades, "This is the Marcus who saved his entire unit at Luguvalium but the Roman officers; they still demoted him."

The shocked room went silent as all eyes remained fixed on Marcus.

"Shit," the man with the scar exclaimed, as he slowly shook his head in disbelief and stared at Marcus with renewed respect. "And here you just walk through our door. Boys, get the man a seat and a drink."

Gratefully Marcus sat down on the proffered chair but he didn't touch the cup of wine that was moved in his direction.

"This is my first time in Rome," Marcus said, turning to look at the eager faces that suddenly surrounded the table, "And I need some advice. If a man wanted to disappear in Rome, what would he have to do?"

"You mean, you want to kill someone?" the man with the scar across his face replied.

"No," Marcus shook his head still speaking in the Batavian language. "If I wanted to vanish into the city and start a new life, how would I go about it, when I know no one whom I can trust and rely on?"

Around the table the Batavian veterans glanced at each other in silence. Then the man with the shrunken face leaned forwards. "You on the run from something, Marcus?" he growled.

"A friend of mine is, she needs to disappear," Marcus replied bluntly.

"She?" one of the Batavians muttered, raising his eyebrows.

"There are many people in Rome who are here because they don't want to be found," the man with the scar interrupted. "Runaway slaves, murderers, debtors unable to pay their debts, foreign spies, Christians, Jews, hell you name it. And the city is an easy place in which to vanish if you have a support group."

The scarred man was staring straight at Marcus. Then he licked his lips. "Newcomers who have no one to support them in this city are fucked," the man snapped. "Let me explain how it works around here. At the top are the rich, the emperor and the senate. They always stick together against the rest of us. You don't fuck with them unless they ask for it. Below them are the ordinary citizens, the merchants and craftsmen, the soldiers, shopkeepers, the lawyers and bankers etc. They like to form guilds that protect their interests. You can rob them once, you can beat them up and maybe you will be able to get away with a murder here and there, but eventually they will gang up on you and then some miserable informant will give you away and they will get their revenge." The scarred veteran gave Marcus a wry smile. "Believe me Marcus, Rome is full of informants ready to sell you to the highest bidder. And below them are the criminal gangs, the unemployed and unemployable, the migrants from the provinces, the scum of the world, most of whom live around here. The gangs need to be watched for they are constantly fighting each other for territory and resources. Whatever you do, don't get caught in their crossfire. They don't care who they kill or harm. They only respect a good, sturdy knife."

"What my friend here is trying to tell you," the man with the shrunken face said interrupting, "Is that you need someone who can watch your back. If your lady friend does not want to be found, exploited and abused, she will need a strong and loyal group of people who will protect her. That's the only way in which she will survive around here."

Marcus remained silent as he took in what had been said. Then he nodded in gratitude.

"One final question," he said rubbing his forehead with his fingers. "If I wanted to arrange a meeting with the Empress Plotina, Trajan's wife. How would I go about it?"

"The Augusta," several voices exclaimed at the same time, surprise written across their faces. "You want an audience with the Empress?"

"I do," Marcus replied.

Smiles creased the faces around him as the veterans turned to look at each other with bemused looks.

"If you go to the imperial palace on the Palatine," the veteran with the scar exclaimed, "they will simply tell you to fuck off. The Empress is a busy lady apparently. But if you really want to speak to her. There is a new ludus, a school for the children of the rich, that has just opened in the Quirinal district and the Augusta goes there every day to collect her cousin's children once their lessons are complete. Your best bet will be to go there and try your luck and speak to her whilst she is collecting the children."

"What do you want to speak to the Augusta about anyway" one of the veterans asked peering at Marcus with interest.

"I haven't made up my mind about that yet," Marcus replied cryptically.

***

It was late in the afternoon when Marcus finally returned to Janus's hostel. The man sitting behind the desk on the ground floor was silent as Marcus strode past and started up the stairs. On the small top floor landing Marcus paused and turned to listen, but no one seemed to have followed him up the stairs. Satisfied Marcus knocked on the door and without waiting entered the room. Instantly he sensed that something was wrong. Petrus was standing beside the open window, his fingers in his hair. He whirled round as he saw Marcus, his face contorted with anguish.

"Esther," Petrus blurted out, "she is gone."

"What?" Marcus shouted in alarm as hastily he turned to look around the empty room.

"I went to sleep," Petrus stammered. "It was just for a short time but when I woke up she was gone. I have no idea where she went."

"Oh, you stupid boy," Marcus hissed, his face darkening, "I told you both to stay here. You were supposed to watch over her. Now think, where could she have gone? Why would she leave without saying anything?"

Beside the window, Petrus helplessly shook his head. "I have no idea, Marcus. I am sorry. What do we do now?"

Chapter Twelve – Women of Rome

It was getting dark when Marcus heard a faint sound outside the door on the landing. Hastily he scrambled to his feet and Petrus did the same. There had been nothing else left to do but wait to see whether Esther would come back. As he glared at the door there came a soft knock. Opening the door Marcus saw Esther standing in the doorway, her head covered by the hood of her cloak. Angrily Marcus grasped hold of her shoulder and propelled her into the room, slamming the door shut behind him. "Where the hell have you been?" he roared, "I told you to stay in this room. Why did you not tell Petrus that you were going somewhere?"

Esther pulled down her hood from over her head and calmly turned to face Marcus.

"You would not have let me go if I had told you," she said in a defiant voice. "There was something that I needed to do."

"What?" Marcus and Petrus cried out at the same time.

Esther took a deep breath and folded her arms across her chest. "You told me once," she said addressing herself to Marcus, "that I was no longer a slave. That I should act like a freeborn woman. Well, I have been trying. I went out to have a look at the house where I was born."

Esther paused as Marcus and Petrus gazed at her in astonishment.

"I went to the house because I hoped to find out a bit more about who my parents were," Esther said quietly and in a dignified voice. "I saw my old mistress. I remember her. She was always kind to me. She is old and frail now but I recognised her. She still lives in the same house. It's on the Aventine hill."

"So, did you speak to her?" Petrus asked.

But Esther shook her head. "No," she muttered, looking away. "There was no opportunity to speak to the woman but it felt good to see her again. If anyone knows anything about my parents, it will be her. My mother and I were slaves in her household for many years."

"You should have told us what you were going to do," Marcus said unhappily. "The city is not a safe place for a single woman to walk about on her own. Especially at night time. This will not happen again."

Esther nodded. "I know," she replied, "but I had to see the house and my old mistress. This is the closest I have ever been to my family. I need to know who they were, Marcus. I have thought about this for so long. I can't stop now. A person who does not know their past, does not know who they themselves are. If it is God's will, then I will discover the truth and be content with who I am."

"This will not happen again," Marcus said angrily, raising his finger in warning. "I haven't come all this way so that you can discover your past. We will meet Abraham, the Christian priest, he will arrange for you to vanish into the Christian community and then Petrus and I are out of here. I have a family waiting for me back on Vectis. I don't have the time or patience for your games."

***

It was morning and a day had passed since Esther had returned. Idly Marcus stood leaning against the brick wall of a building on the Quirinal hill, in the northern district of Rome that abutted onto the city wall. He had been waiting for over an hour already but so far nothing had happened. Just down the noisy, narrow and congested street the tall gates of the ludus, the newly opened school, that the Batavian veterans had told him about, remained firmly barred and closed. Had he mistimed his visit? There was no way of knowing. With a weary, bored sigh, he turned to look around him. The corner of the intersection he'd chosen was busy and in the streets around him people jostled

104

their way past each other. Labourers carrying the tools of their trade, the odd litter-born noble, slaves running errands for their masters; a man leading his horse in the direction of the cattle market. No one paid any attention. Opposite him a woman was operating a fast food stall. It was nothing more than a small handcart on wheels, that was selling pieces of dried fish and other meats, covered in thick helpings of Garum, fermented-fish sauce. The Garum stank to high heaven but no one seemed to mind. The meat however looked rotten and covered in flies but despite its doubtful condition people were happily buying it. As he looked on with a distasteful expression Marcus suddenly realised the reason why Garum must be so popular. For it hid the multitude of rotting sins that lurked inside the meat. With a little disbelieving shake of his head he wrenched his gaze away from the meat and glanced up at the city walls that loomed up behind the buildings across the street. On his morning vigil, he had asked a man how old the walls were but he had not known and neither had the second person he'd asked. It was as if the inhabitants of Rome had forgotten how old their city was. It was a far cry from the people in Londinium, who knew exactly when their city had been founded.

Once more his eyes wondered down the street and came to rest on the tall solid- looking doors of the school. Would the Augusta come today? There had been no time to send a message to Alexandros cooped up on the Hermes in Portus. But as he stood staring at the school gates Marcus sighed again. Since he'd arrived in Rome he was in two minds. If the chance arose and he could catch the empress's attention for a few precious seconds, should he tell her about the voyage of the Hermes to Hyperborea or should he raise the plight of the homeless veterans begging and sleeping on the streets of Rome? He would not be able to raise both issues. Not unless the empress took a shine to him, invited him back to the palace for a drink and asked him to explain his whole life story. Marcus lowered his head and grinned as he imagined that highly unlikely scene. Now, that would be a story to tell the others he thought.

Suddenly from down the street he heard a commotion. Turning to peer in the direction of the commotion he caught sight of the crowd hastily moving aside, as a big, well-dressed man clutching a vine stick, came striding down the narrow street, clearing the path in a loud, confident and commanding voice.

"Make way for the empress, make way for the Augusta," the man cried out.

He was followed by a detachment of soldiers from the Praetorian Guard who came marching down the street in full armour, carrying their shields and spears. And behind them Marcus noticed the grand litter carried by eight litter bearers. A line of stony-faced freedmen armed with sticks, strode along in single file alongside both sides of the litter and bringing up the rear, was another detachment from the Praetorian Guard. A noisy crowd of citizens was following the procession up the street, calling out to the inhabitant of the litter. Along the sides of the street others had stopped to stare as she swept past. Hastily Marcus left his position and crossed the street so that he was pressed up against the wall beside the school gates. He had just made it, when with a creak the gates swung open and two slaves quickly knelt on one knee on both sides of the gate and respectfully lowered their heads. The litter was approaching. Marcus gazed at the white square box. Fine curtains of white silk billowed gently on all four sides of the litter, obscuring the inhabitant from view but through the gaps Marcus caught sight of a plump lady of around forty-five, dressed in a fine, expensive toga. She was lying on a comfortable- looking mattress with a pillow made of silk. Along the street some of the onlookers were calling out, gesturing with their hands as they tried to attract her attention.

"Augusta," Marcus cried out. He surged towards the litter as it was about to enter through the school gates. "How do you sleep at night knowing that many of your faithful veterans are homeless and sleeping on the streets. Have pity on them, Augusta. I beg you."

One of the freedmen shoved Marcus back against the wall and from inside the litter there was no reply or response. Then the litter vanished into the school-yard, the gates slammed shut and the rear-guard of Praetorians took up their position in a solid line along the school entrance, their hard, cold faces staring straight ahead into space. Dejected Marcus shook his head as he stared at the school gates. The Augusta had said nothing. He wasn't even sure that she had heard him. He had wasted the whole morning.

Across the street, the woman selling the rotting meat was laughing at him.

"You think she wants to talk with you," the woman called out. "The Augusta only talks to those who deserve her attention. Not your day is it."

"Shut up," Marcus retorted.

"You will get another chance when she leaves," the meat seller cried, "but she will have the children with her then so her attention will be on them. Come back again tomorrow and buy some of my meat next time. Maybe it will change your luck."

Marcus shook his head in disgust but he didn't move from his position beside the gates. It was a few minutes later when the gates creaked open and a sharp, shouted command made the praetorians form up in the middle of the street, sending anyone unfortunate enough to get in their way tumbling into the dust. As the litter once more appeared, Marcus surged forwards once more but two freedmen swiftly pushed him back.

"Augusta, remember your veterans," Marcus cried out, "They are our best people. They do not deserve to be homeless and sleeping rough."

But from the enclosed litter there was no reply or acknowledgment and swiftly the procession departed down the street in the direction of the Palatine hill. Sourly Marcus watched them go. He was about to have a go at the laughing meat seller when a woman's voice stopped him in his tracks.

"Marcus, Marcus, is that really you?"

Slowly Marcus turned around to look at the woman who had spoken and as he recognised her, a fierce blush appeared on his cheeks. Standing in the school courtyard was a woman in her fifties, clad in a simple black tunica with a fine see through black mourning shawl covering her head. Her greying hair was elegantly done up above her head and fixed with a long bone fibula. The only indication of her status was the array of gleaming amber and gold rings that adorned her fingers. And at her side, she was holding the hand of a little boy of five or six.

"Lady Claudia," Marcus replied, dipping his head with a quick respectful gesture. "You are not mistaken. This is a surprise."

In the school courtyard, Claudia was staring at him in shocked surprise. Then a little teasing smile appeared on her lips and she beckoned for him to come towards her.

"Indeed, this is a most welcome surprise, Marcus. Come on, don't be shy, I won't bite, not this time anyway," Claudia said as the cheeky smile on her lips widened.

Marcus did as she had asked and swiftly the slaves closed and barred the gates behind him leaving him alone with her and the boy. The school yard was small and a few paces away was the entrance to the school building. Claudia's smile was genuine. She took her time, silently looking him up and down, as if he were a prize horse. And as she did Marcus was suddenly transported back twenty years to the Prefect's quarters in the wooden fort at Luguvalium during the great northern rebellion. A stark-naked Claudia, the Legate's wife, was lying on his bed and beckoning him to join her; and he'd joined her. He'd made love to her all night whilst Kyna and Fergus had been sleeping less than a hundred paces away. Hastily Marcus blinked and looked away.

"What are you doing in Rome, my lady?" Marcus said in an uncomfortable voice. "I thought you had made your home in Londinium. I trust that all is well with you and your husband." Marcus cleared his throat awkwardly, "I believe that when we last met, you said that he was a senator, here in Rome."

"Things don't always work out like you would like them to," Claudia replied smoothly. "The school in Londinium is doing just fine as is your son, Ahern. He is a most promising student, Marcus. He is going to be a great man one day."

The smile slowly faded from her face and with a little tap on the boy's shoulder, she sent her student scurrying into the school, leaving her alone with Marcus. Slowly Claudia folded her arms across her chest. "This is my new school," she said indicating the building. "I now have three schools. I am doing well. That's why I am here in Rome and now we are lucky enough to host some of the children of the Imperial family. As to my poor husband, the senator. He is dead. Yes, died just after I arrived in the city. It's such a shame. He had his uses. He was a powerful man, unfaithful but powerful. As you can see I am in mourning for him."

"I am sorry to hear that," Marcus replied lowering his eyes. "How did he die?"

"Someone poisoned him," Claudia said with a breezy sigh as she looked away. "But let's stop talking rubbish Marcus," she snapped, turning to stare at him. "You don't give a damn about my husband and neither do I. Neither of us were faithful to each other as you know. I am glad that he is dead. You were more of a man to me than he ever was."

"I don't think we should talk about this," Marcus muttered as he fixed his eye on Claudia.

"And why not?" Claudia said as she took a step towards him.

"You saved my life and that of my daughter, twenty years ago, when you gave us protection in that fort of yours. What was it called again?"

"Luguvalium," Marcus muttered.

"That's right," Claudia snapped. "It may be twenty years ago, but I remember those days like they were yesterday. Oh, Marcus if only you knew. Those days in that fort with you, they were one of the few times that I have ever truly felt alive."

Claudia chuckled and raised her eyes to the heavens. "Who but you would have the balls to come after me and my daughter and single-handedly rescue us from those rebels. And then you had the guts to tell me off, slap me and embarrass me. Me - a lady of senatorial rank. I could have had you flogged for such behaviour. You must have known that."

"I have a wife," Marcus said in warning. "I have a family. They mean the world to me."

Claudia sighed and turned to look at him.

"I am not trying to steal you away from your wife or family," she snapped impatiently. "I can have any man I like. No, Marcus you misread me. I have no interest or need for your cock. But like I told you when we last saw each other in Londinium, you have an ally in me Marcus and everyone in Rome needs an ally. You are an ambitious man. A man looking to go up in the world but sooner or later such a man must choose who his allies are going to be."

Chapter Thirteen – The Good Christian

"Entrance gate 22, section 9, row 6, seats 12 and 13," Petrus said hastily as he looked down at the numbered pottery shards in his hand. "They gave me these shards. They are our tickets into the Flavian Amphitheatre, called the Colosseum. My brothers told me that we should arrive early and take our seats on the benches where two cocks have been cut into the wood. We are not to sit anywhere else. When the games are over they told me that we should stay in our seats and let the rest of the spectators leave. Abraham will approach us then and we can talk. Those were the instructions. They were very specific about them. Screw up and Abraham would not show they said. That's all. It's a rather strange way in which to arrange a meeting."

Marcus nodded quickly as the two of them strode along the narrow, congested street. It was morning and a couple of days had passed since his encounter with Lady Claudia but there had been little time to dwell on her. For last night, Petrus had returned to the top floor room in a triumphant mood saying that he'd heard from his brothers and that Abraham, the Christian priest had agreed to meet them.

"It doesn't surprise me. You Christians are strange folk but at least you have a sense of humour; two cocks indeed," Marcus muttered, as they pushed their way down the street. "But by meeting in this way, this priest Abraham will be able to observe us for the whole day whilst we have no idea who he is. He is clearly concerned for his own safety and he probably doesn't trust us. It's clever. He has the upper hand. The stands are going to be packed with spectators. We will never know who he is until he shows himself. But when we meet, let me do the talking."

"I can handle it," Petrus snapped, "I set this up. I should be the one doing the talking. You are just the hired muscle here to protect us," and as he said the last sentence, Petrus glanced at

Marcus with a little humorous smile that revealed the excitement that was coursing through him.

Marcus let the remark go with a little shake of his head. He too was strangely excited. Not only was he looking forwards to seeing the Colosseum for the first time, but if the meeting went well he would soon be on his way home.

"Are you sure that we should not take Esther with us?" Petrus asked as the two of them swept out of the Argiletum and into the Forum.

"No, not at this first meeting," Marcus replied, as he gazed up at the magnificent, towering oval-shape of the Flavian Amphitheatre - the Colosseum that rose from the earth, utterly dominating everything around it. "If Abraham agrees to take her into his community then we shall hand her over at a second meeting. But we still don't know who this man is. He could be a murderous, rapist for all we know."

"He is a good Christian," Petrus retorted with an excited grin.

"Let's hope so," Marcus replied, unable to take his eyes off the massive structure of the Colosseum.

As the two of them strode down the Sacred Way, the crowds around them seemed to swell and everyone seemed to be heading in the same direction. A strange excited tension seemed to have made itself master of the crowds, a sense of expectation with a dark, violent undertone. As he wrenched his eyes away from the Colosseum and glanced about, Marcus could see that the crowds already far too large and concentrated for the few visible detachments of the urban cohorts to control and the crowd seemed to know it too. For a moment, they were the masters of the streets and nothing was going to stop them from getting what they had come for.

Passing the Senate House and the Temple of the Vestal Virgins, the crowds swept Marcus and Petrus up the Sacred Way, straight towards the Colosseum and, as they made it to the top of a small rise the great cream coloured, limestone Flavian Amphitheatre appeared before them in its full, magnificent splendour. As he caught sight of it Marcus grunted in disbelief and a tingle of excitement ran down his spine. The oval shaped Colosseum was vast, easily the largest building that he had ever seen and from every access street, crowds of people were streaming towards it. Rising about 160 feet into the air, the three stories of elegantly painted stucco- decorated arcades were surmounted by a podium and an attic. Above the attic hundreds of mast corbels supported a retractable canvas roof. The mass of people assembling around the building was easily in the tens of thousands and the tension and excited buzz was unmistakeable. A series of individual stone posts formed the outer religious perimeter of the building and Marcus could see that people were already queuing to enter the Colosseum through the eighty entrance gates. Squads of soldiers from the Urban and Praetorian guard units were stationed around the entrance and exit gates, their armour, helmets and shields glinting in the morning sunlight.

Grouped directly to the east of the Flavian Amphitheatre, just a short distance beyond the outer perimeter, the proud banners of the gladiator training schools were fluttering in the gentle, cool breeze. Beside the entrance gates to the Ludus Magnus, the Ludus Matutinus and the Gallic and Dacian gladiator-training schools, teams of town criers were standing on top of barrels, shouting out the schedule of the day's games and the name of the benefactor who was paying for it all. Their voices however were barely audible amongst the noise of the surging crowds.

"Remember entrance gate 22, Marcus," Petrus called out as he struggled to stay on his feet amongst the frighteningly-packed mass of moving people.

Marcus wrenched his eyes away from the gladiator schools and turned to stare at the long snaking queues. The four main axial entrances seemed to be reserved for the elite and the wealthy and many of the upper-class citizens seemed to have brought their own chairs and cushions to sit on.

As they approached the outer religious boundary a disappointed and angry cry rose amongst the vast crowds.

"No bread, no free bread. No bread."

The cry spread through the vast crowds of spectators and with the flick of fingers the mood seemed to change slightly from excitement to disappointment.

"Arseholes," a man beside Marcus cried angrily, directing his fury at no one in particular. "They fucked it up again. No free bread handouts, again. What am I supposed to eat today then? It's a disgrace."

Passing the religious boundary, Marcus and Petrus struggled through the crowd until they finally caught sight of the number "22" chiselled into the stone above an entrance gate. When it was their turn to pass through the gate they showed their numbered pottery shards to a slave, who checked the tickets without saying a word. Then they were being pushed up the stone steps towards a passageway. Another flight of steps followed and then another, until they came out onto a long curving passageway with multiple entrances that led out onto the different sections of the stadium. Marcus paused suddenly, unsure of what to do. Pushing past him was a continuous stream of people anxiously looking for their section. More slaves, checking people's tickets and directing them to their seats, were standing beside each entrance that led out onto the terraces. Finally spotting section 9, Marcus beckoned for Petrus to follow him. Showing the numbered pottery shards to one of the slaves Marcus ducked through the short passageway and as he emerged out onto the open terraces, he gasped in amazement. Extending out before him was the interior of the Colosseum and what a sight it was. Stretching for 600 feet in length and 500 feet wide, was a vast open space, with the tiered terraces rising before him, packed with tens of thousands of spectators. Covering most of the top of the amphitheatre, the Velarium, the retractable canvas roof was at its full extent shading the spectators from the sun. Inside the stadium, the noise was already deafening as more and more people streamed out onto the terraces to take their seats.

"Are you going to move or what?" an annoyed voice behind Marcus snapped jolting him into action.

Hastily he turned and finding row 6 he and Petrus edged along the wooden bench until Marcus spotted their numbered seats, 12 and 13. On the plain wooden bench someone had scratched two phallic symbols. Sitting down, Marcus turned to look around him. The section he was in seemed to already contain a couple of hundred people and as he glanced at the faces of the people around him, he knew it would be impossible to pick out Abraham. But the Christian priest must be watching. By now he would know what they looked like. Twisting his head Marcus turned to gaze up at the top of the Colosseum. There was another ring of sections above them but it seemed to be reserved for the poor and for the women, for there was no seating space and the spectators were all standing up.

"This is absolutely amazing," Petrus hissed as he took his seat beside Marcus. "How did they ever manage to build this place?" Marcus did not reply. Instead he leaned forwards and peered down towards the open central arena below him. The sandy space was completely empty and there was not so much as a hint at what the coming spectacle was going to contain. Switching his gaze to the fifteen feet high wall that enclosed the arena, Marcus could see that the elite of Rome had the best seats, closest to the arena itself and that the sections above them seemed to reflect the social class hierarchy of Rome.

"This will be a story to tell the brothers back in Reginorum," Petrus gasped as he stared at the arena, his cheeks blushing with excitement. "I, Petrus, have actually sat in the Colosseum in Rome."

"Remember why we are here," Marcus growled as once again he turned to glance at the faces around him but amongst the hundreds of spectators, no one was paying him any attention. The people's eyes were firmly fixed on the sandy arena below and as the seats slowly filled up the sense of expectation in the crowd continued to grow.

When the games finally began, it was to a loud cacophony of trumpets and as the noise died away the crowds grew quiet. Marcus leaned forwards so that he could get a better view, as a man in a white toga appeared below him in the emperor's personal viewing box and in a loud voice, started to address the crowd. But despite the respectful silence Marcus could barely hear the man.

"Is that the Emperor Trajan?" Marcus asked nudging his neighbour and gesturing at the speaker.

The spectator beside him jutted out his chin. "No, Trajan has left the city for the Dacian frontier," the man replied annoyed at the interruption. "There is a war on, don't you know. That man down there is Gaius Avidius Nigrinus. He's a close friend of the emperor and one of the wealthiest men in Rome. He gets to speak because he is paying for today's show."

For a moment, Marcus studied the distant figure. Then abruptly he turned to glance around at the crowd but he saw no one watching him. And yet Abraham had to be here. Irritably Marcus shook his head and slowly raised his hand in a rude fuck-off gesture. He didn't like not being in control.

Down in the arena the crowds suddenly cheered as through one of the side gates a stream of exotically-clad hunters appeared.

The roars of the crowd grew as the animal hunts reached their climax with the ritual slaying of a huge black bull. Marcus sighed and once more turned to look around as the heralds announced an interval to allow slaves to rush into the arena to remove the carcasses of the slain animals. Along the aisles that separated the sections of the terraces, food sellers swiftly appeared and began to do a brisk trade with the hungry and excited spectators. Marcus was staring up at the sections higher up the stands when the whole Colosseum, some sixty-five thousand or so people suddenly erupted into a huge ecstatic roar. Startled he turned to see what was going on.

In the arena, an opening had appeared in the sand and from the depths below the Colosseum a lift suddenly appeared. Standing on the square elevator as it slowly rose, surrounded by three armed men, was a solitary bearded figure, clad solely in a white loin-cloth. His arms and legs were shackled in iron chains. As Marcus stared down at the scene, the three guards pushed the prisoner out onto the sand and towards the centre of the sand-covered arena and as they did, the roar of the crowd grew. Marcus frowned as he gazed at the man, then slowly his mouth opened, as he understood what was happening. The prisoner was about to be executed. With a final push that sent the man crashing to his knees in the sand, the guards left him and hastily beat a retreat to one of the gates in the side of the arena wall. And as they did the roar of the crowd rose to another pitch as, at the far end of the arena, another gate opened and several lions came bounding into the Colosseum. In the arena, the hapless, solitary, chained prisoner staggered to his feet and turned to face the wild animals. Around Marcus the crowds were going wild, their arms raised above their heads and the noise was deafening. The lions, catching sight of the man lowered their great maned heads and slowly began to advance on the prisoner and as the animals closed with their prey the man calmly stood his ground and raising his shackled arm he made the sign of the cross. At Marcus's side, Petrus suddenly gasped. "He's a Christian," Petrus exclaimed with bulging eyes as he finally realised what was going on.

Marcus did not reply. His eyes were fixed on the Christian down in the arena. The man was about to be torn to shreds by the lions and the crowds were loving it. As he stared at the man's approaching death, Marcus's eyes widened in shock and his cheeks broke into a fierce blush as suddenly the unexpected happened. Around the stadium, the tone of the cries and screams of the sixty-five thousand spectators changed, as down in the arena three young men and one woman suddenly appeared from nowhere and leapt over the wall and into the sandy arena. Ignoring the big starving lions, the four of them ran across the open space and as they reached the martyr they knelt, making the sign of the cross and then reached out to grasp hold of the condemned man's body. On his seat, Marcus abruptly rose to his feet, his eyes suddenly moist and his chest heaving with a strange, unexpected emotion. The four youngsters seemed to have chosen to die with their master. They seemed to be praying. Only once before, many years ago, during the fight to break out from Tara in Hibernia had he seen such devotion to one's comrades and the rawness had awoken something deep inside him. Around Marcus the crowds were screaming at full pitch as the starving lions charged and threw themselves at the disciples. Marcus forced himself to watch the scene as the starving beasts tore the five people to shreds, and as the animals wallowed in their blood and tore chunks of flesh from their bodies, the stadium erupted in an ecstatic scream of approval.

When it was all over and the screams and yelling of the crowd had started to subside Marcus slowly sat back down again, his face ashen. In his seat, Petrus was staring at the gory, bloody scene in stunned, horrified silence. The execution was followed by several gladiatorial fights but Marcus no longer seemed interested in the spectacle. As the crowds around him roared out their approval he turned to gaze at the faces around him, lost in thought. It was only when the games had come to an end and the spectators were rising from their seats and heading for the exit that Marcus seemed to return to his normal self.

"Let's get this done as quickly as possible," he hissed turning to glance at Petrus. "I am sick of this depraved town."

Slowly the crowd dispersed and Marcus was watching them depart when a man suddenly appeared and sat down behind them. Hastily Marcus and Petrus twisted around in their seats and looked up at him. The bearded, simply clad man was studying them with a calm, intelligent expression. He looked around Marcus's age. Then before anyone could say anything he turned his attention towards Petrus and with his hand he made some strange secret signs. Petrus blushed as he quickly repeated the signs with his fingers.

"You must be the Petrus who is so eager to meet me," the man said with a satisfied nod. He spoke in a strange accented Latin. "I am Abraham and you have my attention. So, talk."

Petrus stammered something incoherently and then hastily glanced across at Marcus and as he did, Abraham calmly switched his attention to Marcus studying him with a hint of interest.

"My name is Marcus," Marcus said as he sized up the Christian priest, "Thank you for agreeing to meet us. An unusual place to arrange a meeting but effective. We need your help priest. That is why we are here."

"Many people need help," Abraham replied with a gentle smile. "Some I can help, others I cannot. Why do you come to me?"

Marcus sighed and turned to look away.

"If you don't trust me," Abraham said quietly, "then why do you come to me for help?"

"All right," Marcus growled raising his hand in an annoyed gesture, "That's not what I meant. We need your help, priest. The situation is as follows. We have a woman with us, a pious

119

Christian woman. She used to be a slave but now she is no longer a slave, if you know what I mean. She needs to vanish, disappear. She needs a new home here in Rome, a place where her former master will not be able to find her. Petrus here, believes that you can provide her with a new life amongst your community. That's why we need your help, priest."

For a moment, Abraham said nothing as he took in what had been said. Then calmly he scratched at his beard and fixed his pale eyes on Marcus.

"So where is this woman? Why have you not brought her to me?" Abraham asked.

"You like to take precautions, so do I," Marcus snapped. "For all we know you could be a murderous rapist. We are not handing her over to just anyone. The woman is a good friend. If you agree to take her in, I will arrange for you to meet her tomorrow at a place of my choosing."

"If she is such a good friend, then why don't you look after her yourself?" Abraham said with a slight frown.

"She was born in Rome. She sees this as her home. This is where she wants to be and my home is far to the north," Marcus replied.

"She is able bodied and in good health," Petrus interrupted hastily, "She is capable of working and she will not be a burden on anyone. I promise you. She is a good Christian woman. Her father was a Christian priest who lived here in Rome, many years ago, Nero had him crucified."

"Is that so?" Abraham replied with a sudden spark of interest as he turned to gaze at Petrus. For a moment, his eyes lingered, then slowly Abraham turned to stare at Marcus.

"I was watching you when the wild beasts tore the prisoner to pieces," the Christian priest said with a little smile. "Your reaction was different to that of the crowd. For a while I thought I even saw tears in your eyes. Could it be that you have Christian sympathies?"

"The four disciples, sacrificing themselves so willingly. That was a rare noble act," Marcus said as abruptly he looked away. "Such acts are very rare and should be treated with the respect they deserve." Marcus fell silent. Then he turned on the priest.

"You don't seem so concerned yourself. He was one of your kindred after all, who was executed today."

In his seat, Abraham shrugged and turned to stare down at the arena. "There is nothing new in what you witnessed today. This is the life that we Christians must live and endure here in Rome. One gets immune to it after a while."

Then Abraham gestured at the Colosseum and the terraces that had emptied surprisingly quickly.

"Petrus, I heard you ask how they could have built this place," Abraham said in a calm voice. "Well the Colosseum was funded by the gold that Emperor Vespasian stole from the Jewish Temple in Jerusalem and much of the actual building was constructed by using the muscle power of over a hundred-thousand Jewish prisoners of war. That included my family, bless their souls. This place, this mighty building is nothing more than a symbol of theft and murder, an abomination in the eyes of God and yet," Abraham sighed, "my fellow Romans love it so."

Slowly Abraham turned to look at Marcus.

"If I am going to help you," he said, "then I am going to need to know everything about this woman. I have people who rely on me. I will not put them in danger for you. So, start telling me everything."

Hastily Petrus glanced across at Marcus and gave him a little agreeing nod.

Marcus looked down at the floor. The request seemed fair.

"Her name is Esther," he replied, "And I spoke the truth when I said that she is a runaway slave."

"Why did she runaway? What was the name of her master? Why are you involved?" Abraham said quickly.

Marcus hesitated. Beside him Petrus gave him another encouraging nod.

"Her former master's name was Priscinus," Marcus muttered at last. "He was a wealthy citizen who owned a farm near to my own in Britannia. There was a land dispute between myself and Priscinus and during the dispute Esther murdered her master on the instructions of my sister. I thought the matter was resolved but now the Governor of Britannia has got involved. The Governor was a friend of Priscinus and he has employed a man, a former tax collector named Cunitius, to investigate the matter. That's why we could not stay in Britannia. That is why we came to Rome. Esther needs a new home. A place where no one knows about her past. They will execute her if she is caught. You know what happens when they catch runaway slaves, especially Christian ones."

Marcus fell silent. On his bench above them, Abraham was looking thoughtful.

"So, that is why you are so keen to come all this way and make sure that she is well looked after," the Christian priest said at last, as a little smirk appeared on his lips. "You don't really give a damn about the woman, you just want to make sure that your sister's role in a murder is never revealed."

"That's right," Marcus said turning to face Abraham with a bitter face. "We all do things in life of which we are not proud. So, will you help us?"

Abraham abruptly looked away and for a while he was silent. Then he turned to Marcus and nodded.

"Murder is a sin," he said quietly. "But in these fraught times we Christians must stick together. So, I will help you, Marcus. I will meet you and Esther tomorrow."

Chapter Fourteen – Crossroads

Marcus stood half hidden in the doorway of the alley. Despite the noon heat the hood of his cloak was pulled over his head obscuring most of his face. From his vantage point he had a good view of the entrance to the Last Truffle tavern and the narrow street beyond. Tensely his fingers played with the pommel of his sword that hung from his belt. The time for Abraham to show up had come and gone and still there was no sign of the Christian priest. A day had passed since their meeting high up in the terraces of the Colosseum. Marcus had left the meeting, having arranged for Abraham to meet them in the Last Truffle at noon. He was to come alone and once he was satisfied, Marcus would introduce him to Esther. Except that Marcus had no intention of bringing Esther to the Last Truffle or being there himself. Abraham had been cautious at their first meeting and so he Marcus would be cautious at their second. He still didn't really know whether he could trust the priest. It would be wise to initially watch Abraham from a distance and see whether he had brought anyone with him. Only then, once he was satisfied, would he approach the priest and take him back to the top floor room where Esther and Petrus were waiting. And if Esther agreed they would leave her in Abraham's care and by tomorrow Petrus and he would be on their way to Portus. The thought of heading home brought a little contented look onto Marcus's face.

Further down the alley two women were engaged in a ferocious war of words with each other and their high pitched, annoying voices carried down the alley. He hadn't paid it much attention but now that he thought about it, there was a strange, tense mood in the congested streets and around the neighbourhood. He'd sensed it the moment he'd left his room and had set foot outside. The fact that no free bread had been handed out at yesterday's games had not gone down well with the populace. They had been expecting the bread. And as he contemplated the thought, he was suddenly reminded of Alexandros's warning about the recent riots in the city. Gods, Marcus thought biting his lip, the sooner he got out of Rome the better. The place was nothing more than a nest of filthy, stinking vipers and cut-throats.

Suddenly he froze. Abraham had appeared at the entrance of the Last Truffle and he was alone. For a moment, the priest hesitated as he turned to look around him but he did not see Marcus hidden in the dark doorway. Then boldly the man entered the tavern and vanished from view. Marcus sucked in his breath as he turned to study the street but all seemed normal. It would take Abraham just a few seconds to notice that Marcus was not in the tavern. Would he wait or would he come back outside? In the doorway, Marcus readied himself to move. If Abraham came outside and started to walk away he would follow and catch up with him in the street. At the door of the Last Truffle all was quiet. Suddenly the door opened and Abraham appeared looking a little confused. He took a couple of steps out into the street and shook his head. Marcus was about to leave his doorway when, from out of view, a second man suddenly appeared, sauntering straight towards Abraham and as he did Marcus's eyes widened in shock and horror. It was Cunitius. Startled Marcus staggered back against the door, his heart thumping wildly in his chest. It was Cunitius. There was no mistake. And Cunitius was talking to Abraham.

"Shit," Marcus hissed to himself as he felt his cheeks start to burn. What was going on?

At the entrance to the Last Truffle, Abraham shrugged and gestured at the tavern as Cunitius seemed to listen. Then as if acting upon some finely-honed animal instinct, Cunitius's searching gaze slowly wandered into the alley and towards the doorway where Marcus stood half hidden in the shadows and as his eyes fixed on him, Marcus felt the bile in his throat start to rise. Cunitius had spotted him. He had picked him out from an impossible position.

"There he is, in that doorway," Cunitius roared raising a finger and pointing straight at Marcus. "Seize him!"

Without hesitating Marcus sprang away from the door and raced away down the alley. Behind him he heard loud, angry, shouts and the sound of running feet coming after him. As he shot past the two arguing women, he yanked one of them into the alley and was rewarded by an outraged squeal. Nearly skidding around the corner at the end of the alley, Marcus dashed into a narrow, crowded street but as he did so, coming towards him he saw four, burly-looking armed men, clad in identical white tunics. They raised a cry as they caught sight of him. With a startled yelp, Marcus reversed course and started to run in the opposite direction. Behind him the excited cries of his pursuers filled the street. How many men did Cunitius have? It was impossible to know but the loud shouts of his pursuers seemed to be everywhere. The narrow street was crowded and congested and as he pushed past the pedestrian's, shoving people out of the way, numerous voices cried out in outrage and protest. From a shop a baker suddenly appeared carrying a tray of freshly baked bread that was meant for his stall, but as Marcus barged past he caught the tray with his hand and sent it and the loaves of bread, out of the shocked baker's hands, and flying into the street.

"Seize that man," a voice roared from terrifyingly close behind him, "In the name of Emperor Trajan, seize him. He is a criminal!"

Darting into another alley, Marcus nearly collided with a man leading a donkey towards him. As he raced past, instinctively Marcus lashed out with his heavy army boot, catching the poor beast squarely in its exposed belly and private parts. Loudly braying the animal ripped free from its master's lead and went careering wildly down the alley and into the street. There was no time to see if his pursuers were being slowed down. Gasping for breath Marcus sprinted down the narrow street. Up ahead workmen had erected some wooden scaffolding. A ladder led up to several wooden platforms and the sloping roof of a building. Two workmen were busy replacing the old tiles with brand new ones. Frantically Marcus flung himself onto the ladder and started to climb up it. Down below in the alley he caught a glimpse of his white-clad pursuers surging around the corner and racing towards him. Ignoring the startled cries of the workmen Marcus scrambled onto the first platform and hastily hauled up the ladder. He'd just managed to raise it when he caught sight of Cunitius running towards him. Dropping the ladder onto the platform Marcus grabbed hold of a roof tile, from a neat stack that was standing on the scaffolding, and sent the piece of masonry hurling towards Cunitius. Above him, from the roof, the workmen broke out into an outraged bellow as Marcus sent a furious barrage of roof tiles hurtling down into the alley in the direction of Cunitius and his men. Then, when there was nothing left to throw, he grabbed hold of the ladder that led up to the second scaffolding platform and hastily started to climb. In the alley below Cunitius was yelling orders and as Marcus desperately clambered up onto the second platform, he felt the whole wooden structure start to shake and move. Above him one of the workers was climbing down towards him, cursing and yelling as he did. With a snarl, Marcus leapt across the platform, stooped and with a mighty shove, sent a whole stack of brand new roof tiles crashing down into the alley below. He was rewarded by a scream and a bellow of pain as with a loud crash the masonry smashed to pieces across the ground. As the workman reached the bottom of the ladder and turned to face him Marcus pulled his pugio knife from his belt and held it up to the man's throat.

"Get the fuck out of here," he hissed, "This is not your fight. And tell your friend to leave me alone. Do it!"

Alarmed, the labourer looked down at the knife hovering close to his throat. Then he raised his hands and nodded hastily. Suddenly and without warning the whole wooden-scaffolding structure swayed violently and with a cry the labourer staggered backwards and before Marcus could do anything the man lost his footing and plunged straight to the ground, striking the hard stones with a dull thud. There was no time to see what had become of the labourer. Gasping for breath, Marcus caught hold of the ladder that led up onto the roof and started to climb. And as he reached the sloping, tiled roof the structure of the scaffolding groaned, swayed violently and then with a single splintering crack it toppled sideways down into the alley. With a frantic cry, Marcus flung himself, belly first onto the tiled, sloping roof, clawing at the tiles. Close by the second workman was staring at him in silent, stunned horror. For a moment, Marcus was incapable of doing anything. Gasping for breath he lay clamping himself to the sloping roof as below him the shouts and cries of his pursuers filled the alley. Then something struck the tiles close to his head and with horror Marcus saw that it was a knife.

Hastily he began to clamber up the roof moving on all fours like a spider, his feet slipping and desperately propelling him upwards over the tiles. Another projectile hit the roof close to where his hand had just been. Then he reached the top of the sloped roof and without pausing, he rolled over the top and onto the other side of the roof, but as he did, he lost his grip and with a terrified cry, he went sliding down the side of the roof and over the edge of the building and down into the enclosed courtyard beyond. A line of ropes from which clothes were hanging up to dry, broke his fall and with a horrified yelp he landed with a painful thump onto a table before rolling off it and onto the ground. For a moment, he lay there looking up at the blue sky, too stunned to be able to move. Dimly he was aware of a gathering noise but it was coming from the streets, beyond the buildings. With a groan, he raised his head and hastily checked to see if he was all right and apart from a few bruises and cuts, he was. As he staggered to his feet he caught sight of a small girl staring at him from a doorway. But before he or she could say anything a woman appeared and quickly caught hold of the girl, pulling her into a protective embrace. Suspiciously and nervously she stared at Marcus as slowly she backed away. Outside in the streets the tumult seemed to be growing.

"I mean no harm," Marcus snapped hastily raising his hands.

"Please, which way leads out onto the street? Preferably not in that direction," he added gesturing in the direction of the alley from which he'd just come.

"You don't want to go out into the streets right now Mr," the woman retorted as she continued to back away. "Can't you hear it. There is a riot going on. Best to stay off the streets until it has died down."

"A riot," Marcus frowned. Then as he cocked his head, he heard it too. The sounds of screaming, thuds and things being smashed in the streets. It seemed to be coming from all around. Silently raising his hand to the woman, he crept away towards a doorway and tried the door but it was locked. He paused beside an open window and was about to poke his head through it when he heard an old man's voice.

"No, you don't, I have a hammer," the old man growled in warning.

"All right. All right," Marcus muttered, leaning back against the wall, "I mean no harm. I just want to get out of here. Which way, old man?"

"No way out," the voice growled from inside the room. "No one goes out whilst there is a riot going on. Are you mad? You will find all doors locked and barred. You will just have to wait until it has died down."

"And how long will that take?" Marcus said with a weary sigh.

"I don't know," the old man's voice answered. "The last one took two days. The drunken thugs around here are never content until they have cracked at least a few skulls. In the meantime, you can fix those ropes that you broke in your fall. Those were my washing lines."

***

It was night when Marcus slunk into the crumbling apartment block and hastily mounted the stairs towards the top floor room where he had left Esther and Petrus. The entrance hall of the building was deserted. Outside, the streets of the Subura were littered with broken and smashed debris, broken doors, masonry, overturned street stalls and the occasional pool of blood and lifeless body. The riot seemed to have calmed down after nightfall but here and there loud cries and screams still punctured the night. What had become of Cunitius and his men was anyone's guess, but Marcus guessed that they had not stayed to hang around after the riot had started. As he made it up onto the top floor landing, he paused to catch his breath and listen, but all seemed quiet. Gently knocking on the door, he opened it and carefully slipped inside. In the darkness, he could barely see anything.

"Petrus, Esther," he whispered, "where are you?"

There was no answer from within the room. Quickly Marcus moved around but the room was deserted and completely bare, even Petrus's pack was missing. With a weary grunt, Marcus raised his hand to his forehead to wipe away the sweat. He was exhausted. What had happened to Petrus and Esther? Closing his eyes, he tried to think. What had he told them to do? Suddenly he opened his eyes and swiftly turned and strode towards the open window. Beyond, in the darkness, the contours of the city of Rome were just visible in the moonlight. Poking his head out of the window he turned first to the right and then to the left.

"Petrus, Esther, it's me, Marcus," he whispered into the darkness. "Everything is all right. Where are you?"

In the darkness, nothing moved. Then as he repeated himself, something stirred in the night.

"We're out here, Marcus," a tired and fed-up sounding voice replied. "We have been sitting out here on the roof for nearly the whole fucking day, waiting for you to return. Where have you been, what have you been doing?"

A moment later Marcus saw Petrus crawling towards him followed by Esther.

"Well?" Petrus exclaimed angrily as he clambered through the window and back into the room followed by Esther.

"I think I caused the riot today," Marcus said, leaning back against the wall in relief. Then softly he began to laugh as he allowed the tension, fear and exhaustion to finally seep out of himself.

"You caused the riot?" Petrus hissed raising his eyebrows in disbelief. "Whatever happened to Abraham? You were supposed to bring him here and we were going to leave Esther in his care. What happened?"

"We were betrayed, my friend," Marcus sighed raising his arm and grasping hold of Petrus's shoulder. "Abraham betrayed us. He is clearly not who he claims to be. He showed up at the tavern with Cunitius and his men. They saw me and chased me. I managed to get away and then the riot started. I was lucky."

"Cunitius," Petrus exclaimed, reeling backwards in shock, "Cunitius is here in Rome! How can this be so? How can he have found us so quickly?"

Then before anyone could answer, Petrus groaned and raised both his hands to his head in dismay. "At Hengistbury Head, the blond girl and your friend, the Batavian, Clodovicus; they knew we were heading to Rome. Cunitius must have somehow found out and followed us here. This is my fault. This is all my fault."

Marcus shrugged as he turned to gaze at Esther. "I don't know who Abraham really is," he muttered. "Maybe he is an informant for the state, maybe he truly is who he says he is and sold us out for the reward, it doesn't matter. He and all those Christian brothers of yours are no longer trustworthy. We cannot rely on them anymore. Abraham betrayed us. After our meeting, yesterday in the Colosseum, he must have gone directly to Cunitius and reported what we'd said. And if he knew who Cunitius was and how to find him so quickly, that suggests that our good friend Abraham is no amateur. Maybe he does this for a living?"

"What do you mean, does this for a living?" Esther asked folding her arms across her chest, the darkness covering the anxious look on her face.

"Maybe he is employed to track down and capture unwanted people here in Rome," Marcus replied. "Maybe he is employed by the government to find people like us, runaway slaves, Christians, criminals, spies and send them to the Colosseum for execution. Now that I think about it, he really didn't seem concerned about the execution of those Christians yesterday. That was odd. That behaviour should have been a warning."

Silently Esther came towards Marcus and before he could stop her she placed her arms around him and embraced, pressing her head against his chest.

"Thank you, Marcus," she muttered in a dignified voice as she broke free. "God is wise for he sent you to protect me and you have, both of you have."

Marcus nodded and looked down at the floor.

"Shit," Petrus stammered as he shook his head, "I can't believe this. So, what do we do now? Our only contacts in the city are bust. Should we just leave and find another home for Esther? Should we just go home? I trusted those brothers. I was told that they were reliable. I was assured that Abraham would help us."

"It's not your fault," Marcus said sharply. "Don't beat yourself up about it. We were all fooled and besides, I already gave you a black eye for what happened in Hengistbury Head. I don't have the energy to give you another."

"I do not wish to leave Rome," Esther said in a firm voice. "Maybe the time has come for you two to go back to your home in Britannia. You have done so much for me and I cannot thank you enough. But maybe I should look after myself from now on. This is the city where I was born. This is my home now. I feel it more strongly than ever. I will manage. I will survive on my own. You should go."

But in the gloom Marcus shook his head.

"No," he said in a resigned voice, "I am not going to give up just yet. There is still one option that we have not yet considered."

Chapter Fifteen – The Alliance

It was deepest night when Marcus, leading Petrus and Esther approached the Ludus on the Quirinal hill. Around them the stink of the city was ever present but all was quiet and they had met very few people on their nocturnal journey through the winding streets of Rome. High above in the heavens the stars covered the night sky in a brilliant and fantastic mosaic of tiny pinpricks of light. Feeling his way cautiously along the wall of the narrow street Marcus grunted as in the gloom he finally recognised the tall school gates. Carefully he reached out to give the gates a push but as expected they were locked and barred. Leaning back against the wall he paused. He was learning fast that no one in their right mind left their doors unlocked at night in Rome.

Glancing up at the stars Marcus sighed. They could not stay here out on the streets. No one in their right mind ventured out at night. The night in Rome belonged to the criminals, the rapists, the murderers and thieves and those up to no good. Reaching out he gently knocked on the school gates but there was no response. He tried again but once more the night remained quiet.

"Open the fucking gates, will you, and let us in," Petrus suddenly roared in a loud impatient voice, giving the doors a furious kick.

Startled Marcus turned to stare at the young man, but Petrus's attention was firmly fixed on the school gates, oblivious to his surroundings. And in the courtyard beyond there was a sudden noise and through the cracks in the door, Marcus caught sight of someone holding up a flaming torch.

"Who's there? What do you want? The school is closed," a voice cried angrily.

"We are friends of Lady Claudia," Marcus called out. "Please Sir. There has been a riot and we seek shelter in your school. Lady Claudia knows me. She will vouch for me."

From behind the gates there was no immediate response. Then a voice, much closer now and standing just behind the gates, spoke.

"Lady Claudia is not here. She has a house on the Palatine. Go away. The school is closed."

"No Sir," Marcus insisted shaking his head, "We have no place to go. Please let us in. Lady Claudia will be most displeased if you turn us away. All we ask is a place to stay tonight and in the morning, I shall explain myself to your mistress."

Behind the gates, Marcus sensed the man hesitate. Then with a bad-tempered grumble, something was unfastened and in a few moments the gates swung open a fraction. In the gap an old man appeared, clutching a burning torch and peered suspiciously at Marcus.

"You had better have a good story to tell her," the caretaker grumbled, as silently and without a word the three of them slipped into the school premises and the man slammed the gates shut behind them.

***

Lady Claudia was staring at Marcus with a calm, thoughtful and serious expression as she listened to him. She was clad in a black tunica over which she was wearing a thin cloak and a black mourning-shawl covered her hair. She looked every inch the dutiful, mourning wife of a recently deceased husband. The two of them were alone, standing in her office in the school house. Outside, the voices of several excited children could be heard playing in the school courtyard.

Marcus sighed and looked down at the floor as he finished telling Claudia everything that had happened. He looked exhausted. Ever since he'd first met her some twenty years ago, Lady Claudia had somehow always made him a tick nervous, but after the disaster with Abraham, he no longer had any choice but to throw himself on the woman's mercy.

"You said to me once that if I wanted to go up in this world, that I would need allies," Marcus said, forcing himself to look up at her. "Well here I am. I am officially asking you for help. I wish to be your friend and ally, Lady Claudia."

Opposite him Claudia's face remained unreadable as she studied him. Then her lips parted into a wide smile and suddenly she giggled.

"Oh Marcus," she exclaimed, "you are so sober and formal. There is no need. We are friends and now we are allies. I am glad. I am truly glad that you came to me. Ofcourse I shall help you and your companions. All three of you may stay in my school as long as you like. I shall have food and drink brought to you."

"Thank you," Marcus muttered dipping, his head in gratitude. "We shall only require some time to sort ourselves out. We shall not be a burden on you, lady."

"You will never be a burden on me," Claudia said with a gentle smile, as she slipped her arm around Marcus's arm and began to steer him out of the study and towards the school yard, where the shrieks of the playing children could be heard. "But what you have told me sounds serious," she said as she paused at the outer door leading into the small school courtyard. "This Cunitius sounds like a horrible man and the Governor of Britannia is an arsehole. I met him once. He has hands that like to wander if you know what I mean. He's a beast."

Marcus nodded but did not say anything as he turned to gaze at the children playing in the school yard.

"You are a man who is in trouble," Claudia said as she held onto his arm. "But don't let that worry you Marcus. To an extent, we are all in trouble. Everyone in this city has their own world of little troubles, challenges, fears and secrets. But a true man rises above it all and remains focussed on what really matters."

"And what does really matter?" Marcus murmured.

"Loyalty, Marcus," Claudia answered. "Loyalty to who you are and to your family and friends."

"And what about loyalty to husbands and wives?" Marcus said fixing his eyes firmly on the playing children.

Standing beside Marcus, Claudia chuckled and turned to look at him with an affectionate smile. "Now there is the young Batavian commander I still remember from the fort at Luguvalium," she exclaimed in delight. "That is why I like you. You are never afraid to confront people with the truth, even if they are born several ranks above you. That is why you are priceless, Marcus. You do not fear telling the truth. That is a rare quality in the circles in which I live."

"You didn't answer the question," Marcus said quietly, as he refused to look at her.

In response Claudia turned to gaze at the children. "The truth is that I never loved my husband," she said in a changed voice. "He was not my choice. One day I was told that I was going to marry him and the marriage was arranged by my father and without my consent. It was a marriage of convenience, one that suited my father and my husband. I had absolutely no say in the matter. I had not even met my husband until my wedding day. Yes, Marcus," Claudia sighed as she studied him, "life at the top is not easy. The only thing that we, high-born women of Rome, have any control over, is the choice of poison with which we can despatch our unfaithful, abusing husbands."

"And did you?" Marcus murmured.

At his side, Claudia smiled secretly but did not reply.

"I am sorry," Marcus said. "I should not have asked you that."

"No, you shouldn't have," Claudia replied. "But it doesn't matter. My husband is dead and that is not a bad thing." For a moment, she paused as she gazed at the playing children. "Sometimes, I wish I had been born just a common citizen." Claudia took a deep breath. "Life would be far simpler and more enjoyable if all one had to care about was a farm and one's family. In that respect, you are a lucky man, Marcus, you have everything that can make you happy."

"I have a son," Marcus said. "His name is Fergus. He has been posted to the Dacian frontier with a vexillation from the Twentieth. I worry about him every day. It's hard," he muttered.

At his side, clutching his arm, Claudia nodded.

"Tonight," she said quietly, "Gaius Avidius Nigrinus is giving a party at his house on the Palatine. I would like you to come with me. There are some people that I would like you to meet."

"Nigrinus," Marcus turned to look at Claudia in surprise. "The same man who paid for the games yesterday? One of the wealthiest men in Rome? That Nigrinus?"

"Yes, that's him, he's a good friend of mine. My daughter was married to him briefly before her death," Claudia said looking away. "So, will you come?"

Marcus thought about it for a fraction of a second and nodded.

"Good," Claudia replied. For a long moment, she was silent as if she was remembering something. Then she turned and gave Marcus a sad smile. "Before we go tonight, there is something important that you must understand," she said quietly. "These people who you will meet tonight. They are not just friends. All of us, we form an alliance - a network of people and families that spans the empire, tied together by blood, family, loyalty and friendship. Our alliance includes generals, senators, politicians, governors, merchants, scientists, lawyers, soldiers and yes people like myself. We have thousands of supporters here in Rome and in the provinces. All of us are pledged to support our man and each other. Our alliance, which Nigrinus leads, has supporters in high places right the away across the empire, from Alexandria to the Caledonian frontier." Claudia fixed her eyes on Marcus and suddenly he was aware of something hard and unyielding in her stance. "We are a force. We wield power and influence Marcus - true power that includes the support of five legionary legates, their troops, over a hundred senators and several provincial governors. But we are not the only alliance. There are others, rival networks, some even more powerful than us. We compete with them. And," Claudia paused, "these alliances exist for just one purpose. To make their leader, their man, the next emperor of Rome. For that is the ultimate objective and once our man is emperor, the jobs and positions that are his to appoint, will be given to us, his supporters. That's how it works. So," she added smoothly, "at the party tonight people will want to know where you stand. You need to think about this."

Marcus was silent as he digested what Claudia had just told him.

"It is hard to pledge one's allegiance and support to a man who I have never met," he said at last.

Claudia chuckled. "I thought you would say that," she exclaimed. "But don't worry, I won't force to you to do anything. Just make up your own mind after you have met him. There will be some interesting people there tonight. People who may be able to help you with your own problems back in Britannia. People who have the authority to tell the Governor of Britannia to fuck off and leave you alone. Think about that, but please" - Claudia gently raised her finger to Marcus's mouth, "I want you to do this on your own, with a free mind. We are good people Marcus, we understand that loyalty cannot be forced upon someone. It is your choice to make, your loyalty to give and we want it given freely."

"All right," Marcus nodded, "I shall think about it."

"Good," Claudia exclaimed turning to give him a quick examination, "I shall have some new clothes brought to you. You cannot show up in what you are wearing. I am sorry to say, but you stink Marcus. There are going to be many very important people at tonight's gathering, so I want you to make an impression. And you had better have a shave too, they don't like beards and neither do I."

***

The house on the Palatine hill, the most prestigious address in Rome, was a sumptuous affair just a couple of hundred yards from the vast, forbidding structure of the imperial palace. The small carriage that brought Marcus and Claudia to the house was just large enough to fit them both. As he squeezed out of it and onto the pavement, Marcus could see a line of burning torches lining the entrance to the house. It was already dark and at the entrance a gaggle of people were talking in loud, excited and confident voices, as armed guards and slaves stood motionless to one side, staring silently into space. Lady Claudia came around the side of the carriage and slipping her arm around Marcus's arm she allowed him to lead her towards the doorway into the house. Her face was made up and she looked fantastic in her elegant, stylish tunic and cloak. Her perfume enveloped him and around her neck was a fine necklace of glittering beads and her fingers were adorned with amber and gold rings. The noise of music and the buzz of a hundred voices was spilling out into the night as they approached the doorway.

140

"It is customary," Claudia whispered as they joined the queue to enter the villa, "for a newcomer like yourself to bring a gift for Nigrinus, the host of this party. He will want to know what you bring him?"

Alarmed Marcus turned to look at Claudia. "What, like a cake?" he exclaimed.

Marcus was rewarded with a shriek of laughter from Claudia, and as they gave their names to the house-master and his slaves at the door, she turned to him with an amused look and shook her head.

"No," she whispered, "he will want to know why he is wasting his money and time on you. He will want to know how you are useful to him."

"You could have told me that earlier," Marcus replied as the two of them stepped into an entrance hall. A beautiful and expensive mosaic, depicting a harvest festival with grapes, wine and naked women, welcomed them into the villa. A couple of female slaves were taking the guests cloaks but Marcus waved them away as they came to take his coat.

In the entrance to the main space within the villa, Claudia paused and turned to inspect the multitude and groups of chatting people who stood interspersed throughout the room. At the centre of the large, open space, the roof opened and a square water-basin, used to catch the rainwater, was set into the floor directly below the gap. In a corner, a few musicians were playing on flutes and a giant harp. Incense filled the room, banishing the stink of the city.

"Lady Claudia, mother in law," a voice called out suddenly and before Marcus could react, a handsome, powerfully-built man in his mid-twenties was approaching them. He was clean-shaven and clad in a fine, white toga with a purple stripe running down one side. As Claudia held out her hand, the man kissed it and grinned affectionately.

"Claudia, I am so glad that you are here," the man exclaimed. "I leave for the Dacian frontier within days. Trajan has appointed me as one of his Tribunes. This is probably the last time that I shall see you for a while."

"It is always a pleasure," Claudia replied with a little respectful dip of her head. "Nigrinus, may I introduce a friend of mine. His name is Marcus. He is a retired veteran from Britannia. He is a good friend and many years ago, he saved my life and that of my daughter."

Instinctively Marcus stretched out his hand and to his surprise Nigrinus clasped it in the legionary fashion. For a moment Nigrinus studied him with a curious searching gaze.

"Shit," the patrician muttered at last with a little shake of his head, "so, you are the man who saved both my dead wife and her mother. I have heard a lot about you. You have my gratitude and welcome to my house."

"Thank you, Sir, I am honoured to be here," Marcus replied, awkwardly dipping his head like Claudia had done. "This is my first time in Rome and everything is rather new to me."

"You are a veteran," Nigrinus said sharply, poking his finger at Marcus. "I too have served in the army. Where did you serve?"

"Britannia, Sir," Marcus replied stiffly. "For a short while I was commander of the 2nd Batavian auxiliary cohort. I fought at Mons Graupius with Agricola and then later I was posted to the Danube frontier. I served twenty-three years, Sir."

"Ah, you were with the auxiliary cohorts," Nigrinus said as the interest in his eyes suddenly and rapidly seemed to diminish. "Fine Cohorts, all of them, they do a splendid job, no doubt."

Beside him Marcus sensed Claudia tense.

"The Batavian cohorts are the finest units in the whole army," Marcus spoke proudly, raising his head and meeting Nigrinus's gaze. "They are more than a match for the best legionaries, Sir. During the great northern rebellion, I saved my entire unit from annihilation. The Batavian veterans; they respect me. They will come to my aid if I summon them and there are thousands of them spread across the empire. They are loyal to me, Sir. They are the finest soldiers in the world."

"Is that so," Nigrinus replied stroking his chin as some of his interest re-appeared. "So, tell me Marcus, what do you think of Hadrian?"

"Hadrian, Sir" Marcus frowned in confusion.

"Yes, Hadrian," Nigrinus repeated, "legate of the 1st Legion based at Bonna on the Rhine. What do you think of him?"

For a moment, Marcus looked a little lost. "I think nothing of him, Sir," he said at last, "for I have never met him and have no idea who he is."

Across from Marcus, Nigrinus was studying him carefully. Then gracefully he turned to Claudia and respectfully dipped his head. "You are most welcome in my house, enjoy the party," Nigrinus said as his eyes slipped away towards the next group of guests.

"That was well done," Claudia muttered in relief as the two of them stepped into the room and looked around.

"It was a lie," Marcus whispered uncomfortably. "I may be respected amongst the Batavian community but there is no way that all those veterans would come to me if I called them out to fight. I don't command that kind of influence."

"It doesn't matter," Claudia hissed, as at the same time she managed to smile politely at a couple of men in the corner. "Nigrinus has seen some value in you. That was enough."

"Well that was his gift," Marcus growled as he accepted a drink from one of the slaves and turned to look around the room. "And why was he asking me about Hadrian? Should I know who that man is?"

"Hadrian is our arch rival," Claudia replied smoothly. "He is the enemy. He and Nigrinus hate each other."

"And why is that?" Marcus asked.

"Because if Trajan remains childless," Claudia whispered, leaning in towards Marcus in a conspiratorial manner, "it is most likely that Trajan will proclaim either Nigrinus or Hadrian as the next emperor of Rome. That is what this is all about. Nigrinus and Hadrian are competing for Trajan's favour and blessing. That's why he wanted to know where you stood with Hadrian."

Marcus grunted but said nothing as he turned to look around at the party.

At his side, Claudia sighed and took a sip from her drink as she joined him in looking around the crowded, noisy party.

"You can do anything in this house," she said leaning in towards him. "Follow that corridor over there and if you want sex, there are female and male prostitutes there who will do absolutely anything. If you want to spend the whole night arguing philosophy with the best Greek professors, that is the next room along and, if you fancy re-enacting famous battles from the past with miniature clay soldiers then you can do so at the end of the corridor. Nigrinus caters to all tastes."

"He can afford to," Marcus replied feeling that he was out of his depth amongst these people and the realisation added to his discomfort.

Marcus was standing beside Claudia who was chatting to a couple of toga-dressed senators when a man appeared, clapping his hands and calling out for silence, and as he did an expectant hush descended on the party. Marcus turned to see Nigrinus standing in the middle of the room, looking around at his guests.

"Friends, citizens, supporters," Nigrinus called out, "tonight is a special night for soon I depart to join our dear emperor and my good and old friend Trajan on his campaign against the Dacians. Rome will be victorious, of this I am sure. So, to celebrate this I have laid on a special treat for you all. Cast your minds and hearts back to the very start of our great city, to a time when our heroic ancestors started out on the path to greatness that we enjoy today. All of you, please accompany me out into the garden."

With an excited buzz the crowd of guests began to follow Nigrinus as he led them out into a walled garden. Outside, the pattern of stars decorated the night skies and along the high garden walls, flaming torches burned, illuminating the silent and motionless slaves, who stood against the wall staring into space. But it was not the fine night-sky or the beautiful garden that caught Marcus's attention. It was the silent lines of armed-men, their large legionary shields resting against their legs, that made him grunt in surprise. The men stood shoulder to shoulder and had been arranged in a square, their faces and shields turned inwards towards each other. In the square, open-space beyond the wall of shields, two men, half naked, partially covered in armour and armed with an assortment of exotic weapons and small round shields stood waiting for the guests to appear. And as the crowds of high-born men and women caught sight of the gladiators, a gasp of astonishment and excitement swept through the garden.

"Two men, professionals and masters of their trade," Nigrinus cried out, raising his arms in the air, "will fight to the death tonight. Our ancestors were such men. They never shirked a fight and they knew the price they would pay for defeat. They were men of steel, hard-working farmers but with tender hearts for their families. Tonight, these two gladiators will honour our ancestors and remind us of who we are. For Rome and her children are the greatest people to have walked this world. Long live emperor Trajan and the imperial family."

"Long live emperor Trajan," the crowd of guests roared back enthusiastically as the excitement in the garden grew. "Long live Trajan and the imperial family."

Marcus and Claudia pushed their way through the throng until they had a good view of the enclosed space in which the gladiators would fight.

"A private gladiator fight, that must have cost," a man beside Marcus said with a gleeful expression, as he leaned inwards towards Claudia.

Marcus did not react. He was staring at the gladiators. The men's faces were hidden behind their exotic helmets. As a hush descended on the party the two fighters solemnly bowed towards Nigrinus and then slowly, and with deadly intent, they began to circle each other. As the fight intensified, the guests, their eyes glued to the contest, started to pick sides, shouting encouragements but Marcus did not join in. When, with a ferocious slicing blow, the victor finally brought down his opponent, a loud triumphant roar filled the garden. In the small square arena, the victor raised his bloodied weapon in the air in salute as his opponent lay on the ground, choking to death on his own blood. With cheers and cries the winner was led away and the crowd, resumed their chatter and started to disperse as if nothing had happened. Hastily pushing his way through the wall of armed men and their shields, Marcus hastened towards the fallen gladiator, but he was not the first to reach the dying fighter. An older, bookish and educated-looking man was already kneeling beside the gladiator, cradling the man's head in his arms. Blood was everywhere, staining the grass and the man's fine tunic.

"It's all right boy, it's all right," the older man was muttering in a calm, soothing voice. "Don't be afraid. You fought well, you fought very well. The pain will soon be gone."

Quickly Marcus knelt beside the dying gladiator. The fighter's fingers were shaking and he seemed to be trying to reach for something just out of reach. Hastily Marcus reached out, grabbed the man's sword from where he'd dropped it and pressed the pommel into the dying man's hand. Blood was welling up and gushing from the fighter's mouth.

"Here," Marcus muttered, closing the man's fingers around the pommel, "Go to your gods and be at peace. You fought well. It was just bad luck. There is no shame. You should be proud."

On the ground the dying gladiator's eyes flickered open as the older man gently cradled his head on his lap and stroked his hair. For a moment, the gladiator stared up at Marcus and then slowly, the light faded from his eyes and his head rolled sideways.

With a sigh the older man let go and gently laid the dead man's head onto the grass.

"Barbarism," the man hissed under his breath. "We are supposed to be a civilised people and yet we love killing people for fun. It's a disgrace."

Marcus said nothing as he reached out to close the dead fighter's eyes and straighten his arms alongside his body. Then reaching for his neck, he undid his own cloak and respectfully laid it across the body, covering the man's face. A slave appeared and tried to grasp hold of the dead gladiator's legs but Marcus roughly shoved the slave away.

"Show him some respect, he deserves that much," Marcus growled, rising to his feet, and as he did the slave backed off.

"Thank you," the older man said as he too rose to his feet and stretched out his hand. "My name is Paulinus Picardus Taliare," the man exclaimed. "Thank you for showing such respect to this man. That was good of you. You seem to be the only one around here who cares."

"You knew this fighter?" Marcus muttered as he grasped Paulinus's outstretched arm and then gestured at the dead gladiator.

"No," Paulinus replied with a shake of his head. "But I don't like to see men die needlessly and for entertainment. It is sick, barbaric and a waste of money and we Romans are not barbarians."

"Don't let your host hear you say that," Marcus said as he turned to look at the groups of guests who still lingered in the garden.

"Actually," Paulinus exclaimed, "he knows my position on these matters very well. Nigrinus and I are good friends. I have known him since he was born. I am one of the Prefects, the Praefecti Aerarii Saturni, who run the Aerarium, the state treasury. I am Rome's finance minister."

Marcus frowned as from the corner of his eye he noticed Claudia moving towards him.

"You look after all Rome's money?" he asked.

"I look after all the state assets, liabilities, moneys and taxes that are collected in Italy and the provinces that are controlled by the Senate," Paulinus replied in a prim precise voice. "I and my colleague run the state treasury on behalf of the Senate. I am one of the dedicated band of unrecognised men who ensure that Rome remains a great power. And we manage the equestrian and senatorial lists and property qualifications. I know; I know, it's not as glamourous as being a soldier or army general but my work is equally vital to the health of the empire. After all, if the soldiers don't get paid then there will be no one left to defend the frontiers."

"You manage the equestrian lists?" Marcus asked with sudden interest, "So you decide who gets to be included on the official lists and who gets to be recognised as an equestrian, a knight?"

"That's right," Paulinus replied with a little nod. "I and my colleague keep the lists up to date on behalf of the emperor. We have Trajan's ear when it comes to who is to be officially recognised as a knight or a senator. It is all based on property and wealth qualifications and whether the candidate is of sound repute."

Paulinus paused and gave Marcus a curious look. "Most men find what I do to be a dull, boring job but if you are interested in my work, young man, then I would be happy to show you around the state treasury."

"There you are Marcus," Claudia called out as she approached. Then abruptly she hesitated as she caught sight of the body on the ground and the blood on Marcus's forehead and hands.

"I am glad that I met you Sir," Marcus said giving Paulinus a respectful nod. "And I hope to see you once again, soon." Then without saying another word he hastily strode away towards Claudia.

***

It was nearly dawn when Marcus finally returned alone to the school on the Quirinal hill. As stiffly and wearily he disembarked from the small horse-drawn carriage and nodded his gratitude to Claudia's slave who had brought him home, he was suddenly

149

confronted by Petrus coming straight towards him. In the flickering torch-light Petrus's face looked ashen and as he caught sight of the expression on his face, Marcus stiffened in alarm.

"What now?" he growled.

Petrus shook his head in dismay. "Esther," he groaned, "Esther, she's gone. She has disappeared."

"Oh, for fuck's sake," Marcus growled closing his eyes. "Not again."

Chapter Sixteen – Aerarium Populi Romani

Marcus leant against the wall, watching the loud, excited children through the open window, playing in the school courtyard. It was morning and behind him in the second-floor room that Claudia had given them, a dejected looking Petrus sat slumped on the floor, his back pressed against the wall, as he repeatedly tossed his wooden cross in the air before catching it.

"Maybe we should just go home," Petrus muttered wearily. "She has been gone for a whole day and two full nights. We will never find her, not in a city of a million people. She must have her reasons for leaving us."

"We cannot leave without settling this," Marcus said sternly. "Cunitius is still out there and I told Abraham about our involvement in Priscinus's murder. I gave Cunitius and the Governor of Britannia the closest thing to a confession as one can get. Even if Cunitius does not find Esther, this is not going to go away. The Governor of Britannia knows we were involved. He will move to punish us and take away our farm and maybe even declare us fugitives. And I am not going to run from that sack of shit. No, we cannot give up the fight. We must win. We must be smarter than our opponents. If we leave now, we are finished."

"So, what do we do, Marcus?" Petrus asked in a miserable sounding voice. "Lady Claudia is saying that notices for a reward for Esther's capture are going up on walls across Rome. Cunitius is tightening his net. He must have the backing and support of the imperial prefects who have been left in charge of Rome. You said it yourself, this city is full of informants. How long will it be before some low life arsehole betrays her or our whereabouts?"

"Or," Petrus said quickly, raising a sarcastic finger in the air, "why don't we just find Cunitius and kill him and after that head for Londinium and kill the Governor. That should end our problems and their threat to take possession of our farm."

"Shut up," Marcus hissed irritably as he stared at the children playing in the courtyard. "That is a most stupid idea. We will never even get close to them. No, brute force is not the answer."

Thoughtfully Marcus touched his clean-shaven chin. "If we cannot be the bear then we must be the fox. I have been thinking," he said, turning to look at Petrus. "The way to get what you want in this city is through using connections and politics. That is how the senators and the rich get things done around here. It's all about whom you know and how good your friendship is with them."

"So, whom apart from Lady Claudia do we know who can help us?" Petrus exclaimed, looking baffled. "Nigrinus?"

"No, there is no time; he has already left Rome for the Dacian frontier," Marcus replied, "and besides I am not sure he would want to help us. He's a bit of a dick."

"Who then?"

"Paulinus Picardus Taliare," Marcus exclaimed, as he turned once more to gaze at the children playing in the school yard. "Master of the state treasury and keeper of the equestrian and senatorial lists. I shall try and enlist his aid. If we are going to win, Petrus, then we are not only going to have to get Cunitius off our backs, but also the Governor of Britannia and for that we need a friend with some serious authority. An ally who is capable of telling the Governor to leave us the fuck alone. That is the only way in which we are going to win."

"Shit Marcus," Petrus said, looking up at Marcus with renewed respect and hope. "Do you think that will really work?"

"I don't know but I am going to need Claudia's help," Marcus muttered as he watched her appear in the school yard below and start to usher the children into her school building.

***

The Temple of Saturn stood at the base of the Capitoline hill, its magnificent stone columns portraying a sense of solidity and enduring grandeur. It was still morning as Marcus and Claudia crossed the Forum towards the Temple. The Roman market place and the ancient heart of Rome was overlooked by the numerous solemn and grave looking buildings of the Roman state. The merchants and farmers were out in force, their stalls covering every available inch of space of the area between the Palatine hill and the Capitoline. They clustered around their market stalls doing a feverish and loud trade with the crowds. In the sections reserved for their professions; money lenders were shaking bags of coins to attract borrowers and lawyers and business men were standing on small raised platforms, loudly advertising their skills and services. On the steps of the senate house a group of relaxed-looking senators were gathered together, chatting, their broad purple stripes on their white togas denoting their rank. As Marcus and Claudia stepped out of the way to allow a closed litter and four litter bearers to pass, Marcus turned to gaze warily around him. He had drawn his hood over his head and without his beard he felt strangely naked. But he had seen no sign of Cunitius or his men.

"Relax Marcus," Claudia said quietly, as she took his arm and began to steer him towards the Temple entrance. "Paulinus is a decent man. They say that he is the least corrupt man in Rome and that is quite a title."

"Just as well," Marcus replied, "for someone who looks after the treasury."

The entrance to the Temple of Saturn, god of wealth, was guarded by a detachment from the praetorian guard and to Marcus's surprise the place was busy with lots of people coming and going. At the base of the steps leading into the Temple, several filthy looking beggars were holding out their hands in a pitiful attempt to gain people's attention and mercy. And close by, a temple prostitute was eying up potential customers. As he stepped through the grand entrance doors Marcus gasped in astonishment. Dominating the central hall was the great wooden statue of Saturn, veiled and grasping a giant scythe that loomed over the people. The statue's legs had been bound in wool and several debtors were kneeling before the image, their bodies and arms outstretched and pressed to the floor in a gesture of complete, pleading submission.

At the back of the Temple several doors seemed to give access to more rooms but as Marcus and Claudia approached, their path was swiftly blocked by armed temple guards.

"Paulinus," Claudia said in a sharp commanding voice turning to the guards. "Tell him that Lady Claudia is here and wishes to speak to him."

When at last Paulinus appeared, he dipped his bookish-face gracefully and smoothly kissed Claudia's outstretched hand.

"This is a pleasant surprise," Paulinus exclaimed, glancing quickly at Marcus. "What can I do for you today Lady Claudia?"

"Marcus is my friend," Claudia said with a twinkle in her eye. "You may remember meeting him at Nigrinus's party, during the gladiator fight?"

"Ofcourse I remember him," Paulinus replied with a quizzical expression.

"You mentioned the other night, at Nigrinus's party that you would be happy to show us around the state treasury," Marcus interrupted. "Would now be a good time, Sir?"

Surprised, Paulinus turned to Marcus. Then slowly his face lit up with a wide, good natured grin. "I don't get many people asking me that," the prefect of the state treasury in the Temple of Saturn replied. "Most think my job deadly boring and that all I do all day is count money, but they are gravely mistaken. Money is not boring, I assure you and my work is anything but dull. It is fascinating. The very survival of the empire depends on what we do here. But not many people know that. Come, of course I shall show you around."

And without another word Paulinus turned and enthusiastically gestured for Claudia and Marcus to follow him.

"So, what do you think of Rome, our great city, Marcus?" Paulinus called out as he led them around the statue of Saturn and away down a corridor.

"It smells," Marcus replied as he and Claudia followed Paulinus. "But there is honour and bravery in surprising places, if one knows where to look."

Ahead of him Paulinus laughed but did not turn around.

"That room over there," Paulinus said, pointing at a doorway guarded by two temple guards, as he fumbled for something in his pocket, "is where the imperial gold and silver reserves are stored. Nearly a hundred years ago, during the time of Emperor Augustus, Rome's state income, our gross domestic product, was around five billion denarii and military expenditure was 2.5% of the imperial budget. Today, we are up to six and a half billion denarii with military expenditure of around 2.7%. So, for nearly a hundred years I and my predecessors have managed to keep our costs and debts under control. That's no mean feat, considering how the empire has expanded and our military resources and costs have increased." Paulinus turned to give Marcus a resigned smile. "It would be nice if our work here would one day be recognised. It is just as important as winning wars and battles, but we get no recognition."

With a sigh Paulinus turned away. "The aerarium of course is not the only the state treasury. There are three, believe it or not."

Slotting a key into the lock of one of the doors, Paulinus opened it and stepped into the room beyond. "The Fiscus is the emperor's personal treasury," he called out, "and there is also a military veteran's retirement fund. I and my colleague run the Aerarium which only manages the finances of the provinces controlled by the senate, which is to say southern Gaul, Greece, Italy and parts of Hispania, Asia and Africa. The rest of the empire's provinces are imperial provinces, controlled by the emperor and their tax revenues go straight to the Fiscus."

Stepping into the small, windowless room Marcus saw two youthful, studious men, barely older than boys and clad in simple white tunic's, sitting at a table. The men were hunched over what looked like sheets of papyrus or velum, parched animal skin. Pots of ink and an iron tipped stylus, pen, lay on the table. On the floor lay a crumpled up and discarded pile of papyrus.

"This is where I work most days," Paulinus said as he turned to gaze fondly at the two scribes working away at the table. "I too have enemies whom I must confront every day. They are called corruption and inflation and I hate them. They give me sleepless nights. Corruption is the worst and we must stamp it out wherever we find it for it diverts tax revenues away from vital projects. It is a cancer that threatens to destroy the empire but unfortunately, we are limited in what we can do."

In the doorway, Marcus took a step forwards and peered curiously at the two scribes, trying to work out what they were doing.

"And then there is inflation," Paulinus said with distaste in his voice, "Another worry that keeps me up at night."

Fishing in his pocket the Prefect of the state treasury produced a solitary, silver coin, held it up in the air and then without warning flipped it across at Marcus who hastily caught it in his right hand.

"The great, solid Roman silver coin," Paulinus exclaimed with a little proud nod. "Possibly our greatest invention. The facilitator and reward for long distance trade across the empire, acceptable and exchangeable everywhere. That silver coin makes long-distance trade say between Egypt and Britannia possible and trade is the basis for all wealth. Without trade, we would not be able to tax the merchants, business would not grow and we would have no money with which to pay the legions that defend the frontiers."

Marcus frowned as for a moment he examined the silver coin, then he tossed it back to Paulinus who caught it deftly as if he was picking a fly out of the sky.

"Sounds like you have it all covered," Marcus said turning to look around the room. "So, why the sleepless nights?"

Paulinus sighed and grimaced as he slipped the silver coin back into his pocket. "The silver content of that coin I just showed you," he rasped, "used to be ninety five percent but the silver content is dropping. It is now already below ninety percent. Year by year it is going down, making that fine coin less and less valuable." Standing beside Claudia, Paulinus sighed again. "Essentially what I am trying to say is that the empire is starting to run out of silver and gold so we are using less precious metal in the making of our coins. It means that inflation is rising. It means that trouble is coming. For people are going to start demanding more and more coins for the same goods and transactions."

"The empire is vast," Marcus frowned. "Surely we cannot be running out of silver and gold?"

"And yet we are," Paulinus replied grimly. "I have reported this many times to Trajan himself in person and it seems that finally the emperor is going to do something about it."

"What do you mean?" Marcus asked.

"This Dacian war," Paulinus replied, "do you think this is about some minor border dispute or who has the biggest cock. No, my friend, Trajan, our cunning emperor, has just one thing on his mind and that is the conquest of all those lucrative Dacian gold and silver mines. That's why we are invading Dacia." Paulinus paused and his eyes were suddenly sparkling with excitement. "When all that gold and silver starts rolling into Rome," he said rubbing his hands together, "our financial problems will be delayed by possibly a hundred years. Make no mistake. The empire needs all that gold and silver. We do, we do, we do."

"So, what are you doing here in this room," Marcus asked gesturing at the two scribes working away on the sheets of papyrus and vellum with their iron tipped pens.

"Ah," Paulinus said, "this is where I am preparing a back-up plan in case the invasion goes badly or Trajan has a change of heart. It is my pet project. My assistants here are working on the designs for a new form of money. One that is based not on precious metals like gold or silver but on nothing more than papyrus or velum. It is a work of genius and will provide a solid basis for imperial trade to flourish forever, if only Trajan would accept my proposals."

"Paper money," Marcus slowly shook his head in disbelief. "That will never work. No one would accept it as payment and what about forgeries."

"It will work," Paulinus retorted confidently, "the value of the notes will be officially backed up by a corresponding amount of coin held in the vault of a bank or an authorised money lender. If a person wishes to exchange the notes for gold or silver coins he can do so at any time. It's just a matter of confidence. There is little chance that every man will demand to have his notes exchanged at the same time and the great advantage of this new form of money is that it will cut the bond between trade and the supply of gold and silver. My new currency would increase trade. I am trying to prepare us for the future. But the key ingredient is confidence in my new currency. We must have confidence. And as for forgeries, yes, we would have to be vigilant but my two assistants here are working on the best designs now. I will be presenting the idea to Trajan when he returns from Dacia."

Marcus turned to Claudia and gave her a slightly disbelieving look. Then he turned to look at the prefect of the state treasury.

"I wish you good luck with that," Marcus said as a little sceptical smile appeared on the corner of his lips.

"It is not as outrageous as some of the ideas that my friends are working on," Paulinus said replying with a good-natured smile of his own. "I know some scientists who are experimenting with new weapons, machine operated bolt-throwers, liquid fire that can be squirted from ships, steam-driven devices that can move heavy loads based on the designs of Heron of Alexandria. All these projects will get proper funding if Nigrinus is made emperor after Trajan. Nigrinus is a big supporter of all these ideas. Think about that."

"Heron of Alexandria," Marcus repeated thoughtfully raising his hand to his chin. "I have heard of that name before."

"Your nephew, Ahern, is studying his work in Londinium," Claudia said helpfully. "That's where you heard about Heron."

Marcus nodded. "Of course, that's right."

Standing beside Claudia, Paulinus was watching Marcus closely. Then with a quick snap of his fingers he gestured for his two young assistants to leave the room. And as the men silently trooped out, the prefect of the state treasury turned and closed the door behind him.

"I understand why you may be interested in my work," Paulinus said, turning to Marcus as he quietly folded his arms across his chest, "But maybe now is the time to tell me the real reason why you have come to pay me a visit. It wasn't to hear me blather away about corruption and inflation."

Marcus hesitated and glanced at Claudia.

"You are right, Sir," Marcus said in a grave voice, "I am here because I need your help. I have for some time been involved in a land dispute. Some people are trying to take away my farm and land and recently it has got ugly. It is why I came to Rome, Sir, to petition the authorities to hear my case, for I will not get a fair, impartial hearing back at home."

"Who has been trying to force you off your land?" Paulinus snapped, his face suddenly transformed, stern and authoritative. "The Governor of Britannia and his friends," Marcus replied. "I am afraid that blood has already been shed in defence of my home."

"The Governor of the Province of Britannia," Paulinus replied raising his eyebrows. For a moment, he remained silent. Then he fixed his eyes on Marcus. "And I suppose that you want me to help you settle the case?"

"That's right Sir," Marcus replied lowering his eyes. ""My property, I believe, qualifies me for membership of the equestrian order but the governor is refusing to allow the state surveyors to come and confirm that. He is preventing me from rightfully becoming a knight. Instead the Governor wishes to take my farm for himself so that he can give it to his friends. And now he has produced spurious claims that I was responsible for one of his friend's death but it was they who first resorted to violence. I swear Sir, that the farm was legally given to my father by Agricola, former governor of Britannia. It is ours and I will fight to keep it. It is my home."

"Agricola," Paulinus exclaimed once more raising his eyebrows, "Now there is a name that I have not heard in a long time." Then he sighed. "I trust that you have the legal deeds to the property?"

"I do," Marcus replied hastily, "They bear Agricola's personal stamp. My family and I have owned the property for nearly fifteen years now and before that my father took care of the estate on behalf of Agricola. This is a simple case of attempted theft. The Governor is abusing his position."

"So, what do you want me to do about it?" the Prefect of the state treasury asked.

Quickly Marcus glanced at Claudia. Then he turned to Paulinus and tilted his head. "I understand Sir," Marcus said carefully, "that matters of finance and property are dealt with by the provincial procurator, whose authority is independent and not subordinate to that of the imperial governor. As my land dispute is a financial matter it should therefore come under the jurisdiction of the provincial procurator augusti. In short, the governor is overstepping his authority by getting involved. If you were to raise this matter by for instance writing the Governor a letter making him aware of this fact and raising my indisputable legal property claims, it may help my cause Sir."

"It would not go unnoticed," Claudia said helpfully, turning to gaze at Paulinus.

"You mean," Paulinus said with a stoic expression, "You want me to write a letter to the governor of Britannia telling him to leave you alone."

"That's about right Sir," Marcus nodded.

For a moment Paulinus said nothing as he stared at Marcus. Then a little smile appeared on his lips.

"I appreciate you coming to me with your petition," the prefect said abruptly, "But writing a letter to a man like the governor of

Britannia, a man of consular rank, is no easy thing and not lightly done. I am sorry Marcus but I will not be writing to the governor," Paulinus paused and took a deep breath, "Because, and this is still classified information, the governor of Britannia is being transferred to Cilicia in Asia. Trajan signed the orders before he left for the Dacian frontier. The new governor is already on his way to the province to take up his post."

"Britannia is getting a new governor?" Marcus exclaimed, his eyes widening in surprise.

"That's right," Paulinus nodded, "but like I said, it is not yet public knowledge. The rotation is not unusual, it's just routine. So, it seems that your enemy has been assigned to a new province, his time in Britannia is up. Lucky for you."

Marcus said nothing as he lowered his eyes to the floor and took in what had just been said and as the full realisation finally sank in, he groaned. His journey to Rome had been a waste of time. If he had known, he could have just stayed on Vectis and waited for the Governor to leave his post.

"Your friend," Paulinus said in a measured voice, as he turned to Claudia, "strikes me as being an honourable man, a man who is not corrupt. And this is a good and rare thing indeed. We need more men like him if the empire is to thrive. So, I shall tell you what I will do, Marcus. I shall write a letter to the provincial Procurator in Britannia, who happens to be a good acquaintance of mine, and I shall ask him to personally look into your case. He is a good man, the Procurator, an honest, incorruptible man like myself, and if, and this of course must be contingent on the land surveyor's report, if you qualify for enrolment in the equestrian lists, I shall personally recommend your inclusion to Trajan when the next review is due."

And as he heard those words Marcus's ears suddenly felt as if they were burning. "No," a voice was screaming inside his head. The journey to Rome had not been a waste of time after all.

"Thank you, Sir," Marcus said in a humble voice as he respectfully lowered his head. "That is generous of you and I cannot thank you enough. But there is one final thing, Sir, one final favour I must beg from you."

"And what is that?" Paulinus said with a patient expression.

**

Later as they strode down the steps of the Temple of Saturn and into the bright sunlight Marcus muttered, glancing at Claudia, "I owe you, thank you."

"Yes, you are in my debt," Claudia replied solemnly, "but that is how things are done around here. You belong to Nigrinus's network now. And when the time comes and we need your support you shall give it freely. We have helped you and you will help us. That is all I ask of you Marcus. Break this agreement and you will have no honour, none whatsoever. You may as well go and kill yourself."

Silently Marcus turned to gaze out across the packed Forum. He was still slightly dazed and euphoric from what he'd just heard inside the Temple. His long-cherished ambition of seeing his family go up in the world was now at last a distinct possibility.

"Yes, I am with you," he growled at last, "Nigrinus can count on me when the time comes. You have my word, as a soldier and as a man."

**

Marcus sensed that something was afoot the moment he and Claudia entered the school yard. As the two of them strode towards the school entrance one of Claudia's slaves came hurrying towards her, followed quickly by Petrus. Hastily Marcus gave Petrus a searching look. The boy seemed confused and just shrugged as he noticed Marcus's glance.

"Lady," the slave said respectfully lowering his eyes, "there is a man waiting to see you and your friend. He has been here several hours and refuses to leave. He says that he has an important message for your friend and that he will only deliver it to your friend. I have asked him to wait in the room reserved for special guests."

"We shall be along in a moment," Claudia said, "see to it that our guest is properly provided with drink and food."

"He has refused all refreshments lady," the slave replied hastily. Claudia frowned and glanced across at Marcus who shrugged.

"All right, let's go and see what he wants," Claudia sighed as she handed her cloak to the slave.

As he followed Claudia into the waiting room, Marcus had a strange sensation of having been here once before. Standing quietly and calmly in the centre of the hall, with his hands clasped together was a tall man, clad in a simple, brown cloak with a hood pulled over his head. From beneath his hood two bright blue eyes peered keenly at Marcus.

"Are you Marcus?" the man asked in a soft voice.

"I am. Who are you?" Marcus replied as at his side Claudia was studying the stranger with a frown.

"I bring a message for you, Marcus," the visitor said, staring straight at Marcus, with unblinking eyes. "Esther is well. She is under our protection. She is with us now and we will look after her. No harm has befallen her."

"What," Marcus growled taking a step towards the man. "What have you done with her? Who are you working for? Cunitius? If you so much as touch a hair on her head, I will come for all of you."

But the man with the strange bright blue eyes, calmly shook his head.

"You misunderstand," he said in his quiet voice, clasping his hands together. "It is Esther who asked me to come here. She is with us because she wants to be with us. She has asked to meet you, to say goodbye and to Petrus as well. She says that you have carried out God's work and that she is grateful," and as the man said those words, he slowly made the sign of the cross over his chest.

Chapter Seventeen – Resolution

The tall stranger with the piercing, bright blue eyes had not said a word since they had left Claudia's school. As he led Marcus and Petrus down the alley and into a barber's shop, he just glanced around to make sure that they were following. It was late in the afternoon and the twisting narrow streets of the Aventine hill were busy, noisy and crowded. Cautiously Marcus stepped into the small front room of the shop. It looked just like any of the countless other barbers he had seen. There was nothing here apart from an old, blind man clutching a wooden staff, a couple of chairs and the barber's equipment. Ignoring the old, blind man, the tall stranger silently closed the door behind him. Then quickly he moved through a doorway into the back room, stooped and pulled up the rag that was covering the ground, revealing a trap door set into the stone. Feeling around, the man's fingers found what they were looking for and gently he pushed down on the door. With a little click the trapdoor opened revealing a dark hole that led down into the earth.

"You want us to go down there?" Marcus said glancing at the stranger with a sceptical expression.

"Yes," the man with the bright, blue eyes said calmly. "Esther is waiting for you. Do not fear us Marcus, we mean you no harm."

With a sceptical face, Marcus glanced quickly at Petrus.

"Stay here and keep watch," he muttered. Then as the tall man slipped into the hole in the floor and vanished from view, Marcus sighed and followed. In the dark, Marcus's right hand grasped hold of the side of the wooden ladder and slowly he began to descend. Around him the air grew cooler and as he looked down, he caught the faintest flicker of a reddish light. The vertical shaft did not last long and with a thud his boots landed on a rocky, uneven floor. A short, low passage slanted away and through the tunnel, the flickering reddish light was brighter. Ducking his head, Marcus followed the stranger and finally emerged into a large cavern, cut into the volcanic tufa rock. Oil lamps had been fixed to the rocky walls and in their light, he saw that he was standing in a large cave, hewn from the rock. At the far end of the cave another passage led away into the darkness.

Several people including children, clad in long robes, were quietly standing in the middle of the cavern, seemingly waiting for him. Marcus grunted as amongst them he suddenly caught sight of Esther, holding a small oil lamp in her hand. As she saw him she smiled warmly. Then, in the dim flickering light, she took a step towards him. Her head was covered in a shawl and in her other hand, she was clutching her wooden cross.

"Don't be afraid Marcus," Esther said in a quiet voice, "these people do not mean you or Petrus any harm. They are my friends, my family."

Carefully Marcus's gaze slipped away from Esther and to the group of people gathered around her and as it did, the tall stranger who'd brought him to this subterranean place, stepped across the floor of the cave and joined them. The adults and children, including some very old-looking men and women, were staring at Marcus in a calm, quiet and composed manner that unsettled him.

"Who are you?" Marcus asked suspiciously, "Christians?"

"They are my friends," Esther said, as she reached out and gently touched Marcus on the side of his shoulder. "They are Christians and they have accepted me into their community. They will protect me. I have come home, Marcus."

"What happened to you?" Marcus demanded, rounding on Esther, his eyes flashing angrily. "Why did you have to leave without saying anything? We came all the way to Rome for you. We do not deserve to be treated like this."

"I know," Esther said, lowering her eyes, "You are right. I should not have treated you in this way. But I was worried that you would not let me go, and this is something that I had to do, Marcus, and I am glad that I did."

"What happened to you?" Marcus repeated, staring angrily at Esther.

Standing before him Esther lowered her eyes once more, as behind her the group of people looked on in stoic silence.

"This place," she said, gesturing around her, "this cavern connects to the catacombs of Rome; a vast hidden warren of tunnels that runs right underneath the city. It is in these hidden places that we come to pray. It is in these tunnels and caves that we worship God, baptise our children and bury our dead, whilst we wait for the day, when we shall be able to do so openly and in the light."

Esther paused and glanced round at the people standing behind her.

"They are good people," she said at last, "and I belong here, with them. You have completed your journey, Marcus. You should go home. I know you long to be back with your family. You have done God's work and I am truly grateful but the time to say goodbye has come."

"I don't understand," Marcus said, with a shake of his head, "What happened? How did you manage to find this place; these people?"

"I went back to the house on the Aventine, the place where I was born," Esther replied calmly, turning to gaze at Marcus. "And this time I managed to speak to the the wife of the man whose family once owned my mother and me. She is a righteous person, a good woman and she was kind to me. She told me that after emperor Nero had my father crucified in the arena, Christian people came looking for my mother. When my mother died giving birth to me, these people wanted to take me away. They said that I was a special child. But her husband refused of course. I was his property and he was not going to let me go for nothing. He banned these people from coming to his house; then he died and his wife sold me, when I was a girl, to traders who brought me to Britannia."

"Get to the point," Marcus said.

Opposite him Esther's eyes were suddenly heavy with emotion. "These people who came looking for me," she whispered in a hoarse emotional voice, "they were Christians. Some of them now stand before you, Marcus."

Carefully Esther raised her hand to dab at her face. "They never gave up hope of finding me. So, when my old mistress, bless her soul, made it known to them that I had returned, they came for me, just like they had first tried to do, more than forty years ago. They had never given up hope."

"Why?" Marcus persisted, frowning as he glanced at the silent group of men, women and children clustered behind Esther, before slowly turning to fix his eyes on her. "What is so special about you?"

"It's because of my father; because of who he was. But until yesterday I did not truly know who he was," Esther replied lowering her eyes. "I told you when we were still in Britannia, that my father was a Christian priest and that emperor Nero had him crucified in the arena for that. My father's name was Simon Peter, and he was one of the close friends of Jesus. After the crucifixion of Jesus my father came to Rome and helped found and organise the Christian church here. That is why emperor Nero had him crucified in the arena. I am his daughter. These people are my father's followers and before my father was taken, they promised him that they would protect and take care of his wife and his coming child. That is why they have come to look after me."

Marcus looked at Esther and her people and finally, slowly nodded his head and smiled.

***

The Temple of Saturn was quiet and nearly deserted, as two days later Marcus stood beside the great veiled statue of Saturn, waiting for his visitor to appear. It was early evening and outside in the forum, the merchants and businessmen were breaking down their stalls and going home for the day. At the base of the temple steps the detachment of praetorian guards were still at their posts. Standing beside Marcus, with his arms folded across his chest, Paulinus looked impatient.

"Will he come?" the prefect of the state treasury asked Marcus as he gazed out through the big temple doors and down the steps leading into the forum.

In response Marcus silently gestured at something with his chin. Coming up the steps towards them was a big, broad-shouldered man. Catching sight of Marcus, a contemptuous grin appeared on the man's face. Slowly and without any haste he ambled over towards the two waiting men.

"Hello Cunitius," Marcus said, raising his head and glaring at him.

"So, this is where you have been hiding," Cunitius replied in a contemptuous voice as, with a bemused look, he took his time to glance around the temple. "That was clever. I would have never have suspected. So, imagine my surprise when I received your message that you wanted to meet me here. Have you finally decided to surrender?"

"No," Marcus replied shaking his head.

"My name is Paulinus Picardus Taliare, first prefect of the state treasury," Paulinus said in a harsh, commanding voice as he took a step towards Cunitius. "And you Sir, need to know that this man, Marcus, is now under my protection until his case and petition has been properly examined and reviewed by the procurator augusti of the province of Britannia. If anything were to happen to this man, his family or his friends, you," Paulinus emphasising the words and jabbing a finger at Cunitius, "you will be held personally responsible. Have I made myself clear? Yes or no?"

For a moment, Cunitius hesitated in surprise as he stared at Paulinus. Then rapidly his composure returned.

"I have orders from the imperial governor of Britannia himself," Cunitius replied with a confident smile, "This man here is guilty of harbouring a runaway slave and he is party to the murder of an important Roman citizen. I have all the authority that I need to find and apprehend him."

"No, that is no longer the case," Paulinus replied in a curt voice. "The governor of Britannia has been recalled and his authority in this matter has come to an end. This is now a matter for the procurator in Britannia. He has the proper legal power to conduct this investigation and he will do so. You are to cease your investigation immediately and return to the shit hole from whence you came." And as he spoke, Paulinus took a menacing step towards Cunitius. "Disregard these instructions and you will find yourself on the wrong side of the law with all the consequences that will have for you. Good day to you Sir."

And with that Paulinus abruptly turned on his heels and strode away into the temple.

Cunitius watched him go with a puzzled frown. Then he took a deep breath and turned to gaze at Marcus.

"Made some new friends, have we?" Cunitius sneered.

"What did you do to Clodovicus" Marcus asked menacingly. "If he has been harmed or worse, then your days are numbered."

"Who?" Cunitius snapped, squinting at Marcus with a hostile expression. "Oh, your Batavian friend in Hengistbury Head. No, he still lives. It took me some time to get the truth out of him, tough man he was, but in the end, they all talk. No man can keep a secret forever, not when you know how to coax it out of them."

"You should go home," Marcus said angrily. "Your task here is finished. Fuck off and go home. My business is no longer your concern."

Cunitius's face darkened and slowly he raised a finger and pointed it accusingly at Marcus. "But I still know what your sister, Dylis did," he hissed. "Abraham came to me and told me everything including your confession. I know the part your family played in the murder of Priscinus. You are guilty Marcus, you and your family are guilty of murder and helping a slave runaway. I won't forget, you can count on that. I will not forget."

"You should know that I never wanted this conflict," Marcus spoke in a hard, cold voice. "It was Priscinus who started it and it is he who first resorted to violence. He attacked my family and my farm and destroyed my crops. The man was a greedy arsehole. I tried to negotiate with him but he would not listen. And consider this," Marcus said, "here we are, you having chased me half way across the empire, and we are resolving this dispute in a peaceful manner by talking about it. If you are going to remember anything, then it should be that disputes like these, do not need to be necessarily settled by violence. This is a job for the law, applied by professionals without bias or an interest in the case. And the great thing about this process is that it gives men justice."

Across from Marcus, Cunitius's eye twitched and for a while he was silent as he glared at his opponent. Then abruptly his expression seemed to soften.

"I was just doing my job," Cunitius said as a little bemused smile appeared on his lips and to Marcus's surprise, the man suddenly stretched out his hand. "So, no hard feelings eh? It was never personal. It was just a job. Like I told you at your farm, Priscinus was never a friend of mine. I was telling the truth."

Marcus hesitated. Then with a grunt he clasped Cunitius's hand in a brief handshake.

"So, what about the woman, Esther," Cunitius asked curiously. "Come on, Marcus, I have been hunting you for weeks and I and my men have travelled a long way to find her. Come on, what have you done with her?"

Once more Marcus hesitated, his eyes fixed warily on Cunitius.

"She is dead," he muttered at last, "On our first day in Rome we took a room in the Subura and that night we were robbed. It is a dangerous neighbourhood. Esther took a knife to her chest during the struggle. It was an accident and we burned her body. She is dead. Your search is over. You should go home."

For a moment, Cunitius remained silent. Then slowly he shook his head and the bemused smile re-appeared.

"You are such a lying sack of shit, Marcus," he said.

"Heh arsehole," a voice suddenly called out and from a dimly-lit corner of the temple, Petrus suddenly appeared, sauntering towards Cunitius. In his hand, he was casually twirling his loaded sling.

"Yes, I am talking to you, arsehole," Petrus called out as he stared at Cunitius. "Not so big and strong now are you. And here is some advice for you. Why don't you turn around, walk down those steps and just fuck off and leave us alone! God, I have waited a long time to be able to say those words. So, go on, fuck off."

Cunitius gave Petrus a silent bemused look. Then acknowledging Marcus, he turned away and started down the steps.

"I will be seeing you again, Marcus," Cunitius called out. "And do me a favour, muzzle that boy of yours, he whines too much."

Petrus hissed angrily as he came to stand beside Marcus and the two of them watched Cunitius vanish into the crowds.

"You know," Petrus muttered at last, "Esther was right. God has worked his magic through you Marcus for everything that has happened to us in Rome. It all started with a single act of kindness and generosity." Petrus took a deep breath as he turned to look at Marcus with sudden respect. "If you hadn't stopped to give that army beggar in Portus a coin, we would never have met Valentian, or the Batavians and in turn we would not know about the school, we would not have met Lady Claudia or through her, Paulinus. God was guiding you that day, when you gave that veteran a coin."

Marcus was silent as he stared out into the Roman Forum. Then at last he stirred and laying a hand on Petrus's shoulder he sighed.

"Let's go home."

Chapter Eighteen – On the Frontier

Spring 106 AD - The Province of Lower Pannonia

Fergus stood at the bow of the river barge, holding onto the rigging with one hand and clutching his long wooden optio staff in the other, as he peered at the barbarian shore. Here and there in the dense, impenetrable forests that covered the banks of the Danube, he could see that the winter snows had still not entirely disappeared. It was a fresh, grey overcast morning and in the spring sky, dark rain clouds were rolling in from the north. Around him the barge was packed with heavily armed troops. The silent and pensive looking legionaries, clad in their full armour, were standing in every available piece of space, whilst at their banks, the oarsmen, following the rhythmic beat of a drum, slowly and steadily dipped their oars into the dirty brown river, propelling the ship down the Danube. The steady rhythmic beat of the oarsmen's drum, the splash of the oars and the groan and creak of the vessel were the only sounds on the placid, wide river. Up ahead the next heavily laden transport in the long, Roman-army river convoy was doing the same. The thick rope that linked each barge to the next transport slackened and tightened as it snaked through the water. On the flanks of the convoy, the naval warships of the Danube river fleet, the "Classis Pannonica," provided a protective screen for the troop transports. The ship's artillery, catapults and bolt-throwers were aimed at the barbarian shore, conveying the simple and unmistakable message, to anyone who may have been watching from the forest – "don't fuck with Rome."

Idly, Fergus tapped the wooden deck with his optio's staff as absentmindedly he started to follow the beat of the oarsmen's drum. His red Celtic hair had been cut short and his handsome face was clean shaven, but he seemed weary and his eyes looked sleep-deprived. He was clad in his army uniform and full armour and over the long winter along the Danube frontier, he seemed to have matured. The last vestiges of the boy who had joined the Twentieth Legion two and a half years ago, had gone and there was a new toughness and maturity about him, that had not been there when he'd left Britannia. Around his neck hung the fine-looking circular iron amulet, the Briton charm that Galena, his young wife had given him and which she had said would protect him on his long journey. Fergus sighed as he let go of the rigging and reached up to touch the amulet. It had been over nine months since he had last seen his wife. His child would have been born by now. Anxiously he bit his lip. There had been no news, no letters from Galena, nothing at all. Childbirth was as dangerous as going into battle and the lack of news worried him, but there was nothing that he could do but wait. Harshly he pushed the thoughts of his pregnant wife away and instead turned to inspect the men from the 2nd company, 2nd Cohort of the Twentieth Legion, who were standing packed closely together behind him. The men looked pensive and some of the replacements were giving the river nervous glances, for if they were to fall in, the weight of their armour would take them straight to the bottom. Silently Fergus studied his men. In deepest, coldest winter, with all the senior officers either dead or wounded, he had managed to lead the band of survivors from the diplomatic mission to the Vandals, back to Roman territory. It had been one hell of an achievement and now he was their Optio, second in command of the whole company of eighty-four legionaries. He had received his promotion from none other than the legate of the 1st Legion, Hadrian, himself.

His gaze passed over the faces of his men and here and there one of the fifty veterans, the soldiers who had survived the brutal winter cold, lack of food and the fighting in Germania, acknowledged him with a grin or a wink. Upon their return from the successful diplomatic mission to the Vandals, the company had been brought back up to full strength over the winter with replacements sent from the home base of the Twentieth Legion at Deva Victrix. With them from Britannia had come Lucullus, now recovered from his wounds, to assume command of the company, as the newly promoted Centurion. The rest of winter had been spent preparing for the coming invasion of Dacia. And now the time had finally come Fergus thought. The battle group commander Hadrian had at last received orders to move the 8,000 men of his battle group to the seat of war. The long-awaited invasion of Dacia was to commence before the end of the month. It had been several days since the convoy, carrying the units of the 1st and 20th legions and the infantry companies of the 2nd and 9th cohorts of Batavians had departed Carnuntum on its river journey down the Danube to Aquincum - capital and seat of government of the province of Lower Pannonia. Hadrian himself however would not be leading his men into battle. With the new orders, Fergus had learnt that the legate was to relinquish command of the 1st Legion and take up his post as Governor of the newly created province of Lower Pannonia. The persistent rumour going around the army camps along the Danube was that Emperor Trajan had fallen out with Hadrian and did not want him to take part in the upcoming campaign.

"Fergus, a word," a stern voice said from close by.

Quickly Fergus turned to see Lucullus, the newly promoted centurion, his commanding officer, pushing his way towards him. Lucullus was old, in his forties and his grey, thinning hair covered his head. He looked tired, pale and unwell, as clutching his magnificent red-plumed helmet in one hand, he came up to Fergus and reached out to steady himself by grasping hold of the ship's rigging.

"Sir," Fergus muttered as he glanced at Lucullus.

"I thought you should know," Lucullus said as he turned to gaze at the endless forests that lined the eastern bank of the great river, "when we reach Aquincum, the Legate Hadrian has requested that it is our company that escorts him into the city. He has granted us this honour, so make sure that the men are presentable and ready to go once we reach the town."

"Yes Sir," Fergus nodded, then for a moment, he hesitated. Lucullus was an old-school officer, an aloof, strict disciplinarian who did not mingle with his men or seek their friendship and the relationship between him as commander and his second in command, was still new and rather awkward.

Lucullus nodded and for a while he remained silent as he stood beside Fergus.

"Titus should have been in command of the company," Lucullus muttered at last. "He was the finest soldier that I have ever known. He and I were friends. His death is a blow, a heavy blow, Fergus. He is going to be a hard act to follow."

"I know Sir," Fergus replied looking away. "He was a good man. We shall honour him when we go into battle against the Dacians. This was his company, he made us who we are Sir, but I am also glad to see you have recovered from your wounds. What with Titus dead and Furius honourably discharged, there are not too many familiar faces around here anymore."

Standing beside Fergus, Lucullus nodded gratefully.

"I was an optio for nearly eight years," Lucullus said quietly, "and I would probably have remained an optio for the rest of my time in the army if Titus had not been killed. So, now they have promoted me to centurion, in charge of the whole company. The army," Lucullus said carefully glancing at Fergus, "does not promote men to the rank of centurion until they have served a very considerable time; many years at least. I have served nineteen years Fergus, and my retirement is not far away. There was a time when I scoffed at the idea of retiring but now, now it somehow doesn't sound like such a bad idea."

"I understand, Sir," Fergus said in a stoical, neutral voice.

"When we reach Aquincum," Lucullus replied quietly, "we will be joined by the cavalry squadrons of the 2nd and 9th Batavian auxiliary cohorts; a cohort of Syrian archers and several units of civilian pioneers and engineers. We will be forming the western flank of the main invasion and it's going to be tough. The

Dacian's know the land and they are formidable fighters. They are going to put up a ferocious fight in defence of their freedom, families and homes. Who wouldn't."

"The company will be ready for anything," Fergus replied stiffly. "I know the men, they are a bunch of professionally-trained killers and thugs Sir. They would scare the shit out of me if I was the one facing them. Titus trained us well."

"I know he did," Lucullus muttered. "But I am going to need your help Fergus in commanding them."

Surprised Fergus glanced across at his commanding officer but Lucullus just shrugged and tried to smile.

"You were there when Titus died and I was not," the centurion said simply. "In Germania, in the mountains, you took command when all the officers were either dead or incapacitated and you successfully led the company back to safety. The men, all of them, they owe their lives to you as does Hadrian but that is a different matter. You are a good man, you are a leader, Fergus, and I know that the men respect you. I think they respect you more than they respect me. But you are my second in command. That's why I need your help. The coming war is going to be hard and the performance of our company is going to be all important." Lucullus turned once more to look at Fergus. "I want to survive this war and I want my men to survive this war. So, can we agree on this. The fate and honour of the company and our men is paramount and to keep them alive we, you and I, must work closely together. We must trust each other, Fergus. Any mistakes or misunderstandings between us will get people killed."

"Strict discipline and sensible orders Sir," Fergus said quickly. "That's what we need. And I agree, the performance of the company is our responsibility. I will not let you down. The Dacian's will not know what has hit them."

"Good man," Lucullus murmured, laying a hand on Fergus's shoulder. "Good man," he repeated.

As the Centurion made his way back to where the rest of the company's officers and NCO's were gathered together, Fergus sighed and looked down at the deck of the ship. Lucullus was a good officer, Fergus thought, but ever since the man had arrived to assume command of the company, he had worried that the new centurion did not have the energy or ambition to carry out his duties properly. Then with another weary sigh and a little dismissive gesture, he stooped and reached for something in his marching pack that lay at his feet. Holding up the small wooden letter to the morning light, he turned to gaze fondly at the small, neat and distinctive handwriting. He had read the contents of the letter so often that he could repeat them from memory, but there was something reassuring about staring at his mother Kyna's hand writing. The letter had been handed to him by a Batavian just before the battle group had started out down the Danube and from the date scratched into the soft wood, he could see that it had taken over six months to reach him. As he silently re-read the contents of the letter he grunted. His mother's letter was dated to late summer of the previous year and it told him of the most welcome news that Marcus, his father, had finally returned, alive and well, from his year-long journey to Hyperborea. It was good news, Fergus thought, lowering the letter and clenching the wood in his hand, and good news was to be cherished, always, always, always. But Kyna, his mother had also written that the land dispute was far from settled and that there was a very real possibility that their farm on Vectis, their home, would be taken from them. That thought, the knowledge that his family were in trouble combined with the lack of news from Galena, his wife, had started to keep him up at night and deprive him of sleep.

Chapter Nineteen – Aquincum

The rhythmic crunch and thud of the soldier's iron-studded boots on the gravel reverberated along the straight Roman road. It was around noon and in the sky, the sun had driven the dark clouds from its domain, bathing everything in a brilliant, warm and bright light. Fergus, clad in his army uniform, full body armour and wearing a white focale scarf tied around his neck, strode along at the rear of the small formation. In his hand, he was clutching his long wooden optio's staff. Ahead of him, the ranks of the legionaries of the 2nd company, 2nd Cohort of the Twentieth Legion were marching down the road, eight men abreast and divided into a rear and advance guard. From his position at the back of the column, Fergus could just about see Lucullus's red-plumed helmet and the company's standard leading the men towards the Roman frontier town of Aquincum, that had appeared, half a mile away. The discs and crescent moon symbols on the proud company-standard glinted in the bright sunlight. And sitting on top of their horses, in the gap between the ranks of the rear and advance guard, rode the new governor of Lower Pannonia – Hadrian followed by his staff, bodyguards and two ox-drawn wagons that contained the Governor's personal possessions. Hadrian was sitting bolt upright on his horse and was staring in silence at Aquincum. For a moment, Fergus's eyes lingered on Hadrian. For the past two days and nights he had been waiting to ask something of Hadrian but he'd had no chance to approach the Governor. And as he studied him, Fergus could not help feeling sorry for the man. Adalwolf had told him in confidence that Hadrian had wanted to take part in the Dacian war, for he loved being a soldier and being around soldiers. Hadrian had not wanted this position as governor of Lower Pannonia. Trajan, Adalwolf had said, was deliberately denying Hadrian any chance of winning fame and glory in the upcoming campaign. And as if reading his thoughts, riding at Hadrian's side, Adalwolf, one of the Governor's principal advisers, turned in his saddle to glance back at Fergus bringing up the rear of the escort.

As the procession approached the gates of the old legionary fortress, Fergus noticed to his surprise, the banners of the 2nd Legion Adiutrix, proudly flapping in the wind from the stone ramparts of the playing-card shaped castrum, the legionary fortress. The 2nd Legion had once been based in Britannia and had been the predecessor of the Twentieth Legion at Deva Victrix, until they had transferred to the Danube some twenty years earlier. All around the legionary fortress the civilian town of Aquincum had grown up. To Fergus, the organised, well-constructed and planned Roman-style terraced houses with their neat red-roof tiles, gutters, wooden blinds, sturdy stone walls and paved streets with drainage channels looked, just like the numerous other Roman frontier towns he'd passed through on his long journey from Bonna on the Rhine. Close by in a cleared area of the growing settlement, he could see labourers hard at work on the construction of an amphitheatre. Lucullus's sharp shouted cry brought the company to an abrupt halt just before the gates into the legionary fortress. Fergus craned his neck to see what was going on. Coming out from the fortress towards them was a small welcoming procession of dignitaries, led by a couple of priests carrying something in their hands and as they drew closer, Fergus caught the scent of incense.

As the welcoming committee finished their religious and ceremonial welcome for the new provincial governor, Lucullus's voice rang out once more and with a crunching sound, the company began to enter the fortress.

"What do you mean, she is not here?" Hadrian bellowed angrily at the hapless, shaking and terrified slave. Fergus, his arms folded across his chest, and the rest of the escort, Hadrian's bodyguards, staff, priests and the local dignitaries together with the two ox-drawn wagons, stood gathered around waiting, gazing silently at the miserable looking slave. In front of them was the Principia, the legionary HQ building that stood at the very centre of the army camp and the place from where Hadrian would govern the province. The building however looked deserted and around it, amongst the rows of dreary-looking barracks blocks, only a handful of legionaries were to be seen. The slave had been the only person who had come out of the Principia to greet Hadrian.

"The soldier's my lord, all marched away to war, a few days ago," the slave stammered not daring to look up at the furious looking Hadrian.

"But where is my wife and her servants?" Hadrian roared at the slave. "They were meant to be here days ago. Why are they not here to greet me? Why is there no one here to carry my belongings into the Principia?"

"The Lady has gone swimming in the lake," the slave stammered. "She has taken her servants and slaves with her. She did not tell me when she would be back, my lord."

"The bitch, the fucking bitch," Hadrian snarled, not caring who heard him as he wrenched his eyes away from the slave. "She has done this on purpose. She knew that I would be arriving today."

Furiously Hadrian rounded on the slave.

"Go and find my wife and tell her," he hissed, "that I await her arrival in my quarters and that I expect her to come at once. Now go, go, go, damn you!"

Without hesitating the slave shot away and vanished amongst the barracks blocks. Angrily Hadrian turned and pointed his finger straight at Fergus.

"Fergus," Hadrian snapped, "assign a squad to bring my belongings into the Principia. The rest of you are dismissed for the day. Get pissed or go and fuck something. I don't want to see any of your ugly faces here today."

And with that the Governor turned and swiftly followed by his staff and bodyguards he stamped away and disappeared into the Principia building.

Fergus caught Lucullus's eye but the centurion just shrugged.

"Aledus," Fergus called out, "get your squad to unpack the Governor's belongings and bring his stuff inside."

***

His men had just finished their task when Fergus, standing just outside the entrance to the Principia, noticed an enclosed litter, carried by four sturdy litter-bearers coming towards him. A clutch of female slaves followed on foot, carrying baskets, towels and clothes and from inside the litter Fergus could hear laughter, squeals and loud drunken voices.

"Oh shit," Fergus muttered as he realised what was about to happen, but before he could do anything or warn Aledus, Hadrian was already approaching, drawn by the noise.

And as Hadrian stepped out into the bright sunlight the litter-bearers came to an abrupt awkward halt just a few yards away. From inside the enclosed litter a woman giggled and someone else burped loudly.

"What's the hold up?" a bold drunken-sounding male voice called out. Then an inquisitive young man's face poked out beyond the cloth that covered the litter to see what was going on. As the young handsome man caught sight of Hadrian glaring at him from a few yards away, his face, as if in slow motion, slowly transformed into a look of sheer horror. Then with a wild, terrified yelp, the young man rolled out of the litter and onto the ground and with surprising speed he sprinted off down the street, screaming in terror. Stunned, Fergus watched the man go. The man was stark-naked and a pink ribbon had been tied around his cock.

"What's going on?" a woman called out slurring her words. A moment later a female face poked out from the litter but as she caught sight of Hadrian, her only reaction was to roll her eyes and take a deep, weary breath.

"Oh, it's you, husband," Vibia Sabina, Hadrian's wife called out in a scornful voice. "I thought we were about to be robbed. You gave poor young Antoninus such a fright."

Standing before the litter bearers, Hadrian's face darkened until it seemed he was about to explode with rage.

"You are a disgraceful wife," Hadrian roared as he erupted. "You do this to humiliate me don't you. Well I will not tolerate it any longer. It is time that you started to treat me with respect. I am your husband. I am going to be the next emperor of Rome and I expect your loyalty and devotion. But instead of this you must humiliate me at every occasion. Was that one of your latest boyfriends? I will not have my wife shagging other men in public!"

"Well, maybe I wouldn't do it, if you ever showed some interest in me," Vibia shouted back at her husband in a defiant, angry voice. "And as for shagging, what about all those pretty, slave boys whom you have had. Have you forgotten them? You are just as bad as I am. I will not take any lectures on love from you, husband."

"Take her around the back entrance and dump her into bed," Hadrian roared at the litter-bearers, "And don't let my wife leave her room until she has sobered up. She is a disgrace to me and to Rome."

As the litter-bearers and the clutch of female slaves dutifully turned and began to make their way around the Principia buildings, Hadrian shook his head in silent disgust and turned to step back into his HQ.

"Fergus, you and your men are dismissed, go and get pissed," Hadrian snapped as he passed by Fergus.

"Yes Sir," Fergus replied snapping out a quick salute. "Sir," Fergus hesitated. Now might not be the best time to raise the matter with Hadrian but he was worried that he would not get a second chance and the matter was pressing.

"What is it?" Hadrian paused and turned to glare at him.

"Sir, I have a request," Fergus stammered nervously, "It's about my family, Sir. They own a farm and land back on the island of Vectis in Britannia. In Carnuntum I received a letter from my mother saying that the governor is trying to steal our farm and take it for himself. So, I was wondering Sir. I want to help them. Would you be willing to intervene with the governor of Britannia on my behalf? I mean if you could write him a letter explaining our case, it may help my family. Please Sir, I want to help them, but I don't know what else I can do."

Surprised, Hadrian remained silent as he stared at Fergus. Then he frowned and slowly shook his head.

"You are a good soldier, Fergus," Hadrian replied sharply. "I appreciate what you did in Germania but this is not a matter where I can help you. Your family's land dispute is in Britannia. It is for the authorities in that province to sort it out. I have no jurisdiction. So, no I will not write the governor of Britannia a letter. I am sorry. I wish you the best of luck."

"I understand Sir," Fergus said, trying to hide the disappointment in his voice. "It was worth asking."

"Yes Fergus," Hadrian said as his expression seemed to soften a fraction, "You are right, it was worth asking but the answer is still no."

***

The men of the 2nd company were sitting around in small groups spread out along the road that led the short distance from Aquincum to the battlegroup's camp on the banks of the Danube. It was early evening and it was getting cold. Beside the road, the men were chatting, resting or gambling. Catching sight of his friends Aledus, Catinius and Vittius sitting clustered together with the men of their tent group, Fergus resisted the urge to sit down and take part in their game of chance and money. Instead he forced himself to step out onto the road, poking the gravel with his staff. Hadrian's rejection of his plan to help his family was bad enough but he knew that if he started gambling, it would just make things worse, for he would lose; he always lost. Fergus bit his lip in frustration. He knew he had a weakness for gambling and it had got him into a lot of trouble in Carnuntum a few months back. Hadrian's three hundred denarii bonus, which he'd received upon his return from Germania, had more than compensated for his debts and yet the debacle of going into debt again had left him depressed. He really did need to get a grip on his habit, but resisting the temptation to gamble was a true slogging-match, the outcome of which hung finely balanced on spinning dice. Grimly he turned in the middle of the road and gazed back down the street towards the provincial capital. How long was Lucullus going to make him and the men wait? Their centurion had given no explanation for his absence, except to tell Fergus to keep the company beside the road and wait for him. And that had been more than an hour ago. As he stood in the road clutching his staff, Fergus heard the thud and clatter of hooves. Squinting down the road in the direction of the town he suddenly caught sight of horsemen coming towards him. There were loads of them and as the riders streamed towards him, he recognised the proud Batavian standards carried by the foremost horsemen.

"They must be the Batavian cavalry squadrons Sir, come to join us," one of his squad leaders said as Fergus slowly stepped into the verge. Along the road, many of the legionaries had paused in what they had been doing and had turned to stare in silence at the approaching riders.

As the cavalrymen came trotting past heading in the direction of the battle group's camp, Fergus gazed at the riders with interest. The auxiliaries were clad in their distinctive chain-mail armour and their simple cap-like helmets. These were the Germanic auxiliaries with whom his father Marcus, had spent his entire career. Their reputation as fierce, reliable and loyal warriors preceded them. He had seen that for himself on the diplomatic mission to the Vandals, when part of Hadrian's escort had comprised of a squadron of Batavian riders from his father's old regiment. Acting on some instinct, Fergus raised his arm and hailed one of the cavalry decurion's.

"Friend, do any of you men belong to the 2nd Cohort?" Fergus called out.

"I am from the 9th, so are all these men," the officer replied in a guttural German accent, slowing his horse as Fergus came towards him.

"My father served with the 2nd in Britannia and here on the Danube," Fergus said, as hastily he kept pace with the horseman. "His name is Marcus, he fought at Mons Graupius with Agricola. Have you any post from Britannia? My father uses you Batavians to send me letters. Have you any letters for me? My name is Fergus, Optio in the 2nd company, 2nd Cohort of the Twentieth. Our home base is Deva Victrix in Britannia. I have to ask. We are a long way from our families and we haven't seen them in nearly a year."

The officer glanced at Fergus with interest. Then sadly he shook his head. "I am sorry I wouldn't know," he growled. "But maybe you should ask our standard bearer, Berengar - he knows about such matters. But he's already up ahead so you must wait until you reach the camp."

Dejected Fergus came to a halt, as along the road the hundreds of heavily-armed cavalrymen continued to trot past. Then as the last of the riders disappeared up the dusty road, Fergus saw

Lucullus coming towards him. As their centurion appeared the legionaries along the side of the road rose to their feet and reached for their shields and spears.

"Everything all right Sir?" Fergus said as he smoothly fell in beside his commanding officer as behind them the squad leaders started to yell at their men to form up in the middle of the road.

"All good," Lucullus muttered without glancing at Fergus, "I just needed to visit the whorehouse one more time before we go to war."

***

It was night and in the vast Roman encampment along the banks of the Danube, the rows of white army-tents stretched away into the darkness. Fergus however was sitting outside in the long grass, beside a crackling camp-fire, gazing up at the multitude of stars that covered the heavens. Around him the eighty men from his company were doing the same, huddled under their cloaks and blankets and gathered around their small fires. Some of the legionaries were trying to sleep whilst others were cooking a night-time meal or quietly talking amongst each other. There had been a screw-up by the logistics staff and for some reason the company's tents had not arrived in time so there had been no other option but to spend the night out under the night sky. Luckily the night seemed to look like it would remain dry. Wearily Fergus closed his eyes and lay back in the grass but he could not sleep. It had been a shitty and disappointing day. He hated this time for there was nothing to do and his thoughts always seemed to turn to his family's predicament and his home on Vectis. There nothing he could do to help them, he had told himself a thousand times, but that did not stop him from worrying. Frustrated he ran his hand across his face and through his short red hair. He had to concentrate on what was coming. The company was going to war. He owed it to his men to be sharp and show them that he knew what he was doing.

"Do you boys know where I can find the 2nd company, 2nd Cohort of the Twentieth?" a guttural voice suddenly called out in the darkness. "I am looking for your optio, a man called Fergus."

In response Fergus scrambled to his feet and turned to peer into the darkness in the direction from which the voice had spoken.

"I am Fergus, who wants to know?" he replied in a loud voice.

In the darkness, there was no immediate reply. Then a few moments later a man appeared from the gloom and came stomping towards the small camp fire. Fergus raised his eyebrows in surprise. It was one of the Batavian auxiliaries, clad in his long chain-mail shirt and wearing his cap like helmet.

"Are you Fergus?" the auxiliary exclaimed, examining Fergus carefully. Over his shoulder the man was carrying a leather despatch case, similar to those carried by imperial messengers.

"That's what I said," Fergus growled. "What is going on?"

"My name is Berengar, standard bearer of the 9th cohort of Batavians," the auxiliary replied. "One of my decurion's mentioned that you told him your father served with the 2nd cohort. You asked him if he had any post. I look after such things for our unit, so I checked and I have a letter for you."

"From who?" Fergus blurted out with sudden excitement, "can I see it?"

"It's from a woman," Berengar said guardedly. "Tell me her name and I shall give you the letter. Can't be giving someone else's mail to you, now can I."

"Kyna," Fergus replied hastily but the auxiliary shook his head. "No, that's not the name of the person that's written on the letter," he snapped.

"Galena," Fergus said without hesitation and he was rewarded with a little satisfied grunt from the standard bearer. "I don't want to hear a bad word being muttered about my Batavians from your men, you hear," Berengar muttered, as he handed Fergus a small tablet of thin plywood. "Good night."

Fergus did not watch the auxiliary disappear into the darkness. His eyes were fixed on the small wooden tablet in his hands and his chest was heaving. Receiving post out here on the frontier was as rare as pay day but was it good or bad news? Someone else must have written the letter for Galena, Fergus thought, for his wife had never been taught how to write. It was probably one of the freedmen in Deva who specialised in these services. Around him the men around the camp fire stirred expectantly as they saw what was going on. Taking a deep breath Fergus undid the seal that fastened the tablet together and sat down beside the fire to read.

Galena to her Fergus, greetings
Dearest husband, I write to you with news that I, and our baby daughter are well. I have called her Briana just like you wanted. She is healthy, happy and she has your eyes but no sign of her father's red hair. I miss you, husband. Since you departed, life has been nothing but toil and hard work. My father, Taran says that you will be gone for years but I do not want to believe it. I have taken Briana down to the grove beside the river where we were wed and I have placed a new stone there for every month that you have been away. And when she is older and can understand I shall tell her about you. My grandmother's amulet will protect you dearest husband, of that I am sure, for it has powerful magic. Keep it close and write to me when you can. I stop by the army camp in Deva every day to find out if there is news. I think the guards beside the gate have become sick of the sight of me but I am not the only woman who comes to inquire and I will continue to do so. Farewell then husband, may the guardian spirits watch over you and protect you, Galena and Briana to their Fergus.

"Oh, I think the optio has just received some good news," Vittius called out as a grin appeared on his face.

Around the camp-fire the rest of the men had risen to their feet and were staring at Fergus. News from home was precious, so precious that it was often shared amongst one's friends and comrades.

"I have become a father," Fergus said in a hoarse voice.

Chapter Twenty – Across the Danube

Fergus could see that the battle group's numbers had swollen again as he and Lucullus strode through the army camp towards the HQ tents. Around him the endless lines of white-army tents covered the fields and meadows along the Danube. Further away along the marshy, reed infested banks of the river, birds were circling in the air and Fergus could just about see the line of black boats that formed the boat-bridge across the Danube. Along the approach road that led in the direction of Viminacium and Kostolac, hundreds of carrobalista, artillery and bolt-throwers mounted on wagons, and carts of all shapes and sizes, filled with provisions and supplies, had been parked along the side of the road. It was early evening and two weeks had passed since they had left Aquincum and had marched south, following the course of the Danube. Their route had taken them past the great Roman fortress cities of Sirmium and Singidunum, Belgrade. They had crossed the Sava river on small boats and finally on to Viminacium and the spot along the Danube where the Roman engineers had thrown a bridge of boats across the mighty river. And ever since they had reached this spot, not a day had gone by when some new unit with their equipment had come marching or riding into the battle group's expanding camp. The soldiers seemed to be converging on the pontoon bridge from every corner of the empire. Already Fergus had counted two nearly-complete legions. The 1st Minervia from Bonna and the 2nd Adiutrix from Aquincum, his own vexillation of a thousand men from the Twentieth and another vexillation of legionaries from the 7th Gemina Legion whom had come from Hispania. Then there were the 2nd and 9th Batavian auxiliary cohorts from garrison duty on the Danube; a detachment of mixed infantry and mounted Germanic irregulars; a force of wild, bareheaded Berber light cavalry from North Africa and a corps of civilian pioneers and engineers, together with hundreds of artillery pieces and war machines. And now just that morning, a cohort of Syrian archers, with their strange, pointy helmets and chain-mail armour, had come marching into the camp.

"There must be over twenty thousand of us by now," Fergus muttered, glancing at his commanding officer.

"Oh, it's going to be big all right," Lucullus replied, as they approached the cluster of tents where the battle group's senior commanders were housed. "Trajan has concentrated nearly half of the entire army along the Dacian frontier. We're talking something like a hundred and fifty thousand men. This war is going to be something you will want to tell your grandchildren about. If you are lucky and survive it," the centurion said glancing sideways at Fergus.

***

The officer in command of the whole twenty-thousand strong army stood alone in the centre of the large tent. His chest was covered by a fine looking, tailored, cuirassed muscle armour over which he had draped a long blood-red cloak. In his hand, he was clutching a simple optio's staff. He looked around fifty years old with short white hair and a rugged, sunburnt complexion. Around him the two hundred or so senior officers had gathered in a wide, closely-packed circle as they quietly listened to their commander. Outside it was growing dark and oil lamps and several braziers lit up the general's tent with a flickering, crackling light. In front of Fergus, Lucullus was staring intently at the rough map drawn in the sand. The O group meeting had just started and the tension and excitement amongst the gathered officers was palpable.

"Gentlemen," the general called out, turning to look around at his subordinates, his eyes twinkling and glinting in the flickering light. "Yesterday I received our orders from the emperor. The invasion of Dacia will begin within hours. As of first light, at dawn tomorrow, our troops will begin crossing the Danube in force. Our main objective is King Decebalus's capital of Sarmisegetusa Regia. It is a mountain stronghold, well sited and well defended. I first fought these Dacian's back in Domitian's reign. Expect the enemy to put up a ferocious fight to protect their capital. They know that we are coming for them and they will be fighting for their very survival. Now if you look at the map you can see that Trajan has divided our forces into three columns. The most eastern column will be crossing the river here tonight," the general said tapping the map drawn in the sand with his Optio's staff. They will advance into the heart of Dacia along the valley of the Aluta river and over the Rotherthurm mountain pass. Along the central axis, Trajan, with four legions, will lead the main central assault across the new stone-bridge that was finished last year and will force his way towards the Dacian capital over the Vulcan mountain pass. The plan is to envelope the Dacian capital from three sides, systematically reducing the enemy fortresses as we progress."

The white-haired general paused, as he turned to stare at the rough map drawn in the sand. Then he raised his head. "So, that leaves us, the western column, here at Viminacium. Our orders are to cross the Danube using the pontoon bridge that has already been constructed. Once we are across the river, we shall advance to relieve our garrisons and forts at Arcidava and Tibiscum, building a supply road as we move forwards. Now gentlemen," the general growled, turning to look at the eager faces staring back at him. "The men in those outposts in the Banat region have been more or less cut off and under continuous siege for the whole winter, ever since the war started in the summer of last year. They are in a bad state and several forts have already fallen into enemy hands. Our task will be to quickly relieve them and engage and defeat any Dacian resistance. No Dacian fortress is to be left standing, not a single fort. They are all to be stormed and taken. After we have accomplished that task, we will turn eastwards, entering the Tibiscum river valley here and fight our way through the iron gates and over the mountain pass towards the Dacian fortress of Tapae. Once we are over the mountain pass we will link up with the other two columns and encircle Sarmisegetusa Regia and destroy it."

As the general fell silent the tent also fell silent.

"Questions?" the general called out in a loud voice, as he turned to look around at his officers.

"If my pioneers are to build your road Sir," an officer called out, "they will need protecting. My men are not soldiers Sir. They are engineers, labourers, slaves, POW's. They are not trained to fight. I hate to say it but they will flee at the first sign of trouble."

"Guard detachments will be left along our line of advance to protect your men," the general replied with a reassuring nod.

"What about the enemy Sir," a Centurion called out, "what can you tell us about the Dacian's, their tactics and method of fighting?"

"I have been fighting these barbarians for over fifteen years," the general replied. "Decebalus is a warrior king; he is cunning and he is ruthless. He fought Domitian to a standstill. Last year he sent assassins dressed as Roman soldiers to try and assassinate Trajan. He lured my friend Pompeius Longinus into peace talks and then took him prisoner, hoping to use him as a bargaining tool. Longinus only escaped by killing himself. This is the sort of king that we are dealing with. But the Dacian's respect him. They still have considerable numbers of warriors and a plentiful supply of weapons and gold. Their fortresses are well-built and well positioned. Expect them to fight like wild beasts but this is not going to be a war of open, pitched battles. Dacia is a mountain kingdom filled with treacherous gorges, mountain fortresses, fast-flowing rivers and dense forests. The Dacian's know from experience that they are no match for us in a pitched battle, so they will defend their mountain strongholds and try and ambush us wherever they can. They are past-masters of insurgency tactics. Once we are across the Danube, you will never be safe, not even in the middle of your own camp. Always be on your guard and don't trust what these Dacian's tell or show you. Always get a second opinion. It may save your life."

***

"Up, up. Move it, move it," Fergus cried out in a harsh voice as he hastily strode around amongst the men of his company, shaking and kicking the legionaries to their feet. It was still night and it was drizzling. Around them the darkness blanketed the land and there was no sign of dawn. But the camp was not asleep. In the darkness, the Roman officers were everywhere, shouting orders and all was movement and activity. In the light of hundreds of burning torches, long columns of heavily-armed and laden legionaries were forming up along both sides of the track leading down to the banks of the Danube. The soldiers clad in their armour and helmets and clutching their large shields, covered in their protective hide-covers, stood around in silence as they waited for the order to move. Across their left shoulders, the men were weighed down by their spears and their heavy, sixty-pound, marching packs, which were slung over their shoulders on rods. And spaced out at intervals along the long columns were the legion's stoic mules, heavily laden with tents, cooking-pots, spare weapons, water-skins, mill-stones and other equipment. Further away hidden in the darkness, Fergus could hear the neighing and stamping of hundreds of horses and the groan and rattle of numerous wheels rolling through the mud towards him.

"Company is all present and correct, numbers tally, Sir," the company Tesserarius, the watch commander said, as he hastily came up to Fergus and snapped out a salute. "We are ready to go, Sir."

"Good, let's take our place in the column," Fergus replied with a nod.

As to the east beyond the Danube, the first glimpse of the sun rose above the distant mountains a trumpet rang out across the banks of the river. It was swiftly joined by other trumpets. And as he heard the signal to advance Fergus, standing at the very rear of his company, took a deep breath and blew on his whistle. Around him the other Roman officers were doing the same. Along the muddy track the legionaries raised their large shields off the ground and began to slowly trudge down the slope of the grassy hill, following their centurions and standards, towards the glittering waters of the Danube. Fergus clutching his optio's staff followed, his eyes fixed on the column of heavily-laden troops in front of him. It was his job to make sure that none of the company's men fell out of formation or started going the wrong way. That was when he could use his optio's staff to beat them back into formation, not that the men had ever given him that excuse.

A column of auxiliary cavalry alae, Batavian and Berber, came hastily trotting past the plodding-line of heavy Roman infantry, making towards the boat-bridge. Fergus gazed at them with interest. The savage, wild and exotic looking Berber tribesmen from North Africa were making strange, excited whooping noises as they rode past. Slowly Fergus shook his head. The lightly clad Berbers were riding their small shaggy horses without saddles and reins and seemed to be armed only with multiple light throwing javelins. He had never seen such warriors before.

Up ahead the legionaries had started to cross the four thousand feet long, makeshift wooden pontoon bridge that had been built across the river. The timber bridge was groaning, creaking and swaying slightly as thousands of iron, hobnailed army-boots clattered across it. As he finally approached the riverbank, Fergus could see that the opposite shore of the Danube was obscured by a heavy bank of morning mist. The boat-bridge loomed up before him. Crossing over onto the wooden deck that the Roman engineers had built over the long rows of back-to-back boats, Fergus gazed suspiciously into the brown river water. One false move and the weight of his equipment would mean he would go straight to the bottom of the river. Then resolutely he lifted his head and gazed at the mist-shrouded bank of the Danube ahead of him. Whatever fate awaited him in the mountains of Dacia, he had resolved, he was going to make his grandfather Corbulo and Marcus his father, proud.

Chapter Twenty-One – Early lessons

On the horizon to the north and east Fergus could see the beautiful snow-capped mountains rising six or seven thousand feet. The rugged, boulder-strewn slopes and spurs of the western Carpathian foot hills were heavily covered in thick, brown and green forest and here and there, jagged rock-faces and cliffs jutted out above the trees. It was a cold, fresh and surprisingly clear morning and along the gently sloping, open and lush valley floor, in which he was standing, the white, foaming water from the small river came cascading over the rocks as it twisted and turned on its journey towards the Danube. Idly Fergus adjusted his white focale, neck-scarf and drew his cloak tighter around his body as he slowly made his way along the stream, glancing at the party of pioneers and engineers who were hard at work constructing the road. The dull thud of their pickaxes and shovels, the grunting of the oxen and the rush of the stream filled the valley with noise. Fergus sighed. A full day had passed since he and his company had crossed the boat-bridge and the sense of anti-climax was overwhelming. Instead of fighting their way along the valley towards the besieged Roman fort at Arcidava, he and the company had been assigned to protect this party of road builders, and if there was ever a truly thankless and boring job, then this surely was it Fergus thought. On their march into Dacian territory the previous day, there had been no sightings of the enemy, except for a few mounted scouts who had appeared from the forests to observe the Roman column. But the Dacian's had swiftly melted away again into the trees when a group of Batavian riders had tried to engage them.

Bored, Fergus turned to gaze towards the western horizon. There were no mountains in that direction and from his vantage point, the land seemed flatter and more open as it fell away towards the great Hungarian plains beyond. A couple of hundred yards away, across the sloping and grass-covered valley, the trees of a large, dark and impenetrable-looking forest had pushed their way down the gentle slope towards the river.

For a moment, Fergus turned to study the forest and as he did, he raised his hand to his chin and frowned in sudden concern. The eighty-four legionaries of his company were spread out in small groups along the section of road that was being built. The men were sitting in the grass or standing about looking as bored as he was. Looking troubled, Fergus turned to gaze down the valley and then up it. The party of road builders and his company were the only Roman's in sight.

"What's the matter?" Lucullus asked as the Centurion came up to Fergus and glanced in the direction in which Fergus was staring. "Something wrong, Fergus?"

"I don't like the look of that forest Sir," Fergus said, pointing at the trees. "Maybe we should place a picket along the tree line. Anyone could be watching us from those trees Sir and we are vulnerable out here in the open, scattered about. Maybe we should bring the men in closer together."

Lucullus placed his hands on his hips and grunted as he turned to examine the forest. Then he turned towards the pioneers and grunted again.

"All right do it. Bring the men in closer together. I suppose we just need to guard the road-builders and not the actual road. Hell, they have given us a shit job. This should be a task for an auxiliary unit, not us," the centurion said, with a weary shake of his head. "But maybe tomorrow will be different. And Fergus, the men's next meal will be at noon, not before and no wine until sunset," Lucullus added giving Fergus a little stern nod as he started up the slope towards the two oxen and wagons, which contained the detachments food, wine rations, the pioneer's equipment and a huge heap of stones.

"What about the picket at the edge of the forest, Sir?" Fergus called out.

"Nah, no need, if someone likes to watch us, then let them," Lucullus replied without looking round as he stomped away. "I am not going to spend the day chasing ghosts."

Fergus bit his lip. Then he reached for his whistle that hung on a cord around his neck and gave it several loud blasts. As the scattered groups of legionaries slowly began to drift closer together, Fergus turned to gaze at the pioneers. Some of the road builders were on their knees. One group, working ahead of the rest, was hewing out a trench and layering it with big stones. A second group followed adding broken stones, cement and sand to form a firm base whilst a third group followed the second group, slotting the tightly-fitting paving stones into place. A fourth group was digging a drainage ditch along the side of the road and fitting the kerb stones. The whole work was being overseen by a young, serious-looking engineer who strode in between his men, diligently checking their work. The pioneers progress was slow but steady and as he gazed at them, toiling away, Fergus was suddenly glad that it wasn't him doing this back-breaking work.

It was an hour later when a small sudden movement along the edge of the forest caught Fergus's eye. Alarmed, he straightened up. Amongst the trees a horseman had appeared. The man's horse was covered in fine layers of scale armour and he was holding a long heavy looking-lance. Then before Fergus could react, the rider raised his lance in the air, turned his horse towards the men down in the valley, and to Fergus's amazement, he charged. Moments later the forest erupted with savage screams and yells as forty, heavily-armoured horses and cavalrymen, clutching similar lances, burst from the cover of the trees and came charging into the open valley and towards the spot where Fergus stood rooted to the ground.

"Cataphracts!" a Roman voice screamed. "Sarmatian cataphracts!"

Along the line of the road the pioneers paused and stared in growing dismay at the heavily-armoured Sarmatian cavalry thundering towards them. Then as one, the labourers dropped their tools, broke and fled with loud, terrified screams.

Fergus's eyes widened in horror at the sight. Then he was moving and shouting at his men. There was no time to wait and see what Lucullus was doing.

"Prepare to receive cavalry, repel horsemen, repel horsemen, move, move," he roared, frantically turning on the legionaries around him. For a moment, the men seemed stunned by the surprise assault bearing down on them but it did not last, and as their training and drilling kicked in, the legionaries grabbed their shields and spears and came rushing up to Fergus and hastily began to form their small-square formation. Fergus drew Corbulo's sword and snatched his shield from where it lay on the ground. Around him the legionaries were still frantically forming their small, tight square. The men, standing shoulder to shoulder had split into two ranks, with the front rank down on one knee, protected by their large shields, which overlapped with their neighbours. The legionary spears pointed outwards and the tightly packed square bristled like a hedgehog, a small oasis of safety in the open valley. Dimly Fergus was aware of Lucullus shouting something, but his voice was drowned out by the wild screams and yells of the Sarmatian cavalry, who were now nearly upon them. Wildly Fergus turned and saw that the pioneers were fleeing for their lives, scattered across the valley. He should have ordered them into the middle of the protective square, but there had been no time and now it was too late to call them back. The pioneers were on their own.

"Brace, brace, men, hold, hold your positions, those horses will not charge onto our spears, stay in formation," Lucullus roared from close by, as the last of the company's men came sprinting up into their positions. Fergus turned to stare at the enemy. The forty Sarmatian cataphracts, heavily-armoured horses and their riders, had formed a tight wedge-formation as they came surging towards the tightly-packed square of legionaries. But at the last moment, the Sarmatians veered away from the solid rows of Roman spears and shields and as Fergus stared at them in horrified fascination, the horsemen expertly swept around the flanks of the Roman square and with excited cries and yelps set off in pursuit of the fleeing pioneers. Close by, a solitary spear thudded into one of the legionary's shields and attached to the spear was a man's shrunken, bloody head.

"Fuck," Fergus muttered as his mouth dropped open. But there was no time to stare at the gory sight. Across the valley floor the Sarmatian formation had broken up as the riders began to mow down and slaughter the desperate, fleeing road builders. Fergus's face grew pale as he turned to stare at the massacre. The pioneers stood absolutely no chance against the heavy enemy cavalry and as their terrified screams and cries for pity began to fill the valley, Fergus bit his lip in horror.

"There is nothing we can do for them," Lucullus's harsh panting voice said beside him. "They shouldn't have run. Those Sarmatian horsemen are allies of the Dacian's. My brother has faced them. He said it was not a pleasant experience." Gasping for breath, Lucullus glared at the enemy horsemen and the slaughter that was now taking place across the valley. In his hand the centurion was grasping his sword. Then he wiped the spittle from his mouth with the back of his hand. "Looks like they are just a raiding party," Lucullus growled. "We must stay in formation. That's all we can do. Someone will come to investigate soon or later. We must be patient. To take that lot on, we would need archers, artillery or cavalry and we have none." Then giving Fergus a hasty, grateful-glance Lucullus touched Fergus's shoulder. "That could have been us out there if we hadn't reacted in time. Well done Fergus, well done, you saved us today."

Fergus said nothing as he stood gazing at the massacre. The Sarmatians were now openly showing their contempt by casually trotting around and finishing off and robbing the wounded and dying who were lying scattered across the valley and amongst the rocks of the river. The enemy did not seem the slightest bit concerned by the tightly packed formation of legionaries, huddled together in the grass.

"Shit," Fergus hissed.

Chapter Twenty-Two – The Storming of Berzobis

The Roman fort of Arcidava was a smoking ruin. It was noon as the long column of weary, mud splattered and heavily laden legionaries and their mules silently trudged on along the muddy and slippery track towards the destroyed and ruined gates of the fort. A pillar of black smoke was still rising from the remains of the fort and in the grey overcast sky the wind was driving the rain straight into Fergus's face. The mud was everywhere, caking his boots, smeared into his armour, on his face and in his hair. Three days had passed since their encounter with the Sarmatian cavalry and since that day it had not stopped raining. Tiredly Fergus glanced up at the fort. Sections of the wooden ramparts had been torn down and lay collapsed, broken and splintered in pools of muddy water. And amongst the wreckage lay the debris of war; arrows, discarded swords, broken spears, lost helmets, battered shields and bodies, all testament to the ferocious fighting that had taken place. A feral dog was sniffing around in the debris and at the corners of the fort, the watch towers were nothing more than smouldering, blackened wrecks. But in the one remaining undamaged tower, a Roman banner fluttered proudly in the wind. As Fergus approached the gates a squadron of Batavian horsemen came trotting past, their hooves sending up a shower of mud in their wake.

"What the hell happened here?" Catinius muttered as he turned to stare at the devastation.

No one replied and as Fergus plodded into the fort, he saw the long lines of bodies laid out in rows beside the track and covered with blankets. A group of wounded, exhausted and shattered looking auxiliaries, were sitting together on the ground beside the track, huddled under sodden blankets. They were staring at the column of silent legionaries with dull, shrunken and listless faces as they passed. One of the exhausted survivors with a bloody bandage tied around his forehead, was still clutching his shield with a name scrawled across its front.

"Heh," Aledus called out from further up the column, as he pointed at the man's shield, "Why write a name on your shield?"

"It's the name of our commander," the survivor shouted back. "We wrote his name across our shields because the Dacian's use our equipment. It is the only way we could tell our boys and the enemy apart."

"I was here during the first war. You are marching into hell," another called out in a voice that trembled with emotion. "Good luck to you."

Fergus averted his eyes from the auxiliaries and turned to look up the long column of plodding men who were heading northwards. He had no idea how the war was progressing or whether Rome was winning or losing. There had been no news but they were still advancing and the signs of ferocious Dacian resistance were everywhere. They had all seen the tall, billowing columns of black smoke rising from the mountains in the distance and the pale, shattered faces and bodies of the wounded being transported back to the rear. Tiredly Fergus raised his hand to pick a piece of mud from his eye. Lucullus had told him nothing except to say that the main part of their force was advancing towards the fort at Tibiscum and that their vexillation, the thousand heavy-infantry from the Twentieth, had been given the task of securing their flank by taking a small enemy held fort called Berzobis, wherever the hell that was.

At dusk, as the weary, silent column of some fifteen hundred men, with their mules, wagon mounted artillery, detachment of Syrian archers and Batavian cavalry escort was crossing rolling, open country, a trumpet finally announced the end of the day's march. Relieved the men came to a halt and as the officers began to shout their orders the legionaries led their mules off the track and began to unload their tents and cooking ware. As the soldiers settled down to rest and prepare their evening meals Fergus strode away from the camp and some distance into the grassy fields. Fumbling with his undergarments he finally and with a relieved grunt, had a piss. When he was done, he turned to gaze to the north. In the fading light, the flat open plains were nearly devoid of any trees or cover and they stretched away to the horizon. It was perfect, magnificent horse country, open and covered in lush grass and as he gazed at the fine view, Fergus suddenly noticed a group of horsemen watching him.

"Oh shit," he hissed, stumbling back in fright. Hastily, his eyes fixed on the riders, he started to back away towards the Roman camp but the riders did not move. They seemed content to just watch. Hurrying back to the camp, Fergus called out to warn the sentries and a moment later he caught sight of Lucullus and the company's tesserarius, watch commander.

"Horsemen," Fergus cried out, turning to point in the direction of the watchers. "There are horsemen over there, Sir."

"I know," Lucullus growled turning to stare in the direction in which Fergus was pointing. "Our Batavian scouts say that they have been following us all day. But don't worry, they are not Dacian's. They are Iazyges, barbarians from the steppes and we are not at war with them. They are probably just keeping an eye on us as we are so close to their homeland. The tribune has issued strict instructions that we are to avoid any hostile contact with them."

"Now you tell me," Fergus muttered angrily to himself, as the centurion strode away.

***

Along the river escarpment the legionaries had thrown up a crude, earthen rampart which had been lined at intervals with sharpened, wooden stakes, cut from the nearby forest. The fire-hardened stakes had been thrust into the ground at an angle so that they pointed straight at the enemy, forming a rudimentary barrier. In addition, some of the legionaries had wedged their shields into the top of the rampart, forming a protective wall.

Crouching on the ground, Fergus carefully lifted his head above the earthen rampart and peered at the Dacian held fort that sat on a small rocky rise, just across from the raging, rushing river. A narrow wooden footbridge, only a few feet wide spanned the torrent but there was a gaping hole in the middle, breaking the bridge into two sections and making it impassable. Beyond the bridge, a steep, stony track led the short distance up to the fort's main gate. Peering at the fort, Fergus suddenly hissed as he caught sight of the wooden stake that had been driven into the ground just in front of the enemy gates. Shackled to the stake by his ankles and with his hands tied behind his back was a Roman prisoner. The man was calling out for water, his chin resting on his chest and he looked in a bad way. Crouching beside Fergus, Aledus stirred.

"The sentries spotted him this morning," Aledus muttered. "I think those fuckers are trying to provoke us into sending a rescue party across the river. But that would be a bad idea. Look," he gestured towards the bodies of two legionaries who lay sprawled at the river's edge. Both men had been killed by arrows. "They have the whole river bank covered. Anything that goes over these ramparts is likely to find an arrow with his name on it heading straight towards him."

Fergus did not reply as he stared at the scene. Across the narrow, raging river Berzobis was small, but its wooden ramparts and watch towers looked sturdy and well-designed, making use of the natural contours of the land. As he studied the enemy positions, Fergus suddenly caught sight of the Dacian sentries standing on the ramparts staring back at him. The men's strange domed helmets glinted in the morning sun.

"All right," Fergus murmured at last, lowering his head and laying a hand on Aledus's shoulder, "keep an eye on them but under no circumstances is anyone allowed to go to that prisoner's aid. I don't want any unnecessary casualties. And don't worry about the enemy, once the engineers and artillery men have finished constructing their artillery we are going to pound them to pieces. They don't know it yet," Fergus said in a vengeful voice, "but hell is coming for them."

The Roman officers stood clustered together under the oak tree. It was noon. The young aristocratic tribune in command of the fifteen hundred strong battlegroup was impatiently tapping his fingers against his thigh, as he listened to his senior engineering officer.

"My men should have our war machines and catapults ready by dawn tomorrow, Sir," the engineer was saying. "It does take some time. These are rather heavy and complicated machines, Sir, so we only carry the metal and other crucial parts with us. It would take an army to move them otherwise. So instead, once we are in position we use local materials to reconstruct the machines and disassemble them when we no longer need them. It's just on this occasion my men have had to forage far and wide. But like I said, we should be ready by dawn tomorrow, Sir."

"Good," the tribune snapped turning to look at his two senior centurions. "All right here is the plan. At dawn, tomorrow we are going to pummel them with everything we have got. I want the artillery barrage to last all morning. Then once we have set them alight and torn down their walls, the 2nd cohort will launch a direct assault across the river and storm their front gates. This should draw most of the defenders towards the river side of the fort. Meanwhile the 6th cohort, all five hundred men, will cross the river further downstream and once the signal is given, the 6th will hit the Dacian's in the flank and use their assault ladders to gain access to the fort. Caught between our two forces we shall annihilate them."

"You want my men to storm the fort across the river," Rufus, the senior centurion of the 2nd cohort snapped looking distinctly unhappy as he poked his vine stick into the earth. Standing at Lucullus's side, Fergus glanced quickly at his cohort's commander, hiding his delight that the man had voiced his own concerns. Rufus looked like he was old enough to be the tribune's father. "That river is a torrent Sir," Rufus growled, "we don't even know how deep it is or whether we will be able to cross it in full armour and carrying a shield. Once my men are out in the open they are going to come under a barrage of arrows and that is before they must cross the river and fight their way into the fort. I am sorry Sir, but that sounds like a shit idea. I am not about to sacrifice my men in such a way."

The officers tensed as the O group went very quiet. Across from Fergus, the tribune sighed and placed his hands on his hips.

"There will be no massacre Rufus," the young aristocrat said in a surprisingly calm voice, "and your men will assault those main gates. I will have our Syrian archers line up behind you, so that they can cover your men during the assault and you will also have artillery support. Casualties are to be expected but there can't be more than a few hundred Dacian's inside that fort and we do not have the time to sit here and starve them out. So, is that clear?"

"Sir, I have an idea," Fergus said, boldly raising his hand. At his side, Lucullus turned to glare at him in surprise.

Without waiting for permission to speak, Fergus continued. "Tonight, when it is dark I could take a few men out into the river to see if it is passable, Sir. And I have also been thinking about that bridge. What if we could get a squad to repair it during the night? We would need several long sturdy planks and a single support in the middle of the river. It could be done in one night. The river is not that wide. If it works, we could use the bridge to cross the river and attack those gates."

The twenty or so officers gathered under the oak tree did not at first reply as all eyes turned to stare at Fergus. At Fergus's side, Lucullus at last cleared his throat. "It is worth a try, Sir," Lucullus said turning towards the tribune. "What do we have to lose?"

Around the circle several of the other officers were nodding. The young tribune was gazing at Fergus. Then slowly he too nodded.

"All right make it happen," the tribune growled.

As the O group broke up and the officers headed back to their units, Lucullus turned to give Fergus a wry look.

"That was a brave thing," the centurion said, "volunteering for that mission. So, take a squad and see that it is done properly."

**

The water was freezing cold as Fergus stealthily crept out into the river followed by Aledus and Vittius. It was night and above them the moon had vanished behind the dark clouds, plunging the rushing, noisy river into complete darkness. Anxiously Fergus cast a hasty glance in the direction of Berzobis but there was no sign of any movement or activity from within the fort. Steadying his breathing, Fergus paused, as for a moment he allowed his body to get used to the ice-cold water that was rushing past his knees. The noise from the torrent would hopefully be enough to hide their presence from the Dacian sentries on their ramparts, no more than twenty yards away in the gloom. As he started out again into the middle of the raging torrent he swayed and cursed softly as his boots hit a rock, but he managed to steady himself just in time. The river however did not get much deeper and the strong current had only risen to just below his groin when he finally reached the gap in the bridge. Standing in the middle of the river, Fergus shifted his weight around until he had found a position where he could brace himself against the strong current. Then silently he turned and waited for Aledus and Vittius to join him underneath the bridge. His two comrades were carrying two long, sturdy wooden-logs balanced on their shoulders and weighed down by heavy sandbags at one end. Grimacing and puffing from the exertion they struggling to maintain their footing in the gushing current.

"Brace yourself, find a spot where you can stand," Fergus whispered, as he reached out to take some of the load.

In the darkness, the only reply was a muffled curse.

Looking up Fergus suddenly noticed that the moon had re-appeared from behind the clouds, casting a faint light onto the river. Anxiously he twisted round to stare at the enemy ramparts. If the Dacian's discovered them now their only hope would be to throw themselves into the river and let the current wash them downstream. That however was a dangerous option considering the amount of armour they were wearing. But as the seconds ticked by and the river water rushed past him, nothing happened and all remained as it should.

Suddenly above them on the Roman side of the bridge a face appeared over the edge of the gap. The man was lying flat out on his belly and was peering down at them, as they stood shivering in the water. It was Catinius and he was grinning. Silently Fergus raised his hand and beckoned to his friend. Abruptly Catinius's face vanished and a moment later the first of the long, crude wooden-planks began to unsteadily scrape across the gap in the bridge. Reaching up with both his hands, Fergus caught hold of the plank and guided it onto the Dacian side of the broken bridge. Then another plank appeared and once more Fergus twisted his body in the freezing water and helped guide the plank onto the opposite section of the bridge. Once the final plank had been shoved into position, Fergus felt a body slowly slithering across the repaired bridge above him. Gesturing silently at Aledus and Vittius, he grasped hold of the log supports and pushing the sand bag loaded end into the water, the three of them strained, cursing softly, as they struggled to wedge the wooden posts into the soft river bed and fix the other ends to the planks above their heads. At last they managed it and, panting from the exertion they swayed in the current, as they peered triumphantly at the supports. Above their heads the noise of a hammer striking an iron nail was muffled by a piece of cloth. Fergus paused as the soft hammering continued. They had wrapped a piece of cloth around the hammer to deaden the noise but standing in the open river, exposed as he was, the noise still sounded horribly loud. At last Catinius's face appeared over the side of the narrow footbridge.

"It's done," he hissed in triumph, "let's get the fuck out of here."

Raising his fist in fierce delight, Fergus gave the supports a final check and then silently gestured for his two comrades to head back to the shore. They had done it. They had managed to repair the bridge right under the noses of the enemy. As he gratefully waded out of the river and onto the bank and hastily joined the squad as they clambered back up to their own positions Fergus punched Aledus's shoulder in triumph and was rewarded with a broad grin.

"A tale to tell the grandchildren, Fergus," Aledus whispered happily as they slithered back behind the protection of the earthen embankment.

***

"Release," the officer bellowed.

Seconds later with a whirring noise, the battery of three onagers, heavy catapults, kicked backwards like mules and their projectiles went arching away in the direction of the Dacian fort. Fergus lay pressed up against the earthen rampart staring at the artillery men who were standing around their machines. It was dawn and he and the five hundred or so men from the 2nd cohort crouched or knelt along the entire length of the ramparts ready and waiting for the signal to commence their assault. In the Dacian fort the onager's clay balls, filled with flammable material vanished from view with a loud explosive crash. It was however impossible to see what damage they had done. Then another whirling and twanging noise filled the air, as the battlegroups battery of twelve ballistae and carroballistae opened up, sending a hail of rocks, stones and heavy arrows hurtling towards Berzobis. In the Dacian fort the yells and cries of the defenders plainly carried across the river.

"Reload," the artillery officer roared, "Tighten, release!"

And once more a barrage of clay balls went hurtling through the air and across the river, crashing into the fort and spreading their incendiary contents, which immediately burst into flames. The thump, crack and twang of the bolt throwers and rock hurlers followed. Just behind the line of crouching heavy infantry, the crews of the six scorpions, giant crossbows standing on tripods, swivelled their sniper weapons and sent a barrage of heavy bolts and arrows straight into the nearest Dacian watch tower. The aim of the scorpions was deadly accurate and as Fergus stared at the Dacian fort, one of the heavy bolts caught an unlucky sentry full on in the chest, sending him flying backwards, and over the side of the tall watchtower where he disappeared behind the enemy ramparts.
"Give them hell! Go on. Burn them. Burn them!" a few of the legionaries crouching in the line shouted, shaking their fists in harsh satisfaction.

On and on the artillery barrage went as the ballistae and their wagon mounted counterparts filled the air with missiles and kept up a furious bombardment of the Dacian positions. Across the river, the first columns of billowing black smoke were soon rising into the sky and despite the constant whirring, crack and twang of the Roman artillery and the shouts of the artillerymen, the noise of crackling flames could be heard coming from the fort. Fergus stared at the display in awe. He had never seen such a concentration of artillery. The crews of the scorpions were methodically clearing the watchtowers and ramparts of any Dacian who was foolish enough to show himself and their bolts and heavy arrows were already stuck into the Dacian walls like a pin cushion. An hour passed and then another and still the relentless Roman bombardment continued. Inside the fort the pillars of black smoke grew bigger and flames could be seen leaping skywards. The shrieks and screams of wounded men was plainly audible but despite the carnage that was being inflicted on the enemy, the Dacian walls still stood. As Fergus gazed at the chaos, one of the tall Roman style watchtowers caught fire and became a blazing inferno. Moments later two bodies fell to the ground outside the fort. One of the Dacian's was on fire and as he hit the ground, the man rolled about writhing until one of the Scorpion's impaled him to the ground.

From his position along the escarpment, Fergus could do nothing but stare in awe at the growing chaos across the river and as he gazed at the smoke pouring from the fort he was glad that he was not there having to take this ferocious pounding. Then suddenly to his surprise the main gates into the fort swung open. Fergus's mouth dropped in shock as a small tight group of Dacian's came storming out, trying to cover themselves with their shields as if they were practising a Roman testudo formation. The Dacian's were heading straight for the repaired bridge, contemptuous of the barrage of flying stones, bolts and incendiary projectiles.

"Oh no," Fergus groaned as he suddenly sensed the Dacian's purpose. "Oh no!"

As the small valiant party reached the river's edge, the tight, shield formation burst apart and a man flung himself onto the bridge, smashing a clay amphora filled with liquid onto the planking. A moment later another man clutching a burning torch, hurled it on the planking and with a whoosh the liquid caught fire and the bridge began to burn. In anguish Fergus ran a hand through his hair, as he stared at the growing fire that was engulfing the bridge he and his comrades had just repaired. But there was nothing he could do about it. Catching sight of the Dacian party outside their gates, the scorpion crews swivelled their huge cross bows in their direction and sent a volley of heavy bolts flying towards the enemy. The Dacian's didn't stand a chance. Two of them were killed instantly as the heavy yard long bolts impaled them, whilst a third man's shield was torn from his grasp. As the survivors turned and raced back towards the gates of their fort, one of the onagers landed a direct hit, the clay ball exploding and bursting into flames on impact and setting another of the raiders on fire. Then with a defiant crash the Dacian gates slammed shut. Fergus groaned as he stared at the fire that was engulfing the bridge and from the corner of his eye he saw Aledus stand up and raise his finger at the Dacian's, in a crude gesture as a stream of obscenities escaped from his mouth.

"Fergus, prepare the men, we are going in," Lucullus snapped at him in an urgent voice as the centurion, half bent over, came hurrying down the line. "We go when you hear the trumpet signal. Forget the bridge, we go straight across the river and up to those gates and ramparts. Good luck to you."

Before Fergus could reply, Lucullus was already hurrying away down the line. With a sigh, Fergus turned to look down the line, his chest heaving with sudden adrenaline and fear. It was time.

"Get ready boys," Fergus cried out in a loud voice, "we go in when you hear the trumpet. Keep your shields up and keep your footing in the river. The water will come up to your waist, no higher. Listen to your officers and NCO's and kill anyone who is not one of us. You have trained for this. No one beats us. Now let's finish this."

Along the line, crouching behind the embankment, no one answered him and all eyes remained on the burning, smoking hell across the river.

"Archers, prepare," the officer in command of the hundred Syrian auxiliary archers yelled and like a well-oiled machine, his men positioned just behind the legionaries and clad in their auxiliary chain mail armour and conical helmets, knelt on one knee, strung an arrow and raised their powerful composite bows, pointing them high up at the sky.

In his chest, Fergus felt his heart thumping away as he reached up to grasp hold of Galena's amulet. Hastily he raised it to his lips and kissed the cold, hard iron. Then just as he released the amulet in the distance he heard the unmistakable noise of a trumpet. Taking a deep breath, he fumbled for his whistle, stuck it in his mouth and blew. Then with a harsh cry he rose and started to clamber up the embankment. Along the entire escarpment, the five hundred Roman legionaries rose as one and with a huge roar they surged forwards over their embankment and went charging down towards the river bank. Fergus was one of the first into the water, splashing into the torrent and once more he gasped at the ice coldness. From the Dacian ramparts, there was no immediate response. Then the air above him was suddenly filled with arrows as the Syrian archers hammered the fort. Around Fergus the heavily armed legionaries were surging into the river and frantically wading and struggling towards the opposite shore. The men were holding their shields up above their heads and clutching their spears in the other.

As Fergus reached the opposite shore an arrow thudded into the shield of a man beside him and then another struck a legionary in the arm. Gasping for breath, his chest heaving from the exertion, Fergus clambered up onto the river bank and raised his shield, trying to protect himself as best as he could. Fumbling for his whistle he blew it once more. Then over his head another volley of Syrian arrows went whirling and whining into the Dacian ramparts.

"Move, move," he roared at his troops as if they needed any further encouragement. Then lifting his shield up in front of him Fergus charged towards the enemy gates and as he did he felt the whine of a Dacian arrow as it narrowly missed him. The Dacian gates and walls were still largely intact and as Fergus made it to the relative safety of the wooden palisade he crouched, raising his shield above his head. Hastily he snatched a glance at the river. The torrent was still filled with legionaries struggling to get across and on the steep land in between the

Dacian walls and the river, others were racing towards the cover that the walls provided. Fergus blinked as he caught sight of Lucullus's red plumed helmet and the company's standard amongst them.

"Get those hooks up against the walls," Lucullus roared, as the old man came charging towards the enemy walls, where a growing number of legionaries were taking shelter. Crouching beside the palisade they had raised their shields above their heads. "Pull that wall down, pull it down."

In response, a party of legionaries, clutching long poles which ended in iron hooks, came storming up to the wooden walls and as they did, a volley of Dacian arrows hammered into their shields and the ground around them. Fergus, his chest still heaving, stared at the soldiers as they raised their long poles, grappled hold of the top of the enemy palisade with their iron hooks and began to pull. Straining and grunting the legionaries tugged and tugged but the wooden wall would not budge.

"Put your backs into it," Lucullus roared as he looked up at the enemy rampart. "You are pulling like a bunch of lightweights. I said, bring down that wall! Now fucking well do it! Pull, pull it down."

Without thinking Fergus dropped his shield and lunged forwards, grasping hold of the end of the pole that one of the legionaries was holding. With a furious roar, Fergus threw his weight into the contest and tugged at the pole with all his strength. He was rewarded with a sudden splintering, cracking noise which sent him staggering backwards onto his arse. Around him the legionaries raised a wild, triumphant yell as part of the wooden palisade gave way and tumbled to the ground. Stunned Fergus stared up at the sudden gap that had appeared. Then with a yelp he rolled away and threw himself into the relative safety beside the Dacian ramparts. A few moments later another splintering crack announced the collapse of another part of the enemy ramparts. Hastily Fergus grasped hold of his shield as suddenly, close by, he heard foreign voices. In the growing breach in the wall another segment of the wooden palisade collapsed, leaving a gaping hole in the enemy defences.

"Get in there, get in there, kill everything you meet!" Lucullus roared, pointing at the breach with his sword.

With a loud, vicious cry the legionaries stormed into the breech, like some blood thirsty, unstoppable and enraged armoured beast. Fergus followed. He had drawn his sword and as he charged through the gap, he was hit by a blast of thick, acrid black smoke. Inside the fort the scene was of complete devastation. Every remaining building was on fire, belching out black smoke into the sky and amongst the blackened, broken debris and chaos that littered the ground lay countless broken bodies and dead horses. But the Dacian's were not finished. As the heavy Roman infantry surged into the fort a ferocious cry rose from the massed Dacian ranks and then they charged. Fergus eyes widened in horror as a Dacian warrior came at him wielding a long, two handed, curved, polearm. Desperately he tried to parry the warrior's blow and as his shield made contact, the sharp curved blade of his enemy's weapon struck his shoulder armour, raking the metal down towards his elbow. With a cry, Fergus slammed the boss of his shield into the man's face, forcing him backwards. Then swiftly he followed it up by jabbing at the Dacian with his gladius. He was rewarded with a shrill cry and in front of him the man staggered backwards, bleeding from a wound to his side. The Dacian was wearing no armour whatsoever, nor was he carrying a shield. But before the warrior could come at him again a legionary came at him from out of nowhere and thrust his sword straight into the man's head, killing him instantly.

To Fergus's left ferocious, snarling, screaming hand to hand combat had broken out as the Dacian defenders tried desperately to seal the breach in their walls. But the numbers of legionaries pouring through the breach was growing. Hissing and holding his bloodied sword, suddenly uncaring about what happened to himself, Fergus strode out alone into the heart of the Dacian fort. The black smoke was billowing up from everywhere, obscuring his view and making him want to throw up. Suddenly another group of Dacian's appeared, clustered around a tall man who looked different to the others. As they caught sight of Fergus they charged towards him. The Dacian's were armed with the same, but smaller looking curved blades that the other warrior had, and like him they were wearing no armour nor carrying any shields. Fergus's eyes widened. Then the Dacian's were upon him, forcing him backwards, their curved weapons slashing and hammering into his shield, their wicked curved points threatening to rip his shield from his grasp and disfigure his face, legs and arms. But the assault did not last long. As Fergus stumbled backwards, a group of legionaries came charging into the Dacian's, forcing them back and as Fergus joined the furious, desperate struggle, the legionaries cut the remaining Dacians to pieces. Fergus roared in triumph as the tall Dacian finally staggered backwards, wounded by a blow to his leg and arm. Around Fergus the legionaries were in no mood to take prisoners and as the tall Dacian stumbled backwards, bleeding from multiple wounds in a final act of defiance, he raised his curved weapon and defiantly pointed it at Fergus.

"Bicilis," the warrior screamed in his alien, unintelligible language, "Bicilis," and the word was followed by something else which Fergus also didn't understand.

With a savage cry, Fergus surged forwards, evading the warrior's clumsy, weak attempt to stop him and thrust his sword into the man's throat killing him instantly.

Chapter Twenty-Three – Tibiscum

The Roman fort of Tibiscum looked largely unscathed and intact. The only sign of recent fighting was a torn down section of the wooden wall, which had been blocked by a makeshift barricade of earth, broken wagons and sharpened wooden-stakes. The noise of hammering and sawing coming from the army carpenters who were repairing the wooden palisade, echoed across the fort. It was dawn and a full week had passed since the successful assault and destruction of Berzobis. Along the main track that led to the gates, companies of legionaries and auxiliaries were marching past, led by their standards and centurions. They were followed by trundling ox and horse drawn wagons; groups of filthy mud stained horsemen; and carroballistae, huge artillery cross bows mounted on carts. And all were moving forwards, squelching through the mud, heading east into the rising sun and towards the western spurs of the great snow-capped Carpathian Mountains. Sitting on the backs of the artillery wagons, the artillery-men, their legs dangling into space seemed to be enjoying the sun on their faces. Up on the wooden walkways that lined the wooden ramparts of the fort, the sentries clutching their shields and spears were staring out across the hilly, wooded landscape.

The unshaven, skinny veteran was sitting on a barrel beside a wooden barracks block and in his hand, he was clutching a Dacian curved sword. The veteran had a bandage tied around his head and his dirty army tunic was torn and in need of replacing. Standing around him in a semi-circle with their arms folded across their chests, Fergus and a dozen others from the 2nd company were listening to the veteran with interest.

"I fought them in the first war, a few years ago," the wounded veteran exclaimed with a little solemn nod. "Last year when the new war began, we were the first to be attacked but we held because we knew they were coming. We threw the enemy back. I was here in this fort during the whole winter, when we were besieged and cut off. Some of us ate grass to survive and we had to butcher all our animals. It was grim, boys. If the winter snows had not blocked the mountain passes and prevented the Dacian's from concentrating more men against us, I would not be here talking to you."

The veteran turned to look away as if pushing away some unpleasant memory.

"Now listen boys," the man said abruptly, turning his attention back to his audience. "The Dacians don't fight like we do. Most of them have no armour or shields but they have this," the veteran said, raising his curved Dacian sword. "The dreaded Dacian falx. It's a really nasty piece of kit and they all have it," the veteran exclaimed thrusting the curved sword towards his audience. "It's a bit like a farmer's large sickle. The Dacian's call it the Sica. The curved tip and blade of the sword can get around your shield and rip open your head, face and arms, forcing you to drop your shield or sword. Make no mistake, the Dacian falx is devastatingly effective. With shields and armour their infantry can hold their own against us if they choose to. The falx also comes with a longer and bigger two handed versions," the skinny veteran explained. "That one is like a polearm, five of six feet in length with a curved iron blade. You will shit yourself the first time you see that blade sweeping down on you. It's even more lethal than the Sica but the two-handed ones are generally quite rare and are carried by their nobles and wealthier citizens for they are expensive to make."

The veteran paused to stare at the group of legionaries standing around him.

"So, to counter the falx," the man said tapping his head with his hand, "we fitted re-enforcing iron-straps to our helmets. You will also want to protect your arms and legs with greaves and arm-guards. Use whatever you can find, but do it boys. We learned quickly and that is why I am still alive."

***

Looking tired Fergus sat slumped on the ground, his back resting against the wall of one of the barracks blocks. An army blanket covered his body. It was a warm night but despite his body's fatigue he couldn't sleep. The Roman fort was packed beyond its capacity and many of the men had been forced to sleep outside on the ground. With nearly fifteen hundred men from the vexillation of the Twentieth and their supporting units of Syrian archers, artillerymen, civilian pioneers and several Batavian cavalry squadrons from the 9th auxiliary cohort, the fort was crammed full of troops, animals and war machines. The garrison was far too large to be accommodated amongst the fort's existing barracks blocks and even though, as an optio, he had been offered a place inside one of the blocks, Fergus had given it up to one of the wounded men.

The night was warm and it was dry. Around him the fort of Tibiscum was quiet, except for the odd cough, snoring and shout. Above him in the night-sky a fantastic array of stars covered the heavens. Wearily Fergus replaced the small wooden tablet in the pocket of his army cloak. It was too dark to read the letter from Galena and besides he already knew every word and sentence by heart. Unable to settle down, he reached up to touch the iron, Celtic amulet around his neck and as his fingers traced the cold outline of the charm, he tried to picture what Galena looked like, imagining he was touching her long, blond hair and the curves of her body. Nearby a soldier's snoring however disturbed him and with a sigh, Fergus let go of his amulet and irritably rose to his feet. If he could not sleep, he might as well seek out the company of his old comrades. Striding away towards the eastern ramparts of the Roman fort he found the ladder leading up onto the narrow walkway that ran along the walls. A few burning torches flickered at intervals along the wall. Aledus and his squad had been assigned guard duty along this section of the walls and as Fergus clambered up onto the wall, he caught sight of Aledus and Vittius clutching their shields and spears. The two of them seemed to be discussing something as they peered into the darkness beyond the walls.

"Mind if I join you," Fergus muttered, as he drew his cloak closer across his body and ambled up to the two sentries.

Aledus turned to glance at him. "Can't sleep?" he asked.

"Something like that," Fergus said.

For a while the three of them were silent and further along the walls, Fergus could make out Catinius and the other men from his old tent group, as they silently patrolled the ramparts.

"We were just discussing what we would do when we retire," Aledus said, glancing at Fergus. "Vittius here wants to go to Rome."

"Free bread, games and the pick of the empire's women, my friend," Vittius said turning towards Fergus with a wide grin. "What is there not to like?"

"What?" Fergus frowned, "You are already thinking about retirement? You are what, twenty-one, twenty-two? Bit young to be thinking about that, aren't you?"

"Maybe," Aledus muttered, turning to stare into the darkness, "But we all saw those wounded, the men missing arms and legs. They will never fight again and some of them were our age. So, yes, we are thinking about what we do if the army no longer has any use for us. You must have done the same?"

"I don't try to think about it and neither should you," Fergus replied swiftly. "This is the life that we chose and it's a good life." Wearily Fergus shook his head as he turned to grip the side of the wooden palisade. "You could lose an arm or a leg even if you were working on a farm or as builder. Accidents happen. A whore could give you a disease, the Gods could strike you down with lightning. Shit, boys, those wounded were just unlucky, that's all."

"Are you saying that we are the lucky ones?" Vittius replied with a frown.

"Forget it," Fergus said, waving the question away. Then a moment later a little smile appeared on his lips and he turned to look at his friends. "All right, so what does Catinius want to do when he retires?" Fergus asked.

Aledus leaned in towards Fergus with a conspiratorial manner.

"He told us that he is planning to get laid for the first time," Aledus said, whispering loudly and as he did, a mischievous grin appeared on his lips. "But he is worried that no woman will have him, so it may have to be with a horny goat."

Vittius's roar of laughter shattered the peace and quiet of the night and Fergus too chuckled in amusement.

"What's going on over there?" Catinius's called out in an annoyed voice as he turned to stare in the direction of his three comrades. "Keep it down, we're supposed to be on guard duty. The Tesserarius told us to keep our eyes open."

"We're just discussing goats," Aledus cried in reply, as beside him Vittius sniggered and then hooted with laughter.

"Shit," Fergus muttered, shaking his head with an amused look as he turned to stare out into the night, "A horny goat. That's a good one."

In the darkness beyond the fort a sudden movement and noise caught Fergus' attention and abruptly the amusement vanished from his face and he straightened up.

"What's that?" Fergus growled in alarm as he pointed into the darkness. Then suddenly in the gloom he heard it again, the noise of muffled, running feet. A moment later, in the gloom of the burning torches and starlight, Fergus caught sight of hordes of men racing straight towards the walls of the fort. The men were carrying ladders and they were armed.

"Oh shit," Fergus yelled in alarm as he staggered backwards in fright and yanked his sword from its scabbard, "We are being attacked. Sound the alarm, sound the fucking alarm!"

Beside him Aledus and Vittius were staring into the darkness in stunned horror and for a split moment they were unable to do anything.

"We're under attack!" Fergus roared, pushing his way past his friends as he began to race down the ramparts towards the closest watchtower. "Catinius, sound the fucking alarm, eastern walls! They have ladders. There are hundreds of them!"

Catinius must have heard him, for a few moments later a loud, clanging bell erupted across the fort. Fergus skidded to a halt just as in the darkness, he felt something fly past his face. With a terrified cry, he flung himself down behind the protection of the ramparts, as close by, another missile went hurtling over the wall. He didn't have a shield he suddenly realised in horror. Inside the fort, he could hear confused shouting. Then just a few yards away an assault ladder thudded up against the wall and from the darkness beyond the ramparts, he heard foreign voices and shouts. Then further along the wall another ladder thudded up against the wall and then another and another. In just a few moments the enemy would come pouring over the wall. Resisting the urge to flee, Fergus scrambled on all fours towards the ladder, rose to his feet and frantically fumbled around in the darkness. Then his fingers found the ladder. Below him in the darkness all was movement and in the faint light a startled face suddenly appeared, staring up at him from no more than a few feet away. Fear lent Fergus strength and with a roar his sword slashed downwards at the face, striking the man in the neck. With a groan the Dacian vanished into the night.

There was no time to see what was going on along the rest of the walls. Below him in the darkness the Dacian's were shouting to each other, as along the Roman perimeter more and more assault ladders thudded up against the walls. Grasping the top of the ladder, Fergus strained as he tried to drag the ladder sideways. At the first attempt the weight on the ladder would not budge but then, suddenly reversing direction, Fergus sent the ladder sliding away sideways into the darkness. He was rewarded by a surprised yell and then a splintering crash. Close by, someone was yelling and startled, Fergus realised it was himself. Crouching behind the protection of the ramparts Fergus turned and started towards the next ladder that was only a few yards away but before he could reach it, the first of the Dacian attackers came clambering and tumbling over the side of the wall. Frantically Fergus launched himself at one of the men, stabbing him straight in the chest before he could react. The Dacian collapsed onto the narrow wooden walkway without making a sound. But already more and more Dacian's were appearing on the ramparts, their alien sounding cries and shouts filling the darkness with terror. An attacker, catching sight of Fergus in the gloom, swung at him with his curved falx, forcing Fergus backwards. Eagerly the warrior came on, his falx slashing at Fergus's body. Desperately Fergus tried to lunge at the Dacian but the man gave him no such opportunity. Gasping, his chest heaving from the exertion Fergus was driven backwards. Then from the gloom a sudden roar made his opponent hesitate and glance over his shoulder, but it was already too late for him. From out of the darkness two Roman's came charging down the narrow walkway using their shields and spears like a battering ram and as they did, bodies went bouncing away backwards or over the side of the rampart and into the fort. As the Dacian turned to face the new threat, Fergus sprang forwards and buried his sword into his opponent's body. With a furious yell, Fergus pulled his sword free and kicked the dying man over the side of the walkway and into the fort below.

"Stay with us, Fergus," Aledus yelled, as he and Vittius turned to face the noise coming down the ramparts, "You don't have a shield. We stand a better chance if we stick together. Those fuckers are everywhere."

Fergus was panting, his breath coming in gasps but he said nothing. There was no time to ponder their situation. Down in the Roman camp all was in uproar and confused shouts and screams rent the darkness.

Along the dark narrow walkway, the sound of running feet drew closer and then with a savage cry a party of Dacian's flung themselves upon Aledus. A falx sliced through the air and Aledus shrieked in sudden pain as he stumbled backwards dropping his spear, as he desperately tried to stem the vicious blows that were raining down on him. Lunging forwards Fergus grasped hold of the spear and with a yell he rose just behind Aledus and thrust the weapon over his comrade's shoulder and into the darkness beyond. In the gloom, he felt the point of the spear punch into flesh and a split second later, a man groaned and staggered backwards. Keeping close to Aledus, Fergus jabbed at the darkness again, protected by his friend's body and shield.

"Ah fuck, fuck, fuck," Aledus cried out in pain, "They cut my arm, they cut me."

In the darkness, a Dacian falx slammed into Aledus's shield and with a cry, Fergus responded by jabbing at the darkness beyond with his spear.

"Aledus move forwards, keep your shield up, Vittius cover our arses," Fergus yelled at his two comrades and a moment later the two of them, working together, inched forwards, Aledus protecting them with his shield whilst Fergus, edging along right behind him, stabbed over his friend's shoulder at anything that moved in the darkness. Behind them Fergus could hear Vittius cursing loudly over and over again.

From within the Roman camp a trumpet rang out. And suddenly, down below them Fergus heard Roman voices. The shouts were drawing closer. From the darkness, an enraged Dacian suddenly flung himself at Aledus, roaring in frustration and as his falx forced Aledus and Fergus backwards, Fergus furiously jabbed at him with his spear but missed. Bracing themselves for the next attack, Fergus jabbed blindly into the darkness but his spear made no contact. Slowly the seconds ticked by and no further attack came.

Then Roman voices were coming towards them along the walkways.

"Password! What's the fucking password?" Vittius yelled in a disturbed voice, as in the darkness the noise drew closer. "You don't get to pass without giving me the fucking password."

From the gloom a centurion's plumed helmet appeared. For a moment, the officer hesitated as he peered towards Fergus and his companions.

"Shit, seems some of the guard detail survived," the officer cried out, turning to the men crouching behind him. "It's all right boys," he shouted, turning his attention back towards Fergus. "We have driven them from the camp. The enemy are gone. The attack is over. We won. It's all right, it's all right boys."

"I still want that fucking password," Vittius yelled his voice shaking with emotion.

***

It was dawn and to the east the welcome rays of the sun were already warming up the earth. Tiredly, with red-rimmed eyes, Fergus stepped out of the first aid post to which all the battle group's wounded had been brought and patted Aledus on his shoulder. In response Aledus acknowledged him with a little silent nod. His friend was sitting outside on the ground together with a group of the other less seriously wounded. A white bandage had been wrapped around his arm. The good news was that the wound had not done any serious damage and it would heal given time the doctor had said. In the meantime, Aledus had been placed on light duties. Across from Aledus, Vittius too was sitting on the ground, his knees drawn up under his chin. He was staring silently and fixedly at his boots. Fergus rubbed his tired eyes. Vittius had not uttered a word to anyone since the night assault had been beaten back. The doctor had told Fergus that there was nothing wrong with Vittius but that he was still in shock. Given some rest and time he would return to his usual self.

"Fergus," a voice called out from the track that ran the length of the fort. Looking up Fergus caught sight of Catinius. His friend looked as exhausted as himself. "Lucullus told me to find you," Catinius called out. "He wants you to take a squad to relieve the guards who are looking after the prisoners. They are being held beside the western gate."

Fergus nodded and leaving Aledus behind he strode over towards Catinius.

"All right," he muttered. Then as he was about to set off to the company's quarters, he paused and turned to look back at Catinius.

"Was it you who sounded the alarm? It was quickly done, I remember." Fergus said, gazing at his friend.

"Someone has to be responsible, Sir. We can't all be making jokes and forgetting our duties," Catinius snapped with a serious expression on his face, as he turned and stomped away through the mud.

Fergus watched him go. Then with a little grin he turned away and headed towards his company's quarters.

***

The Dacian prisoners were sitting on the ground in the mud. There were twenty of them and their hands had been tied behind their backs and their ankles were clasped in a long iron slavers-chain that snaked its way through the group. The prisoners looked exhausted and miserable and some of them bore signs of abuse, black eyes, bruises and open wounds from where someone had whipped them. As Fergus approached with the eight-man squad from his company, he suddenly came to an abrupt halt. A few Roman legionaries were standing around guarding the prisoners and amongst them, Fergus suddenly recognised Fronto. The big Tesserarius of the fourth company was clutching a coiled whip in one hand. Catching sight of him, Fronto's lips split into a cold, unwelcoming smile.

"Well, well, look what the dog has found for us," Fronto said, as he glared at Fergus with contempt. "What are you doing here boy?"

"That's no way to address a superior officer," Fergus retorted as he came towards Fronto.

"So what," Fronto said. "Do you think that I am afraid of you? You may have sucked Hadrian's cock to get that promotion but that doesn't mean you are a better man than me. I piss on you."

"I have orders to relieve your men; so get the fuck out of here," Fergus commanded coming up to Fronto and fixing him with a hard, uncompromising stare.

"Gladly, they are all yours," the tesserarius snapped as he raised his hand and gestured at his men. Then without saying another word, he pushed past Fergus and went striding off into the camp, whirling his whip in the air as he went. Annoyed Fergus watched his arch enemy disappear amongst the barracks blocks. Fronto and he shared a long, violent history of conflict that went back to his first days in the legion at Deva Victrix. Fronto's jealousy, unstable and cruel mind and the fierce competition for promotion, had twice pushed Fronto into trying to murder him. And that had not been the only occasion when there had been trouble between them. At Deva, Fronto and his men had beaten up Aledus, putting him in hospital for several weeks and at Bonna on the Rhine the legal accusations against Fergus seemed to have been started by Fronto. And then there was the assassination attempt in the woods at Carnuntum, which although unproven had Fronto's fingers all over it. The second attempt on Fergus's life had been the last straw forcing the senior cohort commanders to promote both and post Fronto to another company. Since then the tesserarius had been keeping a low profile.

With an angry look, Fergus turned away and as the squad took up their posts around the group of prisoners, he placed his hands on his hips and stared at the Dacians. None of the sullen, bloodied prisoners looked back at him and as he walked around the edge of the silent, miserable-looking group, he could see that Fronto had done a good job at terrorising them with his whip and fist. Fergus was about to hand over the guard duty to the decanus in charge of the squad and walk away, when he noticed a small group of officers and civilians approaching.

Curiously Fergus waited as the group halted by the prisoners and the civilian amongst them began to speak to the Dacian's in a foreign language that was completely alien to Fergus. At first the prisoners remained silent, but as the civilian strode in amongst them, talking to them as he did, some of the Dacian's started to answer back in their own language. At last, looking satisfied, the civilian came up to the gaggle of Roman officers and as he did, Fergus edged a little closer so that he could hear what he was saying.

"They don't seem to know much or maybe they are unwilling to tell me," the civilian translator and interrogator exclaimed with a sigh. "They are telling me that their general is called Bicilis and that he is in command of all Dacian forces in this district. It was he who ordered the night attack on our fort. They say that many of the Dacian tribes are deserting King Decebalus and are trying to make peace with Trajan. But Bicilis is loyal to the king. They say he is going to make a last stand at Rosia Montana and that he may try to destroy all the gold and silver mines in that region. They ask you for mercy and water."

"Bicilis," Fergus called out in surprise, as he took a step towards the officers, "Bicilis. I have heard this name before. The defenders at Berzobis, they called out his name too."

The Dacian War – Veteran of Rome Series

Chapter Twenty-Four – Into the Carpathians

To the east in the distance, the Carpathian-mountains rose majestically, their high, indomitable snow-capped peaks lining the horizon. Closer by, the steep slopes of the mountains were covered in dense green forest and rocky outcrops. Spectacular white waterfalls, jagged gorges and here and there a high, well-watered pasture, completed the picture. There was no denying it Fergus thought - the rugged mountains of Dacia were beautiful. The wild, lush meadows and forests were well suited for flocks of sheep, cattle and hunting. As he plodded along the narrow track that clung precipitously to the mountainside, Fergus idly glanced down the steep, rocky, boulder strewn and partly forested mountain slope towards the valley. Far below him a river was twisting and turning along the valley floor as it disappeared towards the west. It was late in the afternoon and the five and a half thousand strong battle group had been toiling up the mountain pass all day. There had been no sign of the enemy but, ever since they had set out from Tibiscum, Fergus had noticed that increasing numbers of Dacian civilians, women, children and the old and sick had appeared on their line of march, begging for food and heaping praise on the Roman invaders. Wearily Fergus turned to look up at the fierce summer sun that mercilessly beat down on him. High in the clear blue sky a hunting bird was lazily circling the column, drifting on the air currents. Then far towards the east he caught sight of a towering column of black smoke rising into the clear, blue sky. For more than five weeks after the night assault, the vexillation of the Twentieth had remained in Tibiscum on garrison duty, as they had defended the strategically important Roman fort and supply base and had waited for new orders to arrive. And as they had waited summer had come.

There had been snippets of news. From Lucullus, Fergus had learnt that the bulk of the Roman forces were continuing their advance towards the east, up the Tibiscus river valley and towards the mountain pass known as the "Iron Gates." The fighting up there is heavy and fiercely contested the centurion had muttered. And from Rufus, the senior centurion of the 2nd cohort, Fergus had learnt that King Decebalus was concentrating most of his remaining forces on defending the approaches to his capital. Rufus had added that it was true that more and more Dacian tribes were trying to surrender. "King Decebalus is finished," the senior centurion had stated in a confident voice. The Dacian's have lost confidence in their king. But that had been several weeks ago, and since then there had been no further news. Then three days ago, the battle group had suddenly received new orders and reinforcements as a complete vexillation from the 7th Gemina Legion from Hispania and four cohorts of the 1st Legion had arrived, together with the infantry companies of the 9th Batavian cohort. The battle group now five and a half thousand strong, was to proceed with all haste across the mountains to the north-east and capture and occupy the important Dacian gold and silver mines around the Dacian fortress of Rosia Montana, a march of some hundred miles deep into enemy territory and across inhospitable mountainous terrain.

Tiredly, Fergus lowered his head. He could not shake the feeling that their new objective had something to do with the information that he'd heard the Dacian prisoners give to their interrogators in Tibiscum. But the news that they were not to take part in the siege and final assault on the Dacian capital of Sarmisegetusa Regia had not bothered the men. Instead the legionaries had seemed thrilled by the news that they were being sent to capture a district filled with gold and silver mines, for the opportunity to loot some of the Dacian treasure would surely arise during the coming fight.

At the very rear of the 2nd company, Fergus continued to trudge on up the steep, rough mountain path. From his position, he had a good view of the eighty men of the company and their mules - one animal for each tent group. If any of the legionaries were to fall out of line or wander off, it was his job to get them back into formation but none of the company had yet given him an excuse to use his staff on their backs. Beyond his company, the long column of legionaries and auxiliaries leading their heavily laden mules, was slowly snaking its way up towards the top of the narrow mountain pass. The rhythmic tramp and crunch of the men's iron-studded boots on the rocky, stony ground and the rolling, grinding clatter of wagon wheels filled his ears. Fergus's face was covered in sweat and dust and he was thirsty but his small water-skin, dangling from his belt, was already empty. On his head, he had fastened small, reinforcing iron strips to his helmet, like most of the men in his company, and along his arms and legs he had fashioned himself some crude iron and leather arm and leg guards. The addition of the new armour had left him looking a rather motley figure, but he was not the only one who had tinkered with his armour and uniform and the senior officers had raised no objections. Over his left shoulder, he was carrying his heavy marching pack, containing his personal belongings. These included his entrenching tools, his cup, blanket and his two-week grain ration together with two spears. And in his left hand, he was clutching his shield covered in its dust jacket, whilst in his right hand he was using his long optio's staff as a walking stick. The weight of all his equipment was just about tolerable but the lack of water was making him irritable.

As Fergus came around a bend in the track he caught sight of a Dacian civilian, an old man with a sunburnt, wrinkled face. The man was clutching a sleek hunting dog tightly by its collar as he stared at the column of heavy Roman infantry plodding past him and up the path. Fergus glanced at the old man as he strode on past and in reply the Dacian called out to him in his unintelligible language. Ignoring the civilian Fergus kept on going up the track.

***

It was early evening and in the lush, high mountain meadow where the senior officers had dictated that the battle group should build the day's marching camp, the men were hard at work constructing their fort. Set out in a typical rectangular playing card shape several thousand legionaries and auxiliaries were busy working on the V shaped ditch, the earthen embankment and the wooden palisade that together formed the outer perimeter. Across the camp the sound of shovels and pick-axes hacking at the earth, shouts, hammering and sawing echoed away across the mountains. Fergus was supervising the squads who were erecting the company's white tents, when close by he suddenly heard raised voices and a heated argument break out. Striding around the edge of one of the raised tents he was confronted by Vittius and another man. The two legionaries were nose to nose in an ugly, aggressive stand off and on the ground, lay a loaf of freshly baked bread.

"What's going on here?" Fergus cried out, as he came towards the two men clutching his wooden staff.

Close by a group of legionaries had paused in their work and were staring at the confrontation.

"This piece of shit here," the aggrieved-sounding man cried out, raising his finger and pointing it menacingly at Vittius, "just tried to steal my bread. The man is a thief."

Confronting him, Vittius hissed and aggressively thrust his face towards his opponent. "Lies," he cried. "This is my bread."

"No, that's not true," one of the company squad leaders called out. "We all saw you take the bread, Vittius. It was not yours."

Slowly as the standoff fell silent, all eyes turned to look at Fergus, waiting for him to say something and make a decision.

"Vittius, did you take that man's bread?" Fergus asked as he came up to the two legionaries and pushed them apart with his staff.

In reply Vittius lowered his eyes and remained silent and Fergus sighed.

"What's going on here?" Lucullus suddenly roared, as the Centurion came striding up, "Why are you men not working? This isn't a fucking holiday camp."

"Vittius here is accused of stealing another man's bread," Fergus called out as he turned to face Lucullus.

Lucullus stopped in his tracks and turned to stare at Vittius.

"Well," the centurion growled, "Is it true Vittius?"

In reply Vittius hissed through clenched teeth but he said nothing as his eyes remained fixed on his boots. Slowly Lucullus shook his head. Then he glanced at Fergus and reaching out, he handed Fergus his vine staff.

"Flog him. Ten lashes on his open back," the Centurion snapped, "And if he does it again it will be fifty lashes and a year's pay. No one steals in my company, is that understood."

Silently Fergus took the Centurion's vine staff. Then he nodded at the squad leader and his men.

"Undo his armour and tunic and hold him down," Fergus said.

From the corner of his eye, Fergus caught sight of Aledus, Catinius and some of the others rushing towards the scene.

"Are you going to strike me," Vittius cried out in sudden anguish as he rounded on Fergus. "I am your friend, I am your friend, Fergus."

Fergus said nothing as the legionaries caught hold of Vittius, roughly forcing him onto the ground and once his bare back was exposed, Fergus raised the centurion's vine staff and brought it down hard on Vittius's back. In response Vittius yelled in pain. Silently and efficiently Fergus administered the punishment beating and when he was finished, Vittius's back was a mass of raw, bleeding lines. Handing the vine staff back to Lucullus, Fergus, his face hard and emotionless, gestured for Aledus to follow him. When the two of them were out of earshot Fergus turned to his friend.

"What the fuck has gotten into Vittius?" he hissed. "Stealing another man's bread. Has he gone insane?"

Aledus took a deep breath and looked away. "He hasn't been the same since that night assault. I think there is something wrong in his head," Aledus said, tapping his head with his finger. "He wakes up in the middle of the night and says crazy shit, like we are all going to die. A lot of what he says doesn't make sense."

"Shit," Fergus muttered shaking his head in bewilderment. Then he rounded on Aledus. "But we can't have this happening again. You heard Lucullus. The centurion will crush him if he shows such disobedience again. You know the rules, you know the punishments." Fergus reached out and poked his finger into Aledus's chest. "You and the boys need to keep an eye on Vittius, don't let him get himself into trouble again. I am counting on you."

**

It was getting dark when Fergus heard a sudden commotion close to the entrance of the marching camp. Turning to peer in the direction of the gates, he saw the sentries running along the top of the newly erected ramparts but there was no general alarm and as the seconds ticked by, the commotion seemed to die down. Finishing the last of his wine ration in one go, he dumped his cup beside his marching pack and with a frown set off to investigate.

As he approached he could see that a large group of Roman soldiers had gathered at the gates and were staring at something or someone. Then the mass of men started to move apart and moments later Fergus caught sight of bearded strangers, wearing Dacian style clothing and domed helmets.

The newcomers were being led towards the tribune's tent in the centre of the camp. Fergus sucked in his breath. The new arrivals were Dacian's. There was no doubt. Hastily he caught hold of a soldier's shoulder and gestured at the strangers.

"What's going on?"

"A party of Dacian's just rode into the camp," the soldier replied, "They say they have come to surrender. They are going to interrogate them now. Looks like we are winning."

Fergus raised his eyebrows as he watched the Dacian's disappear into the tribune's tent. Then with a little shake of his head he turned and headed back towards his own tent.

He was woken by a hand shaking him awake. "Fergus, get up and come and with me," Lucullus growled sternly.

Startled and bleary-eyed, Fergus got to his feet. He was already fully clothed and outside the tent he could see that it was still dark. The camp around him still seemed to be asleep. Lucullus was waiting for him at the entrance to the tent. The centurion already had his armour and helmet on.

"Put it on later," Lucullus snapped as Fergus moved towards where his own armour was lying on the ground, "The tribune is holding an O group. He wants all his centurion's to be present. Something has come up."

"Sir," Fergus replied quietly, as he followed Lucullus out into the early morning darkness. As the two of them strode along the long lines of army tents Fergus hastily glanced at Lucullus.

"I appreciate you asking me to join these O Groups Sir," Fergus said quietly. "I know you don't have to bring your second in command to these meetings. I know many of the other centurions don't."

"Nonsense," Lucullus snapped, his eyes fixed on the tribune's tent up ahead. "If something were to happen to me, then you would have to take over command of the company. So, you may as well know what is going on."

In the darkness, Fergus shrugged. "And what is going on Sir?" he muttered.

But Lucullus did not reply.

Chapter Twenty-Five – In Defence of the Marisus River Valley

The young aristocratic tribune who was in command of the battlegroup was sitting at the rectangular table inside his spacious, richly decorated tent. The commander was playing with the tip of an army pugio - knife. A brazier was burning in one corner, filling the tent with flickering reddish light. Outside it was still dark and the trumpets that would order the camp to wake and rise, had not yet sounded. Around the table, standing facing the young commander were the battle group's senior officers, their plumed-helmets casting shadows against the fabric of the tent. The officers remained silent as they waited for their commander to speak.

"Gentlemen," the tribune said thoughtfully as he played with his knife. "The party of Dacian's who rode into our camp yesterday did so because they wanted to surrender. They say that Decebalus has lost the war. But they have also brought us some news. Today's march will take us down into the Marisus valley and we shall have to cross the Marisus river. The Dacian's tell me that the bridge across the river has been destroyed but that they are willing to show us where we can ford the river. They say that there is a spot a mile or so upstream from the bridge, where the water level is low enough for our wagons to cross. The Dacian's tell me that once we are across the river the shortest and most direct route towards their fortress at Rosia Montana leads through a vast forest. They also tell me that Bicilis, their general, will not contest our river crossing but that he is waiting for us in the forests, along the route that he expects us to take. He plans to ambush us in the forest. His men are already waiting for us."

Seated at his table the young tribune looked up at his officers with a confident but thoughtful expression. "I may well be in command of this battle group but you gentlemen are the army's long-term professionals so I want your opinions on this matter. Can we trust these Dacian's and what they are telling us?"

"Sir," the prefect in command of the 9th cohort of Batavians said in his guttural and heavily accented voice. "My scouts confirm that the bridge has been destroyed. It would take us several days to repair it at least. As for the river ford, this is the first that I have heard of it. My men tell me that they have seen no sign of the enemy since we left Tibiscum. But my cavalry scouts should be able to warn us of any ambush. That's our job."

"Why would he wait for us in the forests when defending the river would make more sense?" a centurion growled. "Bicilis is no fool and he still has considerable support amongst the Dacian tribes. He could be fortifying that ford as we speak. At some point he must make a stand and fight. The Marisus is an obvious place to make that stand."

"Sir," Rufus said in a calm voice, "if the information that these Dacian prisoners have brought us is true, then we should advance in battle formation. Form the column into a hollow square with our baggage-train in the centre of the box and deploy our Batavian cavalry out onto our flanks." Rufus paused to clear his throat. "And if they are wrong and Bicilis has decided to fortify the banks of the Marisus, we shall know soon enough. I would suggest that you send a cavalry force to inspect the river ford. We must cross the river at some point, we don't have a choice. If the scouts think it is passable and there is no sign of the enemy, we cross and immediately fortify ourselves on the opposite bank."

"And if Bicilis contests the river crossing?" the tribune snapped gazing at Rufus thoughtfully.

"If the Dacian's try to prevent us crossing we should hammer them with our artillery and archers and then force a crossing. It can be done," Rufus said in a quiet confident voice. "Our men are ready for anything and the Batavian's are experts at swimming their horses across rivers whilst staying in formation. We would destroy the enemy."

"That will take time though," the tribune replied looking away as he resumed playing with his knife.

For a while the spacious tent remained quiet.

"Once we are across the Marisus," the tribune said thoughtfully, twisting the point of his knife into the wooden table, "the Dacian prisoners tell me that there is another path through the forests which we can take. They are willing to show us the way. It is a longer route and will take us through a gorge and across the tops of the mountains but they say it is safer. Bicilis will not be expecting us to take that route. The Dacian's claim that we shall be able to avoid Bicilis's trap altogether."

The tent remained silent.

"You," the young aristocrat in command of the battlegroup said suddenly pointing straight at Fergus with his knife. "You, who had the bright idea of trying to repair the bridge at Berzobis. What do you think? Should we trust these Dacian's?"

The tips of Fergus's ears were suddenly burning as the assembled officers turned to gaze at him. For a moment, he remained silent, struggling to think of something to say.

"I think Sir," Fergus said straightening up and looking straight at the tribune, "That you should get a second opinion. It may save our lives, Sir."

For a split second the tent remained silent. Then around him the officers burst out laughing and seated at his table the tribune grinned and looked away.

"I am glad to see that you were paying attention when our general gave his speech beside the Danube," the tribune replied. "Unfortunately, I only have one set of Dacian prisoners whom I can ask."

***

It was just after noon as Fergus, plodding along at his usual position at the rear of the company, caught sight of the Marisus through the trees and shrubs that lined its bank. The slow-moving waters of the river glinted and gleamed in the fierce, warm sunlight and a party of water-carriers - slaves, were crouching along its peaceful, open shore, filling their large water skins. In the broad, flattish and open strip of country in which Fergus found himself the river was flowing from east to west. In the distance to the south and north, the horizon was lined by heavily-forested hills and mountains that overlooked the broad river valley. Along the flat, open banks of the river, the long, Roman army columns had turned eastwards and following their officers and proud gleaming standards, were slowly making their way along the southern bank of the river. The trundle and groan of the numerous horse and ox-drawn wagons and the braying of the army mules was mixed with the constant thud of thousands of heavy army boots and the rattle and clinking of equipment.

In front of Fergus quite a few of his men had turned their heads to stare at the cool refreshing water with longing, but no one fell out of the column. Earlier that day they had passed steaming rock pools of hot, natural spring-water and some of the more superstitious souls had hastily averted their eyes, believing the rising steam to be the breath of the gods.

Lifting his gaze, Fergus turned to study the northern bank. The forests seemed thicker to the north and further away from the river the land became progressively more wild, mountainous and rugged. Above the dense canopy of the green and brown forest, a group of black birds, seemingly disturbed by something, rose from their perches and flew away towards the west. Fergus watched them go in silence. Then turning his attention back to the plodding column of heavily laden legionaries in front of him, he noticed a group of Batavian cavalry galloping down the line towards him. The rider's faces were smeared with sweat and dust.

"What news?" Fergus cried out, "Has the enemy blocked the river crossing?"

But as the Batavian's thundered past they did not answer.

It was an hour or so later when he spotted the ruined bridge. As the Roman column in front of him trudged along the southern bank of the Marisus, Fergus turned to stare at the blackened, broken timbers that lay collapsed and sunken into the river. At the point where the bridge spanned the water, the Marisus looked around forty or fifty paces wide. A little further up-stream Fergus suddenly caught sight of a small Dacian village. The timber walls and high, angular thatched roofs of the Dacian huts were clustered together a respectable distance from the river and smoke was rising from one of the huts. At the water's edge, a group of Dacian women and children, clad in their long, colourful robes were staring in silence at the Roman infantry, from across the river. Fergus peered curiously at the Dacian's. Although he could not understand a word of their language, the Dacian civilians they had encountered so far had all seemed to have a proud but resigned attitude. Lucullus had said that after twenty years of near constant fighting with Domitian and now emperor Trajan, the Dacian's had finally accepted that Rome was going to win. But not all had come around to that view Fergus thought, as he glanced back at the destroyed bridge.

As his company finally approached the ford in the river Fergus could hear the shouts of the officers up ahead and from the nearby wood, the sound of axes at work. Abruptly, up ahead Lucullus's loud voice called the company to a halt. Moments later the centurion, in his red plumed helmet, came striding down the ranks of his men towards Fergus.

"What's going on Sir?" Fergus called out as Lucullus approached.

The centurion looked annoyed.

"The river," Lucullus blurted out as he came up to Fergus, "the ford is too deep for our men to cross. Those fucking Dacian's got it wrong. We are going to have to build rafts to get our men across and then once we are on the northern shore the tribune has ordered us to construct our marching camp. Get the men cutting down trees or else we are still going to be here at dusk. Those fucking Dacian's don't realise how much kit we have to carry."

***

Two sturdy ropes had been run across the placid river and in between them, the large rafts were being slowly pulled from one bank to the other by teams of soldiers. It was late and on the northern shore of the Marisus, parties of legionaries and auxiliaries were already hard at work, digging and constructing the day's marching camp. The bulk of the battle group had already been ferried across the river and only the rear guard was left on the southern shore. Fergus crouched on the raft and gazed at the teams pulling them across the river. Around him, the raft was packed with troops and mules and in the water, stripped to their waist several men were standing in the river guiding the raft along on its way. So, he thought, the Dacian's had decided not to contest the river crossing and as he stared at the soldiers labouring to construct the marching camp, Fergus wondered if that was a good or bad thing. Idly he glanced sideways at Vittius who was sitting close by. His friend was staring moodily into the water with an unhappy look. Fergus sighed. Vittius had not said a word to him since he had flogged him.

They were just about to reach the northern bank when a sudden commotion in the meadows beside the river, caught Fergus's attention. Amongst the hundreds of troops working to build the fort a few men were pointing at something across the open, grassy fields. Following their gaze, Fergus stiffened as he saw a small party of horsemen galloping towards the Roman beachhead. The Romans around Fergus had seen the riders too and their alarmed shouts and cries rent the air. As the raft was pulled up onto the bank the troops streamed onto land and

Fergus hastily jumped to the ground, his eyes on the advancing horsemen. One of the riders was holding up a Dacian Draco banner on a pole. The coloured cloth with a gaping, opened mouth, looked like the head of a giant snake as it streamed along in the wind behind the horsemen. And as they came on one of the riders blew on a curved horn.

Advancing to intercept them, a Batavian cavalry squadron came galloping across the fields their hooves throwing up clumps of dirt. But as the Batavians closed with the Dacian horsemen the enemy riders came to a slow halt and raised their arms in a gesture of parley.

"They have come to talk," one of the soldiers standing beside Fergus cried out. And sure enough as the two groups of cavalrymen slowed and cautiously closed with each other, Fergus could see that the Dacians had indeed come with a message. Fascinated, he stared at the scene. Then after no more than a minute, the Dacian horn rang out once more and swiftly the Dacians turned their horses around and rode off towards the edge of the forest from where they had come.

"What was all that about Sir; what did those Dacian riders want?" Fergus called out as he finally found Lucullus standing beside another centurion.

"Bicilis sent them," Lucullus growled. "They were here to deliver a message. Bicilis demands that we immediately retreat across the river. He says that if we don't, none of us will ever see our families again."

***

"All men accounted for Sir, the company is ready to move," the tesserarius said quietly, as he came up to Fergus and saluted.

"Good," Fergus murmured, tell the men to follow the standard bearer. And there is to be no noise, none whatsoever. All right, go."

As the tesserarius vanished into the night, Fergus stooped and raised his heavy marching pack over his shoulder. In the darkness around him, the Roman marching camp was alive with hushed voices and the muffled clink of the men's armour and along the ramparts of the fort, the usual torches were still burning. In the night sky the stars twinkled and gleamed. Dawn was still several hours away but the summer night was warm.

With a sharp, half-shouted command, the columns of heavily laden legionaries began to march out through the gates of their camp. Fergus clutching his shield and long staff fell in at the rear of his company and peered into the darkness ahead. A few burning torches were already moving across the open meadows; northwards and away from the camp and the river and in the dark, he could hear the faint thud of horses' hooves and the trundle of wagon wheels. The battle group was trying to slip away from their camp under the cover of darkness. Tensely Fergus bit his lip. Would the Dacian's notice their departure? The tribune had ordered that the sentries were to remain in the camp until dawn and that the normal camp fires were to be left burning giving the impression that the Romans were still inside. There was no way of knowing whether the ruse would work, but if it did the column would have several hours lead on their enemy. Fergus tightened his grip on his staff. The tribune had decided to believe the Dacian's who had surrendered to him. The column would be taking the longer, harder but safer route across the tops of the mountains and the Dacian's would show them the way.

"Move, move, keep moving," a Roman voice whispered in the darkness as the column of men came plodding past.

At dawn Fergus found himself moving up a narrow-forested path that was leading them straight up into the high mountains. The columns of legionaries were snaking their way in single-file up the slope, one column on each side of the track whilst in between them the battle group's wagons and carts clattered and trundled along. A few men with sprained ankles and the sick and ill were sitting on top of the wagons gazing down at their silent plodding comrades. Ahead, Fergus could see the company's stoical uncomplaining mules, heads down, their backs and sides laden with packs and equipment. The 2nd cohort and one of the cohorts from the 1st Legion had been assigned to bring up the rear of the column and pick up any stragglers who had fallen along the wayside.

Fergus was forcing an auxiliary back onto his feet when behind him, he suddenly heard a cry. Turning to look down the track he saw a group of men hurrying towards the rear guard led by a centurion, easily identifiable by his plumed helmet. It had to be the men who had been left behind to act as sentries in the marching camp. As the Roman's re-joined their comrades Fergus caught sight of one of their men hastening alone up the path towards him. The man looked like he was in a hurry and a leather despatch case was slung over his shoulder.

"What news?" Fergus called out as the man drew level.

"Dacian cavalry were swarming over the fort when we last caught sight of the place," the soldier panted as he shot past up the track. "A damn shame to leave all those fine fortifications in their hands. Keep an eye open for their cavalry. It won't be long before they find us."

**

It was around noon and the company had reached a heavily forested ridge and were moving along a wide, sandy forest track, when a scream suddenly rent the tranquillity. A moment later with a snapping crack, one of the tall pine trees in front of Fergus slowly toppled over and came crashing down onto the path, along which the Roman column was moving. The crash was followed by confused screams and shouts. Fergus came to an abrupt halt. Then the forest around him was filled with more horrible cracking, splintering noises and before he could react, more trees, on both side of the path, began to slowly topple over and crash down onto the legionaries stranded along the sandy track. And, as more trees came crashing down on the path, the

Roman columns on both sides of the track were instantly thrown into a mass of shouting, screaming confusion. Fergus's face went pale as he turned to look left and then right. They were under attack. They were being ambushed. In the forest, he suddenly caught sight of figures flitting away through the trees. Then a legionary brutally thrust him out of the way and he tumbled onto his arse in the sand, as with a creaking, splintering-crash another tree came crashing down onto the path where Fergus had just been standing a second ago.

"We're under attack," a Roman voice roared from close by, "form a shield wall on both sides of the path, move, move!"

Still stunned from his near miss, Fergus scrambled to his feet and grabbed his shield and spear. He was just in time to see a volley of arrows come zipping and whining out of the forest, mowing down and striking a dozen men and a mule across from him. The legionaries screamed and tumbled to the ground. As if in slow motion, Fergus stared at the growing chaos, unable to move and then an arrow struck him on his shoulder armour and bounced away.

"Form a line," a Roman voice was screaming. But there was no question of forming an organised defence. The crashing trees had cut the Roman rear-guard into isolated, confused segments, forming barriers between the men and their comrades. Then from the forest on both sides of the track a great, harsh, triumphant-roar rose and Fergus felt the hair on his neck stand up. Through the trees, racing towards him he caught sight of hundreds and hundreds of running figures. Mastering his shock, Fergus whirled round and roared at the men closest to him. Then the Dacian's were upon him. With a savage cry, Fergus battered away a man with his shield and then flung his spear at another who came charging towards him. The spear caught the warrior in his chest, sending him tumbling and crashing to the ground. Ripping his gladius from its scabbard, Fergus desperately raised his shield as another attacker came at him, wheeling a long two handed falx. Terrified by the huge, wicked curved blade, Fergus stumbled backwards against one of the wagons. With a great furious bellow the bearded warrior came at him again and jumping aside at the last moment Fergus slashed at the Dacian with his sword but missed. All around him the forest track had been turned into a mass of vicious, bloody, snarling and confused brawling bodies as men hacked, stabbed and slashed at each other, in a desperate bid to stay alive. From the corner of his eye, Fergus caught a flash of a centurion's red plumed helmet surrounded by a mass of screaming Dacian warriors.

His Dacian opponent came at him again and this time he was aided by another man. As the curved blade of the falx came swinging towards the side of his shield, Fergus cried out in terror and ducked. Then launching himself forwards, his shoulder pressed up against his shield like a battering ram, he bowled straight into the Dacian warrior and with a yell, both tumbled onto the ground. The man had lost his grip on his falx and Fergus had lost his shield. Snarling the two of them rolled over the ground in a confused mass or arms and legs, as they fought and struggled to get a grip on each other. As he emerged on top, Fergus's fingers desperately clawed at the Dacian's face eliciting a scream of pain. Then yanking his army pugio from his belt, in one smooth move, Fergus rammed the knife into his enemy's head. There was no time to see what was going on around him. From the corner of his eye, a shadow rose above him and suddenly something hard smashed into his ribs knocking him sideways into the blood-stained sand. Groaning and coughing, Fergus tried to rise but the pain in his side was excruciating. Standing over him, a Dacian raised his falx to finish him off but as the man began to bring the weapon down on Fergus's head, a legionary thrust his gladius straight through the man's neck and kicked the dying warrior to the ground.

Staggering to his feet Fergus, hastily reached out and picked up his shield. Around him the forest path was a scene from hell. Bodies and body-parts lay strewn across the sand and amongst them were discarded shields, weapons, dead horses and mules.

Screams, yells and the clash of arms filled the forest with noise. Grimacing with pain, Fergus pressed his hand against his ribs. His armour was stained in blood and seemed to have taken the brunt of the blow, but the blood was not his. Close by a tight-knot of legionaries had formed in the space between two wagons, whose horses lay wounded on the ground, screaming. The men were desperately defending themselves against a large swarm of Dacians, who were threatening to overwhelm them. Suddenly something inside Fergus seemed to snap and his mind filled with rage and energy, an overpowering surge of energy. Stooping, he dropped his shield and instead grasped hold of the Dacian's two handed falx. Then with a roar he threw himself at the Dacians swinging his great two handed weapon at them. Startled, some of the Dacians turned to face him but the men had little in the way of shields and armour and as Fergus brought the great curved blade of the polearm down on them, he cut them to pieces with a savage, furious, bellowing roar. The falx was devastatingly effective and as Fergus advanced towards the legionaries, scything down anyone in his path, the Dacian's seemed to hesitate as they caught sight of Fergus's crazed, blood stained and splattered face bearing down on them. From their position, in between the two wagons, the legionaries suddenly raised a yell and boldly flung their enemy backwards with their shields, their short swords stabbing at the Dacians, as they tried to drive the enemy back. In front of Fergus, a screaming Dacian came charging towards him, his arm raised and clutching an axe but as the man came into range, Fergus's falx swept in and caught his attacker in his side, nearly cutting him in half. A split second later an arrow thudded into the ground beside Fergus and then another struck a dead man in the head. Someone was targeting him. Without looking up Fergus dashed into the cover of the wagons, slicing open a Dacian, whose back was turned to him. Then he was in amongst the relative safety and protection of his comrade's shields.

"To your standard," a Roman voice was yelling from close by, "defend the standard, defend the standard!"

Snatching a glance in the direction from which the voice was shouting, Fergus saw Lucullus crouching on top of one of the wagons. The centurion was still wearing his magnificent red-plumed helmet and he was clutching a shield, from which a solitary arrow protruded. In his other hand, he was holding up the company's banner. Around him a rapidly shrinking number of desperate legionaries were trying to hold off the mass of Dacian's pressing forwards and intent on striking Lucullus down and capturing the company banner. Fergus's surge of energy was fading. There was no way he and the few men with him would be able to fight their way to Lucullus's aid. They could barely hold their own where they were. There were simply too many Dacian's. As if to press home that point, a party of Dacian warriors launched themselves at the men trapped in between the two wagons and with a furious crash they hammered into the line of Roman shields, forcing the legionaries backwards. But nevertheless, he had to try, Fergus thought, as one of his eyes twitched uncontrollably. Clambering onto the wagon and over the corpses of two dead Romans, Fergus leapt down onto the ground and with a scream, his two-handed falx went scything into the enemy ranks. This is crazy, a voice was screaming at him. You are going to get yourself killed. This is insane. Nevertheless, catching sight of Lucullus, Fergus began to move towards him. But as his falx hammered into a Roman shield, which a Dacian had picked up, the blade suddenly broke leaving Fergus clutching the wooden pole. Fool. Now you are going to die a voice was screaming at him. Staggering backwards, Fergus nearly tripped over a corpse. Clutching the stump of the falx he suddenly realised that he had no weapons with which to defend himself. He was going to die here in this forest, right now. Two Dacian's, their faces contorted with rage and hatred came leaping towards him from the forest, their wicked looked falxes gleaming in the sunlight. Defiantly, Fergus raised his broken weapon and screamed at the enemy, baring his teeth. But just as the Dacian's came within striking distance, one of them went tumbling to the ground with a spear protruding from his back and the other swiftly sank to his knees, his hand reaching up to his neck where a long Roman cavalry sword had slashed him. Dazed Fergus stared at the two Batavian riders as they charged past on their horses and on down the path. The Dacian whose neck had been slashed was trying to breath as a great mass of blood was welling up from his neck and from in between his fingers. With a savage cry, Fergus stepped forwards and swung his wooden shaft into the man's head knocking him onto his back with a sickening crack.

Along the edge of the forest, more and more Batavian horsemen were appearing, flowing along and over the fallen trees, their spears and swords stabbing and slashing at the enemy and as Fergus grasped hold of a Dacian falx, he heard a Roman trumpet ringing out in the distance.

The Dacians suddenly seemed to have had enough and as Fergus crouched beside a dead ox and an overturned wagon, he saw them begin to turn and flee into the forest. And as the enemy retreated, the sound of fighting began to slacken until only the hideous screams of the wounded and a few isolated shouts and cries echoed away through the trees. It is over. It is over a voice was screaming at Fergus, as slowly he sank down on his knees in the sand. You are one lucky bastard. Lucky, fool, lucky, fool. Fergus groaned. Then forcing himself to his feet he turned to gaze in the direction in which he had last seen Lucullus and the company standard. The centurion was sitting on top of the stalled wagon and he was still clutching the proud banner. In the sun the standards discs and crescent moon symbols gleamed in the light. Then wrenching his gaze away from Lucullus, Fergus slowly turned to gaze at the utter carnage that stretched away along the forest path. Bodies of men and animals lay strewn everywhere and amongst them, the wounded were shrieking and screaming.

Stumbling towards the spot where Lucullus was sitting, Fergus picked up a discarded shield and then lent back against the wagon, his chest heaving and his hands suddenly shaking. On top of the wagon the Centurion was panting from exertion as he stared blankly at the devastation. Apart from a cut to his arm he looked unhurt.

"I tried to come to your aid Sir," Fergus said, his voice shaking with emotion. "Defend the standard. That's what you said. And our banner did not fall into enemy hands."

Slowly Lucullus raised his hand to wipe something from his face. Then he turned to gaze down at Fergus.

"I saw what you did," he said in a weary, toneless voice. "And I will see that you get rewarded for your actions. That was heroic what you tried to do, foolish but heroic."

Fergus grimaced as the pain in his ribs suddenly returned with a vengeance and hastily he pressed a hand up against his side.

"The fuckers ambushed us," he groaned.

But on top of the wagon Lucullus shook his head. "No," he growled, his face darkening, "We were betrayed. Those Dacian's who surrendered to us. This was their idea all along. I bet it was Bicilis who sent them to us. They led us straight into his ambush. And now," Lucullus snapped, sliding off the wagon and onto the ground, "I am going to personally ram my sword down their throats."

Chapter Twenty-Six – War Crimes

The horse-drawn wagon groaned and swayed as it rolled along the rocky mountain path under the fierce summer sun. Inside the wagon, Fergus could see the fruits of the day's foraging; wicker baskets and Roman style amphorae filled with grain; wine and salt; a chicken-coop containing cackling chickens; a barrel and a solitary fat looking pig. All of it had been taken by force from the Dacian village they had just visited. The battle group had to eat. A couple of Syrian archers clutching their powerful composite bows, sat at the back of the wagon keeping guard and, following the cart, a few legionaries were leading three mooing cows by their halters along the path. Spread out around the wagon and along the track, the sixty legionaries from the 2nd company, led by their centurion and eight mounted Batavian horsemen, plodded along in the dusty, summer heat as they headed back towards their camp, five miles away. Fergus, bringing up the rear of the small foraging party, took a swig of water from his water skin and wiped his lips with the back of his hand. Two weeks had passed since the ambush in the forest. The fighting had cost the battle group two hundred and fifty-five dead including four centurions and over three hundred seriously wounded and nearly all the casualties had been inflicted on the 2nd cohort and the cohort from the 1st Legion. It seemed that the weight of the Dacian attack had fallen on the rear-guard of the Roman column which, according to Rufus, the cohort's most senior officer, meant that Bicilis no longer had enough men to attack the whole Roman battle group. It was scant compensation. A quarter of the wounded were still likely to die from their wounds, a doctor had told Fergus. Grimly he turned to stare at the cows ambling along in front of him, their restless tails swinging about. The ambush had mauled the 2nd cohort, reduced the unit to just three hundred or so men capable of active duty and two companies had lost their standards. His own company had lost seventeen dead and seven men, who were too badly wounded for active service. It had been a bitter blow but at least his friends had survived. Idly Fergus rubbed his hand across his ribs. His armour had saved his life, the doctor had told him and although his ribs were badly bruised, they were not broken and they would heal given time.

Turning to glance at Vittius, who was walking along at the side of the track, Fergus gave him a thoughtful look. Vittius was still refusing to speak to him. His friend had not forgiven him for the flogging.

"Vittius," Fergus called out, beckoning to him. "Come over here and walk with me."

Vittius glanced up and as he caught sight of Fergus, his face seemed to darken. But he did as was asked.

As the two of them strode along together at the very rear of the column, Fergus rounded sharply on his friend.

"What's the matter with you?" Fergus whispered harshly. "Aledus says that you don't talk to anyone anymore and that you keep yourself apart. What's going on?"

"You beat me, Fergus," Vittius hissed through clenched teeth. "I thought I was your friend. You humiliated me in front of the whole company."

"You were caught stealing another man's bread," Fergus retorted. "There were witnesses. You know the rules, you know the punishment for stealing. Lucullus could have chosen a much harsher punishment if he had wanted to. You were lucky. You need to get a grip, Vittius. The boys need you to get a grip."

"I don't care," Vittius snarled turning on Fergus and as he did Fergus, was startled to see real hatred in his friend's eyes. "You humiliated me in front of everyone and I will not forget that. You and I are no longer friends. And if you beat me like that again I swear, Fergus, I will kill you. Watch yourself."

And with that Vittius abruptly stomped away, his iron-studded boots scraping over the rocky path.

Startled, Fergus slowly exhaled as he gazed at Vittius as the man walked away from him. He could have Vittius brought up for a court martial for what he had just said. Threatening a superior officer was a very serious offence but, as he stared at him, Fergus sighed and looked away. He couldn't do that. Vittius was still a friend, despite what he had just said and he was not about to have a friend executed. Aledus was right, Fergus thought, as he slowly shook his head. Ever since the night assault on the fort at Tibiscum, there had been something not quite right in Vittius's head.

The arrow came zipping and whining down on the foraging party and thudded into the shoulder of one of the plodding legionaries. With a loud, painful cry the soldier went crashing backwards onto the ground, clutching his hands to his shoulder-wound. Instantly the company on the mountain track broke into a frenzy of activity, as with loud, startled and alarmed shouts, the men rushed into cover behind boulders, trees and the wagon, or raised their shields and crouched on the ground where they were. Fergus too, raised his shield and hastily peered in the direction from which the projectile had come. On the top of jagged rock formation overlooking the path, he suddenly caught sight of movement but before he could react, another arrow came whining down at the Roman party, striking the horse that was pulling the wagon. The animal shrieked, rose on its hind legs and then as the beast was struck by a second arrow, it collapsed sideways onto the ground, sending the wagon lurching dangerously to one side.

"There they are," a Roman voice roared. "They are up there on the top of those rocks."

"Get them," Lucullus screamed from where he was crouching beside the wagon.

And in response a party of eight legionaries, covering themselves with their shields, dashed across the path towards the cliffs and began to clamber up. On top of the rocks Fergus again saw a flurry of movement. On the track below another arrow slammed into a legionary's shield. Then two figures hastily rose from their sniper's position, their bows clearly visible and vanished from view. Fergus did not move as he searched the trees and boulders but there was no sign of any more trouble. In the road, two of the legionaries dashed across towards their wounded comrade and hastily dragged the groaning man into cover behind the cart. A few minutes later the eight legionaries returned. The decanus, squad leader was shaking his head as he hastened towards Lucullus.

"We lost them Sir, they fled into the woods," the NCO called out. "All right," Lucullus growled, rising stiffly to his feet and turning to stare at the dead horse. "Get that beast out of the way and load that wounded man onto the wagon. We will pull it along ourselves. Now let's get moving. I don't want to be caught out here when it gets dark. Those arseholes may be back."

Fergus rose and as the legionaries hastened to fulfil Lucullus's orders, he turned to gaze up at the cliffs with a sour, annoyed expression. Maybe Rufus was right he thought. Maybe Bicilis did indeed lack the men to stop them, for the Dacian tactics seemed to have become more and more desperate. Since the ambush in the forest there had been no serious Dacian attempt to halt the battle group's advance towards the Rosia Montana gold and silver mines. Instead the Roman columns had found themselves harassed and under almost daily attack from small groups of warriors, who, hidden amongst the trees or crouching on top of cliffs and rocks, had launched their hit and run attacks, before swiftly melting away into the terrain. In every forest, gorge, mountain track and defile that the battle group had advanced through, there had been a small party of Dacian's who had attacked with arrows and spears or had sent big boulders and rocks tumbling down on the advancing Romans. But it was all desperate stuff, Fergus thought with contempt.

The steady trickle of Roman casualties might not be doing anything to improve Roman morale but the hit and run attacks would not win the war. They were a sign of weakness.

It was an hour later when they came across the village. Lucullus, who was leading the foraging party, suddenly raised his hand and the company came to an abrupt halt. Along the track the men hastily crouched behind their shields, their eyes searching the forest for trouble but none came. At the rear of the party, Fergus peered into the trees up ahead. Smoke was billowing up into the sky from a Dacian hut in the woods that was on fire and he could smell the acrid, unpleasant smoke, but all was quiet. Silently Lucullus pumped his fist into the air and began to move forwards along the path and into the village. As Fergus drew closer he caught sight of a dead dog lying beside the track. The settlement was small, no more than a cluster of timber and thatch huts in a forest clearing. Then, as the Romans cautiously and silently advanced into the settlement, Fergus saw the bodies. The women, children, babies and old folk lay in the doorways to their homes, slumped against trees and crumpled on the ground. They were all dead and as Fergus stared at the massacre in mounting horror, he noticed that many of the civilians had been mutilated. A few of the women, their clothing torn and bloodied looked like they had been raped before being murdered. In the centre of the village a wooden stake had been thrust into the ground and on top of it was a man's gory head. Fergus crouched on the ground beside the stake and silently turned to look around him in disgust. Someone had massacred the villagers. The village was completely deserted and everything of value seemed to have been stripped away and taken, leaving just the empty, abandoned homes and the dead.

From the corner of his eye Fergus noticed Lucullus coming towards him. The centurion's face looked grave.

"This is not war," Lucullus hissed angrily. "This is a war crime. Look at these people, women, children, babies, hell Fergus, in their own homes. This is a disgrace."

Fergus nodded in agreement, as around him the legionaries silently began to spread out, cautiously examining the dead and poking around in the deserted huts.

"The fourth company were assigned to forage in this area," Lucullus growled. "This must be their work."

"That's Fronto's company," Fergus snapped, his eyes flashing with sudden anger. "We should report this to Rufus, Sir. Someone must be punished for this."

"Yes," Lucullus nodded, "That's exactly what I want you to do when we get to camp. Find Rufus and report what you have seen here."

***

The Roman battle group's camp had been constructed in a broad, lush and high mountain plateau that was surrounded on three sides by forest, that sloped away down into a valley. Nearby a mountain stream gurgled and twisted its way down into the valley below. As the foraging party emerged from the woods and slowly began to make their way past the numerous, fresh tree-stumps towards the gates of the camp, Fergus gazed up at the massive, lofty, craggy mountain peak that rose above the camp, a half a mile away. The Dacian fortress of Rosia Montana looked magnificent and impregnable, perched high on the rocky summit of the mountain. Its massive stone walls had been expertly built into the natural rock and the sheer, vertical flanks of the mountain, rising some hundred feet into the air, made them impossible to approach. From the battlements, a proud Dacian Draco banner was fluttering in the breeze, the giant opened-jaws of the snake's head glaring in the direction of the Roman fortifications. The only access into the fortress was by way of a narrow, stony track, barely wide enough to allow a single wagon to pass. And it was to this place, the last Dacian

262

stronghold in the district, that Bicilis and his few remaining, loyal men had retreated, to make their final stand.

As Fergus approached the V shaped ditch and the wooden gates of the Roman fort, he glanced at the heads of the four Dacian prisoners who had not managed to get away in time during the ambush in the forest. The bloody, shrivelled heads had been stuck on poles and placed outside the camp gates as a warning to anyone else who might be thinking about similar acts of treachery. Along the earthen ramparts and the wooden palisade that ran along the top, the Roman sentries were keeping a keen eye on the forests. Fergus however, seemed in no mood to acknowledge the welcoming shouts of the sentries as they opened the gates. The 4th company had lost half their men in the ambush, including their centurion and optio and Rufus had placed the remaining survivors under Fronto's temporary command, as he was the company Tesserarius, third in command and most senior surviving officer. He was no stranger to death and war but the massacre of the women and children in the village had shocked Fergus and now he was angry.

***

Stiffly Fronto saluted as he came striding into Rufus's tent and halted before the senior officer of the cohort. Standing beside Rufus, Fergus, his helmet tucked under his arm, glared at Fronto with barely concealed fury. Kneeling on the ground in Rufus's richly decorated tent, a slave was silently mending a tunic with a bone needle and a piece of thread. Catching sight of Fergus, Fronto's face darkened with suspicion. Then swiftly he fixed his eyes on Rufus.

"You called for me, Sir?" Fronto barked.

"That's right," Rufus said sternly, looking Fronto straight in the eye. "This morning I gave you orders to take your company out on a foraging expedition. Did you go to the village which was assigned to you?"

For a moment Fronto hesitated.

"I did Sir," he said at last. "We took what was needed and we returned at once to camp. The quartermasters will vouch for the supplies which we brought back. What is this about Sir?"

"There has been an allegation made against you, Fronto," Rufus snapped. "An allegation that after you took the supplies, you also raped and massacred the entire village. Women, children even babies. Is this true?"

Again, Fronto hesitated and his eyes briefly glanced at Fergus.

"When we arrived in the village," Fronto said, clearing his throat, "there was resistance. The villagers would not let us take their food. They tried to fight us, so yes there were some casualties, Sir."

"Some casualties," Fergus hissed taking a step towards Fronto. "We found that the entire village had been massacred and they did not seem to be armed. Women were raped and children had their throats cut open. Are you saying that your men could not cope with a few unruly, unarmed women and children? This is war crime and you as the senior commanding officer are responsible."

"What do you care about these Dacians?" Fronto snarled, rounding on Fergus. "Those fuckers wiped out half my company and killed some of my friends. They deserve nothing from us."

"Why do I care?" Fergus retorted. "I care because your actions have brought disgrace, shame and disrepute to our banners and our honour. We are soldiers. We are not murderers. Have you no shame? The gods will not look kindly on us for such cowardly action. There will be consequences."

"I do not fear the gods," Fronto snarled contemptuously.

"All right, that will be all Fronto," Rufus growled unhappily. "Dismissed."

As Fronto saluted he gave Fergus a quick, murderous look and then turned and marched out of the tent.

Rufus sighed, stepped over to a table on which stood a bowl of water and carefully began to wash his hands.

"I will report this matter up the chain of command when I get the chance, Fergus," Rufus said, looking down at the water, "But don't expect anything to come of it. The senior commanders are too busy fighting a war. They will not spend much time or thought on this. It won't be a priority. You were right to report this to me but don't expect that anything will happen."

As he emerged from Rufus's tent, Fergus could see that it was getting late. Wearily and deflated he trudged past the rows and rows of white army tents until he came to the spot where the 2nd company had been billeted. Some of the legionaries had already got their cooking fires going and were preparing their evening meal. There was nothing more he could do Fergus thought, but at least he had raised the incident with his senior officers. Rufus was right, the army would report the incident but nothing would come of it for no one would be really interested. *But I am not going to be like Fronto* Fergus thought resolutely, *a man without honour, who is happy to murder women and children.* Corbulo, his grandfather would have turned his back on him if he ever allowed himself to get caught up in something like that. Of that Fergus was sure.

Reporting the outcome of the meeting with Rufus to Lucullus, Fergus finally retreated to the tent he shared with the standard bearer and the company Tesserarius. Stepping inside he reached down to pick up his army blanket and then with a startled cry he staggered backwards in fright. Lying coiled on the ground where he normally slept, was a venomous looking snake.

Stumbling out of the tent Fergus stared at the snake in horror. Then slowly turning his head, Fergus caught sight of Vittius. His friend was standing facing the setting sun, praying to Mithras but as he did he paused and turned to glare at Fergus.

Chapter Twenty-Seven – The Battle for Rosia Montana

The Dacian fortress of Rosia Montana, perching high on its impregnable rocky-summit, loomed over the lines of Roman siege fortifications that sealed it off from the outside world. From the battlements of the fort, the proud Dacian Draco banner still fluttered defiantly in the wind. It was dawn and along the Roman earthen ramparts with their sharpened wooden stakes pointing outwards, Fergus and hundreds of silent legionaries stood waiting, their shields resting at their feet as they gazed at the gates leading into the Dacian redoubt. After nearly two weeks of preparing Fergus thought, the day in which the siege would be decided had finally arrived.

The lofty fortress, with its sheer hundred-foot-high cliffs and walls and single access route, was protected by a twenty foot deep natural gorge that ran along most of its front. The jagged crack in the earth cut straight across the access track that led to the gates of the fortress, cutting off most of the redoubt with a ten-foot wide, gaping hole and making it impossible to approach. At the bottom of the gorge a small stream cascaded down the crack, ending in a spectacular waterfall that crashed down the side of the mountain. Towards the back of the fortress the land fell away steeply to a forested valley, several hundred yards below. As he stared at the gates, Fergus could see that there had once been a bridge spanning the chasm but that the Dacian's seemed to have removed it. Lifting his gaze upwards he could see that the fortress was divided into two levels, an upper level and a lower level connected by a wide staircase, hewn from the rock. From his vantage point too he could clearly see the Dacian archers, standing on their battlements staring back at him.

The two Roman negotiators, one of whom was holding up a flag of truce, were still standing at the edge of the gorge, speaking to a party of Dacian's who had ventured out from behind their gates and were standing on the other side of the gorge. They were however too far away for Fergus to hear what they were saying. Uncomfortably Fergus shifted his weight and touched the pommel of his grandfather's sword as he waited to hear whether the fortress would surrender or not. After the ambush in the forest he had searched for the weapon amongst the bloody carnage and chaos and had finally found Corbulo's old sword underneath a corpse. The sword had once belonged to his grandfather and afterwards to Marcus, his father and now it was his turn to carry it and he would be damned if he was going to lose it.

Fergus blinked. The negotiators were coming back towards the Roman fortifications and on their side of the gorge, the Dacians were hurrying back into their fortress. The negotiations seemed to have come to an end. As the two negotiators hastened through a gap in the Roman siege works, Fergus saw that the men were shaking their heads.

"They refuse to surrender, no surrender," one of the men called out. "They say that they would prefer to fight to the death."

"Fergus, with me," Lucullus commanded as the centurion beckoned for Fergus to follow him.

Quickly the two of them left the siege fortifications and headed back towards the Roman camp on the plateau.

"The tribune is holding a council of war and I want you to be there," Lucullus said as he caught sight of Fergus's questioning look.

***

Inside the tribune's large, plush-looking tent a table had been placed in the centre and on it sat a finely-crafted wooden and stone miniature of the Dacian fortress, complete with the positions of the Roman siege lines. Fergus and the twenty or so other senior officers were standing around the table staring at the model of the fort, as the chief engineering officer of the battle group explained his plan.

"The fortress is built on solid rock," the officer said as he tapped the side of the miniature fortress, "We cannot approach from the rear or the flanks; the valley slopes are too rough and steep. That leaves this section here, directly facing our lines. Now the Dacians have increased the height of their defences by building their walls into the rock. We do not possess anything that will be able to attack those walls, so we must concentrate our efforts on their weakest spot, which are the gates and the walls of the lower level. These are man-made and present the easiest way in which to break into the fortress."

"How will we cross the gorge?" a centurion asked pointing at the crack in the ground that cut across the access track. "How can we attack the gates and walls if we can't even reach them?"

"My engineers have built all kinds of war machines for this purpose," the engineering officer replied confidently. "As the main assault starts, our men will advance up the access track carrying the screens which we have built for this purpose. Our artillery and siege-tower will provide cover. The screens should protect the assault companies from enemy missiles. Once they reach the gorge we will fill in the gap with bundles of wood and stones and place a bridge across the divide. With the assault bridge in place, we shall then wheel our battering ram up to the gates and bring them down. After that we storm and take the fortress."

For a moment, the gathered officers around the table said nothing.

"You are going to need a lot of wood to fill in that gorge," one of the centurion's exclaimed. "How long will this take?"

"Hard to say. It's twenty feet deep and ten feet wide," the engineer shrugged, "we have already prepared the bundles of logs, the hardest part will be bringing them and the bridge up, under those enemy missiles. But it can be done."

"It will be done," the young aristocrat in command of the battle group snapped, as he leaned forwards against the table and stared at the miniature fort. "The Dacians have refused to surrender and we all know what that means. Our laws are clear. From the moment that the head of our battering ram first touches their gates, no one shall be allowed to surrender. All men and boys aged over fourteen will be killed and any women and children will be sold into slavery. That is the right of war, gentlemen. But I want Bicilis," the tribune growled, turning to look at his officers, "Tell your men that whoever brings Bicilis to me, dead or alive, will be rewarded with a bonus of five hundred denarii."

***

The battery of onagers, heavy catapults, kicked backwards with a vicious cracking movement and with a whirring noise, the first of the Roman incendiary missiles went arching through the sky towards the Dacian fortress. Kneeling on one knee, his shield resting against his body, Fergus watched the missiles as they vanished into the Dacian fortress with an explosive crash. The impacts sent groups of birds rising from their perches in the nearby forests. Along the length of the Roman siege fortifications, the silent legionaries were down on one knee as they waited and watched the aerial bombardment as it began to intensify. Suddenly from close by, with a creaking groan and a few shouts, the tall wooden Roman siege tower, thirty feet high with five storeys, began to slowly move forwards through a gap in the siege works. The huge wheeled, swaying tower was being pulled forwards by a team of oxen whilst at the rear, men strained to push it along the specially designed wooden trackway. Fergus looked up at the siege tower in awe, as it loomed over him and slowly began to make its way towards the gorge and the Dacian gates. The men had called the tower "the beast" and the platforms of the tower were bristling with Syrian archers and scorpio's, giant tripod-mounted cross bows. And as the siege tower advanced it was accompanied by detachments of legionaries cautiously moving forwards in compact testudo formations, their shields overlapping to form a magnificent, close protective cover for the men inside the scrums.

When the beast finally came into range of the Dacian gatehouse and walls, the first of the Dacian arrows began to zip across the divide and from the Roman tower, an answering barrage of arrows and heavy scorpion bolts began to pummel the defenders. Hastily decoupling the oxen, the siege tower lurched to an abrupt, swaying halt as the teams of auxiliaries hastily worked to fix the tower into position and lead the animals to the rear. Guarding the tower on the ground, the testudo formations too came to a halt and settled, crouching along the access track like squat, armoured beetles, as over their heads the archery duel and barrage of zipping and whining arrows and missiles intensified.

Along the earthen embankment, Fergus could see his men watching the growing aerial battle. The company had been assigned to guard the Roman siege works and they would not be the first into the fortress. That honour had been given to a cohort from the vexillation of the Seventh Gemina Legion, whose men now crouched in two assault columns directly behind the Roman fortifications. The Spaniards from the Seventh would have the best chance of capturing or killing Bicilis and claiming the five hundred denarii reward, Fergus thought sourly. Five hundred denarii. He licked his lips as over his head another barrage of incendiary missiles went arching towards the Dacian fort. It was a huge sum of money, nearly two year's wages for a common legionary and it had certainly motivated him and the men.

In the gap between the Roman fortifications, the first of the assault parties began to move forwards. The legionaries were holding up large wooden-screens lined in places with iron plates and animal hides. Behind them came a long line of men carrying bundles of wooden-logs and tree-trunks tied together with ropes. Up the track leading to the gorge and the Dacian gates, the Dacians were trying to set the siege tower on fire with oil-soaked rags tied to arrows, but they were having no luck. The vinegar-soaked, uncured animal hides and iron plates protected the wooden tower and it would not catch fire. And as every burning Dacian arrow struck the beast, it was quickly extinguished by slaves who had accompanied the Syrian archers. Eagerly Fergus watched as the assault parties stormed past the tower and the testudo formations and made it to the edge of the gorge, barely thirty feet from the gates. Their light screens however were not a perfect cover and here and there an arrow found its target. And as the assault parties maintained their tenuous position, their comrades hastened forwards with their bundles of logs. Suddenly the Dacian missile barrage seemed to switch to the men racing along the track and a murderous hail of missiles hammered into them, sending men tumbling, shrieking and collapsing to the ground and their wooden-cargoes crashing onto the track. But the Roman assault continued and more men came charging up the track and slowly the gorge began to be filled with wood and logs.

It was noon when the men covering the soldiers beside the gorge slowly began to withdraw, their wooden-screens peppered with arrows and the track around them strewn with corpses, abandoned weapons and blood. From his vantage point Fergus could see that they had done their job and that the gorge was packed with debris. In the Dacian fort a column of black smoke was rising into the sky. And as the Romans slowly withdrew, another party of men moved forwards under the cover of more screens. This group was lugging a twelve-feet long makeshift bridge, made of several layers of tree trunks lashed together. As they approached the gorge, a few brave men covering themselves with shields, clambered across the debris-packed gorge and managed to help slide the new bridge across the ravine, resting it on the wood and logs that filled the gorge. Then they too hastily beat a retreat under a hail of arrows and spears. Fascinated, Fergus stared at the determined, orderly and methodical Roman assault. He had never seen anything like this before. Over his head the whirring projectiles from the Roman artillery went crashing into the Dacian fort with monotonous regularity and from the siege tower, a continuous barrage of arrows and bolts whined into the Dacian ramparts above and beside the gates. Then from the gap between the siege fortifications, a strange shed on wooden-wheels, twenty feet long, with a high, triangular-shaped roof, which was reinforced with animal hides, began to roll towards the gates of the fortress. Open at the front and rear, Fergus caught sight of a massive wooden tree-trunk sticking out of the front like a tortoise's head. But instead of a tortoise the end of the tree trunk was covered by a solid iron battering ram in the shape of a ram's head.

Slowly the battering ram advanced towards the gates and as it did, the five hundred men from the cohort of the 7th Legion began slowly moving up behind it in testudo formation, as they readied themselves to storm the fort. Across the makeshift bridge the battering ram trundled, until it was nearly at the gates and, as it rolled forwards, the Dacian barrage of arrows and spears seemed to grow more desperate and despairing as if everything they had was being flung at the battering ram. Fergus rose to his feet to get a better view as the battering ram came to a halt. The high triangular-shaped roof was protecting the men inside the shed who had to operate the ram. Slowly the head of the tortoise pulled back into the shed, suspended and hanging freely in the air on cables lashing it to another beam above it and then, with a dreadful, inevitable, silent swinging-motion the head of the ram came shooting out of the shed and with a "dull boom" it smashed into the centre of the gates. And as it did, a great cheering roar rose from the Roman lines. Once more the ram's head disappeared into the shed and then with irresistible force it came swinging out again and crashed into the gates, sending a dull booming sound echoing away across the valley. It would not be long now Fergus thought, for nothing could stand up to the door knocker once it was in position. Then just as the ram struck the gates for a third time, a Dacian came leaping over the top of the gate-house and landed spectacularly on top of the triangular roof. Fergus's mouth opened in disbelief as he caught sight of the burning torches in the man's hand. The Romans in the shed could not see the man but it was already too late. With desperate valour, the Dacian clung to the roof of the battering ram as he tried to set fire to the vehicle with his burning torches. Around him Roman arrows started to thud into the roof but the Dacian was not hit and Fergus groaned as he suddenly caught sight of smoke beginning to rise from the Roman war-machine. Then just as the first flames began to leap up into the air, the Dacian was struck by two arrows that sent him spinning off the roof and onto the ground. But the damage had been done and as Fergus looked on in horror, the roof of the battering ram became engulfed in flames and smoke. Once more the ram head battered into the gates. Then the flames and smoke became too much for the men inside to bear and they abandoned the war machine and fled back across the bridge, towards their own lines. Fergus raised his hand to his chin as from the Dacian fortress a great victorious roar rose.

"Well that's fucked things up," a legionary beside Fergus growled in disappointment.

Fergus gazed in silence at the scene as the flames engulfed the whole battering ram, turning it into a blazing inferno and as the smoke began to drift towards him he sighed. It would take days to build another ram. Then just as he thought things could not get worse, through a gap in the billowing smoke he saw the Dacian gates open and a party of men, armed with Roman legionary shields came storming out and up to the wooden bridge. And before the Romans could react, the men had flung burning torches down at the wooden debris that supported the bridge. The thick billowing smoke covered their retreat into the fort and as the Dacians fled back inside, Fergus groaned as he saw that the timber debris too had caught fire.

***

It was night and in the sky the bright full-moon cast its light across the devastation and debris that littered the access track to the gates of the Dacian fortress. The Roman attack had failed and in the pale-moonlight the burned and collapsed remains of the battering ram, bridge and wooden-bundles in the gorge, had been reduced to a smoking, blackened, useless ruin. And across the track that led to the gates of the fortress, birds and other nocturnal scavengers were silently feasting on the corpses of the dead.

Fergus clutching his wooden staff in both hands was checking up on the sentries posted along the earthen, siege fortifications that faced the fortress. The senior officers fearing, a Dacian attack on the siege works had reinforced the embankment with two full companies. Strictly speaking, checking on the sentries was the company Tesserarius's job but tonight Fergus wanted to do it himself. He couldn't sleep and the incident with the snake in his tent had put him on edge and reminded him that his enemies were inside as well as outside the Roman camp. Could Vittius had placed the snake there as a warning or was this Fronto's work? Wearily Fergus trudged on along the embankment. He hated snakes and Vittius knew that, but somehow, he couldn't believe that Vittius would do such a thing despite what the man had said. No one had noticed anyone going into his tent and without a witness there was precious little that he could do, but the episode had unsettled him. So, the previous night he'd spent away from his tent and out in the open but that couldn't last. No, he would have to do something about this situation, but what?

As he passed the tall, dark siege-tower he gazed up at the beast. The tower was peppered with arrows but intact. Once the attack had failed the officers had brought the beast back into the protective embrace of the fortifications. Further back and drawn up in a long, silent menacing row, the onagers and ballistae, catapults faced off in the direction of the enemy. Amongst the big war machines the artillerymen were clustered around their small camp-fires.

Fergus had just checked on the last of his sentry posts when, from the darkness, a band of silent, running-men appeared, storming up the embankment. Stunned and taken completely by surprise, Fergus halted in his tracks. A split moment later the night sky was lit up by a volley of burning arrows that arched straight towards the beast, hammering into its wooden sides.

From the Roman embankment, the startled cries and shouts of alarm rent the night. Close by, the party of attackers who had come out of the darkness had swiftly killed the sentries on the embankment and were already racing towards the line of Roman artillery pieces. We're under attack Fergus suddenly realised in horror. With a surge of energy, he turned and yelled at the men of the 2nd company who were still clustered around their camp fires. Close by in the gloom, a figure came storming over the side of the embankment and without thinking, Fergus swung his wooden staff straight into the man's face, knocking him off his feet and onto his back. Dropping his staff, Fergus drew his gladius and before the man could rise he had stabbed him in the chest. Then with a cry he set off at a run towards the beast where numerous arrows, fitted with burning-rags had got stuck in the wood.

"Protect the siege machines," he roared into the darkness. "They are after the siege tower and our artillery!"

Around him the night was alive with confused yells and shouts and everything seemed to have been thrown into chaos. As he neared the beast he could see that the arrows were already beginning to spread their fire damage. An artilleryman and two Syrian auxiliary archers were already there trying to douse the flames. As Fergus came racing towards them they turned in fright, stumbling backwards as they fumbled for their weapons.

But there was no time to reassure the men. Two Dacians suddenly appeared out of the darkness charging at the beast with desperate valour. The men were clutching spears onto which they had fastened burning, oil-soaked rags and as they appeared, to Fergus's horror, they flung their burning spears at the wooden tower. With an angry roar, Fergus ran at the men. The first Dacian didn't see him coming until it was too late and Fergus stabbed him in his exposed chest. The second man wheeled round in fright and lashed at Fergus with his falx, but in the darkness his aim was poor and as he jabbed at Fergus again, one of Syrian archers rushed at the Dacian and stabbed him in the neck with his knife. The man collapsed to the ground with a horrible, gurgling noise. Fergus leapt towards the tower and with a grunt, he pulled the spears out of the wood and flung them onto the ground.

"Get up onto the higher platforms and put out those fires," he roared at the artilleryman and the two Syrian archers. "What do you use to put out those flames?" Fergus added gasping for breath.

"We use sand, we have buckets, Sir," one of the Syrians replied hastily, in his thick oriental accent.

"Good. Do it. Hurry," Fergus cried as he turned around to stare into the darkness and slowly backed himself up against the beast.

In the darkness, the sound of shouting and screams filled the night but as Fergus stared anxiously into the darkness no more attackers appeared. Then, as the noise swiftly started to diminish, he heard the rattle and clink of armour from close by and a few moments later Lucullus and a dozen heavily-armed legionaries appeared, hastily and protectively swarming around the tall siege tower.

"It's all right Fergus," the centurion cried out as he caught sight of Fergus. "I think we got most of them and the rest seem to have fled back to their fortress. It was only a small raiding party."

"They were after the siege machines," Fergus growled. "They were trying to destroy them."

"I know, I know," Lucullus muttered as he turned to look up at the beast where the Syrians were about to extinguish the last of the burning arrows. "Shit Fergus, did you just save the beast all by yourself?"

"I had help," Fergus gestured at the three men up in the tower.

Lucullus grunted in approval and then he turned, and with uncharacteristic elation the centurion punched him on the shoulder.

"That was well done," Lucullus exclaimed.

"We were beaten today," Fergus replied. "The Dacian's are laughing at us. This was the least that we could do."

"Nonsense," Lucullus replied stoutly, "Today was a setback that's all but it won't stop us. Tomorrow the artillery will resume pounding the enemy and the day after tomorrow, we shall repeat the same assault all over again and this time those gates will fall. The Engineers are already at work constructing a new battering ram. The Dacian's inside that fort have only days left to live."

Chapter Twenty-Eight – Comrades in Arms

From the Dacian fortress the shouting and yelling was growing in intensity and desperation. It was morning and through the clear blue summer sky the Roman projectiles came hurtling and whining into the Dacian fortress, landing with loud explosive crashes and cracks. Fergus and the men from the 2nd company crouched in a long single file along the access track leading to the fortress gates, as they awaited the signal to storm the Dacian stronghold. Their shields were resting against their bodies and the men's armour glinted coldly in the sunlight. Ahead of him Fergus could see the Roman battering ram and as he stared at the massive war machine, the solid-iron ram's head came swinging out of its protective shed and smashed into the Dacian gates. The dull booming crack echoed away across the valley. The triangular roof of the battering ram had been covered in legionary shields and behind the monster, a squad of Syrian archers were covering the roof with their bows. Not long now Fergus thought, as he caught a glimpse of the badly damaged gates. At the head of the Roman assault column Fergus could see Lucullus's red-plumed helmet and the company standard, raised proudly into the air for all to see. On the other side of the track another column of legionaries from a different company were down on one knee, their shields protecting their bodies as they too waited for the order to advance. Over his head another barrage of Roman projectiles went arching towards the Dacian defences and from the tall siege tower, an unrelenting hail of arrows and heavy-bolts pummelled the remaining defenders along the walls. It had taken the battle group only two days to recover from the failure of the first assault. With remorseless determination, the engineers and auxiliaries had once more filled in the gorge and placed a bridge across the gap and now the newly constructed battering ram was about to bring down the Dacian gates.

"Company, prepare!" Lucullus's loud shouting voice rose above the whine of the artillery missiles and the shouts and yells of the defenders.

Fergus tensed and tightened his grip on his spear. The palms of his hands were sweaty and his chest was heaving. Once more the heavy metal battering-ram came swinging out of its shed and as it struck the gates the ram's head kept going and with a splintering crack the mighty gates burst open and collapsed, torn clean from their hinges. The way was open.

"Up, up, company follow me," Lucullus's loud voice was the first to respond. And at the very front of the assault column, Fergus saw the centurion rise and go charging forwards towards the shattered gateway. Behind Lucullus the legionaries raised a triumphant roar, rose, clutching their shields and spear, and went charging after their centurion and company banner. An arrow thudded into the ground narrowly missing the man in front of Fergus. Raising his shield, Fergus ran forwards. In the shattered, debris-strewn gateway Lucullus's red plumed helmet had vanished from view. The desperate Dacian defenders had formed a line to stop the Romans from getting into the fortress, but in the close confines of the gatehouse the more heavily-armoured Romans with their big shields and short stabbing swords had the advantage. As Fergus stormed past the battering ram he saw that the Roman assault had already punched straight through the Dacian defenders, scattering them into small groups, as behind them more and more legionaries poured into the fortress. Then he was through the gatehouse and into the fortress. Fergus was met by a scene from hell. Corpses lay scattered across the ground and some buildings were on fire, belching out thick, black smoke. Wounded men, lying on the ground in pools of blood were screaming in agony but neither side seemed in the mood for mercy. Two yelling Dacian's, their faces contorted in rage, came charging towards Fergus clutching spears and intent on impaling him against the fortress walls. With a savage roar, Fergus flung his spear at one of the men, striking him full in the chest and sending him staggering backwards. The other Dacian's spear slid off Fergus shield and as the man's momentum took him past Fergus, Fergus punched him in his neck with his right hand. Close by, a wounded man was trying to crawl across the bloodstained ground towards where someone had hacked off his arm. On the ramparts above him some Dacian defenders were still at their posts and as he caught sight of them, one of the Dacian's raised his arm to fling a spear down at the Romans surging into the fortress. With a warning yell, Fergus thrust a legionary out of the path and the Dacian's spear thudded harmlessly into the ground. Then a Dacian warrior came at Fergus and the man's axe thudded into Fergus's shield, sending a painful tremor jolting up his arm. With an angry cry, Fergus threw the man backwards with his shield and stabbed at him but missed. Around him the shrieks, screams and yelling of desperate fighting men filled the fortress, but the numbers of Roman legionaries now pouring through the gates was unstoppable. Slowly the Dacian defenders were being driven backwards towards the stairs that had been cut into the rock, and which led to the upper level of the fort.

Suddenly Fergus caught sight of Lucullus's red plumed helmet. The centurion was lying on his side on the ground, his hands pressed to a nasty wound to his leg. At his side lay a dead legionary, felled by a spear. Lucullus was grimacing in pain. Fergus's eyes widened but he resisted the temptation to rush to his commanding officer's aid. Before the battle, Lucullus had given him strict instructions that if something were to happen to him, that he, Fergus should continue the assault at all costs.

"You," Fergus roared grasping holding of a legionary. "Stay with the centurion. Keep him alive. The rest of you follow me. 2nd company with me!"

And without waiting to see whether his men had heard him and were following, he raced towards the nearest ladder that led up onto the parapets. There were few Dacian defenders left on the narrow walkways that ran alongside the walls. As he scrambled up onto the Dacian ramparts, Fergus once more turned and yelled at the men from his company to follow him and in response he saw that a dozen or so men had heard him and were following him up the ladder. Down below in the fortress, the legionaries were slowly but steadily driving the defenders back towards the broad staircase that led up to the upper level.

Rising to his feet, Fergus raced along the walkway, slipping nimbly over the odd corpse that lay scattered across the narrow parapet. On the mountain plateau beyond the fortress, the Roman artillery had ceased their barrage and as they caught sight of legionaries storming along the battlements, the Syrian archers in their siege tower too ceased their shooting. Snatching a look behind him, Fergus saw that he was being followed by a line of legionaries who were moving along the walls in single file, as they strained to keep up with him. And amongst them he caught sight of the company standard, it's discs and crescent-moon symbols on the wooden pole, glinting in the fierce sunlight. Some of his men at least had heard him. Up ahead, the level Dacian battlements ended in a steep staircase, hewn from the rock and at the top of the stairs was a tunnel, cut into the natural rock. The tunnel must lead to the higher level of the fortress. Fergus bit his lip as he moved forwards. If he was wrong, he was going to look like a fool or worse a coward. He had spotted the tunnel cut into the rocks whilst the company had been waiting to assault the gates, and if his guess was correct the tunnel should lead up into the upper section of the fortress, bypassing the rock staircase where the bulk of the Dacian defenders were engaged in a desperate stand. If, Fergus thought, his chest heaving with exertion, if his guess was correct he would be able to lead his men up into the higher level of the fortress and attack the Dacian defenders from the rear.

As Fergus stormed up the rock staircase an arrow struck one of the legionaries behind him and sent the man tumbling and groaning down into the fort below. And a split second later another whining arrow hammered harmlessly into the stone-walls, close to where Fergus had just been. Wildly, Fergus snatched a glance in the direction from which the arrows had come. On the opposite walls, across the width of the fort, a cluster of Dacian archers was kneeling and shooting at the Romans racing along the walkways. Their aim however was partially obscured by the billowing clouds of black smoke. But there was no time to pay them any more attention. As he raced up the stairs, a party of Dacians burst from the tunnel and came charging down the steps towards Fergus. The first man's spear-thrust missed Fergus completely, as at the last moment Fergus twisted sideways, and then with a savage yell he pushed the man off the narrow walkway and down into the fortress below. The second man's falx hammered into Fergus's shield and as it did, Fergus's sword buried itself in the man's chest. With a groan the Dacian dropped his weapon and slowly toppled sideways into the fort. The third man, seeing the fate of his comrades hesitated and jabbed at Fergus with his spear but kept himself out of range of Fergus's bloodied sword. Then just as he was about to jab again, a Roman spear came flying over Fergus's shoulder, missing him by inches but striking the Dacian in his groin. Without hesitating, Fergus leapt forwards and knocked the weapon from the man's hands. Then with a startled cry he slipped and landed on top of the dying Dacian. Fumbling desperately for a grip, Fergus frantically stabbed at his opponent and finally silenced him. Hastily scrambling to his feet, his armour and tunic stained with blood, Fergus turned around and stared with a mixture of horror and fury at the long file of legionaries waiting behind him. The Roman spear had missed him by inches and it had come from one of his own men. An insane thought came to him. Was one of them trying to murder him? Or was it just a well-aimed throw.

There was no time however to dwell on the matter. Down below in the fortress the Dacian defenders were slowly retreating up the staircase. The defenders had managed to form a coherent line and the advantage of having the higher ground was slowing the Roman assault. Leaping over a Dacian corpse, Fergus headed up the remaining steps and then he was inside the tunnel. In the cool darkness, he slowed his pace and raised his shield in front of him. The noise of the fighting sounded distant and as he advanced up the sloping tunnel, he heard the panting breath and the rattle of the legionary's armour as the men followed him into the tunnel. Then suddenly he caught sight of light at the end of the tunnel. Moving towards it Fergus suddenly emerged out onto the battlements of the upper level of the Dacian fortress. A dozen paces away, attached to a wooden pole, was the proud Dacian Draco banner fluttering in the breeze, which he'd seen from outside the fortress. Fergus hissed in delight. He had been right. The tunnel had led them around the Dacian flank and as he realised he'd been right, a fierce sense of elation surged through him. In the open space below him a few Dacians were rushing down to join their comrades on the broad staircase, but apart from them the upper level seemed deserted and unprotected. The walkways that lined the battlements in this part of the fort were less high than in the lower level, being only a yard from the ground. Catching sight of the Romans pouring out of the tunnel on top of the ramparts, a party of Dacians skidded to a halt and broke into loud alarmed shouting.

"Bicilis," Fergus roared as he leapt down from the ramparts and onto the rocky ground. "Where is Bicilis?"

In response, the Dacian's came charging towards him but there were too few of them and as the legionaries came surging past Fergus, the Dacians were swiftly cut to pieces until only a lone survivor remained. The man was holding a Roman shield and in his hand, he was clutching a captured gladius, short sword. With a tired, resigned expression, the man backed away, as Fergus and a group of legionaries closed in on him, trapping him against the battlements of the fortress.

"Where is Bicilis?" Fergus roared again. "We want your commander. Where is he?"

"Bicilis has fled and has taken his family with him," the Dacian snarled suddenly speaking in near-perfect Latin. "He is not here. He's a coward. He is hiding in the gold mines. You will never catch him down in those mines, it's a labyrinth."

Surprised, Fergus raised his eyebrows as he stared at the man. There was something strange and odd about this Dacian.

"How come you speak Latin so well?" Fergus cried out, as he slowly edged closer to the man. "Throw down your sword and tell us what you know and we will let you live," he added hastily.

In reply the man fixed Fergus with a resigned, defiant look. Then with a little, bitter smile he shook his head.

"A man like me cannot surrender," the warrior snapped. "I was a legionary once just like you and there will be no mercy for me. No, I shall see you on the other side in the presence of the gods, Roman." And with that, the man jumped up onto the parapet and with a final, loud, defiant roar he leapt from the battlements and went plunging down towards the valley floor several hundred yards below.

"Shit," Fergus hissed, as he and the other legionaries raced up to the side of the battlements and peered over the side. He had not been expecting to meet Roman deserters inside the Dacian fortress but the man had been right. No captured Roman army deserter would be allowed to live.

With a sigh, Fergus turned away and looked back into the fortress. From the tunnel a continuous stream of legionaries were emerging and hastening down towards the staircase that connected the two levels of the Dacian fortress. The other companies had followed him along the ramparts and as he saw them emerge, Fergus felt a sudden pride. He had led them around the enemy flank. This was all his doing, his achievement, his idea. The fighting would not last long now. It was nearly over. The defenders, caught between the Romans in front and now in their rear, were going to be massacred. His chest heaving from exertion, Fergus suddenly caught sight of Aledus cutting down the Dacian Draco banner from where it had been flying from the battlements and as the colourful cloth fell into his hands, Aledus hastily stuffed the banner into the space between his armour and his tunic. Catching sight of Fergus staring at him, Aledus raised his fist in triumph.

"Battle souvenir Sir," Aledus cried out with a grin. "Their banner belongs to me now. It's mine."

***

Tiredly, Fergus sat on the edge of the battlements of the upper level of the Dacian fortress and gazed out across the beautiful mountainous countryside. From his lofty position, he could see for miles. To the west, the sun was sinking below the horizon but it was still a warm evening. Close by, flying from the wooden post fixed to the hundred feet high fortress walls, the banner of the vexillation of the Twentieth Legion fluttered proudly in the wind. The tribune in command of the battle group, in honour of the units from the Legion who had played a decisive role in capturing the fortress, had granted them this honour. For a single day, the banner of the legionary detachment would fly from the battlements.

Fergus's face was stained with sweat and his body ached with fatigue. Silently he chewed on a piece of bread. The fortress had been taken and the fighting had come to an end and for that he was glad. The carnage around the gates and across the central stairs was truly horrific. In the end, very few of the defenders had tried to surrender and many had died by leaping off the fortress walls just like the Roman deserter had done. But now it was over and the fortress had been given over to the men whom had captured it and the legionaries had wasted no time in swarming over the place, looting and stealing everything of value. But there had been no sign or word about Bicilis's fate. Hungrily, Fergus tore a piece from the loaf of bread and put it in his mouth. None of the small group of Dacian survivors had been able to tell their interrogators what had become of the Dacian commander. Bicilis it seemed had not been present when the final battle had begun. It seemed, Fergus thought with a frown, as he stared at the magnificent view before him, that the Roman deserter had been speaking the truth when the man had said that Bicilis had fled to the gold mines. He'd of course reported the news to his superiors but what happened next was not for him to decide. And then there was Lucullus. Fergus exhaled sharply, closed his eyes and tiredly ran his fingers across his face. The centurion's leg wound was bad, but he would live provided the wound did not get infected the doctor had said. The last view he'd had of Lucullus was of him being carried away by two slaves on a stretcher. And that meant that for the time being the company was his to command, again.

Ten yards away from him, Aledus, Vittius and a few other men from his company were sitting on the rock, gathered around a pile of captured Dacian arm bands, rings, daggers and other looted items. The men were gambling and as Fergus gazed in their direction, Aledus held up a cup, rattled the die inside, and threw them onto the ground. From a doorway in one of the few remaining undamaged Dacian buildings, Catinius suddenly appeared, rolling and pushing a small barrel before him with his feet. He was grinning as he headed towards his comrades.

"Look what I found, boys," Catinius called out gesturing at the barrel, "who fancies getting pissed tonight?"

Fergus finished his bread, rose and headed across to the gamblers. As he sat down beside them, Fergus caught Aledus's eye and some silent, unspoken message was communicated between them.

"Wine, boys, who wants some?" Catinius cried out as he rolled his barrel up to the group and up-ended it. "Where are your cups then?"

"Back with our stuff in the camp," one of the men replied. "And I am in no mood to go and get mine so why don't you just pour the wine into my helmet and I will drink it like that."

"Well done Catinius," Fergus exclaimed as the men took their helmets off and Catinius began to pour the wine directly into them.

"Shit, mine's covered in blood," Aledus muttered unhappily, as he accepted his helmet back.

"It will add to the taste," Catinius said with a smirk. Then he turned to Fergus with a respectful look. "Lucullus is wounded so I guess that makes you the senior officer in the company now. Should we be calling you Sir, Sir?"

"Only if there are other officers around," Fergus said with a good-natured smile. Taking a sip of wine from his helmet he swiftly turned to look around the group.

"So, which arsehole flung that spear over my shoulder when we were charging down those parapets? If it had been a few inches lower, you would have killed me. Come on, I want to know who it was."

"That was me," Aledus said, clearing his throat and raising his hand, "Shit Fergus I know how you run and I wasn't going to miss and I didn't, so what are you moaning about, Sir."

"Hell," Fergus replied looking away and shaking his head. "Remind me to put you at the front of the next assault. I know how you run," he added with a grin, as he made a mockery of Aledus's accent.

The good-natured banter continued and as the wine flowed and the group grew merry and their voices louder, the darkness closed in around them. Slowly the other men drifted away until only Fergus, Catinius, Aledus and Vittius remained. Then as the first of the stars became visible in the night sky Vittius, who had remained quiet for most of the drinking session, rose to his feet. But as he did Fergus quickly gestured at Aledus and the two of them rose and blocked Vittius's path. Swiftly and smoothly Aledus reached down and pulled Vittius's knife and sword from his belt and flung the weapons away and onto the rocky ground. "Where do you think you are going?" Aledus muttered as he squared up to Vittius.

"Sit down, Vittius," Fergus said in a sharp voice. "It is time that we had a chat with you."

For a moment Vittius said nothing as he stared at Aledus. Then heavily he sat back down on the ground and as he did, Catinius reached for his helmet and poured him another generous helping of wine.

"I told Aledus and Catinius about what you said to me the other day," Fergus said quietly and soberly, as he crouched in front of Vittius, "And all three of us are agreed that you are not yourself these days. We are your mates, Vittius. We are having this conversation because we are concerned about you."

"Really?" Vittius snapped with a sarcastic voice. Angrily he tried to rise to his feet but Catinius pushed him gently back to the ground.

"You are not going anywhere until you tell us what is going on with you?" Aledus snapped. "Shit Vittius, if a company loses confidence in the man standing beside him then that company is doomed. You know this."

"What's the matter with you?" Fergus asked in a gentler voice.

On the ground Vittius raised his helmet and poured all the contents down his throat in one go and as he lowered his helmet, Catinius filled it up again with wine. Suddenly Fergus noticed that Vittius's hand was trembling.

Once more Vittius raised his helmet to his lips and poured the contents down his throat, sloshing wine onto his boots. Then he dropped the helmet onto the ground, bowed his head and clasped it in his hands.

"I don't want to die," Vittius whispered, with shaking hands. "I can't sleep. Ever since that night attack in Tibiscum I have had these dreams of my own death. They come every night. They haunt me. They terrorize me."

Suddenly Vittius let go of his head and stared up at Fergus and as he did, Fergus could see that his eyes were red-rimmed and that he was crying.

"I am so sorry Fergus," Vittius gasped as the tears rolled down his cheeks. "I should never have stolen that bread and I should not have spoken to you like that. I am sorry Fergus, forgive me. I am just frightened, I don't want to die."

And as Vittius lowered his head, his body shook and he sobbed uncontrollably. Fergus looked up at Aledus and Catinius and as he did, both of his comrades looked down at their boots in sombre understanding. So, that was what had been behind it all, Fergus thought. Vittius was just frightened, he was scared. With a weary sigh, Fergus laid his hand on Vittius's shoulder and leaned forwards so that his head was resting against that of his comrade. They had all experienced the same fear and terror, it just seemed that some men were better at coping with it than others.

Chapter Twenty-Nine – The Gold Mine

"Right, listen up, all of you," Fergus called out, as he strode down the line of twenty legionaries of the 2nd company who stood facing him. The men were clad in their armour and were clutching their legionary shields. A sturdy rope was tied around the waist of each man, linking him to his neighbour and in their hands the men were all holding unlit torches. One of the men had a coil of spare rope slung over his shoulder. "When we get inside it will be dark, slippery and it will be cold," Fergus cried out. "Watch your step and trust your torches. The rags that are wrapped around their ends are dipped in oil, sulphur and lime and will not go out, even if they come into contact with water, so there is no need to panic down there. The rope will ensure that we do not lose you. It's a maze down there and who knows what creatures may be lurking and hiding in the shadows. I hope none of you are afraid of the dark because we may be gone for several hours." And as Fergus made the remark, a grin appeared on the lips of the men.

"And don't forget, it is five hundred denarii for the man who captures Bicilis," Fergus cried out, as he inspected his men. "He is down there somewhere in those tunnels. We know he is in there and every tunnel exit is being watched. We have him trapped like a rat in a barrel. Now we just have to go in and drag him out."

A month had passed since the successful assault and capture of the Dacian fortress that guarded the gold and silver mining district of Rosia Montana. The battle group had made the captured Dacian fortress their HQ and within days, a dozen or so high-ranking Dacian nobles had arrived at the fortress to surrender. Once they had been rested and had recovered sufficiently from the fighting, the Roman units of the battle group had started to fan out across the mountainous district and the vexillation from the Twentieth Legion had been assigned to guard several gold and silver mines and lead the on-going hunt for the elusive Dacian commander. Many of the Dacian mines that scarred the district were open cast mines, nothing more than trenches dug into the rock which followed the veins of gold and silver, but there were also some deep-gallery mines and it was to these that Bicilis seemed to have fled. From information provided by friendly villagers and Dacian deserters the location, where Bicilis had taken refuge with his family had been narrowed down, to two of these deep mines. The vexillation from the Twentieth had promptly surrounded the mine entrances, posting guards and sending search parties down into the labyrinth of tunnels, galleries and caves that honeycombed the mountains. But so far, they had found nothing. Then just a few days ago, another legionary battle group had come marching past, heading north towards the Dacian settlement of Porolissum that butted up against the edge of the northern Carpathians. And with them the newcomers had brought welcome news. Emperor Trajan and the legions under his personal command had stormed and sacked the Dacian capital of Sarmisegetusa Regia and King Decebalus was on the run. The war it seemed, was coming to an end at last.

For a moment, Fergus paused and glanced up at the fierce August sunlight. The noon heat was making him sweat even when he stood still. He had told no one, but he was terrified of confined spaces and he really didn't want to go down into the mine, but he could not refuse a direct order. Along the earthen embankment and wooden palisade that protected the small Roman camp, the sentries were all watching the search party as they prepared to enter the mine entrance. The twelve white tents of the hundred-odd men of the 2nd and 3rd companies of the 2nd cohort stood in two neat rows and in between them, were the blackened embers of the men's cooking fires. With a resigned sigh, Fergus turned, walked up to where Lucullus was resting and saluted smartly.

"We're ready Sir," Fergus said quietly.

Lucullus was lying stretched out on a comfortable looking divan that had been looted from a deserted Dacian village. One of his legs was wrapped in a bandage and a jug of wine and a pair of crude, wooden crutches sat on the ground beside him.

"Five hundred denarii, that is what the tribune promised," the centurion replied looking up at Fergus. "And remember there are other search parties down there already. This blasted mine has several entrances. The fourth and sixth companies have sent men down as well, so don't kill each other in the dark by accident. That would make us look stupid, Fergus," Lucullus advised.

"We will find him today," Fergus said, with a nod.

Turning away, Fergus gestured to the Dacian guide who would help lead them down into the mine. The man was unarmed except for a burning torch, a small brush and a bucket of red paint that stood at his feet.

"All right, light your torches and let's go," Fergus called out to the twenty legionaries in a loud voice. Lifting the sack that contained spare rags and a small reserve of oil, sulphur and lime, Fergus swung the sack over his shoulder and headed off after the guide. The trapezium-shaped mine entrance was just a few yards from the Roman camp. The dark brooding entrance had been cut straight into the rock face with some skill. And as the silent Dacian guide vanished into it, Fergus cast a final glance at the bright august sun. Then he too stepped through the entrance and into the darkness beyond. In the flickering firelight from the torches, Fergus could see steps, hewn from the rock leading down into the earth.

Following closely behind the guide, Fergus turned to look at the rough, rocky walls of the tunnel as he began to descend.

"How deep are these mines?" he asked quietly, tapping the guide on his shoulder.

The Dacian didn't look round nor did he pause.

"The lowest galleries go down a thousand feet into the earth," the man said in thickly accented and broken Latin. "It is easy to get lost without a guide. Lucky for you, you have the best. I have worked in these mines all my life."

"Shit," Fergus muttered to himself, as he tried to imagine how far a thousand feet would stretch.

The stairs led them down and down into the earth. Then at last, after what seemed an age, the sloping tunnel levelled out and in the flickering light, Fergus could see that they were in a huge natural cavern. Raising his torch, he saw that the cave was at least a dozen yards high and covered in wonderful icicle-shaped stalactites and stalagmites that glinted and gleamed in the torchlight. Some of the pointed tips of the mineral formations nearly reached from the ceiling to the ground and from somewhere in the cool darkness, Fergus could hear the steady drip of water.

"This is the oldest part of the mine," the Dacian guide grunted in his thick accent. "We call it the bat cave. The gold has long been gone from this place."

"The bat cave?" Fergus muttered.

And in response, the guide lifted his torch up to a wall and in the flickering light Fergus suddenly caught sight of thousands of black bats hanging from the ceiling of the cavern. Startled, he took a step backwards and in the gloom the guide sniggered.

"Would Bicilis know the layout of this mine?" Fergus asked trying to hide his embarrassment.

"I don't know this man," the Dacian replied. "But if he has a good guide he will be able to go and hide anywhere inside this tunnel system. Come, we go this way. The others have not been down this passage before."

"Where does it lead?" Fergus asked as he began to follow the guide across the rock and boulder strewn floor of the cavern towards a corner of the cave.

"Down to the lower galleries," the guide replied. "Tell your men that they must bend, the tunnel is going to get low and narrow and it's going to get wet."

As the guide approached the wall of the cavern, he paused and raised his torch revealing another trapezium shaped hole in the rock. Then ducking his head, he entered the passageway and vanished from view.

"Mark it," Fergus muttered, turning to the legionary behind him who was carrying the bucket of red paint, and in response the soldier dipped his brush into the bucket and quickly drew a red II symbol on the wall beside the tunnel entrance.

Stooping, Fergus hastily followed the guide into the tunnel. The ceiling was lower here and he had to bend his head to prevent his helmet from scraping against the jagged, uneven rock ceiling. And as he followed the guide's torch, the tunnel began to slope downwards into the earth, twisting and turning as it went. As they went down the carefully hewn steps, Fergus noticed other tunnels and galleries leading away into the darkness. Here and there they came across some old, rusting and abandoned miner's tools, a broken hammer, a chisel and the handle of a pickaxe. Along the rocky walls, Fergus suddenly noticed a metallic gleam and with a shock he realised that this must be gold. The twisting gallery must be following a gold vein into the depth of the earth. Behind Fergus the legionaries came on, the rattle and clink of their armour the only noise in the claustrophobic tunnel. But as they descended deeper into the earth, Fergus suddenly began to hear a different sound. From somewhere ahead in the darkness beyond the flickering torch light, he could hear the rush and crash of water. It grew steadily louder the further they went. Then at last the guide stepped out into a large chamber and, as he followed and raised his torch in the air, Fergus gasped as he caught sight of the magnificent waterfall cascading onto the rocks. The waterfall was coming from a jagged crack in the rocks, close to the ceiling of the cave and fell a good eight yards into a rock pool. The noise was deafening.

Behind Fergus the legionaries gasped in astonishment as they emerged into the chamber and raised their torches above their heads. In the large, open space, large enough to house a four-storey insulae apartment building, a forest of stalactites and stalagmites glinted and gleamed in the light, which filled the chamber. And running through the middle of it all, from rock pool, to rock pool, was an underground stream. Hastily Fergus took a step forwards and extended his torch, but there was no sign of any human presence.

"They won't be short of drinking water down here," Aledus exclaimed in a loud voice, as he dipped his hand into the gushing underground stream. "Hell, it's freezing!"

"From here we will search the drowning gallery," the guide cried out, as he turned to Fergus, "Tell your men that they are going to get wet."

"The drowning gallery?" Fergus sighed.

"You will see what I mean," the Dacian guide said as, raising his torch, he began to make his way across the vast chamber.

With a certain amount of apprehension, Fergus followed the guide, moving his torch from side to side but he could see no sign that anyone had ever been down here before. Behind him he could hear the legionaries muttering uneasily amongst themselves. This was a world that none of them had ever witnessed before. Up ahead, the guide suddenly paused and crouched and extended his torch towards the cavern wall. For a moment, the Dacian remained silent. Then he rose and turned to Fergus who was standing behind him.

"Someone has been here, recently," the guide hissed. "Look, there is a piece of cloth snagged on one of the rocks."

Fergus lent forwards and peered at the rocks to which the guide was pointing, and there, caught neatly on a sharp jagged edge was a torn piece of clothing. Straightening up, Fergus sucked in his breath.

"Whoever was here used the drowning gallery," the Dacian guide said, pointing at a jagged, dark hole in the wall a couple of yards away. "Its half-submerged in water so we shall have to wade through it. There are more caves beyond; dry caves and there is an airshaft to the surface. It would be an ideal place to hide. And this is not the only way to get to those caves. There are other escape routes."

"So why the hell do we have to get our feet wet Fergus?" Aledus hissed.

Turning around Fergus saw that he had been listening into the conversation. "I don't like this," Aledus muttered, leaning towards Fergus. "It feels a bit like we are about to cross the river Styx and meet the ferryman of the underworld. And if that happens, I am not paying my coin. I am cutting this damned rope and heading straight back the way we have come. And the boys feel the same."

"Shut up and follow me," Fergus snapped irritably, as the guide started out into the dark hole in the chamber wall. Without waiting for an answer Fergus turned, ducked and followed the guide into the tunnel.

"Follow me," Fergus called out as he felt the rope tied to his waist go taught, "There is nothing to fear down here but fear itself. Now move it."

After a moment's hesitation, he felt the rope slacken and behind him the first of the reluctant legionary's torches appeared. Up ahead, the guide had paused to allow Fergus to catch up. Then seeing him approach, he turned and began to wade into the water. Silently Fergus and the legionaries followed and as he waded into the tunnel-water Fergus gasped. It was ice-cold. As he pushed on deeper into the tunnel the still, silent black water rose to his waist but no higher and, holding his torch in the precious space above the water, Fergus doggedly pushed on. Behind him the legionaries were gasping at the cold and muttering uneasily amongst themselves. On and on the guide led them through the half-submerged gallery and as they kept going, a grim determination seemed to come over Fergus. He was not going to leave these mines until he had Bicilis. They had come too far to let him slip away now.

Then just as he thought he could no longer feel his feet, the gallery began to slope upwards and after a while the water level began to drop. Carefully, holding his torch before him, the guide led them up the tunnel and, as Fergus finally waded out of the freezing water, he grunted in relief. The tunnel was taking them upwards. That felt good. A few moments later the guide came to a halt and crouched on the ground moving his torch from left to right and then back again. Behind him Fergus did the same.

"What's the matter?" Fergus muttered.

"We have a decision to make," the guide replied, "The tunnel forks to the left and to the right. Which shall we search first?"

Fergus was about to reply, when a loud high-pitched scream came echoing down the tunnel and, as he heard it, Fergus's eyes bulged in fright. After a brief pause the scream came again, hurtling and echoing down the galleries towards where the terror-stricken Romans crouched along the tunnel floor. And as they heard the second scream some of the men behind Fergus cried out in superstitious terror and tried to make a break for it, but the rope held them back.

"Stay where you are," Fergus cried out, "stay where you are."

Fergus turned to the guide. "That was a woman's scream. I think it came from that direction," he exclaimed pointing to the right.

In reply the guide began to move down the tunnel and as they advanced along the lengthy twisting gallery, Fergus heard the scream again and this time it sounded closer. As they hastened along, Fergus suddenly caught sight of flickering light up ahead but how could this be. Frowning, he followed the guide and suddenly and without warning they emerged into a large chamber. Standing in the middle of the uneven, rocky floor was a group of eight men holding torches, just like those Fergus and his men were holding. They were looking down at a screaming, struggling young woman who lay on the floor. A man was on top of her, trying to tear her clothes from her body and just beyond her, cowering in the flickering torch-light, was a bearded man and two other women. One of the women was clutching a crippled looking boy in her arms.

"What the hell is going on here?" Fergus roared as he dropped his shield, switched his torch to his left hand and drew his sword.

Startled, the group of men backed away as they saw the legionaries emerging from the tunnel opening. On the ground the young woman was still screaming and struggling with the man who was trying to rape her. Then in the flickering light of the torches, Fergus caught sight of the man sitting on top of her. It was Fronto. Sucking in his breath, Fergus advanced towards him and before anyone could react, Fergus's sword was hovering under Fronto's chin, forcing him to look up at Fergus.

"Get up," Fergus hissed. "Make one wrong move and I will cut your throat."

Slowly, his eyes gleaming in the torch light, Fronto raised his hands and got to his feet and as he did, Fergus suddenly kicked him hard in the balls sending Fronto staggering backwards onto the floor with a howl of pain. In response one of Fronto's men moved aggressively towards Fergus, but swiftly Fergus's sword was pointing at the man's chest.

"No, you don't," Fergus snapped, staring at the legionary from the fourth company, "Do you know the penalty for striking a superior officer? That's right. Death by beating. So, go on give it a try."

In the chamber the man glared at Fergus but then silently backed away. On the ground Fronto was groaning and clasping his hands to his groin.

"Disarm these pigs and bind their hands," Fergus snapped at his men who were standing arrayed behind him. "Any resistance, kill them. They are a disgrace to their banners and our gods."

Silently the twenty men from his own company moved forwards across the chamber floor with drawn swords and after an awkward moment, the eight men from the fourth company were disarmed and forced down onto their knees and their hands tied behind their backs with pieces of spare rope.

On the ground the young woman had stopped screaming and had crawled into the arms of one of the other women, where she lay trembling and sobbing. Then before he could turn his attention to them, the bearded man was approaching Fergus. The man was small in stature and looked around fifty and he was utterly worn out.

"My name is Bicilis," the man said in good Latin as he straightened up in front of Fergus. "And I wish to surrender myself and my family to the Emperor Trajan."

"You will surrender to me," Fergus said sternly.

"No Sir," Bicilis replied with a firm shake of his head, "I will surrender only to the Emperor Trajan. I have important news for him - and him alone."

Chapter Thirty – "Let the boy have a share of the glory"

"There seems to be some dispute regarding who captured Bicilis," Lucullus said wearily, rubbing his eyes as he turned to Rufus. "And who will be rewarded the five hundred denarii bonus. Fronto claims he was the first but Fergus says he also has a claim."

Fergus stood stiffly to attention in the cohort commander's tent and, at his side Fronto was doing the same, his hands clenched tightly into fists. A large, dark bruise covered one of Fronto's eyes. Across from them and seated behind a small wooden table, were Lucullus and Rufus and at the entrance to the tent stood a legionary guard. Rufus was studying the two-young officer's sternly. Then slowly he rose to his feet.

"How did you get that bruise, Fronto?" Rufus asked as he came up to stand right in front of the two men.

"In the mine, Fergus here, he hit me Sir," Fronto hissed angrily.

"He hit his head on the rock ceiling whilst I and my men were escorting him out of the mine, Sir," Fergus interrupted. "It was an unfortunate accident."

Rufus grunted as he turned to look at Fergus.

"And what reason," Rufus snapped sternly, "apart from wanting to get a five hundred denarii payment, did you have to bind the Tesserarius and his men's hands and lead them up out of the mine, as if they were common criminals? For Jupiter's sake, Fergus, we are all on the same side here."

"The Tesserarius was trying to rape a woman, Sir," Fergus replied, his eyes staring straight ahead and into space. "Bicilis's daughter. Bicilis and his family were no threat to us. They surrendered willingly. As the most senior officer present I felt it my duty to put an end to the rape attempt, Sir."

"There is nothing illegal about raping and killing the enemy," Fronto hissed. "The Dacians would have done the same if they were Roman women. I did nothing wrong and it was I who captured Bicilis, Sir. I found him cowering in that mine."

"She was not a day over twelve year's old," Fergus cried out, unable to contain his anger. "And you did not capture him; he surrendered to me and my men."

"Silence," Rufus cried, raising his voice as angrily the senior centurion rounded on the two subordinate officers standing before him. "If it wasn't for the fact that you two are the best junior officers in the cohort," Rufus snapped, his eyes blazing, "I would have had you both demoted for the shameful business today. You have made us look like fools with this infighting."

Standing in front of Rufus, both Fergus and Fronto remained silent.

"Fronto," Rufus snapped turning on the Tesserarius, "This is not the first time that allegations of murder and rape have been made against you. I know there is history between you and Fergus that stretches all the way back to Deva, but if there is a repeat of the incident down in the mine then I shall take action. I cannot have my best two officers fighting each other like this. Now get out."

"What about the five hundred denarii bonus," Fronto protested, "It was I who found Bicilis, the reward should be mine, Sir."

"Get out," Rufus roared.

In reply a little colour shot into Fronto's cheeks and hastily he saluted, turned and marched out of the tent.

In the silence that followed Fergus swallowed nervously. Slowly Rufus came up to stand right beside him and glared at him.

"The same goes for you Fergus," Rufus growled in a milder voice. "I cannot have my best two junior officers fighting each other. It is bad for morale and it makes us look stupid. If it happens again you will be punished. Is that clear?"

"Yes Sir," Fergus said stiffly.

Turning away, Rufus glanced at Lucullus who had remained sitting beside the table.

"Fronto is right," Rufus said. "There is no law or rule that says a soldier may not rape or kill the enemy. I cannot punish him for that. But that is not to say that it should occur and personally I feel that treating women in such a way is barbaric. But that is just my opinion. I grew up with four sisters."

Rufus sighed and slowly shook his head.

"The war is nearly over Fergus and soon I expect that we shall be heading back home to Britannia," Rufus said. "So, see to it that you stay away from Fronto and when we get back to Deva I will raise this matter with the camp prefect."

"Thank you, Sir," Fergus muttered.

"Who do you think should be awarded the five hundred denarii bonus for capturing Bicilis?" Lucullus suddenly exclaimed, as he turned to address Fergus.

Fergus lowered his eyes to the ground as he stood to attention and for a while the tent remained silent, as the two centurions gazed at him.

"Fronto found them first Sir," Fergus said at last as he cleared his throat. "We heard the screams and when we arrived he was trying to rape the girl. I put a stop to that." Fergus paused. "If I were you Sir," he said stiffly, "I would divide the five hundred denarii amongst my men and Fronto's men but bar myself and Fronto from receiving anything. The soldiers were just following our orders Sir. They should not be punished for the quarrel that exists between me and Fronto. Divide the money between them Sir. The men will be happy and you will have set an example to the other officers."

Quickly Rufus glanced at Lucullus and for a moment he did not reply.

"Well, well," Rufus said as a faint smile appeared along his lips. "So, you are a diplomat in addition to being a good soldier, Fergus. All right, I shall speak with the tribune and see whether he agrees."

"There is also the matter of what to do with Bicilis and his family," Lucullus said. "Bicilis is refusing to cooperate. He is being a right pain in the arse. He says that he will only surrender to Emperor Trajan in person. He claims to have important information, vital news that Trajan will want to know about. Personally, I think he is just out to save his own skin and that of his family, but he is insisting that he be taken to see the emperor right away. He says it is urgent."

Rufus wrenched his eyes away from Fergus.

"Yes, I have spoken with Bicilis," Rufus said thoughtfully. "The man is the brother-in-law of King Decebalus. The king is on the run, somewhere in these mountains. Maybe Bicilis knows to where the king has fled. It would be a coup if we were the ones to find out where Decebalus has gone. But we must be careful," Rufus added as thoughtfully he rubbed his chin. "I would have liked to have interrogated Bicilis here but he is an important royal captive; a member of King Decebalus's family. If Trajan were to find out that we had kept him here and prevented him from giving his information, the emperor will not be pleased.

Trajan may even think that we were deliberately withholding something from him. No," Rufus said with a resolute shake of his head, "If Bicilis insists on speaking to Trajan, then we should send him to the emperor right away and let him deal with it."

"Trajan is camped in the village of Ranisstorum near the ruins of Sarmisegetusa Regia," Lucullus replied, glancing at Fergus who was still standing to attention. "It's no more than fifty or sixty miles from here. On horseback, with a small escort he could be in the emperor's presence within two days. We could keep his family here as hostages. That should be enough of a guarantee for his good behaviour, although," Lucullus coughed, "I get the impression he is eager to speak to Trajan. You would need the tribune's permission of course."

Once more Rufus rubbed his chin with a thoughtful expression. "No, the tribune does not need to know," Rufus said quietly, "that we have sent Bicilis on to emperor Trajan until after it has occurred. I want the emperor to know that it was our cohort and the vexillation of the Twentieth who captured Bicilis. If we inform the tribune right away, that young arrogant prick will try to steal all our glory and make it his own."

"Then Bicilis's escort will need to come from our own men," Lucullus said. "What about Fergus here? He could lead the escort. After all he caught Bicilis in the first place. It would be a fitting reward for him to be seen leading Bicilis into the emperor's presence? Let the boy have a share of the glory."

"That's a good idea," Rufus muttered as he turned to look at Fergus. "That is a very good idea. Tell me Fergus, do you know how to ride a horse?"

"I have ridden on horses before, Sir," Fergus replied stiffly.

"Good, then it is settled," Rufus said sharply. "I shall write you a letter which I want you to give to the emperor himself if you get the chance. Select a few good men and have them ready to ride out at dawn tomorrow. And Fergus, whatever you do, don't lose Bicilis, that would be very bad for all of us."

Chapter Thirty-One – The Man who has the King's Ear

The cliff tops of the rocky mountain-gorge were covered in bushes and the land looked parched under the fierce august sun. It was afternoon and in the clear blue-sky Fergus could see birds circling high above him, as he slowly rode through the mountain defile. Warily he gazed up at the cliff tops, searching for any unexpected movement or the reflective glint of light on metal that would give away a Dacian ambush. But all seemed quiet and peaceful and for hours now, they had seen no one. Ahead, the small figure of Bicilis sat hunched on his horse and despite the summer heat, the man had wrapped a black cloak around his body and his head was covered with a hood, as if he did not want to be recognised. Fergus peered at him. He had considered binding the man's hands but that would have made it very hard for Bicilis to ride and the Dacian noble did not seem to be interested in escape, so in the end, he had decided against it. If they ran into trouble their best chance would be to gallop away as fast as they could and if Bicilis were to try to escape, Fergus had resolved to kill him. Riding on either side of Bicilis and looking rather ungainly and uncomfortable on their horses were Vittius and Catinius, whilst Aledus led the small party of five down the gorge.

"Fergus," Catinius called out sounding bored, "Do you really think we are going to meet the emperor?"

"Who knows?" Fergus shrugged. "But maybe not. I am sure he is surrounded by his praetorian guards and a host of officials, senators and busy bodies. He's the emperor of Rome, after all."

"I heard he is a soldier just like us," Vittius called out with an amused grin. "And if I get the chance to ask him just one question, it would be: do you prefer the gladius or the Dacian falx?"

"What?" Catinius retorted with a laugh. "You are standing before the most powerful man in the world and that is all you would ask. Ah, shame on you Vittius. You may as well ask Trajan how big his dick is."

"Well what would you ask the emperor - you, who knows everything?" Vittius batted back at Catinius.

But before Catinius could answer the question, further along the gorge Aledus suddenly raised his hand in warning.

Hastily, Fergus urged his horse forwards and rode up to Aledus, who had halted beside a steep, rocky undergrowth-covered slope that fell away into a river valley.

"What is it?" Fergus muttered as he drew level.

But there was no need for Aledus to answer. Fergus grunted and frowned, as in the valley below he suddenly caught sight of the column of civilians, several-hundred strong and accompanied by their cattle, flocks of sheep, barking dogs and a few wagons, upon which were piled all sorts of personal belongings. The multitude was slowly plodding along in the heat, heading eastwards along the valley. And amongst them Fergus caught sight of a small group of men carrying Roman shields and wearing Roman legionary armour.

"They are fleeing," Bicilis said in his thick accent, as he nudged his horse alongside that of Fergus and gazed down at the dispirited-looking column. "They must be hoping to escape your legions, by heading east into the lands of the Roxolani or north to where the Sarmatians and Scythians live. The war is over. My people have given up hope."

"They look like Roman legionaries down there," Vittius muttered, as he pointed at the men clad in the Roman army armour and carrying Roman shields.

"They are deserters," Bicilis sighed, "Roman army deserters who fought for us. King Decebalus bribed them with gold and silver. There are many of them but now, they too must flee. There is no place for them here any longer. Emperor Trajan will take all. The history of my people is finished."

"Is that why you surrendered so easily?" Fergus asked turning to gaze coldly at Bicilis. "When we took your mountain fortress," Fergus said, "you were not even there to defend it. Why should any Dacian fight for you? What kind of commander abandons his men and his home?"

"Ah," Bicilis replied with a weary sigh, as he looked away. "You are young and you are on the winning side. It is easy for you to say such things. But the war with Rome was already lost years ago. My brother in law, King Decebalus, thought he could beat you. He dreamed of conquering Rome and becoming the greatest king Dacia has ever known. But it was a fool's dream and now we must all pay the price. I was the only one who counselled him against making war with Trajan. I said it would lead to this defeat and destruction, but the king and his advisors would not believe me. They preferred war and now we have this catastrophe. But it is not my fault."

"But you still ran away and hid in a mine. That's what a coward would do," Catinius retorted, as he fixed Bicilis with a contemptuous stare.

"I was not only hiding from Rome," Bicilis replied in a quiet, dignified voice. "I have enemies, powerful enemies amongst my own people. Enemies who in this terrible moment of our downfall would wish me and my family harm. The war is lost. Rome will conquer and occupy our land and this is the time when grudges are settled. So," Bicilis sighed wearily, "there is nothing left for me to do but make a bargain with your emperor. I shall persuade Trajan to offer me a position within the Roman administration that will now rule Dacia and I will get a guarantee that my family will be well treated and allowed to live in safety."

"You are betraying your king and you are selling out to save your own skin. Some would say that was dishonourable," Fergus said.

Calmly Bicilis turned to look at Fergus and there was a sudden defiance in his eyes. "I have seen war before you were even born and I am sick of it. I do not want to have my daughters and my son experience what I have seen. My brother-in-law was a fool, an arrogant fool and it is he, who has brought this catastrophe down on his people. He is to blame for this, not I. So, now I am going to make my peace with Trajan and afterwards I am going to get filthily fat and live out my remaining days watching my children grow up."

"Why didn't you flee like they are doing?" Vittius asked pointing at the column of civilians down in the valley.

"Let them run," Bicilis retorted with a contemptuous voice, "but these mountains, these valleys, they are my home and I wish to stay. I do not wish to end my days as a slave in Rome or a refugee in some neighbouring land. No, I am not going anywhere. This is my home."

"You said you wished to make a bargain with Emperor Trajan," Fergus said frowning. "But what do you have to bargain with? Do you know where King Decebalus has fled to? Is that it?" Fergus fixed Bicilis with a cold, hard stare. "Remember, you are our prisoner and if Trajan wanted to, he could have you crucified and tortured. He does need to bargain with you. You mean nothing to him. You are just a Dacian commander who ran away and hid in a mine."

"Yeah," Vittius exclaimed. "Down in the mine, you told us that you had important information. So, what do you know?"

"What I have to discuss with Trajan is none of your concern," Bicilis replied avoiding Fergus's gaze. Then he sighed and turned to look down the mountain pass. "If we want to reach the capital by tomorrow evening, then we should keep going. The capital is in that direction. You have no idea how to get there. And yet you think you are escorting me to the emperor's camp."

***

It was getting late. The five of them were passing through a large forest and looking for a place to make their camp for the night when, once again Aledus, who was out in front, raised his arm in warning. As Fergus nudged his horse alongside his friend, he too saw the smoke rising above the trees.

"What do you think?" Aledus muttered as he examined the forest around them.

Silently Fergus peered into the trees but he could see nothing except for the solitary column of smoke.

"Whoever they are," Fergus replied at last, "they don't seem concerned about being spotted. People can see that smoke from a mile away. "All right," he said, patting Aledus on the shoulder, "take Catinius and try and find out who they are and keep your head down. We will wait for you here."

A few minutes later Aledus and Catinius were back and they looked excited.

"It's all right Fergus," Aledus said, as he rode up to him, "There are about a hundred of them and they are Romans and not just any old army grunts. From our position, we saw what looked like a mixed group of Praetorian cavalry and legionary cavalry. No infantry, all cavalry."

"Praetorian cavalry?" Fergus muttered with a frown. "What are they doing out here? They are elite troops; the emperor's personal horse guards."

"What shall we do Fergus?" Vittius asked.

For a moment, Fergus seemed undecided. Then he glanced at Bicilis, who was sitting hunched on his horse, his dark hood covering his head.

"I suppose it cannot harm us if we join their camp tonight," Fergus said with a sigh. "We should be safer with those cavalrymen and maybe they have news. All right, let's go and join them."

The praetorians and the legionary cavalrymen were in a loud, boisterous and excited mood as they clustered around their small camp fires, preparing their evening meals. It was dark and in the forest clearing, a small stream was tumbling down the side of a slope. Amongst the dark trees, at the edge of the clearing, the cavalry detachment's horses were nosing about, looking for grass to eat. Fergus was silent as he sat on the ground beside a fire and chewed on a piece of game meat. Above him in the clear night sky, the stars were out in force. At his side his companions were devouring their meal and lifting cups of watered-down wine to their lips. All except for Bicilis, who was refusing to eat and seemed to have withdrawn within the hood of his cloak that covered his head. The Dacian noble's legs were bound together with rope, but Fergus had decided against binding his hands. There seemed little chance that Bicilis would try to escape. Across the fire from Fergus and sitting cross-legged on the ground, were several praetorian and legionary troopers, one of whom had a leather bag lying in his lap. The trooper with the bag seemed to be in a very good mood and around him, his companions were laughing and joking.

"My name is Tiberius Claudius Maximus," the trooper said boastfully, pointing a finger at Fergus. "Remember that name. I am going to be famous. Oh yes, you are looking at the face of a man who will be remembered by history."

"What are you famous for?" Fergus replied in a tired, disinterested-sounding voice as beside him he heard Aledus mutter, "for being a prick," under his breath.

In response Tiberius glanced at his comrades sitting around him and they all laughed.

"I am the man who has the king's ear," Tiberius exclaimed with a mischievous grin, as he turned his attention back to Fergus. "Yes, that's right."

Fergus frowned and shook his head. "What do you mean?" he asked.

Carefully Tiberius placed his cup of wine on the ground and then, turning to the bag that lay in his lap, he undid the leather bindings and slowly with both hands, he pulled out a bloodied and gory human head and held it up for all to see.

"I present to you," Tiberius cried out in triumph, "the head of King Decebalus. So, you see my friends, I truly do have the ear of the king," and as Tiberius said those words, his fingers tapped the ear of the head and all around him the men burst out laughing.

Fergus was staring at the gory, human head in stunned silence. Then he shook his head in disbelief.

"That is king Decebalus's head," he exclaimed.

"That's right," Tiberius said proudly showing the head to all the men around him, as if it was a prize trophy. "And I have the king's right arm as well with his rings still attached. We are on our way to present Decebalus's head and arm to Emperor Trajan. The war is over, boys and the king lost."

"The emperor sent us to track down King Decebalus. That's why we are out here," another trooper said. "Our mission was to find the king and capture him alive if possible, but if that was not possible we were to kill him. Those were our orders from Trajan himself. A few days ago, we finally caught up with the king in the mountains to the north of here. He only had a few bodyguards left with him and we killed them. Tiberius here was the first on the scene."

"What happened?" Fergus asked staring at Tiberius from across the camp fire.

"Well," Tiberius sighed as he turned to look down into the flames, "Decebalus was exhausted. I don't think he'd had a proper rest in days. When I got to him he was lying on the ground and he still had his falx and he was wearing one of those peaked Dacian caps on his head. He was alone at this stage and we were on a steep rocky cliff. I had to dismount to get to him. When he saw me he tried to cut his own throat with his falx, but he did a bad job and I was able to get to him before he died." Tiberius paused as he gazed into the fire. Then with a frown he shook his head. "He said something to me before he died, but I do not speak his language so I have no idea what it was that he told me. Anyway, after that I cut off his head and right arm. Trajan will demand proof that it was indeed King Decebalus, who we had caught and killed. There can be no rumours that the king may have escaped. That's why I shall be presenting the head to the emperor in person."

"That is King Decebalus's head, there is no mistake," Bicilis said in a sharp, unhappy voice and as he did, all eyes turned to stare at the Dacian noble.

"Who are you?" Tiberius snapped, his eyes narrowing.

"My name is Bicilis and I am the king's brother-in-law," Bicilis replied, "and if you had any decency you would put that head back in that bag and bury it with honour. That is the king of Dacia you are talking about and he will remain a far greater man than you will ever be."

"Maybe I should cut off your head and present it to the emperor," Tiberius said dropping the king's head on the ground and rising menacingly to his feet.

"No," Fergus said quickly as he too rose to his feet and took a protective step towards where Bicilis was sitting. "This man is my prisoner and no one is going to harm him. I have orders to bring him to the emperor, alive, and that is what I am going to do. And any man who thinks otherwise will find my sword against their throat."

Seated on the ground beside the fire, Bicilis slowly turned his head and glanced at Fergus with an appreciative look before muttering something to himself in his Dacian language.

***

It was still dark when Fergus was woken by a rough hand. As he hastily sat up, in the low, flickering fire light, he saw that it was Catinius.

"Fergus," Catinius whispered in the darkness, "it's Bicilis. He wants to talk to you. He says that's its important. He has been going on and on about speaking to you. The arsehole is getting on my nerves."

"This had better be good," Fergus grunted, unhappy at having been woken up before his watch. Then swiftly he threw aside his army blanket and rose to his feet. Bicilis, Aledus, Catinius and Vittius had found a spot to sleep a little distance away from the camp fires and beside their horses. As he stumbled towards them through the darkness, Fergus quickly rubbed the sleep from his eyes. In the gloom Bicilis was sitting upright and both Aledus and Vittius were wide awake and crouching beside their prisoner.

"What is going on?" Fergus snapped as he came up to the small group.

"We need to leave now," Bicilis said quietly, looking up at Fergus.

"We will leave at dawn," Fergus snapped irritably, "and by evening we should reach the emperor's camp. What is the rush?"

"There is no rush but we are not heading for the emperor's camp," Bicilis whispered in reply.

Fergus grunted in surprise and slowly he crouched, so that his face was level with that of Bicilis. "Really," Fergus exclaimed in a sarcastic voice. "Are you in charge now? I say we leave at dawn and head straight for Trajan's camp. That is what we are going to do. That is what you yourself wanted. Have you really woken me up to tell me this?"

"You haven't asked me why?" Bicilis retorted in a whisper.

"Why?" Fergus hissed.

For a moment Bicilis did not reply and instead he glanced around in the darkness to make sure that they were alone.

"I never managed to thank you," Bicilis whispered, "for saving my daughter from being raped. If you and your men had not shown up in that mine, those Roman soldiers would have gang-raped both my daughter and my wife and probably slit their throats. They owe their lives to you and I am grateful for what you did and for protecting me from that thug last night."

"What has this got to do with not heading to the emperor's camp tomorrow?" Fergus whispered in an annoyed voice.

Once more Bicilis cast a furtive glance around him, but in the darkness the Roman camp was quiet and peaceful, disturbed only by the occasional snoring and the whinny of the cavalry horses. Then conspiratorially, the Dacian noble leaned towards Fergus and in the moonlight his eyes gleamed.

"We shall go to meet emperor Trajan," Bicilis whispered, "not tomorrow but the day after. There is something that I wish to show you four. Something that will change your lives forever."

"What are you talking about?" Aledus muttered.

"You asked me once," Bicilis whispered as he turned to look at Fergus, "what information I had which could be so important to the emperor. Well," Bicilis swallowed, "now that the king is dead, I am the only person who knows where Decebalus has hidden the Dacian state treasury. If we leave now I shall show you where it is. The spot is not far from here, less than a few hour's ride."

"The Dacian state treasury," Catinius whispered, licking his lips. "What, you mean gold and silver and that sort of stuff?"

"That's right," Bicilis nodded. "I shall show you the place where the king had it hidden and you four shall have the chance to take as much gold and silver as you can carry."

In the darkness and crouching beside Bicilis both Aledus and Vittius sharply sucked in their breath and for a moment no one uttered a word or made a noise.

"Why are you doing this?" Fergus whispered at last. "Why are you telling us this now?"

"Because in the mine you saved my family," Bicilis whispered, "and after this is done I shall owe you nothing. You see Roman, I know what you think about me, that I abandoned my troops and fled, but I am an honourable man and this way you shall always remember that it was I who made you rich. I reward those who help me. Now we must leave and you must trust me." For a moment, Fergus stood rooted to the ground by indecision. What Bicilis had just told him sounded too fantastic to be true and yet, and yet, would an extra day's delay to find out really matter?

"Hang on," Aledus whispered in the darkness. "You said we could take as much gold and silver as we could carry. So, how much gold and silver in this state treasury are we talking about? How much of the stuff has the king squirrelled away?"

Bicilis took a deep breath. "King Decabalus's hideaway contains four hundred and ninety-five thousand pounds of gold, over a million pounds of silver and the King's spare robes, sword, old hunting bow and finger rings," he whispered. "There is no treasure in the world like it and it's hidden under a river bed."

Chapter Thirty-Two – The Treasure beneath the River

The Sargetia river gurgled and cascaded over the rocks as it rushed through the forest. Along its low-lying stony banks, the trees came right up to the water's edge. It was getting late in the day as Fergus and his companions watched from the bank as Bicilis slowly edged out into the river. The Dacian had taken off his boots and as he waded out into the middle of the river, Fergus could see that the water only came up to his knees.

"It's worse in the winter and spring when the snows come and melt," Bicilis called out above the rush of the water. "Come in and I will show you where we buried it all. Come on before the light goes completely."

Cautiously Fergus looked around but amongst the forest all was peaceful and quiet and they seemed to be alone. Then gesturing for Catinius to stay behind and guard the horses, he moved towards the water. Without taking off his boots he strode into the river and waded out to where Bicilis was standing in the current. Part of him still could not really believe what the Dacian was telling him. *Four hundred and ninety-five thousand pounds of gold and over a million pounds of silver.* It was too vast a treasure to be able to imagine. As he came up to Bicilis, he heard Aledus and Vittius follow him into the river.

"The king had this section of the river temporarily diverted," Bicilis exclaimed as he looked down at the water, "and then he enlarged a cavity in the river bed and placed all his gold and silver inside, together with a few of his personal effects. He then had it covered with stones and earth and when all was complete, he restored the flow of the river to its original, natural course. The men who did the work were Roman prisoners. Afterwards Decebalus had them all executed so that none would be able to give away the location of the hiding place. And now when you look at the river you would never suspect the treasure that is buried beneath it. This is what I shall use to bargain with, when I meet Trajan. I am sure that the emperor of Rome will want to know the location of Decebalus's treasury. It is the reason why he invaded my country."

Cautiously Fergus looked down at the water. The river was not deep, barely coming up to his knees but amongst the stony rocky riverbed he could see nothing out of the ordinary.

"So where is the treasure?" Aledus said eagerly.

"You are standing on it," Bicilis replied. "The cavity stretches nearly from one side of the river to the other and it's at least fifteen feet deep and twenty yards in length. Like I said, the treasure is huge."

"Jupiter's horny cock," Aledus muttered, as his eyes widened in astonishment.

"How do we get it out" Fergus exclaimed as he poked at a stone with his boot.

"Leave that to me," Bicilis replied confidently.

"Bring it all up," Aledus exclaimed in sudden uncontrollable excitement, "Hell boys, we're rich. We are going to have all the gold that we will ever need. This is a dream. Vittius slap my face and tell me that I am not dreaming."

In response Vittius leaned forwards and slapped Aledus hard across his face and he was rewarded with a painful, happy yelp.

"Shit. It's still true, we're rich, we're rich, we're rich," Aledus gasped, as his eyes bulged in their sockets.

"Calm yourself," Fergus hissed tensely and nervously. But there was no denying it. The thought that soon they would have as much gold as they could carry had completely undone him. It meant, Fergus suddenly realised, that he would now be able to do something for his family back on the Island of Vectis in faraway Britannia. And as the ideas and possibilities tumbled into his mind, he suddenly knew what he would do with this fortune. He would give it to his family for safe keeping and as the thought came to him, he too felt a sudden flood of excitement. Striving to contain himself, Fergus turned to his two companions.

"Listen," he said, "if Bicilis is right and we are able to take away as much gold as we can carry, we are still going to have limit ourselves. Gold is heavy and it makes a noise and we can only carry so much. Have you forgotten our journey into Germania? What do you think the rest of the cohort are going to think when we rock up with saddle bags filled with a fortune? Best outcome is that they are going to want to know where we got it from, worst case scenario is that we have our throats cut in the night and our fortunes stolen."

"Fergus is right," Vittius exclaimed. "Shit, I hadn't thought of that. We shall have to limit ourselves in what we take."

"Fuck that I am not limiting myself, no way," Aledus hissed. "We will never have a chance like this again boys. Our descendants will still be benefiting from what happens here tonight, in a hundred years' time."

"No," Fergus said sharply as he turned towards Aledus and shook his head. "We take only as much as we can carry and as much as we can hide on ourselves. I don't care where you stuff that gold, but no one must know about this. This must remain our secret, between the four of us, forever. No one must know. If word gets out the army will never allow us to keep this treasure. It's too big and I do not want to be watching my back all the time. It also means that we won't be able to spend it when the army is around, because it will raise questions as to how we became so wealthy overnight."

"Fergus is right," Vittius muttered, glancing at Aledus. "This must remain our secret. No one else can know about this."

In the river Aledus lowered his head and stared at the water for a long moment. Then wearily he nodded in agreement.

"Agreeing to keep this our secret is not enough," Fergus said sharply. "All four of us, we must swear an oath, on our honour and our friendship, that none of us shall ever reveal the source of this wealth. Bicilis is right. This is going to change our lives and those of your families. Now swear."

***

The villagers who lived in the tiny Dacian settlement of Ranisstorum must have never experienced anything like this before Fergus thought, as he, Bicilis and his three companions slowly rode through the Roman camp towards the centre of the sea of white, army-tents. The Dacian hamlet, nothing more than a village of wooden and thatched huts, clustered around a stream, had been dwarfed by the vast Roman camp that had suddenly been pitched beside it. Inside the camp, Fergus had noticed and counted numerous unit banners, from which he had deduced that there must be at least two full legions present and numerous, attached auxiliary, Praetorian and cavalry units. That would amount to around fifteen thousand men Fergus thought, as he gazed at the activity around him. At Fergus's side, and riding his horse, Bicilis had his eyes fixed firmly on the horizon. The Dacian nobleman had been silent ever since they had spotted the Roman camp. The time to hand him over was fast approaching, but after the dizzying events of yesterday, Fergus thought, everything had changed in a most spectacular manner and he still couldn't entirely believe it. Cautiously he twisted in his saddle to glance back at Aledus, Catinius and Vittius who were riding side by side. The three young soldiers could not stop grinning, their secret, silent smiles as wide and stupid as imbeciles. Over Catinius's shoulder he had slung a Sarmatian composite bow with a quiver of arrows. Bicilis had pulled the bow from the treasure horde and had told them that the old hunting bow had belonged to king Decebalus and Catinius had promptly made himself its new owner.

"Stop smiling," Fergus hissed tensely, "and start looking serious and normal. People will suspect something is up if you keep looking like that."

Without waiting for an answer, he turned to look ahead towards the section of the camp which seemed to be reserved for the senior officers. The four of them had spent nearly the whole night stuffing and hiding gold coins into every available space of their clothing, army belt, boots, in the lining of their helmets and in the saddle bags of their horses. It had been painstaking, greedy work, but when dawn had come, Fergus had insisted on an inspection to check them to see whether anyone would notice the wealth that they now possessed. They had all passed his inspection but Aledus had still insisted on placing a large bag of coins in a hole underneath a tree, some distance from the river, which he had then marked with a large A. A reserve in case he ever ran out, Aledus had explained. And after that there had been no more talk of whether they would meet the emperor or what they thought of Bicilis. The Dacian had with one single stroke made them all very, very wealthy men. And as he thought about the wealth that was hidden all over his body and in his horse's saddlebags, Fergus too, had to force himself not to smile.

A detachment of Praetorians was guarding the entrance to the camp's principia and as they rode up to the men, a Centurion raised his hand to bring them to a halt and hastily Fergus dismounted, saluted and handed the officer, Rufus's letter.

Fergus, optio, 2nd company, 2nd Cohort, Twentieth Legion reporting the delivery of one high ranking Dacian prisoner as per my orders Sir," Fergus rapped out staring into space.

"A high-ranking Dacian prisoner?" the centurion growled as he took the letter and then glanced from Fergus to Bicilis, who was still sitting on his horse.

"That's right Sir," Fergus said stiffly, "I was ordered to escort him here. His name is Bicilis and he says that he has urgent news for the emperor Trajan. It's all there in the letter, if you care to read it, Sir."

"Alright optio," the centurion said as he gestured at Bicilis to dismount. "We will take it from here. Half the world and their dog would like to have an audience with the emperor, but he is a busy man."

"I think the emperor will want to meet this man," Fergus said boldly. "He is King Decebalus's brother-in-law and he says he knows something important. Something he is only willing to divulge to Trajan."

"This man claims to be the king's brother-in-law?" the centurion exclaimed, as he turned to stare at Bicilis in surprise.

"I am," Bicilis replied, looking down at the centurion from on top of his horse. "and if I do not get my audience with Trajan right away, the consequences will be on your head, Roman."

For a moment, the Praetorian centurion hesitated, as he glanced from Bicilis to Fergus.

"Stay here," the officer growled at last. "I need to speak with the tribune about this. I will be back shortly."

And as the centurion stomped away towards one of the army tents, Bicilis smoothly slid from his horse and turned to face Fergus.

"So, this is goodbye then, Fergus," Bicilis said with a sigh, as he extended his arm. "Today you and Rome are the victors but the day will come when a barbarian prince shall look down upon the smoking ruins of Rome. Maybe not tomorrow or the day after, but one day it will happen. Defeat and death come to us all. Remember that and remember who made you wealthy. But in the meantime, I wish you and your companions all the best."

Fergus looked down at the extended arm and after a moment's hesitation, he gripped the outstretched hand.

"I hope you get your audience with the emperor," Fergus muttered in a neutral voice. "and that you get to grow old, fat and not too afraid of your brother-in-law's vengeful spirit."

For a moment Bicilis's face remained emotionless. Then a little smile appeared on his lips and he laughed.

"Whatever you do," Bicilis said, taking a step towards Fergus and lowering his voice, "Do not go back to the hiding place in the river. That spot will be swarming with Roman troops within a few hours from now. Trust me."

The Praetorian centurion was coming back towards them and at his side was a young, serious looking tribune.

"Maybe we shall meet again," Bicilis said, as he too noticed the approaching officers.

"No, I don't think so," Fergus replied, as he turned away.

Chapter Thirty-Three – Settlement of an old rivalry

"Listen," Fergus said in a patient voice as he, Aledus, Catinius and Vittius crouched together under the great oak tree at the edge of the forest clearing. "Rufus thinks that the war is over and that we shall soon all be heading back to Deva in Britannia. So, here is my plan. Let's bury our big bags of coins here, beneath this tree until we get word that we are moving out. Then once we know we are going, we come back, retrieve the bags and hide them amongst our personal things. There will be less chance of the coins being discovered that way and whilst we are marching, we will be able to keep a better eye on the money."

"We could use the mule to transport the coins," Vittius exclaimed, "I am normally in charge of the beast. I could hide the coins amongst the squad's kit. The other two men in our tent group hate tending to the mule. They would be happy for me to look after the beast all the way to Britannia."

"A bit risky isn't it," Aledus frowned, "What happens if the damn mule gets scared and bolts taking all our money with it. No, I will go with Fergus's plan, but I am not letting any stupid mule look after my coins."

"Dig the damn hole and let's get this done," Fergus snapped, as he rose to his feet and glanced around at the forest.

It was noon and it had taken the four of them three days to cover the fifty or sixty miles on horseback from Ranisstorum to the battle group's camp, amongst the mountains of the Rosia Montana mining district. The company's camp was only half a mile away through the forest. But first things first Fergus thought, as he turned to look at the spot beneath the oak where Aledus and Vittius had begun digging a hole. If anyone in the company found out about the coins it would only cause trouble. Fergus sighed as Catinius passed him on his way into the forest.

"Sorry, I have to piss," Catinius said with a broad smile, as he adjusted his Sarmatian bow across his shoulder.

"Always slacking off when the going gets tough," Fergus called out after him in a good-natured voice. "Are you not worried they will try and nick some of your coins?"

"Nope," Catinius replied, with a shake of his head as he vanished into the forest without looking back.

Patiently Fergus watched as Aledus and Vittius finished digging and stowed the four big bags filled with coins into the hole and swiftly covered it with the excavated soil before rising and stamping the earth down with their feet. The two of them had just ambled over to join Fergus beside the horses, when movement at the edge of the clearing suddenly caught Fergus's eye. From the treeline five men had appeared and were slowly coming towards him and as they did, Fergus groaned. The five were legionaries, clad in full armour and leading them was Fronto.

"Well, well what a surprise to find you out here Fergus," Fronto called out, as he advanced towards Fergus. "Look he has his boys with him."

"What do you want Fronto?" Fergus said sharply.

For a moment Fronto did not reply, as he turned to examine Fergus and his companions with a curious, intrigued look.

"One of my boys here spotted you in the forest," Fronto said with a crooked smile. "So, I thought I would come and see what you were up to and now I am well intrigued, for what may I ask, have you boys been burying beneath that oak over there. Yes, we saw what you were doing. So, come on, what is the big secret?"

Fergus looked away with a pained expression.

"That is none of your goddamn business, arsehole," Aledus cried out. "Now why don't you just turn around and go back to the camp and forget about what you think you just saw."

"You are a funny man," Fronto retorted, glaring at Aledus, "I had forgotten how much fun it was to beat you into hospital, back in Deva. That must have hurt."

"Do you want to have another go?" Aledus snapped angrily, taking a step towards Fronto.

"What we were burying in the ground is none of your concern," Fergus snapped angrily. "And as your superior officer I order you back to the camp. I will not repeat myself. Go!"

"I remember now why I don't like you," Fronto hissed, his face darkening as he raised his hand and pointed a finger at Fergus. "You are an arrogant prick. Always getting in my way and trying to humiliate me. I should have gutted you a long time ago. You think that promotion makes you better than me. You think that I am afraid of you. Think again, arsehole. It is I who is the better man. You don't even deserve to qualify for the legions. You lied on your letter. I know the truth. I know your father was not a Roman citizen when you joined us. I mentioned it to the officers when we were in Bonna but you must have sucked cock to get those allegations dropped. That's what you do Fergus, you suck cock. Well now you are about to suck my cock."

"There is no need to do this," Fergus cried out hastily.

But Fronto was not listening. Turning to glance at the four legionaries with him Fronto nodded grimly.

"Kill them," Fronto hissed. "Kill them all."

With a loud cry the four legionaries drew their swords and charged. In horror Fergus stumbled backwards as he hastily drew his own sword. But as Fronto and his men came storming across the forest clearing towards him, an arrow suddenly came zipping and whining from out of the trees and struck one of the legionaries in his chest, knocking him boldly off his feet and onto his back in the grass. With a howl, Fergus sprang aside, as Fronto lunged at him with his sword. Fronto's face was contorted in rage and hatred.

"I am going to finish what I should have done a long time ago in the Lucky Legionary tavern," Fronto yelled, as spittle flew from his mouth.

From the corner of his eye, Fergus caught sight of Vittius and Aledus desperately trying to defend themselves, as Fronto's three remaining men drove them backwards into the trees. He was on his own.

In front of him Fronto charged again, jabbing at him with his gladius and with a grunt Fergus again sprang aside. Warily the two of them circled each other like gladiators in the arena. Fronto was hissing and snarling, as if possessed by demons and Fergus could see how much he wanted to kill him. The sight scared the shit out of him, but he could not let this man win, not now, not ever. Fronto was nothing more than a murderous bully, a man who thought nothing of raping and murdering women and children. With a savage yell, Fergus attacked, jabbing at Fronto's chest but the man was too quick and he danced away. Then Fronto came at him again and this time he truly went for Fergus and with a wild scream, he crashed into Fergus and the two of them went tumbling to the ground in a confused, screaming and fighting tangle of arms and legs. Over and over the ground the two of them rolled, as they tried desperately to kill each other. From the forest, close by, a high-pitched scream rose before it was abruptly silenced but it was impossible for Fergus to see what was happening to his companions. Desperately Fergus tried to get a hold of Fronto but his opponent was brutally strong and tough. Wheezing as Fronto's hand closed around his throat, Fergus tried to head butt Fronto but he couldn't make it. Shifting his weight, he rolled over but

Fronto forced him backwards and now he was on top and in control. Frantically Fergus struggled to prevent Fronto from stabbing him, but the man's sword-point was inching closer to Fergus's chest and he was having trouble breathing as Fronto's hand tightened its grip on his throat. The man's strength was terrifying and suddenly Fergus realised that he was about to die. But that is not going to happen he thought with savage determination. It was not yet his time. Galena and Briana were waiting for him. They were waiting for him to come home. Snarling and with his strength fading fast, Fergus's left hand let go of the futile attempt to pull Fronto's hand away from his throat and instead dropped down alongside his body. Fronto's hand was slowly strangling him and as his sight began to blur, Fergus scrambled around for his pugio, knife, pulled it from his belt and with a cry brought it swinging upwards and straight into Fronto's head with a sickening thud. Immediately the pressure on his throat slackened and as he gasped for air, Fronto rolled off him and onto his back, his sword falling out of his lifeless hand. Groaning Fergus rolled away and gasping for air, he staggered to his feet. Then with an enraged, savage, hoarse scream he brought his sword straight down through Fronto's neck, sending an arc of blood spurting into his face. But Fergus didn't care. Furiously he kicked at the corpse again and again. Then, as he was about to kick at the corpse again, he heard another terrified scream, which ended in abrupt silence. Horrified he turned around and stumbled into the clearing. The four legionaries who had come with Fronto were all dead, two of them with arrows sticking out of their bodies. But beside a tree, his hands clasped to a wound in his chest, was Vittius. Aledus and Catinius were crouching beside him trying to stem the blood from the nasty looking wound. Catinius's Sarmatian bow was lying on the ground beside him.

"How bad is he?" Fergus blurted out as he staggered up to his friends and in response, Aledus silently shook his head.

"No, we are not going to lose him," Fergus roared. "Not after all that we have been through. The camp is only a half a mile away. Get him onto a horse and take him to the camp doctor and get that wound treated. He is going to live, but you must hurry and don't you dare let him die. Don't you dare!"

"All right Fergus," Aledus said hastily, his own face splattered with blood. "But what shall we tell the doctor and Lucullus? They will want to know why he is wounded and they will want to know where you are."

"Tell them," Fergus gasped as he struggled to think of something. "Tell them that we were attacked by a party of Dacians and that the last you saw of me was when I went rolling away into the undergrowth. I will join you later. I must get rid of these corpses. The army must never know what just happened here, do you understand? Shit," Fergus cried out, as if he had suddenly realised what had just happened, "We just killed five of our own men. The army will execute us for that if they ever found out."

"It was self-defence," Aledus hissed angrily. "Fronto attacked us. We all heard what Fronto said. "Is that arsehole dead?

"I killed him," Fergus nodded with savage delight as he looked down at Vittius, who had his eyes closed and was groaning softly.

Without a further word, Aledus and Catinius lifted Vittius up and carrying him between them, they hastened across towards where their horses were standing tethered to trees. And as he watched them hastily ride away into the forest, Fergus's trembling, shaken hand reached up to touch the iron amulet around his neck.

Chapter Thirty-Four – The Offer

"Is he going to live doc?" Fergus asked quietly, as he, Aledus and Catinius stood in the army tent looking down at Vittius who lay on a camp bed, his body covered in a blanket. The young man's eyes were closed and his face was coated in beads of sweat. The doctor, a Greek civilian, sighed as he came up to the side of the camp bed and looked down at his patient.

"If he survives the night he will stand a chance," the doctor said. "The wound is still fresh and hopefully it will not become infected, but if it does, well then…" the doctor let the sentence hang. "You need to let him get some rest," the doctor added. "I will let you know if there is a change in his condition."

Looking haggard and bruised, Fergus and his two companions emerged from the medical tent in the small camp that the company shared with the 3rd company. And as they did, Lucullus came limping towards them.

"How's our boy?" the centurion muttered as he came to a halt before Fergus.

"The doc thinks he has a chance if he can survive the night," Fergus replied, lowering his eyes to the ground.

"Good, that's good," Lucullus muttered, with a concerned look. Then he turned to look at Fergus.

"You were all lucky to escape those Dacian's," the centurion exclaimed. "It sounds like it was a pretty bad fight. I have sent a message to the other cohort companies to be on their guard. It's a shit way to go, being killed, just as we have won the war. But the good news, boys is that Rufus has heard that we are going home. The decision has been made. As soon as they can move an auxiliary unit up here to replace us, the vexillation will be on its way back to Deva. Hell, if that doesn't cheer you up then nothing will."

"Thank you, Sir," Aledus and Catinius said smartly.

"Ah Fergus, one more thing," Lucullus said as he placed his hand on Fergus's shoulder, preventing him from moving on.

"Whilst you were away," the centurion said, gazing at Fergus with an odd expression, "a man arrived at the battle group HQ. He is looking for you. Says he has come all the way from Aquincum in Lower Pannonia and he claims to have been sent by the Governor of the province, Hadrian. Seems that you have come to the attention of some powerful, important people, Fergus. He wants to talk to you. Would you know what that was about?"

"Hadrian?" Fergus frowned. "I know the governor, Sir," he muttered. "I was with his escort in Germania, but I have no idea what he would want with me. The last time I saw him, he refused to help me."

"Well would you mind clarifying what this is all about?" Lucullus ordered. "The last I heard is that this messenger is on his way over here to speak to you. The officers back at HQ say he does not seem to be the kind who takes no for an answer. Bit of an arrogant arsehole, if you know what I mean."

***

It was dawn, when a slave shook Fergus awake in his tent.

"Sir," the man said, lowering his eyes respectfully. "You need to come to Lucullus's tent right away. There is someone here who wishes to speak to you."

Bleary-eyed Fergus rose from his camp bed and quickly splashed some water over his face from a bowl that was standing on a table, inside the tent. Then he turned to look at the slave, but the man had already disappeared.

Weary and feeling stiff, Fergus emerged into the cool morning and hastened towards Lucullus's tent. A single guard was standing at the entrance to the tent and as he entered, Fergus caught sight of a well-dressed man of around forty, with an array of fine, glinting amber rings on his fingers. The man was talking to Lucullus and the centurion did not look amused. Then as Fergus entered, the stranger turned around and Fergus saw that it was Adalwolf.

"You," Fergus grunted, as he took a step forwards, "What brings you to our camp? You are a long way from Aquincum."

"Well good to see you too," Adalwolf said in his thick Germanic accent and as he did, a smile appeared on his face. For a moment, he examined Fergus. Then he stepped forwards and before Fergus could stop him, the German had embraced him in a tight bear hug.

Releasing Fergus, Adalwolf stepped backwards.

"You are right," he said. "I have travelled a long way to find you and it was not easy. But now I am here and so are you, so we are good. Hadrian sent me to find you. It seems that your exploits here in Dacia have come to his attention." Adalwolf paused and studied Fergus for another moment.

"Hadrian wishes to offer you a job," Adalwolf said abruptly. "He wishes to offer you a place on his staff as his principal bodyguard. The man who used to fulfil this role has become unsuitable and Hadrian needs a new man. He wants you. So, this is the offer that I have come with. What do you say, Fergus?"

"Hadrian wants me to become his bodyguard?" Fergus blurted out in surprise. "What does that mean? He wants me to stand by his bed chamber all night and keep a watch out for ghosts and assassins?"

"The physical protection of the governor would be your main duty, yes, and you would oversee his guard detail and security arrangements," Adalwolf said with a curt nod. "But you fail to see the significance of this role, Fergus. As Hadrian's principal body-guard you will be privy to the man's innermost secrets. The role would be a bit like being a companion and friend to the governor. I think that is what Hadrian has in mind. And Hadrian is an ambitious man. One day he is going to be emperor of Rome. I would urge you to think carefully about this opportunity."

"A companion and a friend?" Fergus repeated, with a suspicious look. Then he turned to glance at Lucullus but the centurion said nothing.

"Would I have to leave the army Sir?" Fergus said straightening up, "Would I have to leave the Twentieth?"

"Well," Adalwolf said carefully, "You should see this more as a permanent secondment into Hadrian's service, Fergus. You will have the benefits of a Beneficiarius, exempt from certain duties. Officially and legally you would still be a member of the Twentieth Legion. You will not receive a discharge but you will also not receive any army pay and obviously, you will no longer be part of your company for operational issues, nor will you be able to stay at Deva."

"And how long would this secondment be for?" Fergus muttered. "Until you die or Hadrian releases you from his service. You shall not have the choice to return to the Twentieth without Hadrian's permission," Adalwolf said sharply. "If you agree, I have been given all necessary authority to get your transfer and secondment approved with the army. Hadrian is most insistent that you join him in Aquincum."

Fergus sighed and looked down at his boots. This was not how he had expected the morning to go and as the silence in the tent lengthened, he felt torn by indecision. The legion was his life.

He had wanted to join his grandfather's unit since he was still a small boy; to make his grandfather proud; to follow in Corbulo's footsteps and now he was here and he had made friends; good friends. But Hadrian was an important, powerful man and Adalwolf was right. The prospects of having such a man as a friend and ally were glittering. It would mean that all kinds of doors and opportunities would open for him and his family. He would probably never get such a chance again, if he turned Hadrian down.

"Fergus," Lucullus said slowly and in a grave voice. "You are the finest optio in the whole Twentieth Legion as far as I am concerned and I would hate to lose you, but if you think that the army will soon promote you to centurion, then you are mistaken. You are too young and there is fierce competition for the limited vacancies. It will easily take you ten years before you would be even considered for a promotion to centurion. You should consider this."

"Thank you," Adawolf said, giving Lucullus a wry look. Then he turned to Fergus. "I must have your answer Fergus. I cannot return to Hadrian without your answer. So, what will it be?"

Fergus groaned inwardly, as he stood rooted to the ground. It was a big decision, one that could send his life in a completely new direction. And as he stood in the tent, he suddenly frowned. What would Corbulo have done? What path would his grandfather have chosen? And as he thought of Corbulo, Fergus sighed. Corbulo would have wanted him to go as high as he could. His grandfather would want him to make something of himself.

"All right," Fergus muttered, turning to face Adalwolf, "Tell Hadrian that I shall accept the secondment on one condition and that condition is non-negotiable."

Chapter Thirty-Five – Efa's wish

Saturnalia, late December 106 AD, The island of Vectis

Marcus laughed at the antics of the four children as they darted into cover behind the bushes and rolled in the thick snowdrifts, seeking advantage in the snowball fight. Marcus was proudly clad in his new tunic with two, vertical narrow, purple-stripes down the side and over that he was wearing a finely tailored sheepskin cloak. Around him the farm was quiet and only the mooing of the cattle in their pens disturbed the fine, crisp, cold winter afternoon. The fresh snowfall blanketed the fields, the roof of the outhouses and the villa, and on the horizon, grey clouds heralded the approach of more snow. From a doorway into the villa Kyna was watching the action with a smile on her face.

Life was good Marcus thought as he looked down at the gold equestrian ring on his finger. Life had never been better. Doors were opening and opportunity beckoned. The future looked bright and hopeful. It may have taken six months but after the land surveyor had produced his report, Marcus had received a letter all the way from Rome. It had come from Paulinus Picardus Tagliare, Prefect of the State Treasury and in it Paulinus had written that Marcus had been officially accepted into the equestrian order. He was now a knight with the right to wear a tunic with a narrow purple stripe down the side and a gold equestrian ring. The symbols of his newly- acquired social rank were just symbols. The real, unseen benefits of being part of the equestrian order was that now it was possible that he would come to the attention of powerful, influential men and that he could be considered for important positions within the provincial hierarchy. And the good news had not stopped there, for within a couple of months after he and Petrus had returned from Rome, the procurator, the most senior financial official in the province of Britannia, had announced that the investigation into Priscinus's death had been halted due to lack of evidence. The threat to his farm had gone and that summer the new harvest had been one of the best on record. And to top it all, news had filtered through during the autumn that the war in Dacia had come to a successful conclusion.

At the corner of the barn, one of Dylis's twins poked her head around the corner and spotting her, Marcus sent a well-aimed snowball hurtling towards her. He was rewarded by an excited shriek. Pretending not to notice little brave Armin charging towards him, Marcus threw up his arms and collapsed into the snow as he was struck by a snowball. With a triumphant cheer, the children came rushing out of their hiding places and began pelting Marcus, as he lay writhing in the snow. Marcus was just about to rise to his feet and do some pelting of his own, when a loud cry from around the front of the house made him hesitate. A few moments later one of the slaves came running through the door, his face lit up with excitement.

"What is going on?" Marcus asked, as he brushed the snow from his cloak and got to his feet.

"Sir, visitors approaching," the slave cried out. "They are coming towards the front gate, I believe Sir," the slave stammered. "I believe Sir that it may be your son, Fergus."

Marcus went very still as he stared at the slave. Then in the doorway he saw Kyna raise a hand to her mouth in shock and swiftly vanish into the corridor. Hastily he hurried after her, followed by the slave and as he came out of the front door, he nearly collided with Dylis and Cunomoltus. Both looked excited as they raced on after Kyna, who was already halfway to the front gates. Anxiously, Marcus paused and turned to search the brilliant, white fields as he too, at a walk, headed for the front gates of his property. And as he did, he suddenly heard Kyna's heartfelt shriek of joy. Coming slowly towards him along the frozen, white track, he suddenly saw two figures on horseback, riding towards the farm. As Marcus made it to the gates, he grunted in disbelief and joy. It was Fergus all right and his son was accompanied by a young woman of around nineteen wearing a cloak and hood that partially covered her blond hair. Strapped across her chest in a sling, the girl was carrying a small child, wrapped in a thick, warm bundle of cloth.

***

"There it is," Fergus cried excitedly, as he sat on his horse and he and Galena slowly made their way down the frozen track. Through the trees the villa and its outhouses had become visible and as he caught sight of them, Fergus felt a strong feeling of nostalgia.

"That's the farm where I grew up," he said, smiling excitedly at Galena. "Oh, you should see it in summer when the forest is a riot of colours and the scent of freshly-cut grass fills the evening air. It's magic."

"I am sure it is beautiful but don't get too attached, Fergus," Galena said with a wise smile. "Remember we cannot stay here forever. We have a long journey ahead if we want to reach Aquincum by the end of spring."

"I know, I know," Fergus said with an eager look on his face. Then he turned and winked at his young wife. "Are you nervous? I mean you will be meeting my family for the first time. They are all right but don't get Petrus started on his god or ask Jowan to explain how he chooses which crops to plant. They will bore you to death. Just a little tip. You have been warned."

"I can handle myself," Galena told him confidently, lifting her chin at her husband. "I managed to give birth and survive the arrival of Briana here. If I can handle that, then I can handle anything. No, the first thing I shall do," Galena said, looking down fondly at Briana, "is to go straight to your mother and give her a kiss. Then after we have been introduced to everyone, I shall tell them that I want five children. And despite being posted to a place a very, long way from my home, I will raise our five children in the manner of my ancestors. But I shall insist that they learn to read and write. That dear husband will not be negotiable."

Fergus grinned and turned to look at the farm as the two, slowly plodding horses started on the final stretch towards the main gates. As he stared at the villa up ahead, a slave hastily climbed down from a small, watch platform and went racing across the snow-covered courtyard and into the house. Fergus watched the man go. Then he sighed and looked down at the two, fat bags that were strapped to his saddle. The bags were filled with Dacian gold, more than enough to make him a very, very wealthy man, but he planned to leave most of it behind here on the family farm. Marcus would be able to make much better use of it than he could, especially now that Kyna's last letter had said that his father had become a knight. It would be his gift to them.

Then as he looked down at the bags, he suddenly lowered his eyes in sombre reflection as his thoughts turned back to Dacia. Despite the doctor's best attempts Vittius had not survived his wounds and they had burned his body outside their camp in the mountains of Dacia. Vittius's death had been a bitter blow, for he had been there from the first day that Fergus had joined the legion. Afterwards Aledus had collected his ashes and interned them in a pot, which he'd said he would carry back to the legionary camp at Deva Victrix. The three of them, Aledus, Catinius and Fergus had agreed that once they had returned to Deva, they would pay for and erect a memorial stone for their lost comrade and that Vittius's share of the Dacian gold and silver would be given to his family. The vexillation's return to the home fortress of the Twentieth Legion had been both a joyous and sombre affair, for nearly half of the legionaries, who had marched out of Deva eighteen months earlier, had not returned from the Dacian war. But all his troubles had melted away when he had seen Galena coming to meet him, carrying Briana in her arms. That had been quite something.

Up ahead in the courtyard of the farm, Fergus's sombre thoughts disappeared as he suddenly caught sight of a woman racing towards him, and with a jolt he realised that it was his mother Kyna. A moment later as Kyna recognised him, she gave a loud, heartfelt cry. Behind her, more figures were emerging from the house and running across the snow towards him and he recognised Dylis, Jowan, Petrus and Cunomoltus.

"Oh boy, my sweet boy, you have come home," Kyna gasped, as she flung her arms around him and refused to let go. The tears of joy were rolling down her cheeks. Then a moment later Fergus was embracing Dylis and Cunomoltus, followed by Petrus and Jowan. Everyone was talking through and over each other in their excitement and eagerness.

But where was Marcus his father? Then Fergus caught sight of him, walking along behind the others, his hand raised in the air in greeting.

***

Marcus paused and reached out to steady himself. Fergus had come home at last. He could not believe it. He watched Fergus dismount and embrace Kyna, followed swiftly by Dylis and then Cunomoltus. Marcus held back a sudden emotion. How long ago was it since he had seen Fergus? It had to be more than two and half years. The boy he'd last seen had become a man. There was no doubt about it. A fine-looking young man with his father's red hair and his mother's big, proud and noble Celtic heart. Marcus began to walk towards the joyous gathering and as he did, he was swiftly overtaken by Petrus and Jowan, who came racing past and burst out into loud cheers as they caught sight of Fergus.

As he approached the ecstatic reunion, Marcus raised his hand in greeting and a big, welcoming smile appeared on his face. Fergus let go of Dylis and came towards him, shaking his head slowly from side to side. "Father," Fergus said stiffly, as the two of them embraced. "It has been too long. It has been too long," he repeated.

"It's good to have you back Fergus," Marcus said. "You have no idea. This is a momentous day son, a momentous day," he repeated, as he clasped his son in his arms. Then hastily he let go of Fergus and stepped aside, so as not to let his emotions overwhelm him.

"Let me introduce you all to my wife Galena and my daughter Briana," Fergus said with a big proud smile. He stepped back and helped Galena down from her horse. And as Galena reached the ground, she went straight up to Kyna and kissed her on the cheek and in reply Kyna, smiled through her tears and reached up to gently stroke Galena's face.

"You are both most welcome, Galena and Briana," Kyna said in a hoarse voice. "Our home is your own home."

"I am afraid that we cannot stay for too long," Fergus said with a sad sigh. "I have given a solemn oath that I will be in Aquincum on the Danube by the end of spring. I am on permanent secondment from the army."

"You are on secondment from the army, so have you left the Twentieth?" Cunomoltus exclaimed raising his eyebrows in surprise.

"No, I am still officially and legally a member of the army but I am on permanent secondment," Fergus replied. "A lot has happened and we have much to catch up on and today is Saturnalia but there will be time for everything."

"Permanent secondment," Marcus said looking at him with a frown. "What does that mean? Did you get an honourable discharge? Are you wounded, sick?"

"Nothing like that father," Fergus said with another sigh, "I am well, healthy and fit but like I said much has happened. I have accepted a new posting which is going to take me away from Britannia. It is a good secondment and I am taking Galena and

Briana with me to Aquincum so that we shall all be together. That was my one condition for accepting this new job. I am to be the principal bodyguard to the Governor of Lower Pannonia. The Governor's name is Publius Aelius Hadrianus and he is going to be the next emperor of Rome."

"Hadrian!" Marcus exclaimed in alarm. "You are going to be Hadrian's bodyguard. Son. That means," Marcus's eyes widened in horror as he suddenly realised the implications. "That means that you are his man now. You are a supporter of Hadrian. The Gods are having a laugh." As he said these words, Marcus felt a deep pit opening within his stomach. How could this be? How could Fergus end up in the political camp that was the sworn enemy of his own political network; the alliance led by Nigrinus. The gods were truly having a laugh.

"It doesn't matter how long you can stay Fergus," Kyna replied, as she wiped away the tears that were still streaming down her cheeks. "I am so glad that you are here, all three of you. You have no idea how much we have all missed you. We have been worried sick, but not today. Today is a joyous day, for you have come home and at last we are all together again."

"You must come and see Efa right away," Dylis cried out, as tears came trickling down her cheeks too. "She does not have much longer to live, Fergus. She is very ill and frail. But she has been waiting for this day. She has been holding out for this day; the day when we are all together again. That was her wish. She will be so pleased to see you and your family. It is the very hope of seeing this day happen that has kept her alive. The doctors say she should have died a year ago. Come, come Fergus, let's get to the house."

As Fergus and Galena were excitedly and loudly escorted through the gates of the farm and on towards the villa, Marcus remained behind, watching Fergus with troubled, worried eyes. As he did, Fergus turned around sharply and gazed back at him with a non-understanding frown. Slowly Marcus turned away towards the distant forest and lifted his eyes to look up at the grey, cold overcast skies. The gods might be having a laugh but they had also kept their side of the bargain he'd struck with them on the beach, more than a year ago. Fergus was alive and he had come home, but as a supporter of Hadrian. Of all the people in the empire, it had to be Hadrian, the arch-enemy of his new friends in Rome. Fate had placed Fergus in an opposing political camp and this was going to cause trouble. He knew it deep down in his bones. Grimly Marcus stared up at the approaching snow clouds. Nevertheless, Fergus had come home and he was alive and that meant that one day the gods would come to collect their payment. For the immortals always did and when the demand came, he would have to pay. And he would pay with his life, for that had been the bargain he'd struck and one did not cheat on the gods.

***

Fergus was swept along towards the villa by his loud, excited family. But as a multitude of voices and questions swirled around him, he turned sharply to look back at Marcus who had remained where he was. What had his father meant by the gods were having a laugh? His reaction was bizarre. Something clearly seemed to be bothering his father and he was fairly certain it had to do with his secondment and new appointment as Hadrian's bodyguard. And as he strode on, looking back at Marcus, he saw his father turn away and look up at the sky with a sombre expression. And as he stared at Marcus in growing puzzlement, Fergus suddenly had the strangest sensation that trouble lay ahead.

***

Efa lay on the bed, covered in thick blankets of animal hides. She looked very frail and weak but as Dylis crouched beside her and whispered something into her ear, she slowly opened her eyes and gazed up at the people crowding around her. They were all there, Marcus, Kyna, Petrus, Cunomoltus, Jowan, Dylis, Fergus and Galena and the four silent children.

"Look," Dylis said, in a voice that was quivering with emotion.

"Look mother, look who has returned home. Look who it is."

Slowly Efa's eyes fixed on Fergus and then she smiled, as he crouched beside her bed and gently took her hand in his.

"Fergus," Efa whispered, in a faint voice. "Fergus."

"We are all here," Dylis gasped. "We are all together again at last, mother. This was your wish, to see us all together again. This is what you have been waiting for. Well we are here now and we are with you. We are with you."

In response Efa slowly moved her head to look at the faces around her and as she did, she smiled gently and happily.

"Yes," she whispered. "We are all here, all here together at last. What a wonderful thing."

For a long moment Efa paused and closed her eyes and for another long moment, it seemed as if she was asleep. Then she opened her eyes again. "If only Corbulo could see you all now," she whispered with a happy smile and in such a faint voice, that she was barely audible. "This was his dream and it became mine and when I am gone it must become yours. It must belong to all of you. Stick together and don't let go of each other, that is what Corbulo would say. He was the love of my life, the love of my life, the love of my life."

AUTHOR'S NOTES

Rome fought three wars with Dacia. The first with emperor Domitian (86-88 AD) which ended in an ignominious truce. This war and the initial Roman military defeats was the reason why one of the four legions then based in Britain, the II Adiutrix, was transferred to the Danube and never returned to Britain. This reduction in the Roman military resources in Britain was a significant factor in the Roman withdrawal from Scotland. This is reflected in the abandonment of the Roman legionary fortress at Inchtuthil. The next Dacian war was fought between emperor Trajan and king Decebalus (101-102 AD) and resulted in Decebalus suing for peace and agreeing to become a Roman vassal and the placing of Roman forts in his territory. This was the war in which Marcus served with his 2nd Batavian auxiliary cohort and where he lost the three fingers on his left hand. The events described in this book are about Trajan's 2nd Dacian war (summer 105 – summer 106 AD) which resulted in the complete destruction of an independent Dacian state, the enslavement of over 100,000 Dacian captives and the death of king Decebalus. From the end of this war until 275 AD Dacia and its mines will be a Roman province.

Regards the place names mentioned in this book I have tried to use the Latin names wherever I could but sometimes it was impossible to find a Roman name for something so I have then used the later names, an example being Hengistbury Head which has obvious Angle and Saxon connotations. Concerning the Dacian treasure buried underneath the Sargetia river this has been estimated to have been in the region of 165 tons of gold and 330 tons of silver. I also looked up how long it would take to travel from London to Rome in those days and found a fantastic online tool called ORBIS created by a team of historians and IT professionals at Stanford University. ORBIS allows you to calculate the fastest and most cost-effective way and route in which to travel between cities and places within the Roman Empire. It is the route suggested by ORBIS that Marcus takes when he heads for Rome. Tiberius Claudius Maximus was a real cavalry trooper and it was indeed he who cut off King Decebalus's head. We know this because his grave stone has been found in Greece on which he records his exploits. Bicilis too was a real person but the only thing we know about him is that he betrayed the location of the Dacian treasure horde to Trajan.

The Veteran of Rome series will extend to nine books in all after which the series will finish. The next book, Veteran of Rome 7 will be published at the start of September 2017.

William Kelso
London, April 2017

MAJOR PARTICIPANTS IN THE DACIAN WAR

Abraham, Christian priest living in Rome

Adalwolf, German amber and slave trader, but also guide, advisor and translator for Hadrian.

Ahern, Kyna's son by another man. Jowan adopted him.

Aledus, Londinium-born legionary friend of Fergus, squad leader

Alexandros, Greek captain of the Hermes that sailed to Hyperborea

Bicilis, Dacian brother in law to King Decebalus

Briana, New born daughter of Fergus

Catinius, Friend of Fergus and a Legionary.

Lady Claudia, A high born aristocrat and old acquaintance of Marcus

Clodovicus, Retired Batavian army soldier living at Hengistbury Head.

Cunitius, A private investigator and representative of Marcus's enemies

Cunomoltus, Marcus's half-brother.

Decebalus, King of the Dacians.

Dylis, Younger half-sister of Marcus, adopted by Corbulo.

Efa, Wife of Corbulo, step-mother of Marcus.

Plotina Pompeia, Empress of Rome, Emperor Trajan's wife

Fronto, Fergus's rival and company Tesserarius in the fourth company

Nigrinus, Leading citizen in Rome and close friend of Trajan

Galena, Wife of Fergus

Jowan, Husband of Dylis.

Kyna, Wife of Marcus, mother of Fergus.

Lucullus, Centurion in command of the 2nd company

Ninian, Marcus's broker and agent with the merchants in Reginorum

Paulinus Picardus Taliare, One of Rome's finance ministers, in charge of the state treasury

Petrus, The Christian boy who Corbulo had rescued from certain death in Londinium nearly twenty years earlier.

Rufus, Senior centurion of the 2nd cohort, Twentieth Legion

Trajan, Emperor of Rome from AD 98 to 117
Vibia Sabina, Hadrian's wife
Vittius, Friend of Fergus and a legionary in the 2nd company.

GLOSSARY

Aerarium, State treasury for Senatorial provinces
Aesculapius, The god of healing
Agrimensore, A land surveyor.
Armorica, Region of north-west France
Aquincum, Modern Budapest, Hungary
Arcidava, Fort in the Banat region of Dacia
Argiletum, Street of the booksellers in ancient Rome.
Ballistae, Roman artillery catapult
Banat, Region of Dacia, Romania and Serbia
Berzobis, Fort in the Banat region of Dacia
Bonnensis, Bonn, Germany. Full name.
Burdigala, Roman city close to modern Bordeaux, France
Capitoline Hill, One of the seven hills of ancient Rome
Carnuntum, Roman settlement just east of Vienna, Austria
Carrobalista, Mobile Roman artillery catapult
Castra, Fort.
Cavalry alae, A Roman cavalry unit
Centurion, Roman officer in charge of a company of about 80 legionaries.
Cilicia, Roman province in modern Turkey
Classis Pannonica, Roman fleet based on the Danube at Carnuntum
Cohort, Roman military unit equivalent to a battalion of around 500 men. Ten cohorts make up a legion.
Colonia Agrippina, Cologne, Germany.
Contubernium, Eight-man legionary infantry squad. Barrack room/tent group room
Cornicen, Trumpeter.
Cuirassed armour, Expensive chest armour that followed the muscles of the chest
Currach, Celtic boat.
Dacia(n), The area in Romania where the Dacians lived.
Decanus, Corporal, squad leader
Decurion, Roman cavalry officer.
Denarii, Roman money.
Deva Victrix, Chester, UK.

Domitian, Emperor from AD 81 - 96
Draco banner, Dacian coloured banner made of cloth
Emporium, Marketplace
Equestrian Order, The Order of Knights – minor Roman aristocracy
Equites, Individual men of the Equestrian Order.
Falx, Curved Dacian sword.
Fibula, A brooch or pin used by the Romans to fasten clothing.
Fiscus, The Roman state treasury controlled by the emperor and not the senate
Focale, Roman army neck scarf
Fortuna, The Goddess of Fortune.
Forum Boarium, The ancient cattle market of Rome
Forum Romanum, Political centre of ancient Rome, area of government buildings
Frisii, Tribe of Frisians who lived in the northern Netherlands
Gades, Cadiz, southern Spain
Garum, Roman fermented fish sauce.
Gladius, Standard Roman army short stabbing sword.
Greaves, Armour that protects the legs
Hengistbury Head, Ancient Celtic trading post near Christchurch, UK.
Hibernia, Ireland.
Hispania, Spain.
Hyperborea, Mythical land beyond the north wind.
Imaginifer, Roman army standard bearer carrying an image of the Emperor.
Insulae, Roman multi-storey apartment buildings
Janus, God of boundaries.
Jupiter Optimus Maximus, Patron god of Rome
Kostolac, City in Serbia
Lares, Roman guardian deities.
Iazyges, Barbarian tribe, roughly in modern Hungary
Legate, Roman officer in command of a Legion
Liburnian, A small Roman ship
Limes, Frontier zone of the Roman Empire.
Londinium, London, UK.

Lower Pannonia, Roman province in and around Hungary/Serbia and Croatia.

Ludus, School

Lugii, Vandals, barbarian tribe in central Europe.

Luguvalium, Carlisle, UK.

Marcomanni, Barbarian tribe whom lived north of the Danube in modern day Austria

Massalia, Marseille, France

Middle Sea, Mediterranean Sea,

Mogontiacum, Mainz, Germany.

Mons Graupius, Roman/Scottish battlefield in Scotland

Munifex, Private non-specialist Roman Legionary.

Noviomagus Reginorum, Chichester, UK.

Numerii, Germanic irregular soldiers allied to Rome.

O group meeting, Modern British army slang for group meeting of officers

Onagers, Heavy Roman artillery catapults

Optio, Roman army officer, second in command of a Company.

Ostia, Original seaport of Rome

Pilum/pila, Roman legionary spear(s).

Porolissum, Settlement in northern Dacia/Romania

Portus Augusti, The new seaport of ancient Rome

Portus Tiberinus, Rome's Tiber river port

Praefecti Aeranii Saturni, Rome's finance ministers

Prefect, Roman officer in command of an auxiliary cohort or civil magistrate.

Praetorian Guard, Emperor's personal guard units

Principia, HQ building in a Roman army camp/fortress.

Pugio, Roman army dagger.

Quadi, Germanic tribe living along the Danube

Ranisstorum, Unknown place somewhere in Romania but recorded on the grave stone of Tiberius Claudius Maximus as the place to which he brought King Decebalus's severed head and personally presented it to Emperor Trajan

Rosia Montana, Ancient gold and silver mining district in Romania/Dacia

Roxolani, Barbarian tribe in eastern Romania
Rutipiae, Richborough, Kent, UK.
Sacred Way, Important road in ancient Rome
Sarmatians, Barbarian allies of the Dacians
Sarmatian cataphracts, Heavily armoured Sarmatian cavalry
Sarmisegetusa Regia, Capital city of ancient Dacia
Saturn, God of wealth
Saturnalia, Roman festival in late December
Scythians, Barbarian tribes, modern Ukraine and Russia
Singidunum, Belgrade.
Sirmium, The ancient city of Sirmium on the Danube
SPQR, Senate and People of Rome.
Stola, Woman's cloak
Styx river, Mythical river you cross with the help of a ferryman as you enter the underworld.
Stylus, Roman pen
Subura, Slum neighbourhood in central Rome
Tapae, Dacian fort at the entrance to the iron gates pass
Tara, Seat of the High King of Hibernia, north-west of Dublin, Ireland.
Tesserarius, Roman army watch/guard officer, third in line of company command
Tessera tile, A small stone carried by the Tesserarius on which the daily password was written down
Testudo formation, Roman army formation and tactic
Tibiscum, Fort in Dacia
Military Tribune, A senior Roman army officer
Urban cohorts, A kind of anti-riot police force in ancient Rome
Island of Vectis, Isle of Wight, UK.
Velarium, Retractable canvas roof over the Roman colosseum.
Velum, Parched animal skin used as writing paper
Vestal Virgins, Female priestesses of ancient Rome
Vexillatio(n), Temporary Roman army detachment.

37413384R00206

Printed in Great Britain
by Amazon